I0710515

When it's impossible to forget...

THE LAST PROMISE YOU MADE

LJ EVANS

When it's impossible to forget…

The Last Promise You Made

L J Evans

This book is a work of fiction. While reference might be made to actual historical events or existing people and locations, the events, names, characters, places, and incidents are either the product of the author's imagination or are used fictitiously, and any resemblance to actual persons, living or dead, business establishments, events, or locales is entirely coincidental.

LJ EVANS BOOKS

www.ljevansbooks.com

Cover Design: © Emily Wittig Designs

Cover Images: © iStock | Cristalov, Lara_Uhryn

Chapter Title Images: iStock | BarvArt

Developmental Editing: Evans Editing and Michelle Fewer

Line, Copy Editing, & Proofing: HEA Author Services, Jenn Lockwood Editing, Karen Hrdlicka, Stephanie Feissner

ISBN: 978-1-962499-16-3

Library of Congress Cataloging in process.

Dedication

*For everyone who thinks their happily ever after is lost,
may you find it when you least expect it.*

For Ceci, we love you and miss you.

*For Stephanie, Kathryn, and Erika, who got me through
some dark days
and believed in me when I'd lost faith.*

Chapter One

Ryder

WHAT HURTS THE MOST
Performed by Rascal Flatts

When I dragged myself out of bed, I had no idea I'd be holding a funeral for a crow before the day was over. I'd been given marching orders from my mother to stop the birds from eating the last of her crabapples. To ensure they were extra sweet, she'd waited to harvest them until after the first snow, and now the damn beasts were taunting us, feasting on the fruit as if it had appeared from thin air in the middle of our Tennessee winter.

I was late getting to the ranch due to a mess-up with the plumbing supplies I'd ordered, so even though I didn't swing by the house, I could still practically hear Mama huffing while she watched the birds destroy the last of her fruit. Forcing aside my frustration at the morning's delays, I stomped into the ranch's office and grabbed my shotgun from the lockbox. I loaded it, pocketed another box of ammo, and headed out. My long stride took me past the immaculately maintained blue-and-white barn with its intricately twined metal H near the roofline. Like every other addition I'd made to the family property, it had been carefully and purposefully crafted to portray the elegance our guests looked for in a luxury resort. These days, the ranch was far removed from the dusty, worn-down farm it had once been.

As I rounded the barn, my feet ground to a halt. The view bled the last of my frustration out of me as I took a deep, cleansing breath. Nothing could beat this. Nothing. Year-round, the ranch was picturesque—worthy of a postcard even—but with a peaceful dusting of snow on the fields, it held extra magic. The bare oaks slumbered under the thin blanket of white while jade peeked from beneath the frozen layer on the evergreens. The low slope of the heather-gray mountains turned the view into a smoky watercolor painting, the pastel blue of the sky blending in with the hills.

The sun was doing its best to bring the temperatures up into the livable range, and I closed my eyes, raising my face to the timid warmth as I breathed in the ranch air I loved. The only thing I treasured more was my family. I wouldn't give this life up for anything. Not for my long-ago dreams of architecture and design. Not for a random woman who came and went from my life in the flash of an eye. Nothing would take me from this place.

The entire morning full of annoyances left me on the next exhale. Hitching the gun over my shoulder, I strode over the field, boots crunching on the ice clinging to the sleeping grass.

The crabapple trees were just past the main pasture near the empty guest cabins. During this time of year, no smoke curled from their chimneys, and their fall-toned, craftsman-style fronts were a stark contrast to the black and white of the January landscape. Next to the ten completed cabins, two new ones sat in various stages of undress, awaiting roofs and siding.

An all-too-familiar feeling of regret attempted to worm its way in through the peace the view had settled in my veins. If I hadn't been blinded by love, those last two cabins would have been built years ago. But they were here now and would be ready for our new season when it began in April.

Even knowing Grandfather Hatley was likely rolling over in his grave at what we'd done to the property, the transition from a cattle ranch to a dude ranch had kept the land in the Hatley name. And we'd managed to hold on to pieces of a working farm in order to give our guests the full ranch experience. We'd simply added on the outdoor resort activities they craved. Whitewater rafting, horseback riding, and hiking adventures were what drew people to us for repeated stays, along with Mama's hearty, down-home meals to which she'd added a modern flair.

As I neared the crabapple trees, the half dozen crows feasting on the remaining fruit lifted their beaks in an unspoken dare. I'd bought a sound gun late last year that had kept the birds away from most of the crops, but the damn thing had died just before Christmas and was sitting in Willy Tate's garage, waiting for him to fix it. Willy worked slow as molasses these days, grieving a relationship that had disappeared years ago.

I was probably the only soul in Willow Creek who understood Willy's continued mourning. I wasn't sure my soul would ever stop howling for what I'd lost. But dwelling on the past would do nothing except make me long to lose myself in alcohol or sex or both, and that wasn't going to happen with a week's worth of work piling up.

I lifted the shotgun, aiming for the tops of the trees, intending only to scare the beasts away. I'd hunted with my dad and grandfather as a kid, but I'd never quite gotten a stomach for the killing. Maybe that was why I wasn't overly sad when we'd sold off our remaining beef cattle and stuck to a handful of dairy cows.

Just as I pulled the trigger, one of the damn birds took flight. Crap timing meant the pellets collided with the bird's chest, and it plummeted to the earth several yards away.

A high-pitched shriek broke through the air, and I whirled around, coming face-to-face with my niece, Mila. Disappointment radiated from her hazel eyes. The dark brows that didn't match her honey-wheat-colored hair were lifted in shock.

My heart kicked into gear. Not only because of the look she was sending me but also from the memories of her last experience with guns a mere fourteen months ago.

I took a step toward her, gentling my voice and saying, "What are you doing out here, kiddo?"

Instead of replying, she took off running for the farmhouse with her blond braids flying and her cowboy boots kicking up snow and dirt.

"Shit!" I looked back at the laughing birds before hauling my ass across the field after her.

She was faster than any six-year-old had a right to be, and I hadn't quite caught up to her by the time she rounded the barn, passed the brick-and-ivy front of the Sweet Willow Restaurant, and banged up the steps of the wraparound porch on the farmhouse I'd grown up in. The blue siding and white trim echoed the sky above it where smoke puffed out of a pair of chimneys on opposite sides of the gray shake roof. Shiny and spiffed up these days, the home had sat in that exact spot for near on two hundred years.

I hollered out for Mila to stop once more, but she ignored me, pushing inside with me on her heels.

"Nana!" she screamed. "You have to punish Uncle Ryder!"

There was a hitch to her voice that threatened tears and made my chest squeeze tight as my mother squatted down to pull my distraught niece into her arms. Flour sifted through the air, catching in a beam of sunshine from the large windows over the farm-style sink and casting them in a hazy halo.

"Bug-a-boo, what on earth?" Mama asked, brows drawing together.

"I do *not* like Uncle Ryder anymore. He is mean, mean, mean!"

A sob escaped her chest that tortured me a bit more as my mama met my gaze over the top of Mila's head. Her bright-blue eyes, the same color as mine, widened in concern. The hint of wrinkles around the corners of her mouth was more evident as she frowned at me.

I pulled my black cowboy hat off, running a hand through my thick waves the same chestnut color as my mother's before gray had decided to weave its way into hers.

"Why was she out by the crabapples?" I asked. None of us had truly let Mila out of our sight since an asshole gang member had taken her and my sister at gunpoint, put a bullet in Sadie's thigh, and tried to use Mila as leverage against my brother several months ago.

Mama finally caught on to what had happened as her eyes landed on my shotgun just as Mila let out another devastating sob. "He *killed* a bird, Nana! A beautiful black bird!"

I moved toward them, and Mila shied away from me, causing my heart to twist a bit more.

"I thought we were just scaring the crows off?" Mama asked.

"Scaring them *was* the plan. I can't help that one of them flew right into the shot."

"You're awful, Uncle Ryder! You killed a poor, hopeless little birdie!"

"I think you mean helpless," Mama responded, her lips twitching as she realized what had happened.

I squatted down, eyes meeting Mila's tear-filled ones. "I wasn't trying to hurt him, kiddo. The sound gun that's been scaring them off is broken, and I was just trying to make a loud noise. What happened was an accident."

"It was?"

I dragged a hand over the scruff that was turning into a beard I kept meaning to shave off and said, "Sure was."

"His family is going to miss him. You need to apologize to them."

"Well, the crows weren't supposed to be eating Nana's crabapples to begin with. This is like...your dad arresting someone for breaking the law."

"Daddy doesn't *kill* people!"

I met my mama's gaze, and neither of us mentioned the man who'd taken Mila and who'd been shot in the ravine before dying at the hospital.

"What do you think Uncle Ryder should do to make amends?" Mama asked.

I groaned internally. Knowing Mila, she was going to come up with a harebrained scheme involving rainbows and unicorns. Maybe even pixie dust. Something nearly impossible.

My niece stepped toward me, her gaze still sad but determined as she patted my arm. "You need to have a funeral for him so his family can say goodbye."

I looked up at Mama to see her eyes twinkling with humor just as my brother walked into the room, demanding to know what was going on. As Mama explained what had happened, his blue eyes crinkled, and he chuckled, making me want to punch him in the nose and add another crook to the one I'd given him when we were younger.

"Let me go dig a hole." I sighed. "Maybe you and Nana can come up with some words to say." Maddox let out a half-laugh, half-cough, and I gave him a one-fingered wave over the top of the women's heads. "Just for that, you can help dig the hole."

Maddox pointed to the bronze star glowing on his chest. "I'm on duty. Was just dropping Mila off for the day."

"You're the sheriff. No one is going to give you a lecture if you're a few minutes late."

"Gotta set a good example for my team."

I wanted to grab him, put him in a headlock, rub his dark-blond hair noogie-style, and mess up his perfectly ironed, khaki-colored shirt and green pants.

He picked up his Winter County Sheriff's hat from the coat rack. "I'll see you tonight, Bug-a-boo. Don't give Nana too hard of a time, but make sure Uncle Ryder follows your instructions about the funeral to a T."

I grunted in protest, following him out the door.

Once outside, I slammed my fist into his shoulder. "Damn you."

"Don't blame me. You're the crap shot who took out a

bird."

"The bird flew into the shot!"

He chuckled, heading for his truck. He glanced at my step-side pickup glistening like root beer on ice sitting next to it. "I hate to admit it, because it's a Chevy, but Willy did a great job fixing the C10 up. I wasn't sure he'd be able to with all the bullet holes riddling it."

The truck had been shot up after a woman tailing a U.S. Secret Service agent and his rockstar protectee had caught up to them while they'd been staying at the ranch. The agent had handed me the registration as a way of apologizing for destroying a whole section of the fence he'd run through in his attempt to get away. We'd seen a bit too much action at the ranch in the last couple of years. We were due some peace and quiet.

"Where's McK today?" I asked.

"She took a shift at the hospital for another doctor."

When McKenna had shown up months ago, I hadn't thought it would end well for Maddox. I hadn't expected her to give up her life in California to finish her residency in the one state she'd run from as a teen. Seeing the love bloom between them again had opened old wounds in my chest.

I couldn't—wouldn't—be like my brother, who'd gone from swearing off anything serious to falling right back head-over-heels for the one woman who'd wounded him to begin with. I'd never forgive Ravyn for what she'd done to me and my family, and I didn't plan on getting hooked up with anyone again. While I saw nothing wrong with losing myself in the scent and feel of soft curves for a few hours, I wasn't getting roped into thoughts of forever after.

My brother got in his truck, tooted the horn as a goodbye, and I strode back to the barn to find what I needed to bury a damn bird. After replacing the shotgun with a shovel, I grabbed an empty feed sack and went back to the crabapple trees. I about destroyed my hands and shoulders digging a hole in the frozen earth for a damned crow.

I picked up the dead bird with a gloved hand, dropped

it into the sack, and stuck the bag in the ground. Last thing I needed was for Mila to see the bloody bird and burst into tears all over again. By the time I was done, I was sweaty and cussing the crows all over again as a line of the black beasts watched me from the trees.

I could almost hear them cackling.

When I looked back at the barn, Mila and Mama were making their way across the field. My niece had her two rainbow unicorns tucked in her armpits and a leftover poinsettia plant from the holidays in her hands.

When they reached me, my mama handed me a piece of paper.

"What's this?"

"Last rites."

Her eyes were glittering with laughter. Had it really only been an hour or so ago that I'd been looking at the ranch and thinking how much I loved my family?

Mama hit play on her phone, and Irish funeral music streamed out of it. I nearly choked out a curse before looking down at Mila's wide, innocent eyes. Gritting my teeth, I ripped the paper from my mother's hands.

I silently read what they'd come up with, grinding my teeth over the sweet words for a pest who shouldn't have been in the trees to begin with.

"To the damn bird I accidentally killed," I growled out, and Mila interrupted me with a huff.

"You owe a dollar for the swear jar, Uncle Ryder. And you don't sound sorry at all. You have to feel it"—she reached up and patted my chest—"in here."

I met my mama's gaze with a glower that promised retribution. She hid her smile behind her hand. I cleared my throat, looked skyward for help that wouldn't come, and then started over. "To the sweet crow that was ripped from his life too soon by an evil shot by a careless human."

I somehow got through the rest of it to Mila's satisfaction and helped her stuff a little cross in the ground supported by the poinsettia while Mama held her unicorns. When we stood back up, Mila looked at me with her hands on her hips and said, "Now promise you'll *never* kill another living thing again, Uncle Ryder."

My stomach turned. We lived on a ranch. Animals sometimes needed to be put down. It was part of the cycle, but as I looked into her innocent face, I knew I wouldn't be able to tell her no. It would cost me a pretty penny to keep that promise if I had to hire someone to do the work for me. Still, I sighed and said, "All right, Bug-a-boo. No animal will be harmed by these hands again."

She stuck out her little finger. "Pinky promise?"

When my large finger twined with her tiny one, my chest filled with an unexpected ache. An ache for something I'd once thought I'd have but had lost. Something I'd sworn to never let into my life again—a wife and a child.

Chapter Two

Gia

SOMETHIN' BAD

Performed by Miranda Lambert and Carrie Underwood

The scene was about as ugly as it could get. The woman's hands were shredded, and vicious cuts sliced her chest, blood pouring from them onto a hotel carpet already stained dark with old spills. The crime scene investigators would be hard-pressed to sort through the evidence and figure out what was related to the murder and what was residual from years' worth of guests who'd stayed at the cheap motel on the outskirts of Denver.

The victim was dark-haired, in her early thirties, with a wild beauty evident even with the shadows under her eyes and the blotchiness of her skin. My gut twisted with something close to guilt. She'd been on the run, and I'd been one of the people chasing her.

My jaw clenched tight. Another woman's death that would haunt me.

Logically, I knew neither this woman nor the one in D.C. two months ago had been my fault. Their deaths came from conspiring with one of the largest, most vile cartels in the Americas. The Lovatos had their hands in everything from drugs to guns to financial schemes, and they were known for ruthlessly eliminating not only the competition but any traitors or weak links.

The question was which one Anna Smith had been.

If she'd been the organization's genius technophile, like I thought, she'd had years of the Lovatos' secrets at her disposal. Had she decided to trade in on them? Or had the screw-up in D.C. placed a black mark on her that couldn't be removed?

The CSI who was bent over her turned to look up at me. "Not sure what happened here." He waved over the blood on her chest. "Looks like something was dragged over her after she died."

"Any ID?" I asked.

He shook his head. "And good luck getting a solid one based on facial recognition. She's had work done, specifically to the nose-bridge area."

The region where the nose, eyes, and forehead intersected was key to facial recognition software. I scanned her again, noticing the long strands of purple in her otherwise nearly black hair and the way it had been styled to cover at least one eye. She was also wearing a harsh concealer that contrasted with her skin tone. These were all things known to confuse the software.

"Okay if I move this?" I asked, leaning down and waving a gloved hand over the purple strand sticking to her lips. He nodded, and I pushed it aside. Her face was frozen in a look that was hard to identify. Fear. Regret. Worry.

I snapped a picture of the woman, wondering if this was truly the elusive Anna Smith we'd been tracking through several countries or just some sad woman with the same name. Anna had been nothing more than a name—a ghostlike apparition—for three years, disappearing every time we caught up to her. Even her name had been an alias we could only track back eight years. Before today, there'd been no image of her anywhere, leaving her a question mark on the board in the conference room of the multi-agency task force in D.C. Maybe now that we had prints and a face, we'd come up with something more.

Rory might be able to manipulate Anna's image enough for us to see what she'd looked like before the cosmetic work, and once we had that, our new analyst would scour every nook and cranny of the internet for Anna's deconstructed face. Rory was better at hacking and pulling puzzle pieces together than just about anyone I'd ever encountered. If she couldn't turn over a hidden rock and discover the truth of Anna, no one could.

Rory may not be the Q to my James Bond, but I'd come to count on her more than the fictional character ever had on his head of research and development—and definitely more than the loner Jason Bourne had ever counted on anyone. If my life were really a novel, like Jack Reacher or Jane Blond or any of the four J-spy heroes who'd influenced my life and my career, Rory might have played the traitorous villain. Except, I'd witnessed her being the exact opposite of a villain last November.

I stood, dragging my eyes around the room, noting there was no computer. No electronic equipment at all. Not even a phone. An open suitcase full of clothes looked like it had been ransacked in the closet, but other than that, the room was empty.

My gaze returned to the victim lying on the floor with her hand extended toward the bed skirt where the white sole of a shoe was just barely visible. As I bent to reach for it, the shoe disappeared. My lungs froze, my body stilled, and my mind went into overdrive.

Local police had been the first on the scene. Sitting in the chief of police's office, I'd been explaining about our multi-agency task force and trying to convince him to lend me some of his patrols to scour the streets for a woman we didn't even have a picture of when he'd gotten the call about the murder. As soon as Anna's name had left his lips, I'd jumped into the agency's Escalade and headed for the motel room she'd rented. CSI had already been processing the scene when I'd arrived.

I slowly turned, tapping the tech on the shoulder. When his eyes met mine, I tipped my head toward the bed.

"Room was cleared, right?" I asked.

His gaze widened, but he nodded.

I pointed at the bed and then back at the cop standing watch at the door. He didn't hesitate, bounding to his feet and whispering something to the officer as I pulled my Glock from the waistband at my back.

I reached for the bed skirt, saying calmly, "Come out nice and slow."

Nothing. Not even a hint of movement. Had I imagined it? The space between the bed frame and the floor was mere inches. I wasn't sure a person could actually slide under it, which was probably why the officers clearing the room hadn't thought to check.

I pantomimed flipping the mattress to the two men and aimed my gun as they lifted it and flung it toward the back wall.

Underneath was a tangled detritus of garbage and dust balls, and in the middle of it lay a little girl. She was curled up in the fetal position, eyes wide with fear, and cheeks tear-stained. She ducked her face into her arms protectively.

What in the actual hell?

My heart skittered around in my chest, and chills coasted up my spine. We had a witness. A witness to a Lovato assassination. If we could find whoever did this and tie them to the cartel, it would be another huge win. Another chunk in the cartel's shell.

But what had she actually seen? Would she be able to help us at all? My stomach fell… What would happen to her if the Lovatos found out she'd seen their assassin?

I put my gun away and stepped over the bed frame into the debris surrounding her. "Hey, it's okay. You're safe."

My words made her flinch, and she drew her legs and arms impossibly closer to her body, as if willing herself to disappear. She was trembling. I could almost smell the fear radiating from her.

Cautiously, I eased closer. "My name is Gia. I'm an…officer. I promise you're safe now. No one is going to hurt you. I won't let them."

The little girl's eyes peeked out from beneath strands of long black hair. She had the same warm brown eyes as the dead woman. Except, the anguish and terror in the child's eyes weren't frozen in death.

I swallowed hard, squatting so I was closer to her level.

"What's your name?"

She shook her head violently. The CSI tech shifted, and the child's eyes darted to him. Seeing both men hovering, she jerked into action, scurrying backward toward the wall. Once she hit it, she wrapped her arms around her legs again, her gaze shifting between us in fear.

"They're with the police," I told her gently. "They're the good guys. No one here is going to hurt you."

She didn't look like she believed me. Her look darted to the door.

"You want to leave?"

She nodded.

"I can take you somewhere safe."

Her eyes landed on the dead woman, and a sob broke from her tiny chest. Tears poured over her lashes and down a cheek smeared with blood. She buried her face in her knees, her skinny shoulders shaking.

Fuck.

I wasn't a kid person. My interactions with them were always awkward and choppy. My mom was desperate for either my brother or me to give her grandbabies, but she wasn't getting them from me for multiple reasons. I loved my life working undercover for the National Security Agency and had no plans of slowing down or staying in one location long enough for family life to get its hooks in me.

As I lowered myself to my knees, I blocked the child's view of the dead body. I might have been screwing with evidence, but I was more worried about getting the little girl away from here than protecting what could be found in the trash around her.

I glanced at the men. "We can't let anyone see her. No one can know she was here." I hesitated for a beat. "Get me one of the housekeeping carts."

The officer left the room at a jog.

I turned back to the child, doing my best to soothe her and promising again to take her somewhere safe. She didn't respond, but she lifted her head, eyes meeting mine in a way that let me know she'd at least heard me. I kept talking softly, and by the time the officer returned with the cart, her shoulders had dropped from her ears. I told her my plan to keep her hidden by bundling her into the laundry bin and wheeling the entire cart into the back of the CSI van where we'd take her to the police station.

When I reached out my gloved hand, she just stared at it.

I moved closer, keeping my voice and expression as gentle as possible. "You can't stay here. I think you know that, right?"

Her gaze did another search of the room, tears still slowly rolling down her sweet face. Finally, she nodded in agreement.

I extended my hand again, and this time, she accepted it. As she stood, I saw blood coated her T-shirt and her arms. None of it appeared to be coming from her, so if I had to guess, I'd say it explained the smear along the victim's chest.

She'd hugged the dead woman to her.

Double fuck.

Standing, the child seemed somehow even smaller. She was old enough to have lost the tubbiness of toddlerhood, but not old enough for hormones to have found her, so maybe six or seven.

I helped her over the bed frame and started toward the cart the officer had placed between us and Anna Smith. We'd just gotten to it when the little girl pulled away from me and ran to the closet and the ransacked suitcase.

To my surprise, she pulled back the inner lining and withdrew a letter-sized envelope. She pressed it to her chest and then turned wide eyes at me in a face as beautiful as the murder victim's. They had the same high cheekbones and pointed chins with a fragile, haunted look to their frames—birds with broken wings.

I pushed the cart closer to her. "Is it okay if I lift you up? Put you inside?" When she didn't respond, I mimed lifting her into the empty laundry basket.

She gave a barely perceptible nod, and I put my hands around her waist and raised her up. She seemed impossibly light as I set her inside. The sense of fragility hit me all over again and, along with it, a deep-seated need to protect her. She sat, still clinging to the envelope before pulling her knees up against her body once more.

"We're going to cover you with some blankets, okay?" She just stared at me, and I turned to the officer, saying, "Get some from the next room."

He left and came back, and between the two of us, we settled the blankets over her head.

The room faced the parking lot on the first floor, and the CSI van was parked mere feet away. The officer and I rolled the cart to it, lifting it into the back, and I followed it inside. No way was I leaving her. No way I'd let an eyewitness out of my sight, regardless of her age.

I looked out at the officer from the back of the van, eyeing his nametag for the first time. "Officer Ramirez, we need someone to take us to the station immediately."

He went to radio it in, and I stopped him. "No. Not over the scanner."

He stared at me for a second and then headed off.

It was barely two minutes later before he returned, climbing into the driver's seat and pulling us out of the lot. News vans were parked across the street, and a horde of bystanders stood gaping just beyond the yellow crime-scene tape. I tried to reassure myself that there was no way any of them could have seen the child. No way for them to suspect we were hiding a little girl inside.

As we drove, I talked to her, even though I couldn't see her. I kept reassuring her she was safe, reassuring her that whatever had happened, she was going to be okay. Words I shouldn't have been promising, but couldn't stop myself from offering.

When we got to the downtown precinct, Ramirez drove us to a side entrance and straight into a bay in the department's garage. I waited until the metal door clanged on the cement behind us before uncovering her. I helped her out of the cart, squatting in front of her.

"We're going into the police station now. It'll be safe for you there, but it might be loud and busy. We'll find somewhere quiet for you and me to sit and talk about what happened. Do you think you can do that? Tell me what you saw?"

Her eyes grew wide, and she shook her head, fear scrolling over her features once more.

"That's okay, kiddo. It's okay. How about we just get you inside safe and sound for now?"

I offered her my still-gloved hand, and she took it, clinging to it so tightly it almost hurt.

We made our way out of the van, up the steps, and into the building with Ramirez following us.

"I need somewhere she'll be comfortable," I told him.

"We've got interrogation rooms, a conference room, or the lunchroom."

I rolled my eyes at him as none of those places would make this scared girl relax.

"Assistant Chief's office?" he offered. "He's on vacation. There's a couch in there."

"That'll work."

He led us up the stairs and down the hall. The sounds of the station grew on us. Laughter and yelling. Doors slamming. Chairs skidding across the floor. A drunken shout from somewhere deeper inside. The little girl cowered, pushing herself into my leg. I pulled her closer, my arm tightening around her shoulders.

When we made it inside the assistant chief's office, I led her to a couch shoved up against a wall of glass that showed the bullpen teeming with activity. The rest of the office's furniture was bland and functional. Government-issued minimalism that made the gray leather sofa stand out as wildly luxurious.

I went to the metal blinds, shutting out the chaos of the bullpen before turning to the officer and saying, "We need blankets. Water. Maybe something to eat."

Ramirez nodded and left, shutting the door behind him. Immediately, the noise level dropped to a muffled buzz. The guy was younger than me, probably just out of the academy, which was why he'd been guarding the hotel door, but he'd kept his wits together and helped me sneak the little girl out. My instincts said he was going to make a good cop.

By now, I'd worked with enough of them to know the difference. I was only twenty-seven, but I'd seen more things in my four years on the job than most people saw in their lifetime. Ugly and evil things. My dad had tried to ask me about it at Christmas, worried by the seriousness in my eyes, but I'd blown his questions off. He'd given me a look that the soldiers under his command would have trembled at, but that hadn't made me budge.

Even though my family had watched me grow up wanting to be a spy, my dad was the only one who actually knew my job as an agricultural journalist was a front. I wasn't sure if he knew which agency I worked for, but then again, as Vice Chief of the National Guard Bureau, he might have pulled enough strings to find out the truth. Either way, he hadn't shared the news with my former-Secret-Service-agent brother or my mother. I didn't know who would get in more trouble if Mom ever found out—me for lying, or Dad for keeping the secret.

My gaze returned to the little girl who'd curled into herself once again. Her knees were up at her chest, arms wrapped around them. She had a pair of Vans on her feet with smiling cat faces. They were a bit dirty, but not old. Blood was spattered on the sides of them—evidence we'd need. Her dark-blue jeans and white T-shirt were smeared with blood as well.

My heart nearly gave out as I thought of her watching the woman in the room being sliced up. Thinking of her hugging the dead body to her tiny frame. It was a miracle this girl was alive.

"Can you tell me your name?" I asked.

The little girl looked at me but didn't say anything.

"Can you tell me what that is?" I asked, referring to the letter she clutched, a splotch of red staining the white envelope.

"*Papa.*" The word was a mere whisper. A hint of a Mexican accent gave her voice a soft, rhythmic quality.

I was thankful once more for the painful years I spent in Spanish class and for the undercover work I'd done in South America that had improved my skill with the language. I asked her in Spanish, "Is that a letter *from* him or *for* him?"

The little girl's eyes widened, responding in Spanish. "I find him."

"So you can find him?" My heart sputtered again. "Can I see it? So I can help you find him?"

She looked at the envelope, hesitant and fearful, and then, with a shaking hand, offered it to me.

The writing on the front was bold and feminine, but it was the actual words that hit me like a fist to my solar plexus. *For Ryder Hatley.*

For all of thirty seconds, my lungs forgot to breathe before the air rushed back into them, painful and raw.

Damn it. Damn it all to hell.

After a bust in Lexington had shown a relatively high amount of chemicals used by ranchers in their cattle feed on the money and the drugs, the task force had begun looking for the leader of the Lovatos at a cattle ranch. We'd divided and conquered. Some individuals went undercover at actual working farms, while I used my fake journalism connections to write an exposé on dude ranches across the country.

Once news broke about a Lovato connection to a biker gang in Willow Creek and a dude ranch there, I'd headed to Tennessee to check it out. But after spending a few weeks at the ranch, I'd cleared the Hatleys of any involvement. Sheriff Hatley was a by-the-book, upstanding kind of guy, and the resort his family ran had been theirs for generations. The money they were pulling in could all be tied neatly back to their legitimate business. The place was thriving but not overly flush.

And yet, I now held a letter in my hand that proved there was a connection.

Something I'd obviously missed. This was a direct link from the Lovatos to the ranch's manager. The person in charge. The guy who'd gotten a burr up his ass about my questions and been angry enough to cage me against a wall when he'd caught me snooping in his office.

Blue eyes as clear as an evening sky and yet somehow still stormy flashed across my mind.

Blue eyes and dark hair that fell softly over a brow in a way that had my fingers itching to push it away.

A square jaw layered with stubble and a smile that both lit me up and made me want to wipe it off. A hard smile from lips that had punished me for daring him. For taunting him.

Lips that had liquified my insides right before he'd pushed me away as if I'd betrayed him. As if I'd had the worst kind of contagious disease.

I cleared my throat. "This man. Ryder. He's your father?"

At first, she didn't move at all, but then she gave a slight nod.

"And the woman in the hotel. She was your mama?"

The little girl's eyes flooded. She nodded again, buried her face, and sobbed, shoulders shaking violently. I moved instantaneously, pulling her into me and holding on while she cried. A piece of me wanted to cry too. I wasn't sure if it was in anger or frustration or hurt. Or maybe all three combined.

The last thing I wanted was to see Ryder Hatley again.

I certainly didn't want to show up with a little girl in tow who was supposedly his.

A child he hadn't told a soul he had.

A child I couldn't understand him having and not loving when I'd seen him shower his niece with so much affection it had made me ache for things I'd sworn I'd never want.

I looked down at the letter. I had to read it because it was part of my job, and yet, it felt like another violation Ryder would somehow hold me responsible for. Whatever was in the envelope—whatever it said—I had a sneaking suspicion it was going to change everything. Not only for the task force but for me.

Chapter Three

Ryder

After a long, tedious afternoon working on the two new cabins, I should have been wiped out and more than ready to head home and fall into bed. Instead, I was weirdly wired. Something about Mila and the crow had sunk into me, and I ached for things I knew better than to want.

What I needed was to get laid. A single night lost in soft skin that would rip any thoughts of a pair of dark-haired beauties who haunted me from my mind. Except, I hadn't been able to close the deal with any woman in months. After Ravyn left, it had been easy to get lost in others. It had felt like vengeance. These days, it wasn't my ex-fiancée who held me back. Instead, it was a damn journalist who'd stayed at the ranch long enough to get caught snooping in my office.

A woman with hair so dark it looked like midnight skies and eyes that mysteriously changed from green to brown depending on the light. A woman who'd briefly made my deadened heart trip out a new pulse before she'd disappeared without so much as a goodbye.

Gia Kent's vanishing act was a warning I needed to heed. A warning to keep my lips and hands to myself when it came to her. Thank God we hadn't shared more than a single damn kiss. Because just that one had left me singed with the taste for her I couldn't quite shed.

Maybe tonight I could finally leave her behind. Find some relief in someone who didn't stir that ridiculous organ inside my chest. Relief with a side dish of peace rather than torment.

I passed on Mama's offer for dinner, saying I'd grab something in town, got in my truck, and headed for Willow Creek. As I passed the town's sign at the city limits, my lips curled upward.

Willow Creek—home of football heroes, rock stars, and ranchers.

The sign was only a couple of decades old, created after the band Watery Reflection built a compound above the lake. Our town was as proud of our celebrities as Bell Buckle was of their RC Cola and Moon Pies. The stadium at the high school was named after a dead football star, and the area behind the lake was now known as *Watery Reflection Hill.* We were proud of those ties to our community, but we were also protective of our famous folk. If the press came nosing around, we shut them down as fast as a raccoon opens a garbage can.

The quaint, old-time vibe of our downtown drew artists, photographers, and even film crews. The plethora of church steeples peeking over the rooftops, the cobblestone streets hinting of long-forgotten carriages, and the sidewalks strewn with lantern-shaped lampposts made it Hallmark-card perfect. Graceful weeping willow trees were mixed in with the magnolias on every corner, filling the air with scent and color when they bloomed. The storefronts were sun-worn brick with white columns and black shutters, and their lead-glass windows turned the street into a mass of gold and crystalized rainbows in the sunset.

I parked my pickup out front of Willy's garage, hoping to put a burr in his butt about the sound gun. When I noticed the sign saying he'd closed early, I groaned, knowing exactly where he'd headed. I wasn't sure I was ready for Drunk Willy tonight.

I made my way to the edge of town and Uncle Phil's bar. McFlannigan's had been in Willow Creek for over a century. Whispers about every generation of McFlannigan owning the place were almost legendary in this neck of the woods.

I pushed open the carved doors to reveal a pub that would have been better suited to the Irish countryside than the wilds of Tennessee. Old-world charm, etched-glass mirrors, and rich woods filled the space. The sound of the live band hit me, and I barely held back yet another groan. I'd forgotten what day of the week it was. Thursday night meant two-dollar beers and line-dancing competitions that turned the town into rabid dogs.

As I made my way to the bar top, my gaze settled on Willy. His mammoth shoulders were hunched, and a beer was cradled in his hands as he watched the locals slapping their hands and twirling about the dance floor. The crowd's flannel, dark-wash jeans, and cowboy boots seemed at odds to the old-world-style dark paneling and faded green wallpaper lining the walls.

I tossed my hat on the lacquered mahogany and swung myself onto the stool next to Willy.

"You get around to fixing my sound gun yet?"

Willy nodded. "I'll drive it out to you tomorrow."

Sadie slid a beer toward me, and I met my sister's eyes with a twist of my lips. "What if I wanted whiskey tonight?"

"You'll get beer and like it," she tossed back, lips twitching as she wiped her hands on a towel.

My sister was a vivacious brunette in her twenties with a pixie haircut and the McFlannigan pale skin and blue eyes. Eyes that used to dance with an impish delight but were often hidden these days behind a simmering frustration. It was one of the aftereffects of being shot while protecting Mila. Another was the limp that showed up when the damage to her nicked femoral nerve flared. Stuck at home while recovering, she'd dropped out of college and given up her promising career on the world dart circuit. My opinion—

that I wisely kept to myself—was that she'd started working at Uncle Phil's simply out of a desperate need to escape Mama's clucking.

My neck burned as if I was being watched, and when I turned my head, I caught a blond woman in a tight sweater dress, staring me down. She screamed city girl with her expensive bag hanging from the back of the stool and her spiked heels dangling from her toes. Tourist. Here for the snowy mountain vibe and the antique stores that graced our streets.

I raised my glass, smiled, and thought briefly about sauntering over to her side of the bar. She was exactly what I needed. The complete opposite of the two dark-haired beauties who'd tortured my memories all day. I could lose myself in this woman. Find release and satisfaction without any emotions attached to it. I'd give her a memorable night to tell her friends about when she returned to her real life.

"No," Sadie said, smacking my arm with the bar towel.

I grunted out my disapproval, catching the towel, twisting it easily from her hand, and then attempting to flick her with it. My sister danced back with a little chuckle.

"What happened to the Sadie who was always on my side, talking about the joys of the naked flesh and making Gemma and Maddox blush?" One of Sadie's and my favorite shared pastimes was making our siblings uncomfortable, and while I didn't want to think of my youngest sister having sex, I could block it out enough to enjoy harassing our middle siblings.

"Not her, Ryder. Not tonight. Her boyfriend stood her up for a long weekend away where she thought he was going to propose."

"Sounds like the perfect time for me to swoop in. Revenge sex," I teased back, but the idea of it actually turned my stomach a bit. I wanted to forget the woman who'd abandoned me, not be reminded of what it felt like to be left behind.

Uncle Phil sauntered behind the bar to join Sadie. As

he was only thirteen years older than Mama, most people thought he was her brother rather than Mama's uncle. He had dark hair that I suspected he dyed, the McFlannigan eyes we'd all inherited, and a stomach that had expanded over his belt in the last couple of years. He normally smelled like cigarettes, whiskey, and cheap cologne, and he had a reputation for being a bit of a ladies' man back in the day, who had turned sort of sleazy as he'd aged. A wave of alarm hit me, wondering if that was what my nieces and nephews would think of me in another thirty years. The decrepit uncle who hit on women too young for him while trying to relive his glory days of sex and rock and roll.

It took any ideas I'd had left about one night in the arms of the blonde and turned them to ash in my mouth.

But what else was there for me? I wasn't going down the path of a relationship again. I'd had my chance, and it had disappeared.

Color-changing eyes and lips that burned taunted me. Eyes that had nothing to do with Ravyn's dark ones. These were all snarky defiance with a rebellious boldness that had all but screamed from Gia when I'd caught her red-handed going through my office, making me want to punish her and devour her at the same time.

Uncle Phil put his arm around Sadie and squeezed. "Your sister looks good back here, doesn't she? Like Sarah all over again."

Sadie and I shared a look. Granny Mc had lived and breathed the bar, spending more time here than anywhere else. She'd had a stroke in the office and died before the EMTs could get her to the hospital. Everyone had said she'd gone out just like she would have wanted, breathing in the bar's aroma. My siblings and I had all worked at the bar at different times growing up, especially in those years when things had been all but desperate at the ranch, but I didn't want this to be my sister's life. She had a future outside of this town and this bar. She just needed to be reminded of it.

Sadie slipped out of our uncle's hold, slid an empty pint glass his way, and said, "On that note, I'm out. I have a song calling my name. I was only covering until Ted came back from his break, so now that you're here, you can do it."

Uncle Phil wiped his arm over his forehead, and I noted, with a bit of concern, that his face was sweatier than normal. It was a cold night and warm bar, but he looked like he'd been working out with a boxing buddy.

"Fine, fine, go have a bit of fun, but you're on the schedule tomorrow."

Sadie just waved at him as she started toward the crowded dance floor. I swung off the stool and caught up to her, grabbing her arm and twirling her toward me. "What are you doing here, Sassypants?"

"I was attempting to dance," she said.

"You know what I mean."

Her eyes turned shadowed, and she didn't say anything. She looked like she had when she was four, and I'd found her with her finger in one of Mama's freshly baked olallieberry pies. Defiant and guilty all at the same time.

"When you going back to school?" I demanded.

"I'm not."

My jaw clenched, and when I started to say something, she cut me off. "Don't start. You dropped out and never went back."

"Totally different."

She huffed. "How is it any different?"

"I wasn't using the ranch to hide. I came back with a plan to save it."

"I'm not hiding, you big jerk. I'm recovering from being shot!"

I rubbed my hand over my stubble. Fuck.

"I'll give you that, Sads, but don't you think it's time to move on now? Get your life back?"

Her eyes narrowed in on me, and I felt the first tremor of something that wasn't fear but was close. Sadie could be deadly when she struck. I'd witnessed it many more times than I could count, but I wasn't usually on the receiving end. She and I had always been a team, ganging up on the others even though she was a decade younger than me.

"You ever going to move on, Ryder? Get your life back? Or are you going to let what Ravyn did leave you with as many invisible scars as I have visible ones?"

My chest squeezed tight. No one in my family seemed to get the truth. Like the rest of the men in my family, I was a one-woman man. Soulmates might be a little too touchy-feely of a label, but it was the truth. My parents, my grandparents, and my brother had all been the same way. One person. One lifetime. Unfortunately for me, it just so happened that the woman who'd been mine had lied, stolen, and left. That didn't make her any less the one I'd given my heart to.

I didn't own it anymore. It wasn't mine. I'd given it away.

Love had come and gone from my life. I'd missed my chance.

"Don't throw what happened with her at me just because you're pissed that I'm right," I grunted out. "Your leg is better, damn it. Pick up a dart. Get a UTK course catalog. Do something, but do *not* get stuck in this town, tending bar so Uncle Phil can get drunk and smoke himself into his grave."

She glowered at me for a moment before that impish look came back into her eyes. "I'll make you a deal." I knew I wasn't going to like it, but I bit my tongue and waited for the rest. "You go out on a date—a real date with a woman who isn't just passing through town—and I'll start throwing again."

I wanted to agree. A date was nothing. A mere exchange of a meal and a few hours of my time. I could do that if it meant getting Sadie moving again, couldn't I?

Eyes the color of the fields in the fall flickered through my mind again.

I'd kissed Gia and been filled with ideas of dates. Filled

with multiple thoughts of having her not just in my arms but at my side, riding along with me in my truck with the wind blowing through her hair. I'd had visions of champagne picnics on the hillside overlooking the lake and her writhing below me in bed.

It had been terrifying.

It was still terrifying.

Sadie's expression turned sad the longer I went without agreeing. Finally, she patted me gently on the arm.

"We both have some healing to do. Pushing isn't the answer for either of us."

Then, she turned toward the dance floor, sliding in next to some of my parents' friends who owned a ranch down the way. A smile filled her face that I knew was fake as she did a three-step move with the rest of the crowd.

I'd been okay with the path I'd chosen. I believed the ranch was all I needed. The ranch and my family. But as my gaze drifted to Uncle Phil again, watching him laugh at something Willy said before I turned back to my sister as she spun to the beat of the music, my heart lurched. That ache I'd been feeling all day bloomed stronger.

Goddamn, Sadie.

Maybe she was right.

Maybe I did need to move on. But I was damned if I knew what that really meant, because the one thing Sadie wanted for me was the one thing fate had already taken away.

Chapter Four

Gia

Normally, I chased down every lead on the Lovatos with a fierce and unforgiving determination. But as I stared at the letter with Ryder Hatley's name on it, I wanted to run far away in the opposite direction. It irritated me. It shamed me.

Still, I stared at the letter without opening it until the little girl had fallen asleep.

Then, I forced myself to break the seal, scanning the letter with a heart that banged so fiercely it threatened to escape my chest. A heart that fell, twisting and turning, as I read the contents. At least the letter explained why Ryder had never mentioned to a single human that he had a child—he hadn't known. And yet, here was a girl, seven years old, named Addy according to the letter, who was his.

I didn't know if I felt sorry for the man, angered on his behalf, frustrated I'd have to investigate him all over again, or a bit panicked at the idea of seeing him once more. No man had ever made me feel the complicated waves of emotion he had. Attraction so strong my body felt it might die of neglect the longer we went without touching. Lust that had burned me from the inside out when our lips had briefly met. Annoyance that he saw me as some meddlesome journalist. Irritation that he treated me—like all women who weren't his family—as if I should come with a warning label.

I'd have to bottle up every single one of those emotions he caused to rip through me because I would definitely be seeing him—and sticking around because I wasn't handing the little girl off to someone and walking away. I wasn't letting Addy out of my sight until I knew exactly what she'd seen and how much danger she really was in. And if there was even a remote chance she had the information the letter insinuated her mom had left behind, that danger could be extreme. So, I'd stay with her until I was one-hundred-and-fifty-percent sure she was safe from the long reach of the Lovatos.

Anna's letter had indicated she'd collected an insurance policy to use against the cartel that Addy would have. But the way the room had been ransacked, leaving nothing but a handful of clothes and the little girl behind, it meant the killer had likely taken whatever leverage Anna had gathered with him. Frustration bled through me. Every time we got a solid lead, it disappeared.

Beneath the blue emergency blanket Ramirez had brought in, Addy still wore her blood-stained clothes. We'd need to collect those and get her cleaned up, but it could wait until she woke, and until I could call my boss and figure out how to get the girl to the Hatleys and what exactly I could tell them about the situation.

I stepped just outside the door where I was still visible through the clear glass in case Addy woke and panicked. I wanted her to know she had someone here who would protect her.

To do so, I had to keep any knowledge of her and her whereabouts to the absolute minimum. I'd already stressed that fact to Officer Ramirez, asking him to pass the word along to the crime scene tech and lead detective at the scene—a message I'd also make sure extended to their chief.

I called Rory before my boss. "I'm sending you a photo of a woman who signed into a motel in Denver under the name Anna Smith. She's had facial work done. We need to deconstruct it and get a clear image of what she looked like before."

"Good evening, G. Long time no hear. How are you? I'm fine, thanks."

I sighed. "I'm sorry I don't have time for pleasantries, Rory. This is top priority."

All teasing left her voice as she asked, "You actually found the elusive Anna?"

The woman who'd written the letter had signed her name Ravyn. I wasn't sure that was her real name any more than Anna was.

"Too bad she's dead," I said, letting out a frustrated sigh.

Rory was silent for a beat before she said, "Well, hell. Are you sure it's her?"

"While the name is common enough, the way she was murdered, the vicious cuts down her torso, is classic Lovato. Plus, she left a letter."

"Damn. Does Leland know?"

"He'll be my next call." I hesitated, chest constricting as I debated telling Leland and Rory about Addy. It wasn't that I didn't trust either of them, but the only way to keep a secret was to tell absolutely no one. Everyone, even the best secret keepers, eventually told someone. Unfortunately, I needed my immediate team to know why I was heading to Tennessee in such a hurry, and I needed their eyes and ears listening for any talk of a child on the Lovato end. So, I took a deep breath and said, "We found a little girl in Anna's room."

Rory inhaled sharply. "Was she—"

"She's alive. I think she saw it all while hiding under the bed. She's not talking yet. Seriously traumatized and scared, but she was still savvy enough to pull out a hidden letter her mom had left in case of an emergency. Whoever Anna was, she'd sunk in to the child what to do if the worst happened." I went on to explain what the letter revealed about Ryder and the information Ravyn had been collecting, but that it was probably gone along with Anna's laptop. Rory swore under her breath.

"So, you're taking her to Willow Creek?"

Rory hadn't been with the NSA when I'd been in Tennessee last summer, but she'd been brought up to speed on every aspect of our case with the Lovatos, including the possible connection to the Eastern Dude Ranchers Association and my time exploring the five-star resorts. Nothing had panned out, but we still had task force members undercover at regular cattle ranches across the country and several undercover with Lovato street gangs.

"Yes. At some point, Child Protective Services will need to get involved," I answered. "But that means paperwork and a shit ton of people who would know about her. I don't know how Anna Smith…or Ravyn…or whoever she really is kept the girl off the Lovatos' radar, but she did. We need to do the same until we know exactly what Addy saw. I don't even want to tell the task force. You, me, Leland, and the couple of local cops who helped me sneak her out of the hotel are it. I'm hoping that taking her to her father and helping her feel safe might get her to open up about what happened."

"The poor little thing," Rory said softly. "Legal is going to have a fit once they find out you took her without notifying CPS."

"Hopefully, everyone will be so happy we've brought the Lovatos down that it'll slip through the cracks."

"Good luck with that."

My chest tightened another notch. Doing this, keeping her hidden, could end up costing me my job if it went wrong, but I knew with an instinct that had kept me safe many times before that we needed to conceal her for a little longer. I'd deal with the consequences later. "Keep me updated on any progress you make with Anna's image."

"Hey, G?"

"Yeah?"

"Thanks for trusting me with this."

I heard the remaining insecurities in her voice. The doubts that had been placed there because she'd stumbled into a Lovato operation that had gone bad. But Rory was damn good at what she did, and she couldn't have done much differently without understanding the full scope of evil that trailed the cartel. "I brought you in for a reason. Not only can I trust you, but I also know you won't stop until we end the cartel once and for all."

We hung up, and I placed a similar call to my boss, who was at home with his wife, daughter, and two sons. Ken Leland had once been a top NSA operative in the Special Collection Service. But after he'd met his wife, he'd asked to be transferred to headquarters so he could stay closer to home. While I respected what he did as my boss, he no longer had any of the thrill—or the satisfaction—that came from being in the field. The intense, holding-your-breath moments that made my pulse quicken were exactly what I'd craved ever since I'd seen my first spy movie.

I'd told Leland once that I didn't know how he'd given it up, and he'd simply said I'd understand someday when I found my partner. But I had no intention of falling in love and letting feelings for another human dictate my life choices. I'd seen what it had done to my mom, how she'd given up everything to traipse around after my dad and his military career. And as much as I loved my father, I certainly wasn't going to do to a family what he'd done to us.

Love was a burden I didn't want or need. I certainly wouldn't risk the career I'd built for it.

Blue eyes glowering below the brim of a cowboy hat flashed at me once again, as if taunting me, but I simply pushed the image of Ryder Hatley aside. As tempting as he'd been, sex with him would have been a mistake. Letting even a tiny iota of a thought that there could ever be something more between us take hold would have been an even bigger one. Not only because of who he was, and how his family was tied to this case, but because our worlds would never meld. It was more than me being a city girl and him being a country boy. It was my career choice and vagabond lifestyle versus a man with deep-seated roots.

If I had a choice, I'd never go back to Willow Creek and the temptation he posed. But right now, the only thing that mattered was keeping Addy safe. Hiding her out in the middle of nowhere was a good idea. If I could find out what exactly the Hatleys had to do with Anna and the Lovatos at the same time, even better. And if there was a chance the little girl still had the insurance policy Anna had talked about, I'd find it.

When I said as much to Leland, he agreed, and we made the necessary plans.

After we'd talked through all the next steps, I turned back to the glass door and watched Addy sleep. Something in my chest threatened to crack open. Doors I'd firmly held shut. I wished I could take away what she'd been through. I wished I didn't have to make her relive it by asking her what had happened, but we needed her story. Not just for the case, but to protect her. But how the hell was I going to get her to open up when I knew nothing about kids?

The crime scene tech who'd been at the scene hurried down the hall toward me with a black backpack in hand. He held it out.

"This must be the little girl's. I thought she might need something familiar, so I got the okay to hand it off to her." My heart leaped, wondering just what secrets it might hold, before the hope was whooshed away as he continued, "There's nothing much in it except some kid clothes, a Nintendo Switch, and a couple of books. We documented everything and fingerprinted it all. There were a couple of long black hairs that could be the vic's or the girl's. We'll need her prints and DNA to exclude it."

I'd go through the items myself. See if there was anything hidden in code. "Thanks. Did Ramirez tell you we can't talk about her?"

He nodded.

"I'm not a crime scene expert, but I can collect her

clothes and the samples if you get me the supplies."

"I'll bring everything back."

He darted down the hall and returned with a paper bag full of items. When I walked into the office, Addy was awake. Wide, teary eyes peeked out from beneath the edge of the blanket.

"Hey," I said quietly in Spanish. "You hungry?"

She shrugged. I handed her a water bottle Ramirez had brought in with the blanket.

"At least drink some water."

She looked at it warily, and my stomach churned some more. How bad had her life been that she already doubted beverages given to her?

I poured some of it into a coffee cup on the back counter, drank it, and then handed her the bottle. She accepted it and drank thirstily before her eyes landed on the backpack I had flung over one shoulder.

"This is yours, right?" I asked, sliding it off and bringing it to her.

She reached out and pulled it to her.

"It has some clothes in it. I need to take the ones you have on for the police. For their investigation. It would really help if you could tell us what happened."

She closed her eyes and shook her head so violently I thought she'd pass out.

"Okay," I said softly. "But we still need to get you changed and cleaned up a bit."

She looked down at her blood-stained hands and clothes, and tears welled in her eyes once more. Then, she stood up, her gaze darting around, and I wasn't sure if she was trying to figure out a way to escape or looking for a bathroom.

"Let's go find a bathroom," I offered.

I glanced out the door and did my best to keep her hidden against the wall as I led her to the women's restroom.

I locked the door behind us and then talked Addy through the photos I needed to take and the scraping of her hands for evidence. After a moment of hesitation, I skipped the DNA test. I couldn't afford to have her in the system yet. While she went into a stall to change into clean clothes, I took everything out of the backpack. The books would have to be scanned. The Switch searched. But nothing here seemed to scream insurance policy.

As Addy came out of the bathroom, I took the bloody clothes and bagged them along with the rest of the items I'd collected. The little girl stood near the sink, and I was hit again by how small she was. She couldn't even reach the faucets. I lifted her up onto the counter, and she caught sight of herself in the mirror and froze for a moment. Then, she reached for the soap and water, scrubbing her face and hands as more tears rolled down her cheeks.

I thought my heart might break.

The entire scene was brutally sad, but it also proved just how resilient the fragile-looking girl was. Not a bird with a broken wing, but a hooded pitohui bird, looking beautiful and innocent but containing one of the deadliest toxins on Earth.

I'd need her strength—that poison—to help me bring down the cartel.

We'd been searching for the key for years. None of us would have expected it to come in the form of a seven-year-old girl.

♫ ♫ ♫

When I was on the job, I normally moved fast, efficiently, and silently. A combination of the four J-named spies that I'd grown up loving. Traveling with Addy meant slowing down enough to explain every step to her.

She refused to talk about what happened in the hotel room—basically refused to talk at all—and I didn't push. Not even when the Denver police chief had huffed and puffed and tried to thrust his limited power at me. I needed the child to trust me, and I might not know a lot about kids, but I knew being a bully wasn't the way to do it. Instead, I had to prove I was safe. Prove that I had her best interests at heart. That meant doing what her mother had wanted by taking her to her father.

When I told Addy the plan, she seemed nervous, but there was also curiosity in her eyes. I wasn't sure what Anna-Ravyn had told her daughter about her father, but she obviously hadn't known he lived in Tennessee as she'd been surprised when I told her that was where we were headed.

Leland arranged for an agency plane to pick us up in the middle of the night at the Space Force base outside Aurora. I drove us straight onto the tarmac, leaving the government-issued SUV for someone else to take care of. Addy's gaze darted around as she took in the airfield, the plane, and the steps leading into it, but she slid her hand into mine and let me guide her inside. The pilots were already seated behind closed doors when we boarded the plane. They wouldn't be able to identify their passengers if questioned, which was exactly what I'd needed.

I'd picked up burgers, fries, and shakes at a twenty-four-hour fast-food place close to the base, and we spent the first few minutes of the two-hour flight eating in silence.

"You're not allergic to any of that, are you?" I belatedly asked, continuing in the Spanish that seemed to resonate with her the most.

Her tiny lips twitched, but she shook her head.

I wanted to ask if her mom let her eat junk food but then decided bringing up the woman she'd seen viciously murdered probably wasn't the best idea.

"Do you know anything about your dad?"

She hesitated, head tilting sideways before saying, "*Bueno.*"

I almost choked on the fry I was eating. Thoughts of all the ways Ryder Hatley could be good struck me—many of which were not appropriate for a conversation with his tiny daughter.

"I've met him," I told Addy, and her eyes grew wider. "His family owns a ranch."

At the word ranch, panic washed over her face, and she dropped her food, shrinking back into her seat and bringing her knees to her chest again. Another puzzle for me to try and figure out, but it had me thinking the task force's search for the Lovato leader on a cattle farm wasn't as far off as some members might have thought.

"Your dad's brother is the county sheriff. He'd be your Uncle Maddox," I continued as if Addy hadn't closed down. "He has a little girl a year or so younger than you. Her name is Mila. I guess that makes her your cousin."

The fear retreated from her eyes as curiosity regained strength.

"She's quite a little character," I said with a grin, thinking of the blond-haired whirlwind I'd met several times when staying at the Hatley Ranch. Mila had introduced herself, shown me all the horses, and tried to convince me unicorns were real all in a matter of a few minutes. "She's kind of the opposite of you. A bubble full of energy. Really loud. Talks superfast. She's at the ranch all the time, helping her grandmother—your grandmother—make pies and stuff. You'll never have to worry about carrying on a conversation if she's in the room."

This time, I got an actual grin before it slipped away again.

"Anything else you want to know about your dad or your family?" I asked.

She looked like she had a thousand questions but, instead, shook her head.

My phone buzzed, and I saw a text from Rory. It was a modified image of Anna-Ravyn that she said she was running facial recognition on. The woman's bridge line had been altered significantly as well as the line of her cheeks and the tilt of her nose. I wanted to show it to Addy and ask if it was what her mom had looked like before, but until the medical examiner finished with the body, I wasn't sure how long ago the work had been done. Addy might have only known her mom the way we'd found her.

"You should probably get some sleep," I told her, nodding toward the couch behind us.

She looked at it but didn't do as I'd suggested. Instead, she opened her backpack and pulled out the Nintendo Switch. She held up a charger, looking around. I helped her find a spot to plug it in and then asked to see the device before she played. She handed it over hesitantly.

I snooped around the files on the device, hacking into the code, but there didn't seem to be anything there. I dug around the menus and code some more while Addy watched me with more patience than any kid I'd encountered. I wanted to go through it some more, but I was afraid if I did, it might mess up the little girl's games, and right now, this was the only thing she had left from her old life. So, reluctantly, I gave it back to her.

We spent the rest of the trip lost in our separate electronics.

When we landed outside Knoxville, the pilots waited inside the cabin while Addy and I gathered our things. I had her pull the hood up on her sweatshirt and led her down the steps to where Leland had another SUV waiting for me. It was a black Escalade that looked almost identical to the one in Denver, except this one had a child's booster seat in the back. I hadn't even thought about needing one when I'd driven Addy from Denver to the Space Force base. Clearly, no one was going to award me any gold stars for parenting.

Addy buckled herself in, and we headed toward Willow Creek. My nerves were unaccountably jittery, especially considering I'd been in much worse situations, like the time I'd been surrounded by guerillas in South America. And yet, one little girl and the man I was driving her to had my insides flip-flopping like I was facing an MK47 while holding only a knife.

Needing a distraction from my thoughts, I switched the radio on. A twangy voice and guitar solo filled the air.

"You like country music?" I asked, and Addy shrugged. "The place we're heading…the people there eat it up like it's homemade chocolate chip cookies. I like it myself, even when it can be pretty corny. When I was in high school, I made my older brother take line-dancing lessons with me."

In the rearview mirror, I saw her lips twitch again, and I wanted to make her smile fully, to somehow lighten her load, even if it was only for a few moments.

"My brother swore he hated every second of it and that he hated country music, but I caught him swinging his hips to Carrie Underwood at Christmas. His fiancée gave him a hard time about it too, because she's a rock star. You ever heard of The Painted Daisies?"

She nodded her head furiously, lips quivering upward.

"His girlfriend is Leya, but I'd bet a deluxe tablet that you're an Adria Rojas fan," I said, and she nodded again. "Badas—cool drummer. You look a bit like her."

That got me a full smile. It was sweet and stunning and beautiful.

I wanted to tell her she looked more like her mom than Adria and that they both made the drummer look ordinary instead of the beauty queen she'd once been. And I'd know. I'd met her in person once as part of our joint operations with the CIA. She was gorgeous, no question about it, but Addy and her mother had something hard to name. The altered image of Anna that Rory had shown me had made the woman more stunning instead of less.

I understood completely why a man like Ryder Hatley would have been attracted to her, slept with her, and made a baby with her. What I didn't understand was the spike of pain it sliced through me at the thought of them together. Neither Ryder nor Anna-Ravyn had anything to do with me, and certainly not years ago when they'd made Addy. I would have been in college—still fresh-eyed and idealistic. Even back then, Ryder was not the kind of guy I would have been drawn to. Grumpy and growling had never been my thing. I liked wide smiles, humor, and easy-going demeanors.

Eventually, Addy nodded off, her little head dropping to the side. It wouldn't take us long to get to Willow Creek, but she'd at least get a couple hours of rest. With only the quiet of the radio breaking the silence, I turned my thoughts to the best way to tell Ryder about his daughter. The truth was, no matter how I said it, he'd react badly. He didn't trust me, so telling him about Addy would go over like a skunk at a birthday party. He'd reject the idea as fast as I introduced it, and I didn't want the tension between Ryder and me to make Addy feel like her dad didn't want her.

The idea of her being hurt by him curled through me like a venomous snake. In mere hours, I felt more protective of the kid than I did anyone but my family. I wasn't sure if that was a good or bad thing. It could impair my judgment if push came to shove. I'd just have to keep that fact in mind.

As we neared Willow Creek, I realized there was an easier way for me to deal with Ryder. Someone he'd believe way more than me. So instead of driving directly to the Hatley Ranch, I headed for the sheriff's station and Ryder's brother. The Hatley siblings were close. They looked out for each other in the same way my brother and I did. If Holden showed up with news I had a kid, I'd believe him even if it was physically impossible for me to have had one and not know. I shuddered at even the possibility of having a baby.

It was hard enough figuring out what to do with the seven-year-old in the back seat, who'd only be my responsibility long enough to ensure she was safe. Right now, that meant trusting the sheriff with the truth and hoping to hell my instincts about him were right.

From Anna's letter, it didn't seem like the Hatleys were connected to the Lovatos. Instead, it seemed like Anna was trying to protect Ryder and his family from them, but the Hatleys had still had two close brushes with the cartel. It was suspicious enough for me to keep my guard up. Suspicious enough that I'd have to dig through their pasts and their finances all over again. If someone in the family, or even near them, worked for the cartel and heard about Addy, they'd make a beeline for Tennessee to grab her. If they thought she had something on them that Anna had left behind, they'd do even worse.

That wasn't going to happen on my watch.

The sun was just rising over the horizon as I drove down the cobblestone streets of Willow Creek and pulled into a slot at the sheriff's station next to a department-issued F150 I'd seen Maddox driving. It was early for him to be at work, but I was relieved to find him there. When I turned off the car and looked back at Addy, she was rubbing small hands over large eyes. It took her a minute to figure out where she was, and raw anguish crossed her tiny face before her gaze met mine.

"It's going to be okay," I told her. "I know you're scared and sad. I know you're hurting. You're probably going to feel that way for a long time, but I also know, it'll get better."

I was speaking out of my ass. I hadn't lost anyone close to me. I'd had a couple bad breakups over the years, but that wasn't the same. The only people in my family who'd died were my grandparents on my mom's side, but that had happened when I was little more than a toddler. I'd loved them in a distant way you were supposed to love people who were related to you, but I hadn't grieved them. Not the way this little girl was grieving for her mom.

I swallowed hard, got out of the car, and went around to open Addy's door. She jumped down, shouldering the backpack that was almost as big as her, and slid her hand into mine. It screamed a trust I certainly hadn't earned yet. My throat closed a bit as we headed toward the station doors.

As we entered, an older woman with pale-gray eyes and hair so white it was almost see-through rose from behind the counter. She looked from me to Addy and back.

"Can I help you?"

"I need to talk to the sheriff," I told her. I flipped out my badge, showing it to her. "It's urgent."

She scanned the badge, raised a brow, looked down at

Addy, and then headed for an office door at the back. She was only inside a few minutes before she came out again, followed by Maddox Hatley. He had a leaner frame than his brother and dark-blond, almost caramel-colored hair, whereas Ryder's was dark-brown chocolate. But they shared a tan, square jaw, aquiline nose, and clear blue eyes. I'd never seen the sheriff's gaze spark with danger the way Ryder's had, but then again, I'd never been on Maddox's bad side the way I'd been on his brother's.

"Is there somewhere Addy can wait safely?" I asked the two adults.

They exchanged a look, and then the older woman held out a hand to the little girl. "I'm Amy. We have donuts and hot chocolate in the break room. You interested?"

Addy squeezed my hand tightly, stepping closer to me. I squatted down and looked straight into her eyes in a way I hoped would be reassuring. "I have to talk to the sheriff before we can take you to your dad. I won't be long. I promise, and I'll be right there." I pointed to the office door. "If you feel worried or scared, you just come barreling in there no matter what, okay?"

It took her several seconds before she gave a slow nod.

When she removed her hand from mine and took a tentative step toward Amy, I felt a strange loss I couldn't explain. Loss that was followed by worry as I watched the older woman lead Addy down the hall to an open door revealing a fridge and a microwave. I reminded myself that she was safe here. No one knew who she was, and yet the same nervousness I'd tried to shake on the drive pounded through my veins even stronger.

Maddox waved me toward his office, and I followed him in. When he went to shut the door, I asked him to leave it open. "Just in case she needs me."

He nodded.

"It's Gia, right? You stayed at the ranch last year. Got under my brother's skin a bit." His eyes twinkled as if the idea brought him a lot of joy.

"I did."

"Thought you were an agricultural journalist or something like that. Amy said you had a fed badge."

"NSA, Special Collection Service. I've been undercover for a while."

"And you were looking for something at our ranch?" He crossed his arms over his chest, immediately defensive, causing the tension in the room to grow.

"Yes."

"What the hell?"

"You'd just had a good tangle with the Lovatos, and I'm part of a multi-agency task force slated with bringing them down."

He rubbed his stubbled chin and made his way to his desk, lowering himself into the seat behind it. I did the same to the hard plastic one in front.

"The man running the West Gears made the mistake of trying to hook up with them. Since he died, the bikers have returned to their normal stupidity. Irritating stuff but nothing serious," he acknowledged.

I didn't agree or disagree, and that annoyed him.

"What brings you back with a little girl in tow?"

I told him the basics. How I'd been chasing another lead and found a woman dead in a hotel room in Colorado. Then, I told him how the little girl had been hiding and had likely witnessed the whole thing.

"Okay?" he prompted with confusion written on his face.

"The little girl had a letter that basically said if anything happened to her mom, we were to take her to her dad."

"And he lives here? Is he a member of the West Gears?"

"No," I responded, hesitating for a beat. "He's your brother."

Shock trailed over Maddox's face for a second, and

then he started laughing.

"Oh hell. I almost believed you for a moment. Who put you up to this? Ryder? Sadie? Jesus."

I pulled a copy of the letter from my pocket. The original was with forensics in Denver, but I'd photographed it and made several copies. I pushed one over the desk at him.

"I wish I was kidding."

His smile disappeared, and he picked the letter up as if it was a hairy-legged tarantula. As he read it, his expression turned dark.

"If there'd been any other name on that letter, I still would have insisted you were kidding. But Ravyn? Fuck." He shook his head. "Ryder would never use her as a joke. None of us would. We don't even speak her name. She nearly destroyed him when she took off two days before they were going to be married, with a chunk of the ranch's cash in her pocket. She left nothing behind but a letter that said she'd lost his baby. Fuck…fuck, fuck, fuck."

He banged the desk, emphasizing the words, and the sound echoed through me.

No wonder Ryder Hatley didn't trust women all that much. No wonder he'd looked at me like I was the devil when he'd caught me snooping. No wonder he'd kissed me and all but tossed me aside, afraid to get close to someone he knew was lying and looked like she'd been stealing.

I hadn't stolen, but I had lied.

And I would again.

And he knew it.

Chapter Five

Ryder

SOME THINGS I'LL NEVER KNOW
Performed by Teddy Swims with Maren Morris

A storm was due later this week, and we were trying to protect the two new cabins as best we could by laying the plywood for the roof, so when my phone played my brother's text tone, I ignored it. Shawn and I ran our nail guns along the boards, and the sound echoed through the meadows and out toward the mountains covered in mist. Something about the scent of lumber and winter in the air felt like comfort and home almost as much as the smell of horses and hay.

Once upon a time, I'd thought I'd spend the majority of my days on job sites like this, but the dream of being an architectural engineer had been short-lived. It wasn't one I regretted giving up. In some ways, all that studying had shown me where I actually belonged.

Maddox's text tone jingled again, followed immediately by the harsh ring of an actual call.

Once we had the board secure, I stood. The rooftop view of the sun cresting over the hills added to my feelings of comfort and belonging.

I ripped my phone from the pocket of my work jacket, growling out, "What the fuck is so urgent?"

"Ry…" Maddox's tone was serious, and the way he petered off made the hair on the back of my neck stand up.

"What's wrong? Is it Sadie? Gemma?"

"No. Everyone in the family is fine. This… It's about…" Maddox was stumbling over his words when normally he was quick-witted and snarky enough to keep us both on our toes. A sudden heaviness settled over me.

"Tell me what's wrong."

"I need you to come to the station."

Whatever it was, my brother was having trouble holding it together. In two large strides, I was at the ladder, one-handing it down. "I'm on my way." I jumped past the final rungs to the ground, ended the call, and hollered to Shawn. "I gotta head into town. Call Ramon and see if he can give you a hand finishing up."

I barely heard his response as I cut across the field at a jog. My gaze flicked to the farmhouse and the smoke spiraling into the crisp air, and I debated whether I should take the time to see if my parents knew what was going on. But Maddox had asked me to come, not them, which meant if they didn't know what was going on, there was a reason for it. I slid into the seat of my Chevy and turned the key I'd left in the ignition. The engine rumbled to life, vibrating through me. The loose gravel on the freshly sealed asphalt kicked up as I tore toward the gates.

Maddox had said everyone in the family was okay, so what did that leave?

My mind drew a blank. What could possibly have rattled my calm-and-collected brother so much that he hadn't been able to get his words out?

The minutes it took to drive into town crawled by, making me punch the accelerator that much harder.

As I whirled into an open spot in front of the station, I noted the black Escalade that screamed *government* parked next to the sheriff's truck Maddox drove. We'd seen plenty of similar vehicles a few months back when The Painted Daisies and their bodyguards had flown through town. Nothing good had happened with the band here, and it only made my hackles rise. I jumped out of the truck, barely remembering to pocket the key this time, and raced into the building.

Amy wasn't at the front desk, but I could hear her soft voice chattering away from the break room. I pushed past the swinging half gate into the bullpen with its small gathering of metal desks and stalked toward Maddox's open office door. My lips tilted up at the sign reading, *Sheriff Maddox Hatley*. He was the youngest sheriff the county had seen, but he did the job with more heart and dedication than any officer of the law I'd ever encountered. His job had changed all of us when it brought Mila into our lives after he'd found her screaming in squalor, left by her addict mother. He'd adopted her and made her his without blinking, and now I couldn't imagine our family without my niece in it.

"What's wrong?" I demanded as I strode into the room. My feet came to an immediate halt as I laid eyes on the woman leaning up against a file cabinet on the opposite wall. Her dark hair, just short of black, was drawn away from her face in a tight ponytail. Thick brows gracefully arched over large, color-changing eyes that were flashing the amber hue of whiskey and sin as they landed on me.

She was wearing all black from her head all the way down to a pair of bright-blue cowboy boots I'd once teased her about. Her tight sweater accentuated a lean body with small curves that my hands ached to touch and had my alarm bells screaming a warning louder than my home security system.

Waves of emotions flew through me. Anger. Frustration. Lust. Concern. I wanted to yank her to me and get another taste of those naturally red lips, while at the same time, I wanted to take her by the shoulders and show her the door and the road out of town.

Gia was dangerous. She had secrets. She'd lied. She'd snooped.

And she'd tasted like sugar and spice and everything naughty rather than nice.

Which made her treacherous.

The thoughts I'd had the night before at the bar made her even more so. I'd been relieved when I'd found out Gia had taken off months ago. Even more relieved when her return reservation had been taken over by her brother and the rock star he was protecting.

I didn't have the time or energy for a woman who couldn't be trusted.

I liked my moments with a woman to be sweet, brief, and full of satisfaction before we both went our separate ways. This woman…there was nothing sweet about her.

"What the hell is she doing here?" I growled out. Rather than my comment angering her, her lips twitched ever so slightly, and that only pissed me off more.

"Gia isn't an agricultural journalist, Ryder." Maddox's tone was smooth and gentle, as if he was trying to calm a spooked horse.

I tore my gaze from Gia to my brother. Concern was written all over his face, and I realized, with a sudden swoop of my stomach, it was for me, but damned if I could figure out why.

"No shit," I said, eyes flipping between the two of them again.

"She works for the NSA."

That did surprise me. I'd highly suspected her job was a front. I just hadn't been sure if it was for a con she'd hoped to play on the hick ranch family or something more sinister. I definitely hadn't pegged her as a fed.

"What's the NSA doing in Willow Creek?" I addressed the question to her, but it was my brother who answered.

"Working a multi-agency case against the Lovatos."

Fuck. If that asshole, Chainsaw, wasn't already dead, I'd want to shoot him all over again. Our little town, our little county, had the normal petty crimes of most small communities, but we hadn't been in the line of fire for anything serious until the idiot had tried to tie the local biker club with the cartel.

I crossed my arms over my chest, widened my stance, and shot Gia a look with narrowed eyes. "And you thought, what? Our ranch was involved? That's why I caught you snooping through our shit?"

"Yes," she finally spoke. A clipped, single syllable, but the sound of her voice went straight to my dick. My body craved hearing that word on repeat as she chanted it over and over with me pummeling into her.

My jaw tightened. I pulled my gaze from hers, determined to not look at her again as I focused on my brother. "So she thinks she's got some type of goddamn proof? If there's anything at the ranch tying us to the Lovatos, she planted it there."

Maddox ran a hand through his wavy hair.

"I don't even know where to start, Ryder." He glanced down at a folded piece of paper and then looked back up at me with eyes that were hurting. My brother was in pain, and that caused some of the heat inside me to simmer down.

"Mads," I said, stepping toward the desk. "Just lay it out. Whatever it is, we'll figure it out together. All of us. As a family. Like we always have."

His throat bobbed, and then he said, "This is about Ravyn."

Her name knifed through me, tearing at scars that were healed, but just barely. Maddox would never bring her up. Never. Not unless he had to. My skin broke out in goosebumps. Dread. Premonition. Something hitting me so strong I knew, somehow, the woman who'd once altered my entire world was going to do it again.

"What'd she do now?" I growled out. "And why the fuck do we care?"

"She's dead," he said softly.

For several long beats, I couldn't quite comprehend what he'd said. Any of the times I'd let myself think of my ex-fiancée, I'd imagined throwing in her face how little she'd affected us after she'd gone. How the trauma she'd tried to aim had missed its mark. How my life was so much fucking better without her in it than with a lying, cheating, stealing con artist at my side. But never once had I imagined her dead.

I forced myself to speak. Forced my voice to be bland and cold as I repeated, "Again, why would we care?"

"She was working for the Lovatos," Gia said from off to the side. I didn't turn my head. I ignored her, eyes locked on my brother instead. "But she did something to piss them off, because they slaughtered her. Tore her open from throat to belly button, multiple times. And her hands—"

"I'll say it for a third time—why do we care?" I cut her off as images I didn't want flew through me. Ravyn with her dark curly hair swirling about her and flashing brown eyes smiling. Her luscious curves moving over me, skin glowing in the moonlight. The feel of her thighs around me as my hand settled over her lower abdomen where she'd told me our child was growing.

Everything had been heightened the night she'd told me about the baby. The smells. The sounds. The feel of our bodies. The wool of the blanket beneath me. The stars spread out like their own canvas above her. She'd blended in with the night sky and yet stood out like a glowing apparition. A ghost who had stolen my heart and then left with it in her pocket, along with a ring that had been in our family for generations and the money we'd borrowed to build the cabins.

That image of her, sexily moving above me, dissolved into one that contained blood and long slashes against smooth skin.

Bile hit the back of my throat. My fists tightened, nails biting into skin.

Maddox picked up the paper he'd been eyeing a moment before. "She left this letter for you. I guess it was tucked away in case something bad happened to her."

He slid it across his desk at me, and I took a step back.

No way. No way was I letting her worm her way into my head from the grave. It took me years to recover enough that I could laugh and joke with my family again. Years until I could look at another woman and not feel like I was cheating on the one who'd stolen more than money from me. A woman who'd stolen my future. A family of my own. A wife and a child.

Behind me, another body ran into the room. For a second, because it was a tiny human being, I thought it was Mila coming to say hello to my brother. But as the little girl ran across the room to Gia, my heart stopped completely. She threw her arms around Gia's legs, and Gia's hand went to the top of her head. She spoke to her in Spanish in a soothing tone I'd never heard come from Gia's mouth, but I'd heard plenty of times from Ravyn.

When the little girl turned, I thought I might be dreaming, because Ravyn looked up at me from the child's face. Dark brows. Beautiful brown eyes flecked with black. Hair that was black and shiny. Heart-shaped curves to her sharp jawline and full pink lips. She was Ravyn's mini-me.

The girl was small, about the same size as my niece, but her eyes—eyes that once had looked at me with such wisdom and sorrow from her mother's face—looked at me the same way now. Eyes far older than any child this age had the right to be.

This age…

Fuck! How old was she?

My heart thudded again. A pained, harsh rhythm that felt like it might break my rib cage.

"You know I wouldn't do this to you unless it was absolutely necessary, Ryder." My brother was talking, but my gaze was still on the little girl.

The child looked up at Gia and then back to me. A curious, cautious word slipped from her lips. "Papa?"

I crashed backward into the wall as if I'd been hit by a sledgehammer. Maddox was out of his chair in a flash, coming to my side. My brain was screaming. Denials.

Heartache. Fury.

No.

Fuck no.

She'd lost the baby. Lost. The. Baby.

Maddox tried to reach for me, and I pushed his hand away.

"No." Even to me, my voice sounded like the howl of a wounded animal. It caused the little girl to flinch, turning into Gia's leg. Gia glared at me before lifting the child into her arms. The girl wrapped her hands around Gia's neck, burying her face. And all I felt was relief because Ravyn's eyes were no longer haunting me.

"Nice job, asshole," Gia said, then turned to my brother. "We'll be in the breakroom. Make sure he gets his shit together."

She stormed past me, shoulder brushing against my arm and causing awareness to rush through my veins. I instantly wanted to demand they both come back. The woman who screamed danger and the child with the face of my former lover.

Fury stopped me. Fury for everyone, but mostly for Ravyn. The same fury I'd felt the day she'd left. The day of our rehearsal dinner. The day she'd torn the ground out from beneath me.

Maddox dragged a hand over his face. "Well, hell."

I shoved at him, the buttons of his uniform shirt biting into my palms. "Yeah, what the hell, Maddox? What the fuck would possess you to even think…" I couldn't say any of the words. They got jammed in my throat like a beaver's dam.

My brother slammed the paper he was holding into my chest. "Read it. Then, we'll talk."

I yanked it from his grip. That same dread that had filled me moments before rippled up my spine again. When I glanced down and saw the handwriting, nausea flew through me. It was as familiar as my own. She'd left me hundreds of notes in the months we'd been together. All over the place. On the coffeepot, the toothpaste, and the stall door in the barn. Each one written on brightly colored neon sticky notes that had brought more joy to my soul than I'd thought possible. I'd felt so damn lucky. So damn sure I'd found the woman who would be at my side through thick and thin, just like my parents had found each other.

Maddox walked out the door as I stared at the familiar, flowery strokes of half-cursive, half-print. The first five words had me wanting to ball the letter up and toss it away. But whatever was inside it, whatever she had to say…my brother felt I needed to see it.

The little girl's face swam in front of me for a heartbeat before I focused again on the words.

My dearest Ryder, mi corazón,

I'm sorry for so many things. Things I know you don't want to hear but are still true. I'm sorry for allowing us to fall in love to begin with. For pretending I could escape my bonds. For taking the joy and caring you offered and turning it into heartache and loss.

But the thing I regret most is lying to you about our child. For telling you I'd lost her when I hadn't.

I looked up, throat bobbing. The old grief welled through me all over again. I'd read a similar letter. But that one had said the exact opposite. She'd said she'd miscarried and that she couldn't stay with me because looking at me every day would only serve to remind her of the loss that sat between us. And I'd called her a coward. Screamed it to the trees and the sky because she hadn't been there to hear it.

At the time, when I realized they'd found me, I panicked. I knew if I stayed, they would kill you, me, the baby, and your family. So, I did the only thing I could. I traded my soul so everyone could live. I've kept Addy close, watching over her and ensuring the wolves stayed just far enough away that their teeth could never quite find purchase. But sometimes, in the dark of another long, sleepless night, I wonder if she would have been safer in the haven your family once offered me. Sometimes, I wonder if running away with her was just another selfish moment I allowed myself—maybe keeping her was as bad as allowing you to love me to begin with.

The deal I made with those holding my chains was that I would do their dirty work, but I would not live under their roof. I would do it from a location of my choosing. Whenever they tried to lure me out, lure me to them, I moved. It allowed me to keep Addy from them. I'm fairly certain they don't know she exists. Or they didn't. But as you're reading this letter, I don't know what happened to cause her to show up on your doorstep. They've either taken me, or I'm dead. In either case, she may be running from the very same wolves I tried to hide her from. Hide you from.

What I need you to know, what I plead for you to believe, is that I love you. I will always love you. There has never been anyone else for me. Only you. And I love our child, if possible, even more.

Our precious little girl has somehow, even with our life on the run, kept your verve for life and your sense of humor. When she smiles, I see you. I hope she's still able to smile when she finds you. I hope the black of my world hasn't forever darkened hers.

As I write this and put the letter where only Addy knows, I am sure of one thing. I know you will protect her with every fiber, every breath in your being.

And I'm sorry to say you may have to.

I won't say their name here in case there's a chance to keep you both safe from them. I've been building something for years, before I even found you, something I hope you can trade your lives for if they do show up at your door. It's an insurance policy of sorts. If you have Addy, you'll have it, but don't use it unless they come for you. It'll be so much better for everyone if they don't know either of you exists.

I won't ask for your forgiveness because I understand there is no redeeming myself for any of the things I've done. But I know there was a time when our love meant everything to you, and I call on those feelings to be your guide as I beg you not to hold my mistakes against our daughter. Please give her freely the love you once gave me. Please let her see the Ryder Hatley I fell head over heels for. The person who allowed me to forget briefly what I'd escaped. The person who allowed me to hope for something better than the life I'd found myself living.

Sincerely, regretfully, and with all the love I still feel for you,

Ravyn

My jaw was clenched so tight I thought my teeth might crack. I balled the paper in my hand, crumpling the words that were tearing apart my walls and my scars and making them bleed fresh and new. How dare she talk of loving me! How dare she!

Fuck.

I closed my eyes, leaning back against the wall.

She'd been running. Running scared. And she hadn't trusted me enough to tell me. Hadn't believed we could face it together. What did that say about me? About us? Could I even believe her? She'd lied about everything before. Maybe this was just one more lie. Maybe she just needed some damn sucker to take in her child if she ended up dead because she was working with a fucking cartel. Maybe I was the only damn sucker she could think of.

And yet, that thought didn't ring true either.

The girl…Addy…she looked a little small to be the right age. She looked like my niece, and Mila had been born a whole year after our baby would have been. But Ravyn had been small as well. She'd been over a foot shorter than me. When we'd been together, I'd loved the difference in our sizes. Loved that I could maneuver her body, set her on me, hold her up, and get lost in her fairylike quality while embedding myself in her.

A simple DNA test would show whether or not she was lying this time.

Whatever the truth, Addy had been told I was her father.

She was here, and her mother had been slaughtered.

My stomach lurched.

Had she seen it?

Had that little girl watched as someone cut open her mother?

Chapter Six

Ryder

GET OFF ON THE PAIN
Performed by Gary Allan

More pain carved its way through me at the thought of Addy watching her mother being killed. It was as if the knife that had cut Ravyn had found its way inside me, slicing away at what was left of my emotions.

What should I do?

I turned my head to find Maddox had come back. He was standing in the doorway, eyes sad instead of sparkling as they normally were. No ribbing. No teasing. Just a mirror of pain. Once upon a time, we'd commiserated over the loss of the women we loved.

He'd gotten his back, and I'd told him he'd done something I could never do…forgive.

Now I didn't have to worry about ever getting that chance.

Ravyn was dead.

Her child—our child?—was here.

"I'm sorry," Maddox said quietly.

My jaw worked. Tears pricked my eyes, which I refused to let fall.

"She was working for the Lovatos?" My voice sounded distant, cold, faraway, but it was either that or bleed emotions all over the floor.

"Gia seems to think so."

Gia. Another dark-haired liar.

When I didn't say anything, Maddox continued, "She can't tell me a lot because their investigation is on a need-to-know basis, but she says Ravyn was some sort of computer genius, running a lot of the cartel's business from behind the scenes."

She'd been wildly good with numbers, websites, and software. Dad and I had hired her because of those skills. We'd needed an office-manager-slash-marketing-manager-slash-accountant. Someone who could do a little bit of everything for the little we were offering. Ravyn had shown up seeming like a godsend.

"The letter." I swallowed hard over a lump that appeared, pushing past it. "She made it sound like they were making her do it."

He shrugged. "I don't know the details. I'm not sure the task force does either."

"What do I do?"

My brother met my gaze, and the eyes meeting mine held a steeliness that was rarely aimed at me.

"Meet your daughter. Take care of her. Keep her safe."

"I want a DNA test," I replied.

"I think that's smart."

"But you think she's mine?"

Maddox ran a hand over his face again. "I think she looks like Ravyn. I think she's the right age, if she's seven. I think it would've been possible—but not likely—for her to get pregnant with some other guy's kid that quickly after she left here."

That thought was a bitter pill. I'd purposefully pushed thoughts of Ravyn with some other guy out of my head whenever they had tried to poke at the corners of my mind. I'd wanted to pretend she'd never existed. This caused something akin to guilt to waft through me. Guilt I didn't owe, and shouldn't have, but still did.

"Okay." I exhaled.

Maddox searched my face. For what, I wasn't sure, but he nodded. "Let me get them back in here."

He left, and I had mere seconds to prepare myself for the shock of seeing Ravyn's face all over again. The little girl was still clinging to Gia. Both with heavy brows, thick lashes, and dark hair. They were similar enough that they could be related. Except, Gia was taller than Ravyn had been. Leaner. Small, tight curves to Ravyn's voluptuousness.

Gia and Addy had their cheeks pushed together, and they were both tense and taut. Gia's shoulders were drawn back, as if ready for a fight...or maybe she was just uncomfortable with a child clinging to her. Maybe she didn't know what to do with a kid any more than I did. All I knew was how to spoil a child—I did that regularly enough with Mila—but I didn't know shit about raising one. My little brother was the family man, not me. I never intended to have kids after what I'd lost.

I stuck out my hand like an idiot and said, "I'm Ryder."

The girl hesitated before removing one of her hands from Gia's neck, sliding her tiny palm into mine, shaking it, and saying, "Addy."

In those two syllables, I heard the same rhythm to her speech that had been in Ravyn's. It came from growing up speaking two languages, she'd told me. She'd been born and raised in the United States, but her father was from Mexico. Her family had spoken both English and Spanish, switching back and forth with an easy fluidity, sometimes within the same sentence.

With me, Ravyn had mostly spoken English, as my Spanish had topped off with the basic two years required in high school. But when we were making love, when her emotions poured from her, she'd slip into Spanish as if it were the language of her heart. I'd learned a little more of it from her. Not much. And most of it was now forgotten.

I let go of the little girl's hand and looked from her to

Gia and then my brother and back. "What now?"

Gia's eyes narrowed. "Now, we take her home."

My chest tightened again. "We?"

Gia knelt, placing Addy on her feet. She spoke to her in a rapid-fire Spanish that spoke of years of use. Addy looked from her to me and then back. She picked up a backpack that looked almost as big as she was and stepped out of the room, sitting down on a chair just outside the office door, and pulled out a gaming device from within the bag's depths.

Gia shut the door, turning to look at Maddox and me with an attitude that screamed defiance, as if she already suspected we wouldn't like or agree to what she had to say.

"I'm not leaving her until I know she's safe."

My chest heaved. I didn't know what that meant. Gia had said, "Take Addy home," in the same sentence as the word "we," but before I could think of the right questions to ask, she continued, "She's spoken maybe a dozen or so words since we found her in the hotel room. She was hiding under the bed in a space that would barely fit a book. She had her mother's blood on her. I don't know what she saw, but I do know if the Lovatos even suspect she was in that room, they'll be looking for her. And if Ravyn was able to hand off something to her that could be used as leverage that they didn't take from the room already, they'll be even more desperate. The cartel doesn't leave loose ends."

"They'd kill a kid?" The words were out before I could take them back.

"They'd kill their own child if it meant keeping their secrets."

My gut turned nastily. Was Addy someone in the cartel's kid rather than mine?

"Who knows she's here?" Maddox asked.

"I kept the knowledge of her existence down to a minimum. There are six people besides those of us in this room who know, and only three of them know the contents of that letter. I trust my boss and my teammate with my life, but the Lovatos have a way of getting information that should be secure."

"You think they'll come for her?" I grunted out.

"Even if she didn't see anything, they don't know that. Only time will tell if they find out about her, if she saw anything, or if her mother really gave her something we can use. So, until we know otherwise, we have to assume she's at risk."

I looked through the window of the door to the tiny child with her head bent over the device, and dark fury welled through me again—this time, at the idea of anyone trying to hurt her.

"You didn't find anything on her? That Ravyn left?" Maddox asked.

"Nothing in the hotel room. But then again, none of the electronics she needed to do her job were there either. So, they could have taken whatever proof she'd gathered with them after they killed her. All that was in Addy's backpack were clothes, two books, some personal hygiene items, and that Nintendo. As you might imagine, tech is kind of our thing in the NSA, so I explored it a bit before I let her have it. I don't think anything is there, but I'll take a better look later. I think it's fairly new as there are only a couple games on it, or maybe they didn't have the money to buy more."

I instantly wanted to buy Addy a dozen games. Maybe a hundred. Give her a whole damn room full of them. Give her a room full of rainbows and sparkles just like Mila's room at Maddox's place.

"Last I heard, no one's been able to identify the head of the cartel. Just a large base of foot soldiers," Maddox said.

"We've had some leads, and we were working a source, but every time we think we're getting somewhere, the person we've got our sights on winds up dead."

"The task force has a leak?"

"It may not be a direct leak. I'm not putting it past the Lovatos to have paid informants within multiple agencies, but it's also much more likely that, with her skills, Anna—Ravyn—opened a door directly into some federal systems."

For some reason, Gia's calm, her almost lackadaisical attitude about it all, pissed me off. "What you're telling me is you have nothing? There's no end in sight? This child could be in danger for years—which means her being here could put my entire family at risk."

"She *is* your family," Gia snapped.

"So you and a thief say," I growled back.

"Take a breath," Maddox demanded, looking between us. "We'll run a DNA test, and we'll know for sure."

"You can't do that," Gia said, shaking her head. "I didn't even run her DNA back in Colorado. If you do it now, and there's a match to something in the system, it'll flag something somewhere, and you'll end up with multiple law enforcement agencies and the Lovatos banging down your door."

"She's here. She exists. And everyone in Willow Creek is going to know about it as soon as I show up anywhere with her at my side."

Gia looked as pissed about this as I was about the entire situation. Her jaw worked as she looked out the door at Addy. Then, her chin went up as she turned back to us and said, "We'll say she's mine for now."

I scoffed. Gia didn't look old enough to have a seven-year-old daughter, no matter her confidence and don't-fuck-with-me attitude. "What? You were a teen mom?"

"She's seven, asswipe, not twelve. There are plenty of people who have kids at twenty."

I could feel Maddox watching the bouncing match between Gia and me. I was pretty sure if I looked at him, he would be trying to decide whether to laugh or defend me. The laugh was probably winning.

"Addy and I can stay in one of the guest cabins at the ranch. You can get to know each other without the pressure of living under the same roof. I can make sure she's safe.

We all get what we want."

I was just about to retort with something along the lines of *when hell froze over* when my brother's soft voice stopped me. "Except for her. I'm pretty sure all she wants is her mother back."

And that seemed to take the bluster out of all of us.

A little girl had lost her mother. Maybe witnessed her being killed. I thought about Mila's traumatized tears after she'd seen me accidentally kill the crow yesterday. What Addy may have seen…it made acid burn through my stomach faster than lye through grease. Who might come after her—and Gia as she stood watching over a child who might be mine…I couldn't even think it all the way through.

"The cabins aren't fit for anyone right now. Construction is going on all around them with the additions we're putting up," I grunted out. "You'll stay with me."

Gia's eyes widened, and her breath hitched. And damn, did I want her breath to hitch for all the wrong reasons, which meant inviting her into my home, into the place I'd never taken any woman, was as wrong as it was right.

"People will talk, Ryder," Maddox said. "You know what they'll say."

Gia's gaze met mine. I wasn't sure if it was resignation or a dare that burned in them.

"Let 'em talk," I said quietly.

I'd walked into the sheriff's office with dread and premonition following me, but all I felt right now was resolve. If someone came after Addy, and Gia because of it, then I'd be there with my damn gun, defending them. I had no doubt this confident, smart, lean-muscled undercover agent had been trained to protect herself and might be able to guard Addy with more skill than me, but I'd be another body between them and her. I'd be the one thing the little girl could depend on.

"What about Dad and Mama? Our family?" Maddox asked.

"We'll tell them the truth," I said, meeting his gaze with a sure one.

"I don't think it's wise to tell more people who she really is," Gia said, arms across her chest.

"I'm not a liar. I don't lie to the people I care about. Let the rest of the town think what they want, but I won't be anything but honest with the people who matter to me."

Maddox looked over at Gia. "If you and a little girl all but move in with Ryder without telling our family the truth, they're going to roll out the welcome mat and start planning a wedding."

Gia grimaced, and her cheeks flushed ever so slightly. "I'm not moving in. We'll just say we needed a place to stay, and Ryder offered."

"You don't get a say in what I tell my family," I growled.

"And you don't get to put her and an entire operation at risk just to relieve your conscience."

Maddox huffed out a mix of laughter and exasperation before saying, "I'm not sure this is a good idea. While it would be entertaining to watch the two of you go at it, that little girl needs peace around her, not a constant battle."

It shut us both up once again.

After a long moment, I uttered words I wasn't sure I felt but was convinced I had to try. "He's right. Truce?" I offered her my hand.

She stared at it for a long time and then took it. Heat swept over my palm, up my wrist, and along my arm. We both pulled away quickly, and Gia rubbed her hand along her thigh, proving that what I'd felt every time she was in the same vicinity as me plagued her as well. But I was a grown-ass man. I could ignore the unwanted attraction. Gia Kent would be there for a matter of days, just long enough to ascertain if the Lovatos were coming for Addy or not.

Then she'd be gone, and I'd try to figure out what pieces of my life were left and how to pull them all together.

Chapter Seven

Gia

AMEN

Performed by Alana Springsteen

𝒟espite having graduated summa cum laude from college and being commended multiple times for keeping my wits about me on the job, I felt like an idiot as Addy and I followed Ryder to his home. Staying with him was a bad idea. An epically bad idea.

The way my body had sparked and burned at our simple handshake was proof.

I glanced at Addy in her booster seat in the back. She was staring out the window at idyllic views of cows and horses roaming over white-fenced fields. What would it be like for her to grow up here? Learning to ride horses, playing in the lake on hot, humid summer days, surrounded by a family who loved each other enough to stay rather than leave.

My family loved each other and would be there in a flash if one of us needed something, but my brother and I had followed in our father's footsteps by putting our country before our relationships. As adults, we rarely saw each other, and we definitely didn't know how to stay.

Except, my parents had now lived in Virginia for longer than they'd lived anywhere in their marriage. After moving three times during my last three years of high school, Mom had finally reached a breaking point, and Dad swore he'd retire before he'd move again. Mom had finally been able to watch the gardens she put her heart into mature and bloom just like she'd designed. She'd found friends and kept them, whereas I had done the opposite.

We'd moved so many times growing up that I'd seen friends as temporary fixtures, toys that got switched out as you outgrew them. And during my high school years, being the new face each fall had been pure torture. I'd been the geeky loner with a love of spy novels and movies that had neared obsession territory.

We blew past the driveway to Hatley Ranch and the stone pillars holding a carved wrought iron masterpiece with the name of the ranch twirled below the silhouette of a bucking bronco. While I'd known Ryder didn't live on the main grounds of the ranch, I'd never gotten to his place last year. After he'd found me snooping in his office, it would have completely blown my cover if I'd shown up at his house too.

Ryder's turn signal blinked just before he pulled down a gravel drive tucked between several tall, southern magnolias that would bloom in a few weeks. The road wound through more thick foliage, including several live oak trees with enormous limbs crawling along the ground like octopus arms. A rustic, red covered bridge only large enough for a single vehicle to cross at a time covered the creek and led to a slight rise on the other side.

When the house finally came into view, shock roared through me.

The research I'd done on the family before I'd ever set foot in Willow Creek had uncovered that he'd designed and built the house himself. He'd gone to college to be an architect but had dropped out to come home and help the failing ranch. So, while I knew he'd built the house, I'd expected it to be something more along the lines of the family's two-story farmhouse or a rustic log cabin and not the glass marvel standing in front of me.

The entire building was made primarily of windows with hints of sleek pine and river rock peeking out. The slant of the roof echoed the slope of the mountains beyond it before dropping off and giving way to tranquil valley views of not just the Hatley land but also the lake in the distance.

It was art in the form of a building. It was breathtaking.

The grumpy cowboy had created this from nothing more than his imagination and the land. What did that say about him?

My heart was slamming weirdly in my chest as we followed the curve of the driveway to the side of the house where a three-car garage was attached to the main structure by a glass breezeway.

All three doors rolled up at the same time, and Ryder drove the pickup into the first bay. In the second slot was an old-school muscle car my brother would drool over, and the third was empty. It was perhaps the cleanest garage I'd ever seen. No shelves of sports equipment or yard tools. Several large, standing toolboxes that looked almost brand new were scattered amongst sleek cupboards that blended in with the walls. Nothing was out of place, and everything was sparkling clean.

Ryder slid out of the truck and waved me into the last slot.

I pulled in, trying to gather my wits.

Ryder opened the back passenger door for Addy as I climbed out. The two of them stared at each other as if taking each other's measure. I popped the Escalade's tailgate, pulled out a small duffel I used as my go-bag, and joined them.

Addy unlatched her buckle and went to grab the backpack right as Ryder did. Their hands collided, and the little girl jerked away as if burned. A shadow of concern flickered over Ryder's face.

He slung the backpack over his shoulder and offered Addy his hand.

She didn't take it.

He backed up, cleared his throat, and said, "Come on

in, and we'll get you settled."

Addy jumped to the ground and looked at me with wide, nervous eyes.

"It's okay," I said in Spanish. "I'm not going anywhere."

Ryder hit a button on the wall to close the garage doors and then led us into the glass breezeway. The ceiling was made of pine planks, glimmering with gold and lacquered until it was almost as shiny as the glass itself. Large slabs of slate beneath our feet mimicked the stone of the mountains.

Addy's hand slid into mine, and I looked down at her. She was as overwhelmed by the place as I was.

Ryder unlocked a second door and waved us through. We entered a mudroom of sorts where he hung his hat. His hair was barely mussed beneath it, but he still ran a hand through it, and I sensed he was as nervous as the rest of us.

The mudroom opened into a kitchen with oversized, professional-looking steel appliances and two walls of glass. The slate floor tiles were repeated on a smaller scale in the backsplash, as if mimicking the boulders visible outside the windows. The vaulted pine ceiling rose like trees to where whispers of blue sky and puffy clouds danced across the largest skylights I'd ever seen in a home. A long counter of shiny wood divided the kitchen from a living area reached via two stone steps.

The entire house felt as if the outdoors had grown into it, or vice versa. A seamless blending of nature and home that was only accentuated by the earth tones of the leather furniture and the large tree trunk coffee table.

No art hung on any of the handful of walls that weren't glass. The house didn't need it. The view was clearly intended to be the primary decoration.

"Holy sh—cow." The words finally slipped out of me as I stared out at the valley from what felt like the treetops.

Addy squeezed my hand, and we both turned our heads in Ryder's direction.

He was standing on another pair of stone steps leading toward the foyer with its large double doors of glass and wrought iron gleaming behind him. That nervousness I'd witnessed in the mudroom seemed to have grown. I'd seen him growly. Snarly. Angry. But not uncertain. And it pricked at something deep inside me that wanted to comfort him. An unwanted softness that I didn't let into my life often.

Addy and I moved through the room to join him on the steps.

"Where do you watch TV?" I asked.

His lips twitched slightly. "Honestly, I don't watch much, and if I want to catch a game, it's usually at the bar, my parents' place, or Maddox's. But there is a television in the game room downstairs."

"Games?" Addy's ears perked up.

His eyes gentled as he took her in. "It's one of my niece's favorite rooms. Let me show you to your bedrooms first, and then I'll take you there."

In the entryway, he pointed to a curved staircase going down. "Game room is there." He went in the opposite direction, climbing four short steps into another hallway. The left side was made of glass, the right of pine walls and doors.

"Half bath," he said, waving a hand at the first door. "My office," he explained, pointing to a set of double doors. "Up here is the bedroom wing."

We mounted another set of short steps that allowed the house to flow with the natural slope of the hillside. He opened the first door, and we walked into a mint-green-and-cream haven larger than my first apartment.

A four-poster bed of wrought iron carved to look like trees was piled with soft linens and butted up against a wall that mimicked moss-covered stone. A dresser, love seat, and writing desk took up the wall across from it. The showcase was once again the windows, where the view was of a grove of ancient live oaks with the sprawling limbs we'd seen along the drive immersed with weeping willows that were still bare. They'd be feathery and green once spring hit, and waking up here would feel like sleeping in a tree house.

"Bathroom and closet are through there." He pointed to a door and then looked at me. "Should be plenty of towels and bath products, but Sadie's been in and out this year whenever Mama's hovering got to be too much, so let me know if you need something."

Okay, then. This stunning room was mine for the next few days.

I swallowed hard, dropped my duffel on the bed, and then followed Ryder out of the room with Addy still clinging to my hand as if I was the last thing keeping her standing. Or maybe she was stabilizing me. I wasn't sure which.

Just like I wasn't sure why Ryder's carefully crafted home was impacting me so much. It was as if he'd thrown a rock into the sleeping pool of my emotions, and the ripples were slowly expanding, taking over in a way I didn't like.

The next room over was done in soft blues and cream. The bed had a canopy of lace, and above it, the ceiling was painted like a spring sky. The recessed lighting hit the clouds, making them glow as if from an unseen sun.

"Bathroom and closet again." Ryder pointed to another door. He looked down at Addy. "My niece, Mila, likes this room best, so I thought you might like it too. She likes waking up to the ducks and geese on the trout pond." He pointed out the windows to where a small pond sat nestled amongst the trees.

It was as if each room was a picture box showcasing another scene.

Another piece of art assembled from nature.

The man before me had seen it, sculpted it, and then carefully embedded his home into it.

I'd never expected to find an artist under all that flannel and denim.

Ryder put Addy's backpack down on a tufted blue

velvet bench at the foot of the bed, and she eyed it as if she didn't want to leave it there. I squeezed her hand, and her eyes met mine.

"It's okay. You're safe here. Your things are safe here."

She hesitated before nodding.

"Does she only speak Spanish?" Ryder asked, concern in his voice. I'd almost forgotten I was still using it with her.

I looked from him to Addy. "You speak both English and Spanish, right?"

She stepped closer to me once more but nodded.

Ryder squatted in front of her. "That's probably good. I don't know much Spanish. But maybe you can teach me? Your mo—" He winced and changed directions. "I was learning some a long time ago, but I've forgotten a lot of it."

The silence left behind turned awkward. She didn't trust him because she'd been trained to distrust everyone. The fact that she was clinging to me had much more to do with how I'd found her than an actual belief that I was safe.

"Let's take in the game room, shall we?" he asked.

She nodded furiously.

We stepped out of the room, and she looked back at the door, eyeing all the ones along the hall and another set of steps leading to another glass breezeway.

"My room's up there." He gestured to the stairs. "If you need anything at night, that's where I'll be."

As Addy shifted from foot to foot, Ryder looked at me, and I saw not just nervousness but helplessness on his face. He was lost. He had no idea how to become a father to a seven-year-old. And not just any little girl. One who'd been traumatized, living a life on the outskirts of society. Who knew what she'd seen, even before yesterday?

I didn't want my heart to soften even more toward him, but it did.

Ryder led us back to the curved staircase and down into a long basement taking up the same amount of space as the kitchen and living area above it. Deep brown leather couches screaming comfort faced a ginormous television built into a wall of teak cabinets. The shelves were packed with entertainment equipment in all varieties, books, and board games. In the far corner of the room was an ancient jukebox and several old-school, free-standing video game units—*Pac-Man* and *Frogger*—as well as a pinball machine. A pool table, dart board, and heavily lacquered bar finished up the man-cave dream.

Addy let go of my hand and ran straight for the machines in the corner.

"Play?" she asked, hand waving at the *Pac-Man* game.

Ryder's mouth curved upward, lips almost too pretty to be a man's with a strong M shape at the top tucked inside scruff that was approaching a full beard. It was clipped neat and tight, and I realized suddenly that the facial hair wasn't just overgrowth he hadn't shaved but purposeful. Clean lines and curves.

Ryder Hatley wanted the world to think he was a rough-and-tumble cowboy, dressed in worn work clothes and well-used boots, and more interested in crops and cattle than glamour and glitz. But this house, the business he ran, the well-groomed beard…they all screamed precision and control, a planning and artistry that was not in the least bit backwater rancher with his head stuck in the hay.

Ryder strode over to a bowl on the bar, fished a bunch of gold coins from inside it, and then headed for the *Pac-Man* machine.

He waved at the bowl, saying, "Tokens. If we run out, let me know. I'll open the machine and get them back out."

He pushed a coin into the slot, and the machine came alive, music and beeps taking over the room. Addy smiled, but when she moved in front of it, she could barely reach the buttons.

"Hold on," he said before turning around and heading for a closet just off a hallway. He came back with a step stool he set down for her. Addy climbed on, hit the start button, and then lost herself in the game. A little laugh escaped her as the yellow character almost got caught in a corner. Her hands were fast. Her face alight. It was the most alive I'd seen her since I'd pulled her from under the bed in the hotel room. My heart twisted.

Ryder stepped back, joining me as we watched her play.

When she lost, she put in another coin from the stack of tokens he'd left for her and started again.

"What's down there?" I asked, chin nodding toward the hallway.

"Unfinished rooms."

"More bedrooms?" I asked.

He nodded, looking uncomfortable before saying, "Ravyn wanted a large family."

My pulse skittered again, that same strange, offbeat staccato that had started when we'd pulled up to the house. It was as if I couldn't find a stable, solid pattern anymore. As if I was perpetually off-kilter here.

"You built the house with her?"

"No. Didn't have the money back then. We'd drawn up the plans together though. Just dreaming at the time. I made some changes once I had the funds to make it happen, but I kept the extra rooms in case someone else ended up living here and needed the space. They're unfinished for now."

"The land belongs to your family, so you wouldn't sell, right?" I asked.

"No. But someday, Sadie or Gemma might want to settle here. Or Maddox and McK might get tired of living downtown." He shrugged.

"Where would you go?"

He pushed his hands into the front pockets of his jeans and rocked a little back and forth. "We have plenty of land. There's an old cabin up along the ridgeline." He pointed across the valley to where the hillside curved upward. "I could fix it up or tear it down, build a two-room place. This is all a bit much for just me." He looked at Addy as he added,

"I had no plans for it ever to be more."

That little soft spot in my heart grew another notch. I wanted to hate the way he was responsible for spreading it, but the idea that this man would give the home he'd lovingly designed and built to his family, because he didn't believe he'd ever have his own to fill it, made me unexpectedly sad. He wasn't like me, who'd never had plans to settle down or have kids. He'd very much had those hopes, and they'd been ripped away. Anna-Ravyn-whoever-she-was had broken him, and the only way you got *that* broken was if you loved with every piece of you and had it torn away.

I couldn't imagine the grumpy rancher I'd met loving anyone that much.

And yet, here was the proof. A home that was a work of art built with love in mind.

I didn't want to be wrong about him any more than I wanted to have anything in common with him. But the solitary life Ryder had chosen was what I'd elected as well. I'd thought my job, my parents, and my brother would be enough. But catching a glimpse into Ryder's life, absent of anything more, felt unexpectedly lonely. I practically ached at the mere glimpse of it, causing doubts about my choices to whisper through me, and all I could do was shove them aside before they could take purchase and grow into something more.

Chapter Eight

Ryder

STAND

Performed by Rascal Flatts

I wasn't sure why I'd given Gia that much insight into my past and my once-planned future. Maybe it was because my emotions were running high. Maybe it was because my life had just been upended, and I might be looking at a very different future than the one I'd envisioned ever since Ravyn had left.

I cleared my throat and headed for the bar.

"Water? Soda?" I asked.

"Water would be great," Gia said.

"Topo Sabores?" Addy looked over at me, a hopeful expression on her face. I looked at Gia for clarification.

"It's a soda in Mexico. Orange is the most known flavor. Doesn't have as much sugar as Crush or Fanta."

I had a list growing in my head of things I needed to get. Toys. Clothes. Books. Video games. And now, orange soda.

"I have root beer or ginger ale," I said.

By the look on Addy's face, I might as well have offered her slimy spinach.

I took three bottles of water from the fridge, twisted off the caps, handed one to Gia, and then set one down by Addy. I glanced at her score, and surprise shifted through me.

"Sadie is going to be pi—upset that you're about to beat her. She's had the high score for years."

"Sadie?" Addy asked, the name coming haltingly from her lips.

"She's my sister…" I almost added she was Addy's aunt, but then I held back. What would happen if we did the DNA test and this little girl wasn't mine? What would I do? What would we all do if she eased herself into our hearts and then was taken away to live with her real father? What if her real dad was a member of the cartel? One of the ones who Gia had said would kill their own kid to keep their secrets?

Acid burned through my stomach at that thought.

My phone rang, and I pulled it out of my pocket. I grimaced at the picture of my mother, ignoring it because I didn't know how to break this news to her yet. Mama had grieved the loss of Ravyn and her first grandchild more than anyone except me. It wasn't just that she'd loved Ravyn and lost her. It was that she'd also seen me hurting and that had added to her pain. A mother's love at work.

Had Ravyn loved Addy that much? I wanted to believe the little girl had received at least that from the life Ravyn had chosen for them.

Gia had taken a seat on one of the high-backed barstools, and as I joined her, I said more to myself than her, "What kind of existence could she possibly have had? Always moving. Running with fear chasing them."

Gia shifted, uncomfortable for some unknown reason, before she raised her chin. "There are positives to moving around."

I turned toward her a bit more, and our knees bumped. Heat and awareness flashed through me.

"Like what?" I asked.

"Resilience. Independence."

"Firsthand experience with this, I take it?"

"My dad was in the military. We moved a lot. Three times in high school alone."

I couldn't imagine being torn out of my safety zone at that tumultuous time in my life. My friends and family had grounded me. Instead of letting sympathy she wouldn't want break free, I asked a question instead. "Military dad, Secret Service agent brother, and you're an NSA analyst. Are your parents proud or concerned that you followed in those footsteps?"

She shifted, discomfort growing. She didn't want to talk about herself. "Holden is former Secret Service. And my mom and brother think I work for an agricultural journal just like you did."

I stared at her for a long beat before her words settled in. All the reasons not to trust her leaped back to life. She didn't just lie to strangers for a living. She lied to the people she loved most. What did that do to a person? How did it twist their values…shift the lines they weren't willing to cross?

My expression must have given my thoughts away, because she huffed and said, "It's better this way. Mom doesn't worry, and my brother doesn't meddle."

I raised a brow, and she crossed her arms over her chest before turning those green-and-amber eyes away to watch Addy. As I took in her profile, I realized she looked tired. There were dark circles I hadn't noticed earlier below her lashes. She was paler than when I'd seen her last. In the months since she'd been here, she'd grown tauter, more muscled. As if she'd done nothing but work out as she scurried from place to place. As if life had hit her hard along the way.

I imagined chasing a drug cartel across the globe could do that to you. I imagined Ravyn's brutalized body wasn't the only one Gia had seen. It infuriated me for some reason—the idea of Gia seeing evil every day. I much preferred the concept of her hunting down the latest and greatest in agricultural technologies than facing the devil. And if it bothered me, a virtual stranger, I could imagine it would torture a family who loved her.

None of my family liked the idea of Maddox facing

guns and bad guys either, but that wouldn't cause him to lie to us about what he was doing. Pretend to be someone he wasn't.

The ease with which she seemed to lie raised all my red flags.

I could admit I didn't trust any woman easily. I'd earned the mistrust after watching Maddox be burned by the woman he'd loved most and then personally feeling the brutal hand of Ravyn's betrayal. Even still, I knew not every female was out to steal and cheat and leave, but I also wasn't sure how to get over it enough to give my heart away again.

A heart I'd thought I could only give once and was no longer mine.

I thought back to the letter and Ravyn's words about having always loved me.

Maybe she had. Maybe I'd had the misfortune of being her one true love, just as she'd had the misfortune of being mine.

That didn't bring me any comfort.

The silence grew as Gia and I watched Addy slide another token into the machine, and in that silence, my doubts and alarm bells grew.

Every time lust flared hard and heavy between us, I had to remember the ease with which she'd acknowledged keeping secrets from her loved ones. Every time that heart of mine tried to wiggle in my chest and tell me I still owned it after all, I had to remember Gia Kent wasn't the one to give it to. She wouldn't care if she left a torn-up soul behind her any more than her brother had cared about the torn-up fields and fences he'd left strewn in his wake.

I stood, stepping away from her so our knees no longer touched. So I could clear my head and my soul of the darts she was sending my way, unintentionally or not.

"We need to get our stories straight, not only for my family but for anyone in Willow Creek who asks."

"I've been thinking about what you said, and I'm not

agreeing that Addy is too old to be mine." She shot me a look that told me not to gloat about being right. "But your family has already met me and my brother. It would be a hard pill to swallow if I suddenly said I had a child. I'm thinking…maybe she's my cousin. I'm watching her for a couple months because of a nasty divorce?"

I wasn't going to lie to my family, but I passed over that for the moment, saying, "We can tell anyone in town who asks that her mama is in rehab."

Gia's head tilted. "Rehab. That's a good one. And the dad is an ex-con. It would be a reason for them to stay alert in case someone from the Lovatos comes sniffing."

That thought twisted my gut tighter. Maybe I should take Addy and Gia and skip town for a few weeks. But the list of things I needed to get done at the ranch was a mile long, and if I suddenly decided to take a vacation in the middle of the construction, all the tongues in Willow Creek would wag.

"I know you don't like the idea, and I even understand your concerns, but I'm telling my family the truth. They'll all take what I tell them to the grave if it means protecting her."

Gia snorted. "Your niece finds out, and she'll scream from the top of the hills that she has a cousin."

She wasn't wrong.

"My parents and siblings at least. I won't lie to them. That's only four people, seeing as Maddox already knows."

Gia sighed. "That's four on top of the six I told before arriving here, plus Maddox, you, and me. The only way to keep a secret is not to tell it."

I stepped back toward her, lowering my voice so my words wouldn't be heard by the little girl at the machine. "If you didn't want anyone to know, you shouldn't have brought her here. If she's mine, like Ravyn claimed, I won't keep that from my family. People in town can remain in the dark for now, but I won't keep it a secret forever. I guess that means you need to do your job and figure out a way to keep her safe by shutting down the Lovatos once and for all."

Her eyes narrowed, flashing like a thunderstorm, but she was calm when she said quietly, "Look, asswipe, I've just spent the last three years of my life hunting the Lovatos. I will end them, but this isn't like your brother being able to drive up to the West Gears clubhouse and cuffing them for possession. We've got multiple agents in multiple agencies working nearly twenty-four seven on this case. I've come close to knocking them down several times. And she," Gia said as she tipped her head toward Addy, "just may be the key to finally unlocking all the doors."

Her calm words triggered something inside me. She was talking about a child—fuck, my child. "She isn't just some random piece of evidence. She's a human being."

Gia stood, pushing herself into my space, slamming a finger into my chest, and every nerve ending in my body came alive. Her voice was a low, barely audible growl as she said, "Fuck you."

Then, she forced her way around me and strode to Addy's side.

She talked to her in Spanish, her voice a low hum with none of the anger she'd just shown me. She gave her a squeeze on the shoulder and then headed for the stairs.

My pulse raced. Was she leaving?

"Where are you going?" I demanded.

Addy was watching her just as intensely as I was. Gia turned at the base of the stairs. "I need to make a few calls. To do my job." She stressed the last few syllables, tossing my words at me. "I'll just be upstairs in my room."

Her fancy blue boots clanged on the metal staircase as she disappeared.

When I looked back at Addy, she had an almost panicked look on her face. I took a step toward her, and instead of easing her alarm, it seemed to grow. My hands clenched tight. If this was Mila, I'd tease her out of her fear with comments about her stuffed unicorns and the bacon she adored, or by challenging her to a poker match with M&M's at stake. This quiet, afraid child I didn't know what to do with.

I shoved my hands into my pockets, rocking. "You like video games."

She glanced at the *Pac-Man* machine, then back at me, nodding.

"Gia said you only have a couple on your Switch. Would you like to get a few more?"

Addy didn't move at all for a long moment and then shrugged.

"I can take you shopping tomorrow. We can get some items to make your room seem like your own. Did you have to leave your toys and clothes behind?"

She shifted from foot to foot and then, with sad eyes, said quietly, "Balam."

I puzzled over that for too long before admitting, "I don't know what that means."

She tilted her head. "*El jaguar.*"

"Jaguar?" I thought of the way Mila never went anywhere without the two unicorns she loved. "It was a stuffed animal? A toy?"

She nodded.

Damn. What would my niece do if she lost those unicorns? She'd be hysterical. No one would be able to console her.

I jerked my phone from my back pocket, opening up the online shopping app everyone hated to love. "It won't be the same. It won't be *your* jaguar, but maybe we can find a similar one."

I waved the phone in her direction, and she hesitated before stepping off the stool and coming over to me cautiously. She eyed the stairs as if she needed to have an escape route planned, and my heart nearly seized. I wanted to curse Ravyn all over again.

I typed in the search engine and the feed was flooded

with stuffed animals. Some were jaguars. Some were other kinds of stuffed cats. I held out the phone, saying, "You pick one."

Her eyes grew large, and she carefully took it from my hand, scrolling upward with the ease of someone accustomed to electronics. Ravyn had been good with all things tech. Had she been teaching Addy also? What other things had she learned that I'd missed out on? Frustration and anger welled that I tucked away so I wouldn't scare this timid child.

We'd had several shy horses on the ranch over the years, and I'd slowly won them over. I could do it with this little girl too. It required slow, patient steps.

Addy's fingers came to a stop, and she turned the screen to show me the item with hope in her eyes. It looked more leopard than jaguar to me, but it appeared as soft and cuddly as Mila's unicorns.

I reached out carefully, taking the phone back. "Okay. Let's see how fast we can get it here." I added it to the shopping cart, hoping in vain for same-day delivery, but we rarely got anything that quickly in Willow Creek. "It's on its way. It'll be here tomorrow."

She smiled, and it lit up her face. She practically glowed. It snatched my breath away and tugged at something inside me. Affection maybe. A protective instinct. It seemed impossible because I didn't know her, didn't even know if she was really mine…and yet I felt tied to her already by just the simple idea she could be.

If Ravyn had stayed. If she'd delivered this beautiful little girl with me in the hospital room, holding her hand and encouraging her. If I'd watched the child grow from a tiny bundle of impossibly small fingers and toes into a diapered toddler crawling across the floor, what would I have felt?

People said the first time they held their baby, they were overcome with an abundance of love. A knowledge that they'd do anything—kill, steal, maim—for the baby. I hadn't been given that chance. I'd been told my child died before ever having a chance to breathe.

My jaw worked as Addy and I stared at each other.

Was she wondering something similar? About what it would have been like to grow up with a mother *and* a father? What it would have been like to have two people you could count on?

My phone rang again. My mother had an intuition that was almost otherworldly sometimes.

"What's up?" I asked.

"You tell me. I just took lunch out to you and Shawn, only to have him tell me you took off like a bat out of hell this morning, and he hasn't heard from you since. Plus, you ignored my call earlier. What's going on?"

I looked at the little girl in front of me—the quiet, skittish thing—and wondered how she'd react if my loud, messy hugger of a family showed up, trying to welcome her.

"Hold on a sec," I said. I put Mama on mute even as she objected. "You want to play some more?" I waved my hand at the machines. "While I make you lunch?" I pointed upward to where the kitchen was.

She shrugged. The smile and momentary glow disappeared behind a blank face. I wanted to curse at myself and my mama. We'd taken a tentative step while talking about the stuffed animal only to have her retreat again.

"I'll be right upstairs if you need me," I told her.

She turned back to the *Pac-Man* machine and inserted a token. I made my way over to the staircase, and when I looked back, I saw her face in the reflection of the screen. She was watching me. My insides twisted again as I jogged up the stairs and into the kitchen.

I took Mama off mute and said, "Maddox called and needed me to come into town," as I scoured my pantry and fridge.

"What's wrong with Maddox? Is it Mila? McK?"

"No. Everyone is fine." Except, everyone wasn't. Ravyn was dead. Her child was lost and scared. I was a mess.

I leaned my palms on the countertop and took in a huge breath, trying to steady the runaway feelings inside me. I finally admitted, "That's not exactly true."

"Ryder. You're really worrying me here."

I spilled everything—the letter, Addy, and why she was in danger with the Lovatos, along with how Gia was here, trying to untangle the web that surrounded the child. Well, I didn't use Gia's name. I couldn't. My family had given me too much shit about her the last time she'd been here. Instead, I just ended with the fact that the undercover agent and Addy were both at my house.

Mama was mostly silent while I talked, exuding an exclamation or a garbled noise here and there, doing what my mother did best—listen with love.

I turned on the griddle and grabbed cheese, butter, and bread.

"I don't know what to do," I told her. "So, I'm making her grilled cheese because that's pretty much the only food I have in the house and one of the few things I can cook." I assembled three sandwiches, and set them on the stovetop before leaning back against the island and asking quietly, "What do I do?"

Mama's voice was full of emotions when she answered, "Sounds like you're already doing it, honey. You're showing her she's safe. Showing her she'll be cared for."

"But what if…" I wasn't sure I could say it.

"What if she isn't really yours?"

I didn't respond. I wasn't sure I could. Instead, I scrubbed a hand over my face and the layer of scruff I'd shaped into some sort of half-assed beard that morning.

"Do you ever think of Mila as anything but Maddox's daughter?" Mama asked gently.

"No." My response was instantaneous.

"Sounds like this little girl has lived through more than anyone should have to. Sounds like she needs a safe place to land. A place to be loved and cared for. And I know my son can give that to her.”

My throat just about closed. “I don’t know anything about raising a child. I don’t know how…”

“You do. You have so much love in that heart of yours. You’ve just locked it up for a while, and I understand why. But it’s time to open the door again.”

Silence followed. Her words felt eerily reminiscent of my thoughts since my talk with Sadie. What was really the truth? Was it that I didn’t know how or that I wasn’t willing to open myself up again? What if I fell in love all over again—this time with a child who got ripped away from me? When Ravyn had told me she was pregnant, I’d seen nothing more than a grayscale image of a bean growing inside her and had fallen head over heels. When I’d lost the baby, it had nearly destroyed me, and it had been nothing more than an image and an idea. What would I do if the reality of a living, breathing child was torn away?

“We’re all going to want to meet her,” Mama said.

“If everyone shows up at once, it’ll scare her.”

“We’ll ease her into the crowd one or two at a time. Dad and I will bring dinner over tonight.”

The relief that hit me at the idea of my parents coming over made me feel a bit cowardly. But having them there would be a buffer of sorts. Plus, it meant I didn’t have to figure out what to feed the two women who’d invaded my house with their intense presence.

“Okay,” I agreed.

“You want me to tell the girls?”

I’d known Mama would tell Dad. They didn’t keep secrets from each other. Growing up, we’d known if you told one, you were telling them both, but I hadn’t thought about telling Sadie and Gemma. The idea of having to repeat my story all over again was almost too much for me.

“That would be appreciated,” I answered.

“Okay. Go flip the sandwiches before you burn them. We’ll see you tonight.”

Shit. I turned back to the griddle, grabbed a spatula from the holder next to it, and turned the sandwiches. They were a little dark, but not burned.

"Mama," I said.

"Yeah?"

"Thanks."

"I wish I had recorded this. Your siblings will never believe me when I tell them you got all mushy and cried."

"I didn't cry," I groused.

She chuckled, and it did exactly what she'd intended—it lifted my heart just a teeny-tiny bit.

Enough for me to breathe again.

I'd figure this out like I had every other crisis in my life—by making a plan and seeing it through one step at a time—with my family at my side.

Chapter Nine

Emiliano

TROUBLE ABOUT MY SOUL

Performed by The Trishas

I thrust the man up against the side of the barn with my forearm shoved into his throat. He let out a garbled noise, yanking at my arm, but I didn't budge. I used my free hand to open the switchblade I'd taken from my father and wave it casually before his eyes.

"Explain to me how this happened," I demanded.

Before he could reply, I shoved harder into his neck. He gasped. Even without me cutting off the air to his lungs, his eyes had been little slits, shoved close to his nose. They'd always screamed untrustworthy, but I'd paid him enough to ensure a beacon of loyalty. I'd paid him not to fuck up.

Fury washed over me as I poked the tip of the knife into his cheek, instantly drawing blood. I eased up the pressure on his throat just enough for him to speak.

"Talk."

"She came at me with a knife first."

"You shouldn't have been in the room with her. You were to take it without her knowing."

His eyes drifted to the side and back, and I knew. This little weasel of a man had wanted a piece of her. Wanted to put his dick inside her. Wanted to take what was never intended to be his. The edge of my knife slid downward. The man didn't cry out, but his eyes narrowed until they were almost nonexistent as blood dripped over his chin.

"She stole from you." He gasped as I varied the pressure on his throat. "I did what you asked. I got it back."

"I needed her alive."

"*Jefe*, you are smarter than her. You do not need her."

If he thought flattery would save him, he was wrong. I *was* smarter than Natalia. I'd always been smarter and more patient than her, but she'd had a skill I'd needed. She'd taken my ideas and made them a reality by carefully applying zeroes and ones. My mistake had been in forgetting her persistence. Forgetting how good she was at hiding that stubbornness under a mask of serene acceptance.

While I'd stormed at our family's dark secrets with brutal force, she'd quietly slid out from beneath them. I should have known better than to assume she'd accept the bonds I put on her any more than she'd accepted our father's.

My anger grew. At myself for the error. At her for her lack of loyalty.

She'd forgotten the promises of our youth.

The promises we'd made while bleeding together…or while playing together. Father had tried to use stories of a big cat that lived in the forest around our compound in Mexico to keep us from wandering away. Instead, we'd used the idea of Balam to hone our skills, biding our time 'til we could use them against our father. I'd enjoyed the hunting, the stalking, the kill. She'd enjoyed the hiding, the camouflaging in the trees, and stealing away in the night.

Now, there would be no more hiding for her. No more escape.

It wasn't only sorrow that tried to worm itself into my heart, but disappointment.

Both emotions only fueled my rage at the man I had pinned to the wall of the barn.

His muscles, his skills, were nothing compared to mine. He was in my territory. Mine.

"You brought everything from the room?" I asked as my knife tip settled on his pulse.

"Yes. Except a suitcase with only clothes in it."

"Nothing at the scene can tie you to this?"

"I know what I'm doing." He hissed out the words while attempting to put some distance between his neck and the knife digging into his skin.

"*Bueno*," I said calmly.

At the same time as I released him, I moved the blade across his jugular. Blood spurted out, hitting my white button-down, ruining it. I let the man fall to the dirt, bending only to wipe my knife off on his hideous, army-green jacket.

I turned to Julio, who'd been waiting off to the side. His eyes held mine. Not a flicker of disgust or surprise in them. Nothing but calm. I should have sent him after Natalia, but I needed him here. He was the only person I truly trusted.

"Bring the items from his car to my office and then deal with this," I said.

I strode away from the barn, with its forest-green slates and river rock, toward the main house. The sprawling single-story building was carved into the mountainside and had been in my mother's family for dozens of generations. Just like the nearly forty thousand acres of land had belonged to them. Land that belonged to me much more than it had ever belonged to my father—a man who'd married into it.

I'd taken it back from my father in the way my ancestors had defended it from the white invaders, cleansing the blood he'd spilled onto the soil by shedding his on top of it. It was his penance for what he'd done to me. To Natalia. Our home no longer haunted me as my sister said it haunted her. I'd shaped it into another tool I could wield in a way my visionless, brute of a father would never have been able to see.

I walked up the stone steps, smooth from decades of use, through the wide brass doors carved with motifs of warriors, and into the marble-floored entry. I tapped a code into the box next to a set of black doors, pressed my eye to the retinal scanner that popped up, and strode down the corridor on the other side. The main residence now held guests spring through fall, but these private areas, with their sleek black-and-white marble floors and walls, were all mine. Soothing. Colorless. Cool.

At the end of the corridor, I repeated the code and eye scan, opening another set of black doors into the monochrome luxury of my bedroom. I'd enjoyed ripping out the old master suite with my bare hands and sledgehammers. I'd enjoyed filling it with the most expensive fabrics and materials I could find, knowing just how much my father would have hated it. How he would have screamed at the expense.

I stepped into the white marble bathroom, shedding the blood-stained clothes.

In the mirror, my gaze skipped over my black hair, nearly black eyes, and pale-white skin to land on the blood on my cheek. It was the only color in the room.

It made me furious.

I turned, heading for the shower. I left it on cold, scrubbing at my skin until I could be sure the taint had been removed. My body shivered, and I fought back the reaction. I'd made a mistake. When was the last time I could say I'd done that?

Father.

I gritted my teeth.

I stepped out, drying off and dressing in a pair of black slacks. I couldn't face the row of white shirts. Atonement had to be made before I wore them again. Errors had to be cleansed. My hands went to the first of a dozen black button-downs, pulling one off the hanger and carefully tucking it into the pants. I double-knotted my shoes, which were shined to perfection, and made my way from the bedroom to the study next door.

Black shelves lined the walls running from the floor up to the vaulted, black-lacquered ceiling. Every single book had a cover that was a shade of black, white, or gray. They matched the black marble floor, partially covered with a white, woven rug handmade in Morocco, and the white armchairs taken from a French chateau. They sat perfectly perpendicular to the ebony desk I'd commissioned, carved with the same motifs of ancient Mayan warriors who graced the front doors.

I ignored the desk, even though I was craving to sit there, just as I itched to bring the next CEO to their knees by undoing his company line of code by line of code. Instead, I went to the side table where Julio had brought in the items Vito had retrieved from Natalia's hotel room.

The pile looked large for the side table but was small considering it contained the entirety of her life. Two laptops, a copy of the golden box we'd created together, three burner phones, fake IDs, and credit cards sat beside over three thousand dollars in cash. Inside a black backpack, I found a handful of clothes in bright colors that assaulted my eyes. I lifted them to my nose, catching a hint of geraniums. Something deep and visceral inside me woke. A longing I thought I'd burned from my soul. Then, I reminded myself that she'd tried to turn on me. After all I'd done for her. For us. After the revenge I'd executed on our behalf, she'd turned her back anyway.

I welcomed the hatred that coursed through me.

After shoving the clothes back into the backpack, I turned on the laptop. I opened the golden box, withdrew the terabyte drive, and used the code I knew like the back of my hand to explore what Natalia had been working on. My excitement grew as I followed the lines. She'd been close. Closer than she'd led me to believe. More betrayal. Losing her life was the consequence she'd paid. But if she'd been going to die, it should have been at my hands. The princess should have been killed by the king, not some nameless, low-life scum.

The computer screen went dark, a single blinking cursor appearing.

I tried several passwords, and when those didn't work, I typed in code we'd used to break into some of the most secure systems in the world.

Nothing. The cursor just stared at me. Taunting me.

If I wasn't so infuriated, I would have smiled. I would have felt some pride at how good she'd become.

I'd need her key. She would have kept it close, knowing she could use it as leverage. Perhaps it was camouflaged just like the jaguar we'd played at being. I carefully went through the other electronics and found nothing. My eyes landed on the backpack. I pulled it closer, tossing the clothes aside once again, digging farther, and stilling as my fingers hit something soft and furry.

I pulled it out, and a flicker of triumph bled through me.

It was a sign. It was as if thinking of the cat had brought it to life.

My ancestors were speaking to me. They wanted me to succeed.

I used my knife to slice the stuffed animal open from head to tail, pulling out stuffing, searching every nook for what she'd hidden. I grew both frustrated and intrigued when I found nothing. Why would she have the stupid toy if it wasn't to hide the key?

When I emptied the remaining items and found a kid's T-shirt at the bottom, the realization hit me, followed by surprise. This was the reason she'd been so determined to stay anywhere but here. Not because of the nightmares she said surrounded her whenever she came home, but because of a child.

She should have known better than to hide it from me.

I always discovered the truth.

It was what I'd been made for.

I was the sword.

I was the fire.

I was retribution.

For the first time all day, a slow smile found its way over my lips.

Chapter Ten

Gia

HIGH ROAD

Performed by Kelly Clarkson

I paced the length of the mint room, ignoring the simplistic beauty of it while I listened to the update from Rory. She'd had no hits yet from the facial recognition software on the modified picture of Ravyn. It didn't seem possible. There should have been something by now, and yet we were no closer to unwinding her identity than we'd been when we'd known her as Anna Smith. Even putting in the name Ravyn Clark had yielded little. She'd appeared out of nowhere ten years ago and disappeared not even three years later. She was as much of an enigma as Anna.

"She had to have hired someone to make her IDs," I said.

"Or she made them herself. She was a tech genius. Hell, the bank in the Caymans didn't even know the Lovatos had the account she'd assembled there."

"Still, she'd need the right equipment, and that can be expensive. No. She hired someone to print them even if she created the backstop herself."

"I'll see what I can dig up from our list of known forgers. Has Addy said anything else?" Rory asked.

"I haven't wanted to ask her about what happened again. Not after she shut down on me. She's been through so much in the last twenty-four hours."

"How'd Ryder take the news?"

"Like he'd been shot in the chest." We were both silent for a moment. "Check in with the Denver PD for me. See if they have any new information."

"While waiting for a facial recognition hit, I examined the camera footage from stores and streetlights near the motel. I might have identified the vehicle the suspect was driving," Rory said.

I inhaled sharply, a chill washing over me. "Really?"

"I shouldn't have said anything yet, as I'm not a hundred-percent sure, but I'm tracking it down."

A prick of hope surged. "I feel like we're close. Closer than we were even in D.C. in November."

Rory was quiet, and I wished I hadn't brought it up. She'd come out of the situation alive, but we'd lost the best lead we'd ever had when the woman working with Anna and the Lovatos had been killed before we could interrogate her. For months, we'd followed that lead, watching as she'd run some of the cartel's offshore accounts, funneling money to gangs, assassins, and more, all while pretending to work for Rory's dad's private security business.

"Chanel was good, but the more I unraveled her work from her iPad and the computer in Dad's office, it was clear she was just using someone else's code," Rory explained. "She didn't always get it right and left behind a trail I don't think Anna would have. Which got me thinking… Have you ever heard of the Houdini box?"

"Like the famous magician?"

"Amongst technophiles, there's a myth about a box or a code that can be created to break into any system, run any program, and leave no trace behind. Like magic. Can you imagine one set of code being able to communicate with and get into and out of any system in the world?"

"I can imagine how dangerous that would be. There have been many books and movies written about it because it's scary enough to cause mass panic," I said. "You think Anna was working on something like this?"

"I think Anna and the cartel have been using something like it for a while. Perfecting it. Tweaking it. Not only because of the way they got into the bank in the Caymans but also the way they seem one step ahead of every agency that comes at them. They could be in the U.S. Customs system, which would allow them to approve shipments in and out of the country without a hiccup. And the identity theft scheme they ran? They broke into records all over the place."

Even though I'd hinted at the idea of them having a worm in our computer systems to Maddox and Ryder, I'd hoped it wasn't true. What Rory was suggesting was even worse. Scary as fuck to think of a cartel being able to get into any system in the world. "You think it's why they killed Anna now? She was done with the code? She completed it?"

"I don't know. But if she did finish it, killing her was a mistake. She would have had some crazy-ass encryption on it. They wouldn't be able to use it without knowing the key, some kind of cipher she would have developed to keep it out of the wrong hands."

"She was working for the wrong hands."

"But she controlled it."

"You're trying to make her into some Robin Hood sitting in the middle of an evil cartel."

"That's because I think she was," Rory said. "I've been poking into some of the leads the task force got last year and her coding that was dropped here and there that we thought we lucked into. I'm almost certain she gave it up on purpose. If she had an actual working Houdini box, G, they could have already dismantled the entire world's infrastructure. Military systems. Banking. Internet. Primary services. Emergency services. But they haven't."

"Because she wouldn't let them?"

"Or she hadn't told them she'd created the final piece. Maybe the cartel got suspicious or simply got tired of waiting. Maybe they thought they could find someone else to finish it for them. I don't have an answer to those questions."

"In Ravyn's letter, she talks about an insurance policy she left with Addy." Goosebumps popped up along my skin.

"I know."

Damn. If that was the case, and if the Lovatos got even a hint at Addy being alive, they'd send everything they had after her. Suddenly, coming to Willow Creek and handing her over to Ryder felt like a huge mistake. It put everyone here at risk in addition to the little girl. I'd wanted Addy to feel safe so she'd tell us what she knew, but maybe I'd done the opposite.

"I shouldn't have come here," I said on a long exhale.

"We have no reason to suspect they know about Addy. And all of this is just wild conjecture on my part. We need to find proof before we leap off the deep end."

"You need to present your idea to the task force."

"Me?"

"Yes, you. It's your theory. They'll have questions I won't be able to answer." Noise from down the hall in the kitchen brought me back to where I was. My hand went to my Glock tucked beneath my shirt at the back, and then I heard the deep timbre of Ryder's voice. "I gotta go. I have to make sure a certain growly rancher truly understands how quiet we need to keep this."

Rory made a noise that sounded like she was trying to hold back a laugh. "Good luck with that."

We hung up, and I stared at the tangle of limbs and leaves outside the window. Exhaustion wound through me. With sleep out of the question at the moment, I needed food and a gallon of caffeine to tide me over.

I went into the bathroom and cringed at the image in the mirror. This was what running for almost two days straight looked like. The walk-in shower with cream tile flecked with gold called to me, but even if I washed off the sweat and dust of the last forty-eight hours, I had no clean clothes in my go bag. I needed to do laundry or get some new things. So, instead of stepping into the luxurious shower, I splashed water on my face, straightened my ponytail, and added another layer of deodorant to the pile I'd already applied.

I'd gone longer than this without showering or changing clothes. Venezuela had been the worst. I'd been stuck for almost a week in the middle of guerilla territory with Gary, who had been pretending to be my cameraman, and a SEAL team. The lack of a shower and clean clothes hadn't seemed important when we were in the middle of the jungle, following a tracker I'd placed on a stolen rifle. But here, in the middle of the spotless elegance of Ryder's home, with his neatness and control on display, my days-old clothes and unwashed body made me feel like I stood out like an ant on vanilla ice cream. But I had bigger things to worry about than what Ryder Hatley thought of my run-down appearance.

I made my way out of the bedroom and into the main living area to see Ryder leaning up against the counter with his phone to his ear. My pulse spiked, worry cresting that he was already telling people about Addy. I wanted to strangle him, even if I understood his reasoning. He'd just had his world turned upside down, and he would rely on his family to help him through it. I just wasn't sure his daughter could afford it.

His voice cracked as I heard him say, "I don't know anything about raising a child. I don't know how…"

My body froze, knowing he'd hate me hearing his torn admission. He'd hate me seeing his moment of weakness, and yet, I wished he hadn't trailed off. I wished he'd finished the sentence so I could see beneath the grumpy veneer once again to the tantalizing truth of the man under it.

I snapped myself out of that chain of thought as quickly as I entered it. What I didn't have time for was to be tantalized and tempted. I had a little girl to protect and a cartel to take down. The only thing that was important was making sure everyone he told was on board with the seriousness of the situation.

I made my way through the living area on quiet feet as he finished up his discussion and flipped what looked like grilled cheese sandwiches onto three waiting plates.

"I really wish you hadn't done that," I said.

He startled, whirling around, spatula in hand. His eyes narrowed on me. "Done what?"

"Told your mom."

Instead of replying, he slid the plates onto the island across from the tall barstools. "Do you want to get Addy? She seems to react better to you right now."

"You're not going to respond?"

"I don't believe in repeating arguments, especially when they won't end any different. I won't lie to my family. That's all there is to say."

"You're putting her at risk to soothe your conscience. What I just learned…" I shook my head, trailing off. I couldn't talk to him about the case.

"What you just learned?" he asked, crossing his arms over his enormous chest, the flannel working double-time to contain the muscles beneath it. Muscles I knew were rock solid from the one time I'd been pressed up tight against them. I swallowed hard and looked away.

"That little insurance policy Ravyn left behind? If it's what we think it is, it won't just be the Lovatos who come looking. It'll be every criminal organization and government in the world."

His jaw worked, hands digging into his arms. "What is it?"

I shook my head. "Not going there. But I think this was a bad idea. I think I should take Addy somewhere we can have a full team protecting her."

"Unless we can figure out what she has and hand it off to you and your pals at the NSA. Then she won't be in any danger, right?"

"They might not know we found it and still come looking."

"I'm sure you and your cronies can find a way to leak it so they know you have it instead of her."

If Rory was right, and Ravyn had been working on a Houdini box, and Addy had the key, we could absolutely drop hints that we'd found it. But it meant figuring out whether Addy really had it before they came looking. I wasn't sure how to do that when all I'd gotten from the little girl was a handful of words.

"We need to get her to trust us," I said softly.

He gave a curt nod, gaze drifting over to the entryway and the stairs that led down into the game room before they came back to lock on me.

The air shifted between us—the same enticing spark I'd felt last year and in every touch today. It was laced with danger and mistrust but also a passion I'd never experienced except in that singular angry kiss we'd shared. My eyes fell to his mouth, and when I jerked them back up, I swore his lips twitched.

I whirled around, heading for the stairs, saying, "I'll go get her."

I slid quietly into the basement, immediately searching the far corner where the video game machines were. My heart skittered around in my chest when she wasn't there. I scoured the room. "Addy?" I called. "*Dónde estás?*"

Nothing.

I tried not to panic. There were no outside doors in the basement. No windows were open.

I called her name again.

Ryder's booted feet hit the stairs, and I met his gaze.

"Where is she?" he asked.

I didn't answer. I started for the hall and the unfinished rooms he'd mentioned. We both called her name only to get nothing in response. The three rooms along the hallway were hung with sheetrock but no tape or texture. Empty spaces that felt sad now I knew why they'd been left this way. As I came out of one room, Ryder came out of the last.

His eyes reflected the same panic I felt welling in me.

We raced back down the hall where he pulled open the closet he'd gotten the step stool from, but she wasn't there. Where the hell was she? The image of how I'd found her, hidden under the bed in the motel room, hit me. She'd been taught to squeeze into small spaces. I ran to the entertainment center, opening cabinet doors as Ryder went behind the bar.

"Gia," his voice was barely a whisper, and I slowly closed the cupboard and turned to him. He closed his eyes, as if in pain, before opening them and meeting mine across the distance. He nodded down at something. I jogged over to see she'd tucked herself onto an open shelf. I didn't know if it had been empty before or if she'd moved everything, but she'd curled herself into the space, knees to her chest, just like I'd found her under the bed. Her chest was moving in a slow rhythm, dark lashes standing out against pale skin.

Tears pricked my eyes, and when I met Ryder's, I could tell he was fighting back his own.

It was all so wrong. So horribly wrong for her to have to hide like this to feel safe.

Ryder's face turned dark with an anger I'd seen when he'd caught me in the ranch office. Except, this time, the fury wasn't directed at me. It was directed at the woman who'd promised him everything before ripping it away.

While I couldn't put myself in his shoes enough to empathize with him, I could sympathize. I'd had my blind love ripped away once by someone. No matter how much I'd insisted earlier that moving around could build resilience and independence, it had been cruel of Ravyn to do this. To make her daughter live this kind of life and to deny Ryder a child he would have showered with even more love than I'd seen him shower on his niece.

I lived in a world of grays, where black and white didn't have a place, but even if Ravyn had lived, there would have been nothing she could have told me that would have justified this. It was just wrong.

Chapter Eleven

Ryder

WEIGHT OF YOUR WORLD
Performed by Chris Stapleton

When Ravyn had left, I'd been devastated. Sorrow deeper than anything I'd ever experienced in my life had filled my soul. And then, when I'd realized she'd stolen money from the ranch and taken our great-grandmother's ring, I'd been furious, both at myself for trusting her and at her for using me. I'd felt duped. I'd felt like the biggest idiot to have ever been conned. Because that was what I'd seen it as—a con.

That fury was nothing compared to what raged through me at finding Addy asleep on a shelf behind the bar. It felt like a tornado was going to spin out of my chest, whip everything in the room up, and tear out of the house, through the fields, and into the sky.

I wanted to punish Ravyn. I wanted to inflict some kind of injury on her.

And yet, she was already dead.

My jaw worked overtime as I fought back frustration and rage and sadness so deep it felt like it had taken root in my soul.

I squatted, taking in the closed eyes of the little girl in front of me. Dark lashes against cheeks just shy of too thin. Soft pink lips barely parted. Hands clenched tight around her knees. She looked so sweet and so goddamn tormented.

Fuck.

Fuck.

Fuck.

I went to pick her up, to move her, to carry her up to the blue-cloud room Mila loved, but Gia stopped me with a hand on my arm.

"You'll scare her," she whispered.

She motioned for me to come out from behind the bar. I looked from Addy to her and then rose, stepping away and saying, "I can't leave her like that."

"I can guarantee you she's used to sleeping in worse places."

"Worse? Than a fucking shelf?"

"I think it was Ravyn's way of keeping her safe in case something happened while Ravyn was sleeping."

"Don't even try to justify this with damn talk of resilience."

Gia shook her head violently. "I'm not agreeing with what she did. But what I *am* saying is, given the circumstances they were in, at least she was concerned enough to teach her how to stay alive."

Noise behind me had me turning my head to find Addy standing at the edge of the bar, rubbing tired eyes. She couldn't have slept for longer than a handful of minutes. Her eyes were so shadowed they looked bruised. When was the last time she'd had a full night's sleep? Had she *ever* had one?

Maddox had found Mila at one year old, in a dirty diaper, filth all around her, and yet finding Addy like this somehow felt worse. I wasn't sure how my brother had ever dealt with Mila's biological mom face-to-face after that without wanting to kill her.

As much as I'd hated Ravyn for what she'd done to me, I hadn't put her in the same category as Mila's mom. Maybe I'd loved Ravyn too much to call her what she actually was. Maybe I'd wanted to justify my love. Maybe I hadn't wanted to believe I could love evil.

But God…what I felt right now…

I stepped toward Addy, lowering myself on my haunches to meet her gaze straight on.

"I want you to know…you never have to sleep like that again." I tilted my head toward the bar. "Ever." My voice shook, and the emotion in it seemed to cause her to retreat into herself. I forced myself to stay calm. "The bed in the room I showed you? That's yours. I promise you you'll always be safe there. Always."

And I meant it. I meant it with a surety that I'd go to my grave defending.

I could practically hear Gia's voice in my head, telling me Addy wasn't going to just trust what I said simply because I said it. I'd have to prove it to her. But hell, how did I do that?

"Are you hungry?" I asked, changing the subject until I could figure out the answer.

Addy nodded.

I breathed out, "Do you like grilled cheese?"

She nodded again.

"Well, okay, then. Let's go get them before they cool off too much."

I stood and offered my hand, but she didn't take it. She pulled her hands back to her chest. I didn't let it put me off. Slow and steady. Calm and sure, just like winning over a shy filly. One confident, trustworthy action at a time.

♫ ♫ ♫

As we ate our sandwiches, Addy's eyes kept drooping. Every time it happened, she squirmed on the barstool and dug her nails into her wrist as if forcing herself to stay awake. It made the food I'd eaten turn into a congealed mass inside me.

When she'd almost finished her sandwich, I said, "My

parents—your grandparents—are coming to dinner. They want to meet you." Her eyes grew wide. "I know you're pretty tired. Maybe…shall we get you unpacked and then you could get a few hours of rest before they come?"

She fiddled with the last piece of her bread and then shrugged.

Gia took our plates and placed them in the dishwasher as if she'd lived in my house for years, and that thought stuck inside me right along with the congealed mass Addy had created.

The three of us made our way down the hall to the blue-cloud room. Addy unzipped the backpack and pulled a handful of items out, including another change of clothes and a bag with toothpaste, a toothbrush, and some hair care items. She watched me carefully as I helped her assemble the items in the walk-in closet and on the counter in the bathroom. The meager belongings looked pitiful, especially when thinking about them in comparison to Mila's closet brimming with items at my brother's place.

"You don't have any pajamas. I can bring you one of my T-shirts for tonight. Tomorrow, we'll go shopping."

"I have to do a load of laundry myself. Maybe if you brought Addy the T-shirt now, I could wash what she has on with my things," Gia offered. "Would that be okay?" she asked the little girl.

Addy didn't look comfortable, but she didn't say no.

"Let me get it," I said, turning and jogging out of the room.

When I came back, the two of them were sitting on the bed with one of the books that had been in the backpack. It was a book I knew well from Mila. *The Day the Dragons Saved the Universe* was a favorite in my brother's household, right along with *The Day the Unicorns Saved the World*.

"Your cousin Mila loves that book too," I told her. She looked up at me wide-eyed. "You won't meet her today. But soon."

I handed her a long-sleeved T-shirt. She went to the bathroom with it and came out looking even smaller and more fragile dwarfed by my shirt. It fell almost to her toes.

Addy handed Gia the clothes she'd been wearing and eyed the bed. I pulled back the covers, and she crawled in. I wanted to brush her hair out of her face. I wanted to soothe her. Pat her. Hug her. Something. But she hadn't even wanted to take my hand downstairs. So, instead, I put her backpack on the floor beside her and the books and her Switch on the nightstand.

When I turned back, she was looking at the windows, brows drawn together. The walls and walls of glass that made up my home were the exact opposite of what someone used to hiding would want. I pulled a remote from a drawer in the nightstand and hit a button. Shades rolled down from their hidden spot in the ceiling, dimming the room and keeping the outside world away.

"This button," I said and showed her, "opens or closes the blinds."

I set the remote with her things.

"I know you don't know me, Addy. I know you don't know this house or the people who live on the ranch, but I promise you, everyone you meet will do whatever it takes to keep you safe. You'll be okay in this bed. No one is going to come in and take you from it. Nothing bad will happen to you while you're sleeping. And if you go somewhere else in the house, if you hide again, it's going to…worry me." What I really wanted to say was it would piss me off, scare the shit out of me, and make me want to bring her mother back to life just so I could scream at her, but none of that would make Addy trust me.

In response, Addy slid down, dark hair resting on the pale-blue pillow. She pulled the covers up, and I barely stopped myself from tucking her in like a burrito in the way Mila loved. Maybe that would just make this little girl feel trapped.

I wanted to give her something to reassure her. To let

her know I'd be there if she needed me. A lifeline of sorts. A phone. My mental shopping list grew. When Maddox had gotten Mila a phone when she started kindergarten, I'd rolled my eyes even though she only had our family's numbers programmed into it and had no internet access. But now I understood why he'd done it.

Gia had already moved to the door, and I followed, glancing back and heart stuttering at the lost look on Addy's face. She fought down her scared damn well, but it was still there in her eyes.

"Do you want the door open or closed?"

"Closed."

I nodded. "If you need anything, I'm here. Gia is here, and you can just come out and get us. I'll be in my office. That's those double doors we passed, but they'll be open. You're always welcome in there."

She nodded, little eyelids already drooping.

We stepped out, and I shut the door behind me. The block of emotions in my chest was trying to unravel. I felt untethered, and if I felt that way, I couldn't imagine what Addy was feeling.

"I should have asked first before offering Addy, but is it okay if I do some laundry?" Gia asked.

"Yep," I said, needing away from Gia as quickly as possible. Needing to get myself in check before she said or did something to unravel me a bit more. "It's up there, the door on the right." I pointed toward the next level that led to my room.

Ravyn had said laundry rooms needed to be by the bedrooms so you didn't have to haul linen and clothes all through the house to get to it, and I'd agreed. So many of the things in my home had been built because of what she'd said. I hadn't sat around in my home, pining for her every day just because we'd designed it together, but ever since Gia and Addy had walked through the door, I couldn't stop thinking of Ravyn. It was as if her ghost had followed them here, tearing open all those scabs, reminding me of things

I'd thought I'd forgotten.

I turned on my heel, heading to my office without another word.

I'd just sat down at my desk and turned on my laptop when my phone dinged.

It was Sadie, texting in the group chat I had with my siblings.

> *SASSYPANTS: If I wasn't so pissed on your behalf, I'd call you a chicken for making Mama tell us what's happened.*

> *GEM MINE: Ry... I just don't have enough words to tell you how sorry I am. For all of it. I can't imagine what you're going through.*

Gemma was going through her own bit of hell at the moment after the asshole actor she'd hooked up with in LA had broken her heart. Maddox and I had wanted to fly out to California and string the guy up by his balls, but Gemma had threatened to disown us if we did. She'd said the best revenge she could get was acting like he didn't even exist. Acting as if he hadn't stomped all over her soul.

> *ME: You can't tell anyone about Addy. She's in a lot of danger, and until we figure out how to get her out of it, no one can know about her.*

Maddox came back instantly.

> *WOODY: Gia find out something else since we talked?*

I groaned, knowing immediately our youngest sister was going to latch on to that name I'd purposefully held back from Mama.

> *SASSYPANTS: Gia? Our Gia? Holy shit! Gia is the undercover agent who brought Addy to*

you? I knew there was more to her than just that journalist gig she offered up.

ME: Leave it to Woody to give me up. There's a reason you earned that nickname.

WOODY: How was I to know you didn't tell Mama she was here? But you know, NOT telling anyone about her speaks louder than you actually saying her name.

SASSYPANTS: Say her name, big brother. Say. Her. Name. I dare you!

ME: Fuck you all. I have more important shit to think about than some lying, sneaky brunette who just dropped a bomb on my world.

GEMMA: Can you call it lying if she was undercover?

SASSYPANTS: We all know Ry would love to help her "under the covers." Question is, could he handle it? Could he handle even more? Like, say an actual date?

I tossed my phone to the side with a disgusted sigh. I concentrated on typing up a list of things I needed to get for Addy. Clothes. Toys. Phone. Bath stuff. More books. Video games. I wanted to spoil her, shower her with all the things Mila had and more. Plus, I needed more than bread, cheese, eggs, and beer in my refrigerator. I needed fruits and vegetables and healthy shit. I never really had a lot of food in the house because, more often than not, I ate at the ranch or in town.

My phone buzzed a few more times, but I just ignored it.

After making the shopping list, I opened the accounting system for the ranch. Ever since Ravyn had stolen from us,

I'd been handling all the financials myself. No way I could trust someone else with it, not after I'd cost us so much already. We were in far better shape than I would have expected us to be not quite eight years after taking that hit. We'd paid off all our loans, generated a decent salary for me and my parents, invested for a rainy day, and were now able to build the final two cabins we'd had to put off.

When I'd first presented my idea to my parents about transitioning the farm to a dude ranch, they'd laughed. But after I'd shown them the studies done by the Eastern Dude Ranchers' Association and told them how it had saved many landholders with properties even bigger than ours from losing some or all their land, they'd gotten on board fairly quickly. If the black blot of trusting Ravyn hadn't been hanging over me, I'd be immensely proud of what we'd accomplished with me at the helm.

My eyes slid to the framed drawings on the wall—designs of the cabins, the restaurant's façade, and the remodel of the barn—all done in pencil and ink with my name scrawled along the bottom. They were good, but the reality was better.

My gaze settled on the largest frame holding a drawing of my home with the mountains sloped up behind it. I may have given up my old dreams, but I'd still had a chance to build something here. I didn't regret the years of college I'd skipped or the dozen more I would have had to spend at an apprenticeship in order to make a mark in the world of architects.

I was happy. Satisfied with the life I was living.

But in less than twenty-four hours, a hole had been torn through the fabric of my contentment. Now, I could see all the things that were missing instead of all the things that satisfied me.

A quiet knock brought my head up to where Gia stood framed in the doorway. The wall of glass behind her cast a glow around her, making her dark hair shimmer with silver and calling attention to her curves. Surrounded by the halo of light, all she needed was a sword in her hand to pass for an avenging angel.

My body instantly reacted to the vision, longing seeping through my veins. I ached to feel every curve and hard plane of her pressed up against me. I wanted to be surrounded by the feel and scent and warmth of her. Even now, months after I'd kissed her, I swore her sweet fragrance was still wrapped around me like a spell. The scent of her reminded me of my best fall memories—apple picking and hay rides, pine trees and the first rains of the season.

Change.

My first instinct when I'd found her sneaking around in the ranch office was to yank her away and call Maddox to arrest her. But as soon as her slim, muscled frame had collided with mine, I'd ignited. The haughty toss of her chin, the way her shoulders drew back, and the tease she'd sent my way had me slamming her up against the wall and punishing her with my mouth instead of a jail cell.

As if she was remembering that moment too, Gia's gaze fell to my lips.

It shouldn't give me as much pleasure as it did, knowing she was thinking about it as well. Thinking about how her hands had slid under my Henley, burning my skin, or how her hips had ground into mine, as if she was greedy for release. Her full, rosy lips had parted, tongue licking into my mouth. We'd tangled and fought for control, each of us demanding the other give and neither acquiescing. I'd been two seconds from tearing open the buttons on her shirt to feast on the taut tips beneath when voices from outside had pulled us both to our senses, dragging us apart with chests heaving.

Desire and regret had hovered in the air around us like a third person.

It clung to the air now as well. My eyes drifted slowly down her body. Was she braless today as she had been then, or had that been simply a way to distract me if she'd been caught? I swallowed hard, jerking my gaze away from her and to the stack of mail sitting on the desk.

It was filled with mostly bills and an invitation to the Kentucky Art Institute's charity gala being sponsored by the president of the Eastern Dude Ranchers' Association. I'd gone to one of Jaime's charity balls before and hated it. It wasn't just the tuxedos and fake smiles I despised. It was the unrealistic views of the politicians and millionaires who showed up to supposedly support whatever the latest, hippest cause was, only to leave the event behind and undermine it the very next day with their personal lifestyles and political decisions.

"What do you want?" I asked when Gia took two long-legged strides into the room.

"Is there anyone working for you who might be involved with the Lovatos?"

"No."

"You need to seriously think about this, not just give me a knee-jerk response."

"No one here is working for the Lovatos," I growled.

"You didn't expect Mila's mom or Ravyn to be working with them either."

My chest burned with humiliation, but I bit my cheek and said nothing.

She rode over my silence. "In an effort to be transparent, I'm just letting you know I'll be delving further into the background of all your employees and everyone connected to your family."

That did get a reaction. I rose from my desk and stalked over to her. She didn't back off as I stepped into her space, leaving barely room to breathe between us.

"The only people who have brought the Lovatos to our doors have been women who lied and stole from us. That's more likely to be you than anyone I know."

She didn't jerk away, but I saw the flinch in her eyes.

"We'll be going through your financials too," she continued, as if I hadn't said anything. "So, if there are secrets, you might as well come clean with them now."

I hated that my family's integrity was being called into question and that I was one of the reasons for it. But I wasn't going to let her stand there and accuse us of being dirty. Not after how hard my family and I had labored to get the ranch turned around.

"I hate repeating myself. The only one here with secrets is you."

She stared at me, not backing down an inch, and I didn't know why that turned me on as much as it pissed me off.

"We'll see."

I was two seconds from punishing her for her attitude and her snark with my mouth again when a, "Hello," rang out through the house.

Gia's hand went to her back, lifting her shirt so I saw the butt of a gun for the first time. She was about to pull it when I caught her arm.

"It's my mama. Jesus. Put that thing away."

The coiled tightness that had taken over her body relaxed ever so slightly as she looked up at me with accusation written all along her face. "Who else has a key to your place?"

"Just my parents and my siblings."

"Ryder?" my mama's questioning voice shouted out.

I dropped Gia's arm and hurried into the entry hall. I didn't want Mama to wake Addy, if the little girl had slept at all.

My parents were standing with arms full of reusable grocery bags. I grabbed the ones from my mother, asking, "What the hell is all this?"

"Don't swear at your mother," Dad bit out. His dark hair was pressed down on the sides from where his cowboy hat had sat—an almost permanent look. His pale, blue-gray eyes were concerned as they met mine, worry lines creasing his brow on a face tanned and leathery from a lifetime spent outdoors. His worn flannel shirt and equally worn jeans were near matches to the ones I'd thrown on this morning—work clothes we spent the majority of our days in.

"Where's my new grandbaby?" Mama demanded, searching the quiet of the great room as we walked toward the kitchen with the bags they'd brought.

"She was resting until you burst in here, screaming like a banshee," I groused.

"Ryder," my father warned again, but Mama chuckled.

"Leave him be, Brandon. It's sweet to see him already so concerned about her."

I was concerned. Concerned and terrified. Both were coiled up like a vicious snake nipping at my insides.

Chapter Twelve

Gia

EXCUSE THE MESS

Performed by Ella Langley

I pulled my shirt over my gun as I faced Ryder's parents. The way they were giving him hell was one of the things I liked most about the older couple. They never let any of their kids get the best of them. They gave it back full and hard in a way that always made me smile. The ribbing was full of love but relentless at times.

My family teased each other, especially my brother and me, but my dad was a military man through and through. He'd earned his seriousness right along with the medals pinned to his uniform. But if both our families were stuck in the same room together, they'd probably get along just fine.

That idea made my heart pitter in a strange way and my stomach flop. There would be no reason for my parents to ever meet Ryder's. Once I did my job, once Addy was safe and the Lovatos were brought down, I'd never see the Hatleys again.

Instead of easing the pressure in my chest, that seemed to add to it.

Eva started pulling things from the bags they'd brought. It felt like an entire grocery store's worth of produce along with a few canned goods. It reminded me of our refrigerator growing up, which had always been stocked with healthy options. The refrigerator in the apartment I rented near NSA headquarters had old condiments and a six-pack of Coke.

"It's nice to see you again, Gia. Even if the circumstances are…" Eva trailed off, gaze searching mine before looking away.

Brandon turned from putting some canned goods in the pantry to take me in for the first time since he'd arrived. His heavy brows furrowed together, doubts lingering in the air. I couldn't exactly blame him—or any of them. I'd lied about who I was. But to be fair, I gave the same lie to my family, just like I'd told Ryder.

"It's good to see you too," I said around the lump that formed in my throat. "I'm looking forward to some more of that olallieberry pie." I tilted my head toward Ryder. "I'm going to go check on Addy."

I didn't wait for his approval, taking off down the hall while trying to pull myself together. I heard their whispers behind me, knew they were talking about me, but it didn't matter. I was here to do a job just like any other, and I would.

When I opened the door to Addy's bedroom, the bed was empty. My heart skipped a beat, even as I knew she'd likely just hidden somewhere in the room. Ryder had given her such a pretty speech before about safety and staying in the bed, but I think even he'd realized the words wouldn't matter to Addy. He'd have to earn her trust just as much as I would.

The toilet flushed, and she came out of the bathroom dressed in the other outfit she'd had tucked away in her backpack—black jeans and a red sweater. Her shoes were on again, her backpack was loaded once more, and I'd bet money the toiletry bag Ryder had set on the sink was inside it also. She was prepared to run—go bag at the ready.

Her black hair was brushed, hanging down around her shoulders, and she reminded me of that hooded pitohui bird again. Small and delicate. Underestimated by those who didn't understand how deadly they could be. Was it wrong to hope she had the power, the venom, to bring down an entire cartel? Maybe. Maybe I should have her change her name, obtain some fake documents, and leave her with the Hatleys, buried in a sea of anonymity.

But I couldn't do any of that until I found out what exactly she knew. If this were any other witness, I would have already gotten what I needed from them—through teasing, cajoling, or force. But how did I get the information from a traumatized child?

I pushed back the sudden bitterness I felt toward my job as I said gently, "I know you're scared, but you'll be safe here, especially if I can arrest the people responsible for what happened to your mom. The ones the two of you were running from. You can help me with that, you know."

Her eyes went wide. "Me?"

"Yep. If you can tell me what happened—"

"No." Ryder's deep voice boomed from behind me, and I spun around to see anger flash in his bright-blue eyes. "She's been through enough today. You don't get to demand that of her. And especially not without me here."

I glared. "You wouldn't even be with her if—"

"Stop," Ryder cut me off, looking from me to Addy and back. I turned to see she'd wrapped her arms around her middle, distress obvious. I didn't know if it was at what I'd asked or at our raised voices. He brushed past me, the touch scorching me as much as the fire in his eyes had. He looked down at Addy and said, "When you're ready to tell us what happened, you can. But until then, no one is going to force you to talk. Okay?"

Her gaze flew back and forth between us.

"I catch…bad men?" she asked hesitantly.

"You can help us catch them," I said, even as Ryder grunted his disapproval.

"Right now, you don't need to worry about any of that," he said before I could ask or say anything else. "Right now, my parents are here, and they're really excited to meet you."

"*Mi abuelo y abuela?*"

She sounded so downright hopeful at the idea of having grandparents that it took all my thoughts of the Lovatos and how she might be the key and wiped it away. Ryder was right. I shouldn't have pressed her so soon. I was pissed off at myself and at him.

"Yep," his voice sounded rough, full of emotion, but there was also hesitation in it, as if he wasn't sure himself if they were her grandparents. I couldn't blame him for the doubts, but the thought of Addy meeting everyone, getting her hopes up, and then being tossed aside if a DNA test proved otherwise sliced through me.

Once again, I wondered if bringing her here had been a mistake. I could have kept her somewhere safe, gotten what we needed, and had her DNA tested all before dropping her into the Hatleys' hands. Had the pull I felt toward Ryder influenced my decision? Had I let it cloud my judgment already? Regardless, it was too late to go back. Too late to do anything but move forward.

Ryder reached out his hand for Addy's, and this time, she ever so slowly put her tiny one in his. His jaw worked, and he closed his eyes briefly. When they opened again, our gazes locked. I knew what it felt like to have this child trust you enough to put her hand in yours. She'd done it several times with me now, and the idea that maybe I'd burned that tiny bridge by pushing her made me want to throw up the grilled cheese we'd eaten earlier.

I followed them out of the room and down the glass-walled hall to the kitchen. Eva and Brandon were at work, chopping vegetables with smooth precision. They both stopped what they were doing as we entered, huge smiles taking over their faces. Ryder had his father's smile, right down to the half-dimple in his cheek, but his vivid blue eyes were his mother's. Normally, her eyes were sparkling with a mischief she shared with her youngest daughter, but right now, they were practically glowing with adoration for a child she'd never met.

It tugged at my heart in more unexpected ways.

Both adults squatted down so they were face-to-face

with Addy. She took a half-step closer to Ryder, but then, as if realizing he was a stranger also, froze.

"Hello, sweet girl. It's such a pleasure to meet you," Eva said softly. "I was as tickled as a June bug on a strawberry plant to find out I had another granddaughter. Now, you may not feel like calling me Grandma or even Nana like my other grandbaby does, so you can call me Eva if that makes you more comfortable."

"Eva, breathe," Brandon said, his lips twitching as he turned his pale eyes to the girl. "I'm Brandon. Or Papa."

He stuck a large, calloused hand out. Ryder's hand would look just like it in a few decades. Worn from hard work. Leathery from the sun. I'd had Ryder's hands on me briefly, and I knew they were already strong and firm and sure, and there was nothing soft or gentle about them. They'd demanded things my body had craved to give. I swallowed hard, pushing aside those thoughts and forcing myself to focus on Addy.

The little girl didn't say anything, just stared with a nonemotional look.

"Is Addy your full name, or is it short for something?" Eva asked.

"Adelaide." The whispered name from Addy's lips shocked me. I hadn't even considered that she had another name than the one Anna had given in the letter.

"That's a lovely name," Eva continued to prattle. She gestured toward the cutting board. "Your granddad and I were making dinner. I figured you might like some comfort food tonight. I have a very special mac and cheese that my children always ask for when they're feeling not quite themselves. And a winter vegetable medley that I promise will make you rethink hating veggies like all you young kids swear you do. Plus, I've got olallieberry pie for dessert. I brought two because Gia here…she almost ate a whole one herself the last time she had dinner with us."

Addy's lips twitched into an almost smile.

"My other granddaughter, Mila, loves to cook with me.

Now, don't feel like you have to, as you're the guest of honor today, but would you like to help out a bit?"

"Mama, you sound just like Mila. Dad's right, you need to take a breath," Ryder said. His face turned up in a wry grin that did all sorts of things to the endorphins I was already fighting. Waves of them were crashing over me and threatening to pull me under.

Addy glanced around at all the smiling faces, and her little shoulders relaxed just a hair. It brought tears to my eyes—tears I wasn't fond of shedding—and when I looked back up at Ryder, I could tell he'd noticed the way his daughter had relaxed as well, because his throat bobbed, and his jaw clenched again.

"Cook?" Addy asked quietly.

Eva's face broke into an even larger smile—one so huge I couldn't imagine anyone seeing it and not feeling completely comforted by it.

"Ryder, go get a step stool," Eva instructed.

Ryder didn't even hesitate. He disappeared out the door through the glass walkway leading to the garage. I wasn't sure where he was going to get a step stool in that immaculate space, but he appeared to have them stored somewhere close by, because he came back not even two minutes later with a small, two-step ladder.

He set it by the sink, and Eva supervised as Addy washed her hands. Then, they moved the ladder closer to a bowl Brandon had just dumped noodles into. Eva helped Addy pour other ingredients into it, and the little girl used a large wooden spoon to stir everything up.

I stepped back, suddenly feeling like the intruder I was. This was a family. A family the little girl needed more than she could know. I went to the glass windows on the far side of the living room, where the view of the valley had turned into a new work of art as the sun began to fade behind the hills. Rays shot into the clouds, turning the world into a hazy mosaic. The warm light filled the room until it seemed like we were standing in a shower of gold. There was a dreaminess to the scene that spoke of romantic walks and champagne picnics. Slow, lazy moments that I'd never wanted. And yet, I found myself tempted to take a picture to share it with…someone. I just wasn't sure who.

Holden was busy on tour with Leya and the band. If I sent my mom the picture, she'd ask a thousand questions I couldn't answer without lying about where I was and what I was doing. Dad would want to know what threat he was missing in the photograph. Who else was there? I went to drinks with colleagues occasionally. Found release in the arms of a random guy now and then. But I'd been far too focused on making my childhood spy dreams a reality than on spending time building relationships with anyone. Rory was the closest thing I'd had to a friend in a long time, at least since Gary had quit tagging along with me to parts unknown, and even he hadn't really been all that great of a friend. He'd hated every minute of our jungle hike with the SEALs and turned in his resignation as soon as we'd gotten back.

I swallowed hard, and instead of taking a photo of the stunning view, I brought up my email app on my phone, hoping I'd have more news from Rory or the Denver PD. Anything to bring me back to the job, and the cartel, and what I actually needed to be doing rather than dreaming about romantic sunsets.

To my surprise, Ryder joined me at the windows. The gold from the setting sun coated his skin and made his dark hair glisten with burnished highlights. What would it feel like to run my hand through those thick waves? What would it be like to grip them tight while those firm lips trailed down my body?

When my gaze met his, his eyes were narrowed, as if he'd read my mind, and I flushed. There was nothing wrong with thinking about sex. Nothing to be embarrassed about, and yet the heat filled my cheeks anyway. Maybe it was because I was thinking about bodies entwined when he was probably still irritated at me for questioning Addy.

Instead of mentioning what had happened in her room,

he surprised me by asking, "Is her limited speech because she doesn't know English that well?"

I considered it for a moment before replying, "I don't think so. Even when she talks to me in Spanish, it's the same way. It could be the trauma she experienced. I don't think we'll truly know until she becomes more comfortable with her surroundings."

We both watched as Addy listened to Eva chattering away as they worked. The little girl's shoulders were looser than I'd seen them since I'd pulled her from the hotel room.

"She should see a doctor. Maybe a therapist? Right?" he said.

"Probably. I'm definitely not a kid expert."

"She seemed pretty attached to you at the station."

"Necessity, I'm sure. I am the last person to know what a kid wants."

"You never babysat as a teenager?"

I rolled my eyes at him. "Just because I'm female doesn't mean I automatically babysat. Nor does it automatically mean my ovaries are going to explode if I don't have a baby in the next ten years."

He rubbed a hand along his jaw, partially covering lips twitching at my little tirade.

"Got it. No kids for the snarky undercover agent."

"I didn't say that either." Before the last twenty-four hours with Addy, I would have agreed with him. I'd not seen them in my future, not even with my mom dropping hints to both Holden and me about grandbabies. But holding Addy's hand, feeling the sag of her little body into mine, was enough to make me reconsider my long-term goals. Make me wonder if I was missing out on something the majority of the world seemed to understand—how having a child could be an adventure more worthy than a spy novel.

Ryder's brows dropped together in confusion at my contradictory words, but I couldn't clarify for him, as I was just as confused. Hadn't I known coming here would do strange things to me? That any interaction with Ryder would leave an imprint I wouldn't be able to remove—just like the last time.

A tiny whisper of a giggle broke our silence, and both our heads whipped toward the kitchen. Addy had a smile on her face. A full smile. Wide and beautiful and angelic. It was directed at Brandon, who was standing behind Eva, miming her in a completely clownish way. Even though the twinkle in Eva's eyes showed she knew he was doing it, she continued right on talking and explaining as if she didn't have a clue.

I hated to admit that telling his parents and having them come here might have been the best thing to have happened. They'd relaxed Addy in a way neither Ryder nor I had been able to do with our emotions running so high. The simple lack of expectation had won her over.

My throat clogged.

While my parents had never demanded perfection from me, I'd always demanded it of myself. I hadn't been in clubs or sports in high school with us moving so much, but I'd ensured I had the best grades and top-notch SAT scores in an attempt to offset my deficits in planning for college. I'd driven myself with the skill and smarts of my fictional spy friends motivating me. My brother had done the same, demanding only the best from himself. What did that say about us? About our relationship with our parents? With each other?

I'd never considered myself one of those people with, quote-unquote, "family issues." I'd mostly considered myself lucky to be surrounded by people who loved and cared for each other. Who respected each other. And yet, watching Eva and Brandon charm their quiet grandchild into giggles, it felt like I was watching something I'd never experienced. Some sort of untethered, unlimited love and acceptance. Something rare and beautiful.

I wanted to bask in it. To be covered in it.

"Okay, that's got to bake for a while," Eva said,

handing the glass dish off to Brandon, who put it in the oven with a flourish. "Which means, we have time to get to know each other."

Addy's smile went away, leaving behind a blank expression that was better than the one I'd practiced for years in a mirror. Eva saw it, but she didn't let it stop her from proceeding. She moved away from the counter, heading to the pantry.

"I'll point to the food in here, and you just say yes or no if they're things you like."

Ryder seemed drawn by this conversation and left me to journey back into the kitchen with them. Addy climbed down off the stepladder and followed Eva to the cupboard. Eva pointed at different things, naming off treats and vegetables and things that weren't even there. She waited while Addy nodded, shook her head, or shrugged. They moved to the refrigerator, repeating the process. It was easy to see the things she'd had no experience with. If she'd been on the run with Ravyn for her entire life, they'd hardly been staying places where her mother could cook a four-course meal, and it showed in the way Addy shrugged at many foods.

As I watched, my respect for Eva grew. She'd gotten more out of the little girl in an hour than I had in twenty-four. If the child was going to open up to anyone, it wasn't going to be some snarky NSA analyst. After years of learning to bury my emotions and personality, I was going to have to do the opposite. I was going to have to open myself up for her to trust me.

That sent more waves of fear through me than the gunfire I'd lived through in a South American jungle.

Chapter Thirteen

Ryder

FALL

Performed by Clay Walker

It wasn't just Addy who'd been relaxed and charmed by my parents. It was Gia…and me. The tension that had been in the air since I'd walked into my brother's office that morning had all but disappeared by the time we were laughing over pie and scoops of homemade vanilla ice cream.

Addy still hadn't said more than a word or two, but her shoulders were relaxed, and she'd listened and smiled and even laughed as my parents told her about our family, the ranch, and Mila. They took great pleasure in telling stories about me growing up. I recognized it for what it was—a way to allow the child to get to know me. I was grateful and yet also uncomfortable because it wasn't just Addy hearing those tales. It was the spitfire I was attracted to in ways I hadn't been to any woman since Ravyn…maybe even more than I'd been to Ravyn.

That wiped my smile away.

I collected the dishes and made my way to the kitchen to wash them as I'd done my whole life. The kids always cleaned up—end of story. Gia came in with the last stack, standing by my side, drying the items my mother would have kicked my ass if I'd put in a dishwasher.

The silence should have been awkward between us, and

yet it wasn't. It was as if the spell my mother had cast had brought that temporary truce Gia and I had called in my brother's office into reality. What it didn't do was dull the way my skin buzzed with awareness of her. In fact, it seemed amplified in the quiet as we worked, fingers grazing, shoulders brushing. It was as if we were slow dancing, the heat flickering and growing with each touch.

"Do you like kittens?" Mama asked.

My head jerked back to the table where Addy sat. Through the window behind her, stars sprinkled in the dark sky. Addy gave an excited nod, and I barely bit back a groan. I could not bring a cat home with us. It was fine if they lived in the barn. They kept the rodents and pests down, and the guests loved the idyllic image of them lazing about the farm, but that was where they were supposed to stay. I didn't want my leather furniture torn apart by claws, and I definitely didn't want to clean a litter box. I shoveled enough excrement at the farm without having to do it here too.

"Well, when Ryder brings you over to the ranch tomorrow, you can meet the little bundles the barn cat had. They're only a few weeks old, but their eyes are open, and they're starting to get into mischief. And if animals are your thing, we've got loads more. Horses and cows and even a pen of chickens I sometimes regret keeping, but I love their fresh eggs. I can teach you how to gather them. Mila is always too excited going into the henhouse, and she riles them all up, but I bet you'd be good at it because you're nice and calm."

Addy's eyes went wide.

"We're going shopping tomorrow," I said, drying my hands and heading back to the table. "Addy needs clothes and…well…everything."

"You can come by after you're done shopping. We'll have dinner, and Addy can meet the rest of the family."

"Mama," I lowered my voice, conveying a warning to butt out.

"Don't Mama me. Addy will be fine, won't you?" My

mother looked over to see Addy had retreated again. Her smile was gone, her shoulders were tight once more, and the blank look was back on her face.

Mama's brows furrowed before she squinted at me with a question in her gaze I couldn't answer.

"You're right. I just got overly enthusiastic about having this sweet girl in our lives and wanted everyone else to meet her too. Take your time. We'll be there whenever she's ready." She rose, and my dad did as well. "We'll let y'all tuck in for the night."

I knew my mama well enough to know she was itching to hug Addy, but instead, she lightly touched the little girl's shoulder. "I really am happy you're here. Next time, maybe we'll make chocolate chip cookies. Or snickerdoodles. Those are Mila's favorite."

Silence invaded for the first time since my mother had arrived. The tension came back into the room, and I hated it, wishing to bring back the relaxed air we'd all been wrapped in for a few moments.

"I'll walk you out," I said to my parents.

The three of us headed up the two steps to the entry hall and out the double doors. Dad's faded-blue Dodge pickup was parked out front.

"When you going to give up on that Dodge and finally get a Chevy?" I teased as my father opened the door for my mother. Between my brother, my dad, and me, we represented all three of the main American car manufacturers and harassed each other about it on the regular.

"Dodge was good enough for my daddy, good enough for you to sit your ass on as a kid, and it'll be good enough for me until I'm dead and buried."

"Keep swearing, and Mila is going to be able to pay for college with her swear jar," Mama said as she climbed in with a smile. Then, her face turned serious. "You going to be able to put her to bed okay? Bath and books and cuddles?"

Shit. I hadn't even thought about a nighttime ritual. But I'd babysat for Mila a time or two. I was usually a last resort, but I'd done it. I could handle it with a little girl who was supposed to be mine, couldn't I?

When I nodded, my mother raised a brow and sent a smirk my way, as if she read my hesitation. Dad went around, climbed in the cab, and they both waved as they headed down the gravel drive, tires kicking up dust into the night sky.

When I went back inside, Gia and Addy were at the table, looking at something on Gia's phone, and I instantly went on alert. I'd been pissed when I'd walked into the bedroom earlier to hear Gia questioning her. The little girl could barely talk, let alone tell us what had happened to her.

I only relaxed when Gia said, "You're really good at video games."

As I got closer, I could see there was some kind of brightly colored game on the screen. Candy and objects that Addy was dragging her fingers along.

I ran a hand over my head, scratching at the back of my neck before settling my thumbs into my pockets. "So, I don't know what time you normally go to bed, but it's late, and you've had a long couple of days. Probably should start thinking about heading that way. Maybe a bath?"

I groaned internally. I sounded like a fucking idiot. Wishy-washy. Mila would have already torn my logic to shreds. Instead, Addy handed Gia back her phone, slid out of her seat, and came over to me. We headed down the hallway, and I felt Gia on our heels.

In the bathroom of the blue-cloud room, I searched the cupboards, wondering if Mila had left any bubbles or shampoo here the last time she'd stayed over, but no such luck. All that was in the tub and shower combo was the grown-up stuff my sisters used. Nothing kid-friendly.

I turned the hot water on and looked back at Addy. If she'd been mine since she was a baby, there'd be nothing awkward about this moment. I would have been helping her bathe since she'd had toes and fingers so tiny they were doll-like. Now, I was sure she was as uncomfortable as I was at the idea of her removing her clothes and getting into the water. Gia seemed to understand, compassion crossing her face in a way that settled deep inside. But I wasn't sure Addy would be any more comfortable with Gia just because she was female.

When I looked at the little girl's face, it remained blank and guarded. She had one hand clasped around the other wrist, nails biting into the skin like she'd done earlier to keep herself awake. There were red marks there, as if she'd done it many times, and that upset me all over again.

"I want to help, but I don't have to," I told her. "Gia can…or, I don't know, can you do this on your own?"

She nodded.

"You can do it on your own?"

She nodded again.

"Okay. Why don't Gia and I just wait right outside the door, and if you need us, you can holler or bang on the wall, and we'll come in."

I stepped outside, and Gia followed. I shut the door behind me, listening to the quiet on the other side. It hung on for a long time before the splash of water drifted through the door. My chest burned. My eyes burned. I wasn't sure I could stand much more tug on my emotions in one day. The soft, compassionate look on Gia's face remained, and I hated it. I wanted the fierce, confident look I'd first encountered.

"I'm sorry. This…" She shook her head. "I can't even imagine how hard this is."

I dragged a hand over my clipped beard. There wasn't much to say in response. Each minute seemed excruciating, opening old wounds, opening a heart that had been locked down, all while there was a chance Addy wouldn't even stay with me. We might find out she didn't belong to me at all, and her real dad would come looking for her. Whether he was someone who deserved her or not wouldn't matter. I certainly didn't feel like I deserved the somber and brave little girl I'd witnessed today.

I paced the room while we waited. Eventually, when I was just about ready to go in and make sure everything was okay, Addy came out. Her hair was wet, clinging to her face, and I wasn't quite sure she had gotten all the shampoo out of it, but that was a problem for another day. She was wearing my T-shirt again, and she was shivering.

"Climb on in," I said, pulling the covers back. "You'll warm up right quick."

As I pulled the covers over her, I noticed she'd repacked her backpack. All her belongings were inside it again. That hurt me in ways I wasn't sure I could even speak about.

"Do you want me to read one of your books to you?" I asked.

She shook her head.

More pain spiked through me.

"I'm not as good as my brother at it, but I *can* read." I tried to make it a joke, tried to keep my voice light like Mama had, and I was rewarded with a little twitch of her lips. But she still shook her head again. "Okay, well. Goodnight." I ran a hand over her wet hair, and she withdrew into the pillow. My jaw clenched, but I pulled back quickly, stepping toward the door.

"Goodnight, Addy. I'm just one room over if you need anything. You can come get me or tap on the wall, okay?" Gia said. Addy nodded.

When I got to the door, I realized she might need a million and one nightlights, like my niece. "Do you want a light left on? We can leave the bathroom one on and shut the door so it's sort of like a night light. We can get you one tomorrow."

I was babbling. Like Mila or Mama.

She shook her head.

Okay, then. Dark it was.

"I know meeting me this way must be real hard,

sweetheart, but no matter how it happened, I want you to know, I'm glad you're here. I'm glad to get to know you." My voice was rough with unshed tears I hated showing in front of the calm brunette behind me.

"Papa?" God, that whispered word tore through me in a way I could never have expected.

I swallowed over the lump in my throat to choke out, "Yes?"

"I stay?"

"Yes, sweetheart, you're staying. You're staying, and you're safe."

She nodded again and slid down farther so that the bedding completely covered her head. She was so small, so slight, it almost looked like she wasn't in the bed at all.

My hand shook as I shut off the light and stepped out of the room, closing the door.

Gia's eyes met mine, and I saw tears in hers as well. She pushed her long fingers against her eyelids and then opened them again before saying, "Well, fuck."

I didn't know what else could be said beyond that. If I said anything, I'd lose it. I'd be bawling like Mila when she'd cried over an accidentally shot crow. Gia's warm-eyed gaze seemed to read every single emotion as I experienced it, and I wanted to hate it but couldn't. Instead, I found myself tempted to see if I could lose an entire day's worth of emotions in fierce lips, stroking tongues, and the pounding of skin on skin.

But I wouldn't. Couldn't. Not only because that wouldn't be fair to either of us but because I wasn't sure I could lose myself in her warm embrace and not want to linger there. I'd want something no woman had been able to give me—a person who stuck by me. I certainly wouldn't get it from Gia. She was just like Ravyn in that she'd leave Willow Creek as soon as she got what she needed from us.

So, instead of tempting fate with desires I wouldn't be able to hold back, I turned away and headed up the two steps that led to my room.

My night had been restless. I'd tossed and turned, reliving my life with Ravyn. Reliving the destruction her absence had left in its wake. Getting angry all over again at her stealing from me—this time something so much more important than fucking money. Tortured thoughts ran through my head about how Addy had lived. What she'd witnessed. And behind it all, I was tormented with a burning awareness of a woman lying just down the hall. A woman whose taste I couldn't seem to forget when I'd done just that with the woman I'd thought I'd marry. I'd purposefully scrubbed everything about Ravyn from my daily existence.

The sun hadn't risen, but the sky had started to lighten when I finally gave up on sleep and hit the shower. When I came out of my room, Gia and Addy were in the kitchen, dressed for the day, with Gia at the stove. It was unexpected and disconcerting. Not because it felt wrong to see them there but because it felt right in a way it shouldn't. It launched another dart into my heart I wasn't sure I could remove.

My family had always accused me of being snarly before my first cup of coffee kicked in, but I did my best to keep the growl from my voice as I greeted the two of them. Addy had her Switch in front of her, but her gaze kept darting from it to Gia and then to me.

Our morning went much as the day before had gone— quiet questions and single-word answers exchanged over scrambled eggs and toast. After breakfast was cleared, I said, "Okay, let's hit the mall."

Addy's eyes grew wide, and she slid down from her seat, running back down the hall. Gia and I shared a look, but the little girl came back with her backpack slung over her shoulder. It about killed me to think that she wasn't comfortable enough to leave it here. That she thought she had to have her things with her at all times.

But instead of commenting on it, I headed into the garage with them following me. Gia suggested taking the

Escalade because she already had the booster seat in it. Plus, no one would know her vehicle like they'd know mine if they spotted us in the mall parking lot. Willow Creek didn't have its own mall. We had to drive fifteen minutes to the next town over, but that didn't mean there wouldn't be people there who knew me. I wasn't ready for the questions about Addy. Wasn't ready for the truth or the lies I'd have to tell. So, I caved and got in the SUV with Gia at the wheel.

Sadie was right. I was a chicken.

We'd barely gotten to the end of the driveway before my phone started blowing up. My siblings demanded to know how the night had gone and what my plans were for the day.

I should have been working on the two unfinished cabins, but I hadn't even thought about the construction since I'd gone to bed last night. My mind was with the little girl in the back seat, the seven years I'd lost with her, and the sexy undercover agent who'd seemed all too at home in my house.

The snarl I'd woken up with hadn't disappeared with coffee and breakfast. I was doing my best to keep it under lock and key for Addy's sake, but I didn't need to hide it from my siblings.

> *ME: I don't want to talk. Stop yammering at me.*

> *WOODY: Did you not have coffee yet?*

> *ME: I have things to do. Leave me alone.*

> *SASSYPANTS: Please do not scare that sweet little girl with your assholeness. Mama said she barely talks and spooks at the drop of a hat. I can't even imagine her having to deal with you this morning.*

> *ME: I'm not being an asshole. I'm busy. We're*

heading to the mall.

GEM MINE: Oh no! The mall! You're going to melt as soon as you step foot inside.

SASSYPANTS: I could have gone with you. I could have been a go-between for your mall-hating self and that little girl.

ME: I'm muting this conversation.

SASSYPANTS: Never mind, Mama just reminded me that you have Gia there to be your go-between. Maybe that's why you're excessively growly this morning. It's all that pent-up sexual frustration.

GEM MINE: How many times do I have to tell you I don't like talking about our siblings' sex lives here? It's gross. It's like thinking of Mama and Daddy.

I choked on the sip of coffee I'd taken from the travel mug in my hand.

WOODY: Thanks for that, Gems. I need to go burn every thought from my brain now.

SASSYPANTS: Just go find McK. You won't have any thoughts left then.

GEM MINE: STOP TALKING ABOUT EVERYONE'S SEX LIVES!

SASSYPANTS: I know we're supposed to be all gentle with you because of the dick actor we don't name, Gems, but you're just jealous they're getting some and you're not.

GEM MINE: If you're so comfortable talking

about everyone's sexual exploits, let's talk about yours. When was the last time you got laid, Sadie? Spill the beans.

I shoved the phone in my pocket, unable to read any more. I couldn't think of my sisters in that way without wanting to kill the men in their lives.

When I looked up, Gia's lips were twitching.

"Your family?"

"Sadie doesn't respect anyone's boundaries."

"But you love them," Gia said softly. And for a brief moment, I thought I saw something close to wistfulness cross her face.

"You're not close to your family?" I asked, frowning, thinking of her ex-Secret Service agent brother and his gruff exterior. He hadn't seemed overly friendly, but then again, I hadn't been friendly either after he'd led Maddox in a high-speed chase.

"We're close. We love each other and harass each other in the appropriate sibling fashion, but it's not a constant in-your-face kind of thing like you've got going on with yours. Holden and I are lucky if we remember to check in with each other once a month."

I thought about what that must be like. To have family, but not. I couldn't imagine going more than a day without hearing from mine. Life would feel…empty. I craved the solitude of my home at the end of the weekends or holidays spent hip-to-hip with my family, but it never lasted long. If it did, I was usually the one seeking them out.

I tilted my head, taking in Addy with her gaze stuck to the window. Who would she have to run to when her loneliness got to be too much? She deserved an entire gaggle of siblings and cousins to keep her company. But I couldn't imagine giving her a brother or sister. The cousins would have to do.

I glanced at Gia. She'd said last night that she didn't want kids and then countered it confusingly. I wondered what she'd look like with a round belly pushing against the steering wheel. What it would be like to place my hands on her stomach and feel a baby kicking inside it. Wondered what it would feel like to experience all the things about having a baby I'd lost out on with Addy.

But then I pushed those traitorous thoughts away.

Because even if I opened myself up again to a relationship—and just the idea of it made me nauseated—it certainly wouldn't be with a woman who was going to skip town in a few days. So, if Gia ever did get pregnant, it sure as hell wouldn't be mine.

Chapter Fourteen

Gia

CRY PRETTY

Performed by Carrie Underwood

I pulled into the parking lot of the mall and, out of habit, backed into a slot near the rear so I'd be ready for a quick exit if I needed it. I was surprised at how busy the place was before realizing not only was it Saturday, but it was a rainy weekend sure to keep everyone indoors. People scurried from their cars to the large glass doors, holding umbrellas over their kids' heads.

I didn't have an umbrella. I didn't have anything that was needed to take care of a child.

"Okay, ready to make a run for it?" I asked.

Ryder grunted out a response, jumping out, shoving his hat on his head, and opening the back door for Addy.

I started to open my door but then noticed the little girl hadn't removed her seat belt yet, and, if possible, she looked even stiffer than she ever had.

Raindrops landed on Ryder's black hat as he peered in at her, confusion in his eyes.

"Addy?" he asked.

She sat there, staring straight ahead, not looking at him.

Ryder eased toward her, reaching over her to unbuckle the seat belt, and she pulled back as far as she could into the seat, as if he'd struck her. The clank of the belt hitting the side of the car was as harsh as a gunshot. Ryder looked up at me with raised brows.

"You want to go shopping?" I asked.

She shook her head violently, fearful gaze directed at the mall doors.

"We'll get some more clothes. Some toys. Things to make your room all yours," he said, using a cajoling tone that spun like silk through my veins. I'd have a hard time resisting it if it was directed at me. "You want a new video game, right?"

She looked at him and gave the barest of nods.

"Okay, then." He held out his hand.

She tucked hers under her little thighs.

Ryder frowned. "Can't get a game sitting here, sweetheart." He gently tugged at her arm. The movement had nothing mean or angry or cruel about it. Instead, it was full of tenderness, but Addy screamed as if he'd hit her.

She screamed and screamed and screamed.

Ryder's eyes met mine, a shocked panic wafting between us.

"Addy, calm down," I said softly. "It's okay."

But she didn't. She continued to shriek, adding a kick of her legs to the tantrum that had come from nowhere. A tantrum that seemed so opposite of the quiet, shy, reserved little thing we'd experienced that it was more than baffling—it was scary.

She was so loud it began to draw eyes. A man getting out of a car two spaces over left his family and came striding over. I hustled out of my seat and met him at the front.

"What's going on?" he demanded.

I flashed my badge. "It's all right. I've got everything under control."

He frowned, his gaze darting from Ryder, who was dripping with rain now beside the car, and Addy, still wailing inside it.

"She's okay, I promise."

He looked doubtful but headed off with his wife and kids.

I got back into the front seat, and Ryder joined me. Once all the doors were shut, Addy finally stopped yelling. She retreated into herself, tears dripping down her face, head dropping to a chest that heaved as if she'd run a marathon.

Ryder took off his hat, setting it on the floorboards, before sharing another look with me. He turned backward to take in the obviously distressed little girl.

"Addy, you said you wanted a new video game, right?" he asked.

She didn't look up, but her head bobbed in a yes.

"And maybe some new toys?"

Another bob.

"And some new clothes?" She nodded and finally looked up, tears still pouring from her large brown eyes.

Ryder dragged a hand over his beard. "But you don't want to go into the mall?"

She shook her head violently, eyes getting impossibly larger.

"No one will hurt you in there. I'd be right with you. Gia would be with you. The bad people don't know you're here. You're safe."

Her little chest heaved again, breathing at a pace so wild I was afraid she'd hyperventilate.

"Do you want to try one store? Just one. And if that doesn't work, we can leave," Ryder suggested, that coaxing tone back in his voice.

Her nails were leaving marks in her wrist again as she shook her head.

"Okay," he said. "Sit tight. Gia and I are just going to get out and talk for a minute. You don't have to go anywhere."

He grabbed his hat and slid out. I did the same, and we

met in front of the Escalade.

"What the hell?" he asked quietly.

"I don't know. That… I've never seen anything like it. I don't think this is just her being scared of the people who killed her mom. This is like… I don't know. Maybe she's never been to a mall? Maybe she and her mom always had things delivered? Maybe it's just the unknown?"

Ryder looked toward the mall and the people still darting inside as the rain lightened to a mist. Puddles glimmered along the blacktop, the car lights and the neon signs reflecting in them.

"Yesterday, I ordered her a toy online. A stuffed animal she said she'd lost." His throat bobbed. "I guess we could try it that way. I have no idea what size she wears. Maybe I should have brought Mama or Sadie?"

It stung a bit that I was standing in front of him, and he didn't think I could help him. But to be fair, I was as lost as he was. I watched as a woman walked by, talking on her phone, and an idea hit me.

"Why don't I go in, and I can video call you? She can pick out things as I show them to her?"

"Still don't know what size to get."

I looked into the car. "Well, we can ask her. And if she packed her spare clothes I put back in her room after I finished the laundry, there'd be sizes on those."

Ryder rounded the car, opened the back passenger door opposite Addy, and climbed inside it as I stood looking in at them.

"Gia says she'll go in for us. She can call us on the phone, show us the items in the store, and you can pick things right from here. How does that sound?" he asked.

Addy's little shoulders relaxed ever so slightly, her nails releasing her wrist. She nodded.

"We just need to know what size clothes to get you," he said. "Can I look at your things in your backpack again?"

She nodded.

We pulled out the clothes she'd put inside her go bag, searching for sizes.

"How about your shoes? Can we see them for a second?" he asked.

She pulled one off and handed it to him. We looked around inside it until we found the size, and then he handed it back.

"Okay," I said, taking my phone out of my pocket and handing it over to Ryder. "Put in your number."

We both hesitated as our fingers brushed against each other. My skin broke out in goosebumps. It wasn't just because our skin had touched. This was the idea of his number being on my phone. Of him having mine. As if there was something more between us.

Once he'd added it in, I started to shut the door, and he stopped me, fishing out his wallet and handing over a credit card. "Here. If you have an issue using it, I can show them my ID over the phone."

I took it and jogged toward the mall entrance with the mist coating my makeup-free face.

I went into Target, figuring it would have pretty much everything we needed. First, I headed to the video games because that seemed to hold her interest the most. I dialed Ryder's number, and my heart flipped at the sight of both their faces squished onto the screen.

"Hey," I said. "So, just holler or tap Ryder or whatever when you see something you want."

And that was how we shopped, moving from the video games, down the toy aisle, where she asked for Legos and puzzles with a smile taking over her face. She seemed uninterested in the clothes, but I added a coat, pajamas, underwear, and socks to a pile of jeans, leggings, T-shirts, and sweaters. In the shoe aisle, she only wanted another pair of shoes that looked like her Vans, but I threw in some boots because a girl always needs boots.

"Okay, almost done here," I said. "Let me just grab a couple of things I need." I went to the adult clothing area, throwing in a few items for myself so I didn't need to be washing clothes every other day while I was in town. Ryder didn't say anything, but when I looked at the screen, his eyes narrowed at the cotton underwear I tossed on the pile.

The cart was already overflowing when I breezed by the bedding department, and Ryder hollered at me to go back. He asked Addy what she wanted her room to look like, and she just did what she always did when she didn't know—she shrugged.

"Mila loves rainbows. Is there something you love like that?" he asked.

I scanned the shelves, looking for anything that might intrigue her based on the limited time I'd gotten to know her. I was just about to give up when I saw, shoved at the back of a shelf, a fuzzy blanket with the dragons from the book she'd shown me yesterday. It wasn't large enough for the double bed in the room, but it was something that added color and would be solely hers. I grabbed it without even asking and tossed it on top of the pile.

Then, I pushed the cart in the direction of the checkout.

"Wait, we need shampoo and bubble bath," Ryder said. My lips twitched. It seemed almost impossible to me that this rough, gruff cowboy knew what a little girl needed. It took all those squishy feelings inside me and amplified them.

Addy didn't say what she liked again. She kept shrugging, but I remembered her eyes lighting up at the olallieberry pie the night before and picked up some berry-scented soaps and shampoos as well as a new toothbrush and some colorful headbands and hair ties before once again making my way to the checkout.

The sales clerk's eyes turned wide at my pile. It took almost as long to buy everything as it did to shop, but eventually, I had the cart brimming again and was pushing it out into the parking lot, thankful the rain had stopped completely.

When I made it to the SUV, Ryder jumped out, helping

me load everything into the back. He was smiling. A slow, wide grin that spoke of joy, as if being able to buy these things for the child he hadn't known he had was one of the best things he'd done in a long, long time.

He slammed the back and then looked at me, eyes twinkling. "Thank you."

"I'm glad I could help."

"No…" He shook his head, the smile dimming just barely. "You should have seen her. She was… I don't know how to explain it except the old cliché of a kid in a candy shop. She was…" He stopped and then started again. "And I got to do that for her because of your idea and because you were willing to help us."

That overwhelmed sensation that had been with me ever since finding Anna-Ravyn's note landed deep inside my chest again. I tried to shrug it off. "Just doing my job."

"Don't do that. We both know shopping for a traumatized little girl is not in your job description. But you did it anyway. So, thank you. I don't think I'll ever be able to repay you."

I couldn't look away, even though every instinct in my body was telling me to. He reached out and tucked a lock of hair that had escaped my ponytail behind my ear. My body nearly exploded. I literally vibrated with a need to touch him too. Instead, I stepped away, and he dropped his hand, as if he was as surprised as I was that he'd done it.

"You know how you can pay me back?" I asked. His gaze fell to my lips, which only increased the pulsing in my veins. "Buy me a milkshake at the drive-thru."

His grin returned. "I think I might have just enough money left in my account to be able to get you both a milkshake."

We headed for the car doors, both of us still smiling. When I got in and looked at Addy, she was grinning too.

And somehow, that moment, where joy overtook the seriousness, lodged itself deep inside me, permanently embedding a mark—a memory—I'd never escape.

Ryder directed me to the drive-thru of the local Dairy Queen. When we got to the menu board, he asked Addy what kind of milkshake she wanted, and she beamed at him. "Chocolate."

Ryder sent her a smile that was so large and bright it felt like it could blow out the windows. "That's my girl."

He winked at her, and damn if my heart didn't flip right over.

When the intercom buzzed, and we were asked for our order, I responded with, "Two large chocolate shakes and one large vanilla bean."

"Anything else?"

I looked over only to see a look of horror on Ryder's face that was almost comical. I turned back to the box. "No, that's it."

I was given a total and asked to pull up to the window.

"What?" I said, lips twitching.

"It's a sin," he said quietly. It took me a minute to realize he meant my order because my body was thinking of all the ways it would like to sin with Ryder Hatley. Ways my mind knew better than to want.

"Since when is ordering a vanilla shake a sin?"

"Please tell me you did it as a joke, because chocolate will forever and always be the only right answer when ordering a shake."

I huffed out a laugh, even though I could see he was completely serious. "There's nothing wrong with vanilla, especially the Dairy Queen vanilla bean shakes."

"Vanilla is boring and bland."

I couldn't help but taunt and tease in return. "Chocolate is dominating and overpowering."

He shook his head and ran his palm over the neat beard that was just past scruff. It drew my eyes to his lips, which were tilted upward ever so slightly. Those lips had been strong and confident when they'd found mine, leaving me with no doubts he knew his way around a woman's body.

"When was the last time you tried dominating and overpowering, darlin'?"

His heated gaze fell to my mouth, and it caused my insides to ignite all over again. How could an argument about milkshakes turn so quickly into a flirtation about sex?

"Don't call me darlin'. And believe me, dominating is overrated." I glanced back at Addy, who seemed, thankfully, oblivious to how this conversation had turned on its head.

"Then, you haven't been having the right…milkshakes," he said, lowering his voice until it coasted over me, low and sexy, as if he'd run a finger over my most sensitive parts.

I swallowed hard but was saved from responding when the take-out window opened, and the tray with three shakes was shoved at me.

♫ ♫ ♫

It took another couple of hours to unload, unpack, and put away everything we'd bought in Addy's new room. She wanted to touch each item, as if she couldn't believe it was hers. When I showed her the dragon blanket, she beamed all over again before spreading it carefully on the side of the bed she'd slept on the night before.

The doorbell rang, and Ryder said he'd get it.

I was hanging the last of the clothes when I heard him come back into the room, tearing apart what sounded like cardboard. I stuck my head out of the closet and saw him hand a box to Addy. The little girl peeked inside, and a look of pure delight shot over her face. She reached in and pulled out a stuffed animal. It had spots and tan fur and looked decidedly like a cat—leopard or jaguar or something. She squeezed it to her chest, eyes shutting, relief crossing over her face before she buried her nose in the fur.

"Balam," she said. She opened her eyes and looked up at Ryder. "Thank you."

He nodded.

"Mama pack," she said. "In Mama's bag."

I leaned against the door jamb, heart pounding at the mention of her mother.

Ryder squatted down in front of her. "Your mother had it in her bag?"

She nodded.

I pulled up the inventory of what had been in the hotel room. A stuffed animal was not listed. But then again, there'd been no computer equipment either. Maybe it had been in Ravyn's computer bag that we assumed had been taken by the killer.

"Were the two of you moving again?" he asked.

Her eyes turned cloudy, but she nodded. "Someone knock. I hide."

"Did you always hide?" he asked.

She shrugged but then nodded again.

His gaze darted over her head to mine and then back.

"Did you see who came in?"

"Man. Ugly man. Big nose. Bad shoes."

"Did you see…" I breathed in. "Did you see what he did?"

She froze, eyes filling with tears, but she didn't respond. Either she'd blocked it out, hadn't seen it, or wasn't ready to talk about it. But she'd at least seen him. "We can draw him using the computer, like building an avatar. If we did that, we might be able to catch him. Would you like to help me?"

She slowly nodded again.

"Can you tell me what you meant by bad shoes?"

"Sharp. Like knives."

Ryder and I frowned, and then his eyes went wide. "Hold on." He jogged out of the room.

"You're really brave, Addy. Do you know that? The bravest little girl I've ever met."

She flushed, burying her face in the toy's fur once more.

When Ryder came back, he had an Eastern Dude Ranchers' Association magazine in his hand. On the cover was a tan cowboy boot that someone had filled with flowers. Attached to the boot was a bright silver spur, the edges sharp and spiky.

"Did his shoes have something like this on them?" he asked. Addy saw the spur he was pointing to and shuddered. She bobbed her head yes.

"Some cowboys use them to help guide their horses. I've never liked spurs much, but they don't have to hurt the animals. They can, but they don't have to."

Addy didn't say anything else. She turned back to the bed and sat down, rubbing her hand along the fuzzy blanket while the other hand clung to the stuffed cat. Ryder's gaze locked with mine. His were sad and frustrated, but excitement surged through me. These were new clues, a step in the right direction, especially if we could get a decent image of the perpetrator.

I'd download the app we used to help witnesses with sketches. I wasn't as good at using it as the people who'd been trained on it were, but I didn't think Addy would talk to anyone but Ryder or me. She was barely doing that as it was. Plus, the cowboy boot and spurs led me back to the original reason I'd been pretending to write about the dude ranches to begin with—the chemicals attached to the cattle feed found on the drugs and money in the bust we'd made in Lexington.

"I need to make a few calls and see if I can get my hands on the program for us to build our avatar," I said to Addy and Ryder. Neither of them said anything, and I hurried from the room. A part of me hated leaving the little cloud of joy we'd been wrapped in for a few moments, and a part of me was elated to have some new leads.

Hope rushed through me. Maybe this time, we really would bring the Lovatos down.

Chapter Fifteen

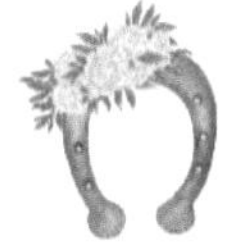

Emiliano

ONE DOWN
Performed by The Trishas

I swirled the dark whiskey around in the crystal glass. The color reminded me of Natalia's eyes. My eyes. Our mother's eyes. I was equal parts furious and impressed. Not only had she encrypted the device in a way that would be nearly impossible for even me to break without the key, but she'd had a child and kept it from me for years. Two points, Natalia.

Except, she should have known better than to play these kinds of games with me. I didn't lose. Ever. I'd already peeled back several of her hidden layers, retracing her footsteps, and revisiting every location I knew she'd lived since I'd brought her back into the fold. The reports my men had gathered after interviewing people in those locations had allowed me to assemble an approximate age and description of the child—a little girl between six and seven years old.

That had been enough for me to know the truth.

It was his. The man she'd nearly given everything up for. The man she'd abandoned me for.

The man I'd promised her I wouldn't touch as long as she stayed where she belonged. With me. With our family.

All promises were off. He was now forfeit.

But for the first time in my life, I regretted slicing

someone's throat. The idiot who'd killed Natalia had to have seen something and not understood it. He'd sworn no one had seen him, so where had the child been? Hiding? Or had Natalia left her with someone? Who? Because I knew for a fact the child hadn't spent all these years with the Tennessee rancher.

I shouldn't have allowed her the little cat-and-mouse game she'd thought she'd been playing with me. It had seemed like such a small concession. A gift I'd granted the sister I'd spent an entire childhood protecting. I'd allowed her to do her job from wherever she wished to save her the pain of reliving our childhood. I hadn't cared if she did her work from Colombia or the Caymans or Montana, as long as she did it. But she'd taken my gift and abused it. She'd made a fool of me.

If any of my other employees had done the same, they'd be dead.

And now she was.

I was still furious that it hadn't been at my own hand. No one had a right to kill my family except me. They were mine to do with as I wanted.

The liquid in the glass taunted me, seeming to reflect the terrified betrayal I'd last seen in Natalia's eyes. Except, she'd been the one to betray *me*. To leave *me*. After all the times I'd protected her, she'd run instead of thanking me for putting an end to decades of abuse.

My hand tightened on the crystal. If I had less control, I'd toss the glass into the fireplace, just to see it shatter. To see the flames flicker with the added fuel.

Instead, I set the glass down slowly, purposefully.

If the child was his, then perhaps that was where I needed to look for her.

Perhaps the child had the key.

That brought a lightness to my heart. I'd take the girl and make her mine. I'd make Natalia's daughter love me. She'd adore me. She'd never betray me like her mother had. Pleasure coursed through me at those thoughts. My sister could toss and turn and burn in her grave, watching from beyond the veil as I turned her daughter against her. As I made her my own.

Chapter Sixteen

Ryder

MADE THAT WAY
Performed by Jordan Davis

$\mathscr{I}$ *looked about Addy's room with* a lightness in my heart that hadn't been there before. It wasn't littered with her personality the way Mila's room was at my brother's, but it was a step in the right direction. There were toys piled in the corners, a dragon blanket on her bed, and the closet now looked like someone actually lived there instead of holding a solitary outfit.

"What would you like to do now?" I asked.

She had the jaguar tucked under her armpit as she dug in her backpack that she'd placed right by the bed again. She came out with the Switch and picked up the two new video games we'd bought.

"You really do like your video games, don't you?" My lips twitched.

She shrugged, but there was a light in her eyes that tugged at me.

"Why don't you bring that into my office? You can play while I get a few things done."

She looked around the room as if she was reluctant to leave, and that made me both happy and sad.

"Scratch that. Stay right here. I'll get my computer and bring it in."

She didn't respond but turned her attention to the video game box, trying to open it. I stepped over, brought out my pocket knife, and went to cut open the plastic and tape. She jerked away from the knife, scooting back onto the bed until she was pressed against the headboard. I cursed inwardly, thinking of what she'd seen happen to her mother. I swallowed over the lump in my throat but finished opening both games for her before setting them on the bed.

After I grabbed the bags of trash we'd filled with tags and plastic, I headed for the door. I looked back to see she was already pushing the game cartridge into the device, and my chest eased ever so slightly.

I hurried out, threw the garbage in the cans outside, grabbed a couple of bottles of water, and stopped by my office to get my laptop. When I came back into Addy's room, her thumbs were moving, and there was a furrow between her brow as she concentrated on the new game.

I kicked off my boots and joined her on the bed, leaning against the headboard.

She stilled when our arms brushed momentarily, but then she settled back into the game.

It was progress.

I opened my emails, working through the small stack that had accumulated since the day before. There was another note from the president of the Eastern Dude Ranchers' Association, asking if I'd received his invitation to the charity gala, and all but insisting I come so we could discuss my future with the association. As much as I hated his events, I wasn't sure I could say no. Or should say no.

Jaime Laredo was not only persuasive, he was usually right. In addition, I owed him. Without the knowledge he'd shared, I wouldn't have been able to save our ranch. These days, he wanted me to step into the treasurer's position that had been vacated due to an unfortunate heart attack, and while I'd never been interested in taking on a leadership role in the association, it was hard to keep turning him down. On the other hand, with Addy being here, I'd have less time and less tolerance for the politics of the association.

I closed the email without responding.

Addy gave out a frustrated grunt, and I looked over to see she'd switched cartridges and was trying to load the second game.

"What's wrong?" I asked.

She tilted the device to me, and I saw an error message stating there wasn't room to load the game. I frowned. "Let me see."

There were only five games there—the four she'd had before and the new one. I flipped through the menus until I found the device's capacity. With a two-terabyte card installed, there should have been plenty of room to load the game. I fiddled around some and then tried to load the game again.

I got the same message.

My phone rang. I handed Addy back the Switch. "Maybe it has a virus, or something's wrong in the settings. We'll figure it out. And if we can't, I'll get you a new one, okay?"

Her shoulders slumped, and I wanted to run out and get her a new one right then.

"You can take off one of the old games and try to put the new one on for now," I suggested before looking down at my phone and seeing my mother's face.

I answered and said, "What's up?"

"I know I said I wouldn't push, but we'd love to have Addy over here for dinner," Mama said.

Other than the huge tantrum Addy had thrown at the mall, we'd had a good day. I didn't want to break the little thread of calm and comfort she seemed to have found— we'd found.

"I'm not sure that's a good idea. We're just getting settled in."

"It'll just be us and Sadie. Just one more person. Dinner is ready and waiting, and after, she can see the kittens. I saw the way her eyes lit up when I mentioned them."

So did I, and I wasn't interested in bringing a cat into the mix. I already had my hands full.

But if we stayed here, I'd have to cook, and while Mama had filled my fridge, I still wasn't sure what I'd make.

"Fine," I groused.

She snorted at my obvious reluctance. "See you soon."

Addy was watching me with curious eyes. "I guess we're going to the ranch for dinner. Mama wants to show you the kittens. It'll be just my parents and my sister Sadie."

Her brows raised, but that blank look that had preceded her terrifying tantrum didn't return.

"Get your shoes and your new coat. I'll go let Gia know." The idea of putting Gia and Sadie in the same room gave me heartburn. My little sister already thought something had happened between Gia and me, and while we had once exchanged a goddamn kiss, it had been punishment more than pleasure. Although, which of us it had really punished was unclear, as I still couldn't escape the taste of her.

I knocked on Gia's bedroom door.

"Yeah?" she hollered. I twisted the knob and stepped inside. She was on the bed, her ponytail now tied into a messy knot on top of her head, and her feet were bare. Bright-pink nail polish glimmered on her toes. The color was somehow surprising when black or a deep purple would have suited her snarky attitude better. Even when I'd thought she was a journalist, there'd been an edge to Gia that had made her seem rough and tumble rather than soft and girlie. And yet, that color felt all girl. All woman.

If it weren't for the computer and papers strewn about her, she'd look like she'd just woken from a nap. My dick responded to the idea of her in bed, soft and warm and messy. My body wanted to push her work aside, take off her clothes, and see what other kinds of mess we could make. My brain told my body to take a cold shower and put as much distance between us as possible. The feelings I was having for her after our day together, along with the hole in my resolve about women and relationships after my talk with Sadie, had my mind screaming danger.

Maybe it was that prick of alarm that had my words coming out colder than I intended when I said, "We're heading to the ranch for dinner. If you're busy, don't feel like you have to come. There's plenty of food in the fridge now that Mama loaded it up."

A look crossed her face that might have been hurt, and I immediately felt like an ass. I wouldn't have gotten through the morning without her, and now I was making it sound like I didn't want her with us. And while it was true, because having Gia with us would allow her to continue chiseling away at the barrier I'd put up between me and my desire for her, it was also equally true that I liked having her around. I liked those flames that licked through me when our skin happened to brush.

"Or come," I grunted out. "Doesn't matter. Either way."

"Wow. How badly did that hurt?" she asked, mischief lighting her eyes, as if there'd never been anything else there a moment before.

I huffed and turned around so I wouldn't be tempted to kiss the look right off her face. "We're leaving in five minutes if you're coming."

"I need ten."

"I can give you seven."

"You're such an ass."

I came out of the room to see Addy wearing the new flowered coat Gia had picked out. She had her backpack on again and the stuffed jaguar in her arms. I wanted to tell her she didn't need to bring the bag with her, but that would likely rip her sense of security away. I'd just have to hope she'd realize soon enough that she didn't need it.

We made our way to the kitchen, and I saw the Escalade key fob on the counter where Gia had dropped it when we'd come in. I picked it up and headed for the garage. I opened the back passenger door of the SUV for Addy, and she climbed in. Then, I went to the driver's side, backed the seat up, and started adjusting the mirrors.

When Gia joined us, she'd brushed her hair back into a smooth ponytail, pulled on a sweatshirt that read University of Pennsylvania, and slid her feet back into the blue cowboy boots she'd had on since I'd seen her in my brother's office. Boots that I'd harassed her about the first time she'd been at the ranch, saying they were what city folk thought actual country folk wore, but they'd never hold up to the rigors of life on the ranch. The boots looked scuffed and worn now, but they also looked like they'd held up just fine, making me wrong about yet another thing when it came to Gia Kent.

When she saw me in the driver's seat, her eyes narrowed. She opened the passenger door, put her hands on her hips, and demanded, "What are you doing driving my car?"

"I don't like being a passenger," I told her.

"Ryder, get out of the driver's seat."

"Climb in. We're already late."

"You're not driving my car."

"It isn't really your car." But it made me wonder what kind of car she actually owned. The last time she'd been here, she'd been in a similar vehicle.

"That isn't the point."

"What is your point?"

"You can't drive a government vehicle."

I put the SUV into reverse and pushed down ever so slightly on the gas so the door bumped into her as it started to move.

"Ryder!"

"Get in, darlin', or you're gonna get run over."

A panicked noise from the back made me turn my eyes to Addy. She was upset, which made me feel like a jerk in a way the argument with Gia hadn't. Arguing with Gia only made me want to shove her up against a wall and kiss her until she gave in. But I hated that I'd upset Addy. Gia had heard the choked noise too. Indecision warred over her features before she huffed and pulled herself into the passenger seat.

"Don't call me darlin'," she hissed, slamming the door with so much force the windows rattled.

"Your boss will dislike you destroying the door more than me driving."

She didn't respond, and I shoved aside what felt like disappointment. I enjoyed sparring with her more than I should have—just like the argument over chocolate and vanilla earlier had made me want to show her just what she was missing, what dominating and overpowering could do for her.

I backed out of the garage and hit the button on the remote on my key chain to shut the door. As we drove down the driveway, Gia turned back and looked at my house for a moment. "Did you set the alarm?"

I unlocked my phone and tossed it at her. "You can turn it on from there."

She found the app with no problem, clicking through the settings before saying, with a hint of surprise, "This is a decent system."

I looked from the road to her and back. "With everything that went down with the West Gears and then The Painted Daisies, we upgraded everywhere on the ranch."

The SUV's headlights reflected off the *Narrow Bridge* sign, and I caught a glimpse of the creek below. It was full after a winter of heavy rains and snows, with more coming. The dark clouds that had started our day were still hanging around. The weather report had said it would hold off tonight, but the air was cold enough that if it did come down, it might just snow. I wondered whether Addy had ever experienced snow. What had she looked like the first time she'd stepped into it? What had the smile on her face looked like when she'd built her first snowman? Had there been joy in her eyes as she'd whooshed down a hill on a sled? My chest tightened. So many firsts I'd lost out on.

The pain of what I'd lost overtook me on the brief drive from my house to the ranch, and the car settled into a gloomy silence I regretted.

I pulled up in one of the empty parking slots in front of the restaurant's darkened windows. In another few months, it would be bustling with activity as the season kicked in, reminding me I really needed to get back to work on the cabins.

When I got out and went around to Addy's door, she was stiff as a board again. My heartbeat picked up pace, wondering if she'd throw another tantrum like the one at the mall. Her eyes were wide, taking in the barn and restaurant and well-lit house.

"I know it looks big," I told her. "But it's just my parents, who you met last night, and Sadie."

Gia stood just behind me as we waited, unsure what would happen.

Slowly, Addy unlatched her seat belt and picked up her bag and her stuffed animal. I helped her out of the car, and to my surprise, she slid her tiny hand into mine, the soft skin rubbing against my calluses. My throat instantly clogged as I gently held onto her fingers, almost afraid they'd disappear.

"You ready?" I asked, looking down into her face.

Her eyes were big in the fading light, but she nodded.

We headed for the wraparound porch and the back door.

The warmth hit us as if we'd opened an oven door, the smell of sugar and cinnamon mixing with the smell of Mama's chili. More comfort food. Rainy day, comfort food.

I took my hat off as we stepped in, hanging it on the coatrack and sliding out of my jacket as I hollered, "We're here."

Rapid footsteps approached, causing Addy to step

behind me. Sadie appeared in the kitchen's archway with an inquisitive look in her eye, head angling to the side to catch sight of Addy, who'd tucked herself behind me. Her face broke into a huge smile with her eyes flashing just like Mama's had the day before. Sadie said softly, but with enthusiasm, "Well, hello there!"

Addy remained still, as if she were invisible.

My sister came closer, leaning over to meet Addy's gaze. "I'm your Aunt Sadie. And while you don't know this yet, I can promise you I'm the fun one. I'm the one you'll come to whenever you want to get into a little trouble, and this one"—she tossed a thumb in my direction—"is being all prickly and growly and saying no."

Addy didn't respond, but Sadie didn't let it stop her.

"You can take your coat and backpack off and hang them right there by the door." Then, my sister stood and turned to Gia. Her smile got even wider, a little dimple appearing. "Well, well, look at what the coyote dragged back onto the ranch. Just couldn't stay away now, could you?"

Gia laughed, reaching over to help Addy with her backpack and jacket.

By the time all their coats were hung, Mama and Dad came in looking disheveled in a way I didn't want to think about.

"You're here!" Mama came closer, bending down to meet Addy in the eye. "What would you like to do first? See the barn and the kittens or the playroom that thinks it's an entire toy store?"

"Maybe we can actually make it into the house first?" I said dryly. Everyone chuckled and backed into the kitchen more. I looked around and said, "I thought you said dinner was ready and waiting?"

Mama looked a bit sheepish. "Well… Once I realized you were really coming, I decided to whip up some cornbread, so we have a few more minutes."

Outside, a bolt of lightning lit up the sky, and barely a

second later, thunder boomed so loud it vibrated the entire house. Addy jumped, moving closer to me. I put my hand slowly around her shoulders. "Just a bit of a storm. Nothing bad."

Hail hit the roof, bouncing off the porch and adding a crescendo of music to the kitchen that had dropped into silence.

Mama took it in stride, sticking out her hand to Addy and saying, "Well, looks like that gives us our answer. Let's go check out the playroom."

Addy looked up at me, and I said, "I'll be right here. I'm not going anywhere. The playroom is upstairs." I pointed above us. "It's in my old bedroom from when I was your age."

Curiosity got the better of her, and she withdrew her hand from mine to stick it in my mother's. I resisted the urge to snatch it back. I'd already lost seven years with her, and I was selfish enough to want every moment for the next seven to be mine. I was already halfway in love with the tiny human being. And that was when the cold reality hit me with the same intensity as the lightning that filled the room. This little girl might not truly belong to me, and yet I was already making plans to keep her. If Ravyn had nearly destroyed me when she left, losing Addy might just finish off the job.

♫ ♫ ♫

After dinner, Sadie and I cleaned up while Mama dragged out photo albums to show Addy—and Gia—pictures of me as a kid. It was supposed to be embarrassing, but I didn't actually care. My childhood had been a good one. I'd gotten up to normal boyish pranks with Maddox. We'd tormented our little sisters in the typical sibling way. We'd been a family. I figured it might be good for Addy to see the love that poured from the pages. Maybe it would make her feel like she'd be safe and loved as well.

I took a dish from Sadie, dried it, and put it up on a top shelf.

"So… How are you really doing?" she asked, all mischievousness gone from her face.

I leaned against the counter, listening to Mama prattle and the nonanswers of Addy. "Feeling a bit like a tadpole put on land before I've grown lungs."

"She doesn't talk much."

"No complete sentences." I went on to describe the tantrum she'd thrown at the mall. "I don't know what it's all about, but if she saw even a portion of what happened to Ravyn…" My throat clogged up like it did every time I thought about it.

Sadie drained the water from the sink, rinsed it out, and took the towel I offered her. She leaned up against the cabinet with me, her once long, lanky body a little rounder these days after all she'd been through.

"I wish Ravyn wasn't dead so I could kill her myself," she said fiercely.

I didn't want to admit how much I'd thought the same thing.

Neither of us said anything for several seconds. Then, Sadie smiled and shoved my shoulder with hers. "And Gia? You put your hands on her yet?"

"Gia is working a case. Nothing more. She'll be gone as soon as she gets what she needs."

"What does she *need*, big brother?"

I whipped the towel out of her hands, twisted it up, and smacked her on the thigh with it. "You've got a one-track mind, Sassypants. I can't even stomach what that means for the guy who eventually falls for you."

The twinkle in her eye dimmed a bit, sarcasm thick as she said, "Sass and scars and flabby skin. He'll be *so* lucky."

I wrapped my arm around her neck, rubbing my knuckles into her hair. "Damn right, he'll be lucky." She fought me off, and we were both smiling until I ruined it by saying, "You're beautiful, Sadie. Inside and out. If a guy can't see that, he isn't worth your time—not even one night's worth of your time."

She grabbed the towel back and flicked it at my abs. "What? You become a dad and turn into a mush monster?"

I growled and made to grab the towel one more time, but she laughed, tossed it on the counter, and skipped out of the kitchen toward the living room.

I followed, rounding the archway and stopping as the image in front of me filled me with warmth. Addy was tucked between Gia and my mother with her jaguar pressed against her chest. Dad was sitting on a chair opposite with the television on low, but he was watching the women rather than the screen. Mama was flipping through an album. Addy kept reaching out to touch the page as Mama told her stories about my siblings and me.

Gia leaned in, checking out a picture of Maddox and me covered in mud from head to toe after we'd gone fishing in a rainstorm and ended up sliding down the hill on our way home. Mama wove the story more, explaining how we'd trailed it through the house, and it had taken days to clean up. Gia's lips were turned upward, face soft and relaxed, and I wondered if that was what she'd look like after she climaxed too—tranquil and sweet and at ease.

Addy stifled a yawn, and it wiped away thoughts I shouldn't have been having about the snarky NSA analyst. I looked at the antique clock on the mantel just as it chimed eight. Day two of parenthood, and I was already screwing up bedtime.

"Okay, I think we better head out. It's been another long day."

Mama patted Addy's leg, and the little girl didn't jump at the touch, which felt like more progress. "Next time you come, I'll show you his awkward teen years. And I think we have some pictures around here of your mama and him."

Addy's eyes turned wide, and my stomach bottomed out. If Mama had a picture of Ravyn, it would be a rare one. I hadn't had the opportunity to burn all images of her after she'd left because Ravyn had rarely let us take them. Just like she'd rarely liked to go out in public. At the time, I thought she was shy. I had been determined to make her feel as beautiful as I thought she was so that she'd want to take pictures with me.

After she'd left, it had been a relief to have so few pictures. I'd wanted to forget there'd ever been a woman named Ravyn who'd been a part of my world. I'd wanted it to be a black hole in my timeline. A before and after where I couldn't remember the in-between.

"Thank you so much for dinner. And the stories," Gia said. "I'm never going to be able to look at Ryder again without laughing at thoughts of him in his birthday suit covered in olallieberry stains."

Mama chuckled, but my body heated all over again at the idea of showing Gia my naked body in a way that would have her begging instead of laughing.

We'd barely shrugged into our coats when headlights flashed through the window, coating us in white light. I narrowed my eyes at Mama. "You said it was just going to be you and Sadie."

Mama nodded, brows drawing together as we watched Maddox's Bronco pull in next to Gia's Escalade.

I took Addy's hand, bracing myself for what was to come. It felt like my brother had barely had time to park before the back door burst open, and Mila bounded in, screaming, "Nana!" at the top of her lungs. Her blond braids bounced around her cherub face, warm honey eyes glinting as she ran headfirst into my mother.

Mama caught her tight, saying, "Why isn't this a nice surprise!"

Mila's gaze went wide as she caught sight of me standing with Gia and Addy. Her eyes dropped to where I held Addy's hand, and she was a breath away from demanding to know what was going on when my mother said, "I thought the three of you were going to the movies."

My brother and McKenna pushed through the doorway covered in rain gear. McKenna was an older version of her little sister. Blond hair, light-brown eyes, heavy brows. She'd grown up in Willow Creek but skedaddled the moment she was eighteen, leaving a broken-hearted Maddox behind. When Maddox had found the baby sister McK hadn't known existed living in squalor, he'd taken her in and made her his own. Eventually, that act had brought them all together.

"We were in the middle of the movie when the electrocity went out at the theater," Mila said.

She rarely got her words mixed up anymore. It was an endearment we all sort of missed. McKenna corrected her, saying, "Electricity."

"That's what I said." Mila turned away from my mother to look at us again. "Who's that?"

I hadn't been prepared for Mila tonight—for her questions or her energy—and I wasn't sure Addy would ever be prepared for my over-the-top niece.

"You might remember Gia. She was here last year," I answered before squeezing Addy's hand and adding, "And this is Addy." I wasn't sure how to explain the rest, because we didn't want Mila blabbing to the world Addy was mine, and yet I didn't want Addy to hear me say she was only there for a little while. I hesitated, and it was Gia who picked up the rest for me.

"We're staying with your Uncle Ryder."

Mila's eyes grew round. "I love staying with Uncle Ryder. He always lets me eat ice cream for breakfast."

Maddox choked, Mama rolled her eyes to the ceiling, and I narrowed my eyes at my niece. "Thanks for ratting me out, kiddo."

Mila's hand went to her mouth. "Oops."

Her gaze dropped to the stuffed animal in Addy's hands, and she grinned, turning back to pull her two rainbow unicorns from McKenna's arms and then skipping back over to us. "You have a stuffed animal too. This is Chester and Charlotte. They're famous. They have a book written about them."

Addy nodded slowly.

"You know the book?" Mila's voice dropped to a whisper. "*The Day the Unicorns Saved the World* is still the bestest book of all the books that exist."

"Dragons," Addy said so quietly that I wasn't sure she'd even spoken.

My niece grinned. "Oh, yes! *The Day the Dragons Saved the Universe* is my second-favorite book. If you like those books, it means we were meant to be friends. Maybe even best friends. And you know what best friends—"

"Breathe, Mila," Maddox said with a soft chuckle.

"But, Daddy, it's true."

I reached down to pick up Addy's backpack and helped her slide it on. "It's late, and we were just leaving."

"No!" Mila cried out just as my mother asked, "What about the kittens?"

"It's rainy and late. We'll come back tomorrow to see the kittens."

"I don't want to go out in the rain again. I'm going to spend the night," Mila said, turning her big round eyes on my mother.

"You don't get to demand it, Bug-a-boo," McK told her with a chagrinned smile. "You need to ask Nana if you can stay. She might be busy and have plans tomorrow."

"I don't," Mama came back without hesitation. She'd never deny time with her grandbaby. It made me ache all over again because she hadn't had the chance to have those moments with Addy. My entire family had been denied what was rightfully theirs. I wanted to hate Ravyn for it all over again, but I wondered how my dislike of the mother she'd loved would impact Addy. And what was the point of continuing to hate a dead woman? It couldn't do anything to her. It would only make Addy and me miserable.

"See!" Mila said, chin jutting out at McK before she turned to Addy. "You should spend the night too. We can build a blanket fort and sleep in it. Chester and Charlotte want to get to know your leopard better."

"Balam. He is a jaguar."

The complete sentence took me by surprise. It seemed like she hadn't uttered a complete one in the entire time she'd been with me.

"That's a super-cool name. You can stay and tell me all about where you got him, and how long you've been friends, and why you're here with Uncle Ryder and Gia."

Addy looked at me, but it wasn't with the pleading eyes that Mila normally gave Maddox when she wanted to stay at my parents' house. Hers looked scared, as if she was afraid I'd actually leave her there. The tightness in my chest grew until I was sure it was going to swallow me whole.

"Maybe next time, kiddo. Addy has had a long couple of days and needs some rest."

Mila's face fell. "Well, if you come to see Nana's kitties tomorrow, I'll be here, and we can become friends then."

Gia thanked my parents once more, Mama hugged me tight, and Dad patted me on my shoulder. Sadie gave me an impish chin nod, head tilting toward Gia, and Mila squeezed my leg before running toward the stairs.

"I'll walk you out," Maddox said, stuffing his hat onto his head.

I slammed my hat on in a similar motion and led Gia and Addy out to the Escalade in the rain. While I opened both passenger side doors at the same time, Gia eased around me to slide into the front. I helped Addy up, watched her buckle her seat belt, and then shut the door all while Maddox watched from the rear of the SUV.

I joined him at the back, stuffing my hands into my pockets to ward off the chill and the wet. Our breath left wisps of white visible in the porch light.

"How are you holding up?" he repeated Sadie's question.

"I'm okay," I said, which wasn't exactly a lie. I had

moments of being okay.

"Look. I know what Gia said about the DNA test, but before you get yourself completely wrapped up, I think you should take one. I have a guy at the lab who runs tests for our department. He said he'd do an off-the-book test for us. You and her. No one else needs to know."

That ache in my chest grew. It was already too late. I'd already gotten wrapped up. In a little over twenty-four hours, I'd fallen hard for a quiet little girl who'd experienced trauma at the hands of the same person who'd handed it to me. It didn't really matter what the DNA test showed, did it? But if it meant I could make sure she was mine and mine for good, then I needed to do it.

I made my way around to the driver's side and turned to meet my brother's hooded gaze. "Arrange it. But I'm not sure it makes a difference."

Chapter Seventeen

Gia

ROLLERCOASTER (FOREVER AND A DAY)
Performed by Brothers Osborne

I'd left the blinds open, watching the thunderstorm as it had breezed through last night, and now the soft sunlight filtered through dripping branches. Mist drifted up from the damp earth, giving the entire scene an otherworldly appearance. It was how I felt. As if being here was an alternate timeline in my life. I had to keep reminding myself to work the case. That I wasn't here just to make sure Ryder and Addy forged a family from the remnants of the one Ravyn had stolen from them.

Even though her letter had said she'd run away to protect them, I wasn't sure how Ravyn had done it. She'd left this honey-like sweetness to live on the run, in cheap hotels and out-of-the-way places. Rory's notion that she was playing Robin Hood, dropping clues for us to follow, only added to the puzzle. Had she been hoping to come back? To return to Ryder and the ranch and the people who'd accepted her with open arms? I didn't want to feel any empathy for the woman, but I did. It hadn't been two days, and already I was being lured by the Southern charm and deep roots of the Hatley family.

I couldn't afford to get too close to this, to feel too many emotions for any of these people. The possessive protectiveness I was already feeling would surely cloud my judgment. And yet, I'd have to be a robot to feel nothing when presented with Addy's quiet bravery and Ryder's brooding acceptance. The sweetness with which he dealt with Addy would stir the coldest of souls.

Frustrated with the situation as much as myself, I rose, showered, and dressed in a pair of jeans and a flannel I'd picked up the day before. I braided my hair to keep it away from my face and went in search of coffee.

Ryder was already in the kitchen. He had on tight jeans and a Henley pushed up at the sleeves, baring corded forearms. The shirt stretched over his wide shoulders, accentuating muscles that came from hard work rather than weights and machines. The entire look was appealing in a way that was dangerous, in a way that reminded me of high school heartbreak.

My first real crush had been the summer after my sophomore year. It was for a boy who'd lived next door and spent all his free time at the rodeo or listening to country music. I'd begged Holden to take line-dancing lessons with me so I could catch the boy's eye come fall. I'd spent the summer learning how to impress him with my dance moves only to have Dad restationed just as the school year had started. I'd had to leave the boy and my moves behind.

"Coffee?" I asked.

Ryder tilted his head toward the old-school pot in the corner. No Keurig here. I'd had to figure it out the morning before, when I'd made myself at home in his kitchen. It should have felt weird, and I'd expected a snarky comment from him when he'd come out of his room, but instead, he'd taken it in stride, as if he'd seen me there a million times before. I hadn't known what to make of it.

"I'd like Addy's help this morning in creating the image of the guy she saw," I told him as I poured a cup.

"I need to get over to the ranch, keep going on the new cabins. Otherwise, they won't be done in time for the guests we already have booked."

"You can go this morning, and I'll bring her over when

we're done."

His brows were hunched together, a scowl replacing the calm that had been on his face. I was tempted to smooth the wrinkles between his eyes with my fingers before the bite in his voice raised my hackles.

"I'm not letting her go through that alone."

"She won't be alone. I'll be with her."

"You're not her family."

The words sliced into me even though they were the truth. The shock of how much it hurt was almost as painful as the words themselves. As soon as I got what I needed from Addy and could ensure she was safe, I'd have to move on. I wouldn't stay. I never did. I didn't *want* to stay. Certainly not here, in the middle of Nowhere, Tennessee.

"Don't act like you've been at her side her entire life, Ryder. You're no more family to her than I am at the moment."

"She's never going to be without a family again. That was true the moment you walked her into my brother's office. It's why you brought her here, isn't it? So you could get what you needed and walk away? I imagine you're really good at it."

"Excuse me?" Why did this man always put me on the defensive? Why did every truth feel like a barb instead of a salve? As if it were a knock to my character instead of what made me excellent at my job.

"Why are you taking offense?" He seemed legitimately puzzled. "That's what your job entails, right? One case closed, and you go on to the next in a new location."

"Yes. But you make it sound like, just because I'm good at my job, it means I don't give a shit about the people involved. As if I simply use them before I disappear."

"Don't you?"

I put down the coffee cup and stepped into his space, poking at his solid chest with my finger. "I care about the people I work with and the individuals impacted by the criminal networks I help unravel, asshole. Hell, I even hired the last person whose world was turned upside down by the Lovatos. I don't use people. I protect them. That's my job."

His eyes narrowed, and he grabbed my wrist, pulling it away so my finger no longer dug into him like an arrow finding its target. The heat of his hands snaked up my arm, over my collarbone, landing in my chest like a spark. The desire I felt when we were like this only irritated me more. I didn't want these feelings. I didn't want him. But just because I didn't want a boyfriend or, God forbid, a husband, it didn't mean I didn't care about people. That I didn't love the people in my life. I might not be able to stick around and shower Addy with the attention she deserved, but I wasn't going to wash my hands of her either.

"You didn't protect us," he growled, and instead of pushing me away, he tugged so I had to step even closer. "In fact, all you did was leave more wreckage in your wake without ever looking back. You gave your reservation to your brother, who traumatized my family all over again with a shoot-out in our front yard, destroying our fence, and our field, and sending Maddox on a wild-goose chase."

"That's hardly my fault. It isn't like I knew the people Holden was running from would find them here. He might have ruined a fence or two, but he was doing everything he could to protect the vice president's daughter. That was mission number one."

I jerked my wrist, trying to step back, but he squeezed tighter, pulling in the opposite direction, and the motion brought me colliding with his body. Hips against hips. Heaving chest against heaving chest. Fire rained through me. Embers threatening to combust.

"You're still the one who sent him to us, knowing it could put us in danger. And after it all went down, we didn't hear a peep from you. Not an 'I'm sorry' or 'Is everyone okay?' So don't give me a line about caring about the people impacted by the criminals you and your brother chase."

His blue eyes sparked, fury and lust combining. The look made me nervous in a way I never was—not when facing a gun or sneaking into a facility to install listening devices. This look…the passion…it threatened to knock open the secret door in my heart I'd kept safely under lock and key ever since it had been brutally stomped on the one time I'd really given it away in college.

I licked my lips, biting down, and his eyes tracked every movement. The punishing kiss he'd given me last summer seemed to bloom between us, and in that moment, I knew the truth. He wasn't pissed at what had gone down with Holden. He was pissed his body reacted to me the way mine did to his. He was furious I'd left and not come back, which made no fucking sense when I knew for a fact he didn't keep women around.

"What are you really upset about, Ryder? That I left or that I didn't show back up? You can't have it both ways."

He looked like I'd hit him. He let go of me, stepping away, and the heat that had threatened to consume us crested and drifted away. For some awful reason I knew I'd regret, I didn't want it to disappear, so instead of letting him escape, I stepped closer, chasing the heat and the spark and backing him into the counter just like he'd done to me in his office.

I fisted his shirt and rose onto my toes so I could bring our mouths closer together. "Is it because you didn't get what you needed from me? You didn't get to finish what you started?"

His gaze dropped to my mouth, and his hands went to my waist. I wasn't sure if he was going to push me away or pull me closer, and I didn't give him a chance to decide. I pressed my lips to his, the firm hard lines turning silky smooth beneath mine. He tasted like coffee and danger and regret. I wasn't sure if it was regret for what was happening or what the aftermath would be.

A mere second was all it took for the surprise of my kiss to wear off and for him to take control. He nipped at my lips with more than just a love bite, and when I gasped, he thrust his tongue inside. And just like last time, there was nothing sweet or tender or kind about his kiss. It was all fiery punishment. Not only for me but for himself. For wanting to play with this flame when we both knew it could do nothing but leave burnt ash in its wake.

He tilted his head, seeking further access, exploring and licking in a way that immediately made my breasts ache and heat pool down deep. He hauled me up against him, the press of his belt buckle in my stomach adding a spike of pain that should have been another warning. That should have been enough to make me step back, and yet I found myself pushing in harder, the sting of it only adding to the longing growing inside for more.

His hips shifted so his legs caged mine, the bulge growing inside his jeans pushing as if it could somehow make its way through layers of denim and brand me. My hands went to his neck, dragging nails into the skin there, and he reciprocated with fingers digging in at my waist.

I'd never been one to play games with sex. I'd never needed ties and bonds to get off, but heaven help me, I wanted this man to tear the clothes from my body and take control. I wanted him to demand I follow his commands. I wanted to forget everything but his words, his taste, his feel. I could spend a lifetime lost in his touch.

That singular thought came down on me like rain on scorched earth.

A lifetime was not in my playbook.

I pushed his hands from my waist, untangled my legs from his, and stepped back.

His eyes were hooded and heavy, his lips red and slick, and a lock of hair dropped over his forehead that I wanted to push away. He gripped the counter, forearms straining, as if he was holding himself up or holding himself back from reaching for me again. And in that moment, fully clothed but straining everywhere for me just like I was straining in every molecule for him, Ryder Hatley became the sexiest human being I'd ever encountered.

Movement behind me broke our gaze. His eyes drifted sideways, and I whirled around to find Addy, fully dressed in some of her new clothes with the new Converse on her feet and her jaguar pressed to her chest. Her backpack was in her other hand.

Ryder stepped toward her. The heat from our kiss was replaced with a look of tenderness as he looked down at her, and I suddenly wanted that softness for my own. I wanted him to look at me with that same concern and affection. With a shock, I realized I was feeling jealous of a seven-year-old, traumatized little girl, and wasn't that just beyond ridiculous?

He cleared his throat and said, "Good morning, Addy. Did you sleep okay?"

She shrugged, putting her backpack on the floor by the edge of the counter. I'd checked on her in the middle of the night. Had he as well? She'd been in the bed, flat as a pancake and almost invisible with the covers pulled over her head, but she'd at least stayed there. She hadn't hidden. In a matter of days, he'd made her feel safe.

"I made breakfast burritos. Do you like salsa?" he asked. She nodded, and he pointed to the counter where there were three different brands and heat levels. "They're not my mama's homemade version, but they're decent."

She pointed to the middle one, and he motioned her over to the plates he'd been assembling before our argument and our heated kiss had distracted him. A kiss I still felt in every single part of me. I'd be feeling and tasting and thinking of it for months. Just like the last one.

He helped her wrap the burrito and got her some juice. I took my plate and coffee and sat at the island on the other side of Addy, using her as a buffer so my body didn't spontaneously combust. It was quiet while we ate, tension drifting through the air that wasn't good for the little girl, but I didn't know how to defuse it.

Ryder pushed his plate back and looked down at her. "My work is at the ranch, and I have a lot I need to do there today. You didn't get to see the kittens, so I thought you might want to come and see them?"

"Okay." Her words were soft and whispery, but they

felt loud because she spoke so little. Normally, if she agreed, she'd just nod. So, getting an actual verbal response felt like a huge step.

When my eyes met his, I knew he felt the same way. His jaw ticked before he said, "Gia needs your help with that sketch of the man in your hotel room first. Do you think you could work on that before we go see the kittens?"

She put her burrito down, looked at her hands, and then glanced from him to me and back down. Then, she let out a shaky little breath and nodded. I wished I didn't need her help. I wished I didn't have to ask her to live through those moments again. I wished I could solve this without her.

"Let me go get my computer," I said, jumping down and heading for the bedroom.

When I came back out, Ryder was washing up. I rejoined Addy at the island, opened my laptop, and brought up the program I needed. We started with a general male face with short brown hair and brown eyes. Then, I asked whether his hair was darker or lighter, shorter or longer, curly or straight before moving on from there. It took us over an hour. I changed the square face to more of an oval. Narrowed his eyes, moving them closer together and thinning them out. Added a rounder, bulbous nose, and heavy brows. Step by step, we moved closer while Ryder joined us and watched.

Maybe because it felt a bit like a computer game, Addy seemed to take it in stride. She clutched Balam to her chest and swung her feet, the toes of her shoes quietly banging into the island. But she didn't freak out, and she didn't cry.

When I'd done all I thought I could do, I pressed the icon that would turn the image into more of a 3D model and then turned the screen to her one more time. She jerked back, and only Ryder's quick move kept her from falling off the stool. She turned, pressing her face into Ryder's arm, and he lifted her off the stool and held her to him.

My lungs forgot to breathe at the image they made wrapped together.

I forced myself to inhale and shifted my gaze back to the computer, saving the image one more time. I worked over the lump in my throat, and said, "Okay. I'll send this off to the team, and see if we can get a bead on who he is. You did an amazing job, Addy. I know I told you this yesterday, but you really are the bravest little girl I've ever met."

Her eyes peeked out from where she was tucked up against Ryder.

"You don't have to talk about him any more today. But just know, the more you can tell us about what happened, the better chance we have of catching him."

"Mama argue," she said softly.

"They argued?"

"She say he not be there. He should go." Addy breathed in and then continued, "He kissed her. Mama mad. Hit him."

"Good for her," I told her, not daring to look at Ryder and break the trance.

"He had knife. Mama fell." Tears filled her eyes, and then they were rolling down her cheeks, and she was crying, quiet little sobs, her body shaking. Ryder held on to her. He held on and kissed the top of her head and whispered soothing sounds and words. Promises of keeping her safe that I desperately hoped we both could keep.

After several seconds, she looked at me again. "I hid. He kicked her. He left..." She sobbed again. "I tried to help."

Ryder squeezed her tight to his chest. "You did real good, sweetheart. Gia's right. You're brave. So very, very brave."

They sat that way, cuddled together, for a long time with him soothing her, and I wished I could do the same. With her. With him. Because the tortured look in his eyes was almost as heartbreaking as hers. I wanted to wipe the agony away from both of them.

But the only thing I could truly do was find the man

who'd done this.

I gritted my teeth and turned back to the computer, determined to get the image out to as many agencies as possible. He'd show up somewhere. Better yet, Rory would figure out who he was, and we'd have every single detail of his life spread out before us.

Chapter Eighteen

Ryder

OPPOSITES ATTRACT
Performed by Jake Bush

As I pulled into the ranch, my emotions were still ping-ponging all over the place. If the kiss with Gia hadn't already shaken me to my core, holding Addy and feeling her little sobs as she'd explained what had happened in the hotel room with Ravyn had shattered what was left of my calm. I felt shaky and unstable. Things I hated. I wanted control and peace. Not the chaos and disorder Gia had thrust into my life just by showing up.

And yet, at the same time, I wouldn't go back and undo it if I could.

Regardless of whether Addy was really mine or not, she was here. She was in my life, and I didn't want that to change. All I wanted was to make her life better. I wanted to make sure she never again lived through anything even close to what she'd experienced hiding under a goddamn bed while her mother was killed.

It made me want to throw up.

I looked over to where Addy sat in the booster on the far side of the bench seat in my truck. We'd left Gia at my house, working to find the murderer. She hadn't wanted to let Addy out of her sight, but we both knew the little girl needed a distraction, an escape from the nightmare she'd walked us through with halted words.

I helped Addy out of the truck, and she reached inside to grab her backpack and put it on again before turning and tucking her hand into mine. Every time she did it, I felt an overwhelming sense of rightness but also an overwhelming sense of responsibility. I couldn't fuck this up, and yet I wasn't sure what the hell I was doing. It continued that ping-ponging in my chest until I thought my rib cage might burst open.

We made our way over to the barn. It hadn't snowed, but the temperature was in the thirties. The leftover puddles had a thin layer of ice, easily broken. The fields beyond the barn were covered with the shimmer of frozen dew. Gray and white clouds blew through the sky, the sun barely getting a chance to warm the earth before it was covered again.

The barn doors were already partially opened, and as we got closer, Mila's and Sadie's voices wafted out to us over the frigid air, accompanied by a soft neigh.

Addy's feet slowed, and I came to a stop, looking down at her.

"It's Mila and Sadie. You met them both last night."

Her face went blank again, tucking her emotions away. It shouldn't be possible for someone so little to be able to do that, and yet she was exceptional at it.

Another gust of wind hit us, and Addy shivered next to me.

"It's warmer in the barn. You can meet the kittens and the horses. Have you ever ridden one?" She shook her head. "Well, we can fix that easily enough."

I pushed open the door some more, the scrape of it echoing through the rafters. The smell of hay and horses hit me. Familiar and soothing. We'd installed solar panels and storage batteries to warm the barn enough that it kept the cold to a minimum. It helped entice the guests into the barn in the early part of the season when we might still have snowy weather, and the animals seemed to appreciate it too.

Sadie's and Mila's voices drifted down from the loft,

and my horse, an all-black mustang, stomped loudly to get my attention. I walked over to her stall, sliding a hand down her neck, and she pushed her nose into me. "Morning, girl. I know you're getting antsy. I hope to take you for a ride soon. But in the meantime, I have someone I'd like you to meet." I gently pulled Addy's hand up to place it on the mare's nose. "Addy, this is Arwen. Arwen, this is Addy."

Addy stilled, and then she let her fingers relax under mine, petting Arwen before withdrawing. "My name," Addy said, and when I didn't seem to understand, she continued, "Adelaide Arwen. My name."

Her words shoved me right back in time to arguing with Ravyn about *The Lord of the Rings* and its epic qualities. Half the horses on the ranch were named after characters and animals in the trilogy. Ravyn had thought it was silly to name the horses after the books. She'd thought the series was boring and overrated. The only thing we'd agreed upon was Liv Tyler's portrayal of Arwen. When I'd teasingly said we could name our daughter after her, she'd given me a flat-lipped, single-syllable answer—a resounding no.

And yet she'd gone and done it anyway.

I cleared my throat. "Well, then, it was fated for you two ladies to meet and get along."

Addy smiled and reached out a hand to pet Arwen again. My horse stood there silently, taking it all in, as if she could read our minds and was trying to soothe us both.

"Addy! You're here!" Mila shouted down from the loft.

We turned to see her peeking over the rail with blades of hay in her hair and clinging to her clothes. In her arms, she had an all-gray kitten who was squirming and wiggling as if determined to escape. Sadie's head appeared behind her, lips turning upward in a smile. "Come on up, and meet the babies."

I led Addy over to the ladder and watched as she carefully pulled herself up. I followed behind her, stooping out of reflex to miss the low rafters. Sadie and Mila had retreated to the back corner. Dust drifted through a single beam of light from the round window in the barn's peak, turning the loft into a collage of hazy shadows.

My sister and niece sat by a crate filled with old rags and blankets from which mews could be heard. Addy and I made our way over. The mama was a gray tabby just like the one Mila was holding, but her kittens were all shades. There was a pure-black one, a white-and-gray one that reminded me of the dapple downstairs, an orange tabby, and a fawn-colored one. They were six weeks old, and I'd have to arrange to get them neutered soon, or we'd have another pile of kittens before we blinked.

"Here." Mila shoved the gray kitten toward Addy, who barely had a chance to stick her hands out and catch the little thing. It wiggled and squirmed, and Addy looked up at me with wide eyes. I helped her adjust it so it was tucked into her arms better.

Mila sat next to Sadie, who was playing with a pipe cleaner the orange tabby was trying desperately to catch.

"Auntie Sadie and I were trying to name them. Do you want to help?"

Addy looked at me, those big round eyes of hers getting even larger, but then she shrugged. My niece didn't even seem to realize Addy hadn't responded.

"Auntie Sadie says we need to understand their personality to find the right name, so we have to play with them first. I really want to name the black one Arturo, after the king dragon in *The Day the Dragons Saved the Universe*. I mean, he even looks like a dragon, don't you think? And maybe we can name the—"

"Breathe, Mila," Sadie and I said at the same time. Mila rolled her eyes, but I swore I saw Addy's lips twitch, and it eased my heart a little bit after the intensity of our morning.

Addy lowered herself to the straw-covered planks next to the crate. The little gray cat escaped, and Addy looked panicked, but Sadie simply picked it up and stuck her in the box with the others. Addy scooted, looking inside. A smile burst over her face as she watched the kittens tumble over each other.

When my gaze met my sister's, we were both grinning too.

"You need to check on the cabins?" Sadie asked, tilting her head toward the area behind the barn where the construction was taking place.

"I should. Shawn sent me some updates yesterday, but I want to make sure the roof kept the worst of the rain out. We were supposed to have the plumbing and electrical finished by next week."

"Go. I'll stay here with the girls."

Addy looked up at me, over to Sadie and Mila, and then back.

I pointed to the round window in the rafters. "I'll just be right out there. You'll be able to see me through that window. You okay with that?"

"Uncle Ryder!" Mila all but screamed. "She's going to be *fine*. She has me and Auntie Sadie and the kitties. She's not a *baby*!"

"Mila," Sadie said, warning. "Not everyone is comfortable around strangers like you."

Even after all she'd been through, Mila was still the least-shy kid I'd ever met. She could talk to a statue and make it talk back.

My niece turned her head to look at Addy, as if seeing her for the first time. "But I'm not a stranger. I'm your friend. We decided last night, remember?"

I held back a little huff of a laugh. I squatted to look Addy in the eyes. "You going to be okay? It'll just be for a few minutes. You can stay right here. No need to go anywhere."

She looked at the cats and Mila and Sadie and then nodded ever so slowly.

"Okay." I backed up and headed for the ladder. "I'll make it real quick. And if you need me, just have Mila scream. She's got a voice loud enough to wake a dead raccoon a county away."

"Uncle Ryder!" Mila objected.

I was smiling as my boots hit the ground. I listened for a minute. Mila was doing all the talking, Sadie adding something here and there. It was good the girls were getting to know each other. Mila had friends, but it wasn't the same as having family at that age. Brothers and sisters…cousins. My heart squeezed. They were cousins. I had a daughter.

Chills coasted up my arms and back.

I was a father.

Even though I'd known it and thought about it ever since walking into the station, it still kept hitting me in the chest at the most random moments. If Ravyn's letter hadn't already convinced me, Addy's middle name certainly had. Maddox had offered to get a DNA test done off the books, and I'd still go through with it, but it wouldn't change anything.

Addy was mine.

♫ ♫ ♫

It took me longer than I'd planned to check on the build. Shawn and Ramon were hard at work when I walked into the newest cabin.

Shawn had grown up in Willow Creek. He was a brown-haired, blue-eyed cowboy who was popular down at my uncle's bar with the locals and the tourists. He was a jack-of-all-trades on the ranch, and I trusted him as far as I trusted anyone but family.

Ramon had been in town for a year or so, moving out of Nashville after trying to make it as a country singer with his down-home, country-star looks and decent voice. He'd said the city life, the pace, the desperation had all been too much for him.

The two men paused their work to walk me through what they'd done over the last two days. Then, we hovered over the plans on a makeshift table built from two sawhorses and a piece of plywood. We talked through the tasks we had to get done before the next inspection, and I felt guilty for leaving them on their own again today.

Building the cabins wasn't a two-man job. Hell, it wasn't even a three-man job. We were already pushed to the limits, but I couldn't leave Addy for long. Not yet. When I explained to them I had some personal stuff going on and hoped to be back at it full time in a day or two, they just brushed it off and told me to take care of whatever I needed to, and they'd be fine. And they would, but the truth was, I liked shaping what I'd designed into reality.

The temperature seemed to have dropped instead of risen as I stepped out of the cabin and headed for the barn again, where Gia was just parking next to my truck. She stepped out, pulling her leather jacket tighter over the lilac-colored flannel she'd had on this morning. It had been soft under my hands, but not nearly as soft as the skin at her waist. Or those silky lips. Those had turned to butter underneath mine.

My pulse picked up at the sight of her.

The second taste of her I'd gotten this morning only had me craving more.

She tucked her hair under a gray knit beanie and headed my way.

"Anything?" I asked.

She shook her head. "Not yet, but we barely released the photo. My coworker, Rory, got a hit on a van she saw at the scene, and they followed that to a suburb of Denver. The local PD is going door-to-door, flashing the picture around to see if we get any leads that way." She looked around. "Where's Addy?"

I tilted my head toward the barn. "I was just heading back in."

As we made our way over, our shoulders brushed, and my body prickled with awareness. There was plenty of space for me to move away, to break the contact, but I didn't. What I really wanted was to grab her hand, push her up against the barn, and continue what we'd started. Instead, I tried to satisfy myself by barely grazing her arm with mine.

We stepped inside to find Sadie filling feed bags for the horses. She waved and then put her fingers to her lips. She pointed upward, and Gia and I stopped and listened.

Mila's voice was the one I heard first, loud and talkative as always, but then, I heard Addy's quiet response. Not just one word. Not even two stuttered ones, but an entire sentence. Several sentences. Shock filled me. I turned to Gia, and her face registered the same surprise.

I moved closer to the ladder, skipping the first creaky rung and pulling myself up until I could peek over the edge. Addy had the gray kitten in her hands again, stroking its fur, a soft smile on her face. She was mid-sentence as I focused on her words. "But the dragons can fly into space, and the unicorns can't, which is why I like the dragons more. They can take you anywhere you need to go. Fly far, far away."

"I don't want to go far away. I would miss McKenna and Daddy and Nana and Papa and my aunts and uncles. Don't you have family that you'd miss?"

"My mama died." Her smile disappeared.

Mila scrabbled to put the kitten she was holding back into the crate and then sat down next to Addy, wrapping her arm around her shoulders. "I'm sorry. You can share my family. You can read about them in the stories I've written. There's one called *The Day the Hatleys Saved Each Other* and *The Day the Hatleys Got Married*. Except, my daddy and McKenna haven't gotten married yet, but they will soon." Mila's head tilted sideways, then she asked, "Is that why you're living with Uncle Ryder? Is he making you his family like my daddy made me his? Because Daddy says Uncle Ryder wouldn't know a—"

"Mila," I warned pulling myself up farther onto the loft. I hadn't wanted to interrupt them. I'd wanted to hear another flurry of complete sentences spoken in Addy's little voice. But who knew what my niece would have said if I'd let her keep going?

She looked at me sheepishly. "Hi, Uncle Ryder. Did you know that Addy's mama died? Are you going to take care of her now? Is she going to live with you?" Her entire face went slack for a moment before joy took over, and she screamed, "Is she going to be my *cousin*?"

Well, hell. That had gone just swimmingly. When I looked over at Addy, her eyes were wide and curious, but there wasn't any fear or sadness.

I swallowed hard, knowing I couldn't lie. I didn't want to. "Yes."

Mila screamed, jumping up and dancing around. She pulled the gray kitten away from Addy, set it in the crate, and then dragged her up and started spinning the two of them around in a chaotic dance.

I slowed them down, hands to shoulders, and squatted before them.

"Mila. This has to be a secret for now. Our family knows, but no one else can."

"But why?" Mila whined.

"Because of what happened to Addy's mama. We need to make sure she's safe."

Mila stilled. Then, she whispered, "Does she have bad men looking for her…like that man…the one who tried to take me and shot Aunt Sadie?"

Addy's eyes turned wide, the fear darting back into them, and I'd never wanted to rewind time faster than I did at that moment. I wanted her relaxed face from moments ago. I wanted the smile and the joy she'd been sharing.

"She's safe here," I said instead of answering my niece directly. I took Addy's hand and tugged her a little closer. "You're safe here."

She didn't respond at all.

Behind the two girls, in the view from the round window, a red Porsche Cayman appeared through the trees on the drive. It stood out amongst the SUVs and trucks that normally littered our yard in the off-season. It would stand out in Willow Creek period, where trucks were the common denominator, the more beat up the better.

"Stay here," I said, and when Addy looked frightened, I nudged her chin with a knuckle. "It's okay. Nothing to worry about."

Then, I hustled down the ladder, jumping down the last few feet and hurrying toward the open barn doors. Sadie and Gia had already turned to watch a tall, dark-haired man unfold himself from the driver's seat of the sports car.

I wasn't sure if I was relieved or not when it was Jaime Laredo's face that turned to meet mine. I was glad it was someone I knew showing up and not someone from Ravyn's shadowy past. But I also knew he'd use his powers of persuasion to get me on board with his plans for the Eastern Dude Ranchers' Association.

I turned to Sadie. "Can you make sure Addy doesn't freak out?"

My sister nodded and turned back into the barn.

"Is that Jaime Laredo?" Gia asked.

I shouldn't have been surprised that she knew him with the research she'd done on dude ranches. I just gave her a curt nod as the man headed toward us. His hair was thick and black, his eyes dark and narrow under finely shaped brows that were almost too thin for the rest of his features. His face was lean and rectangular, his jaw always cleanly shaven. He was tall with a thin build that belied the muscles I knew he had as I'd seen him slinging hay in a T-shirt when I'd gone to his ranch over a decade ago.

The man had been open and generous in sharing his knowledge of dude ranching and luxury resort management when I'd met him. Even though he hadn't gone to college, he was one of the savviest businessmen I knew. Our lack of higher education had been a commonality we'd shared and discussed over whiskey and a good meal. It had become a badge of honor for both of us when we'd turned our family land into wildly successful resorts. His was just five levels up from ours.

"Well, hell, if it isn't Jaime Laredo in the flesh," I said, stepping toward him.

He raised a brow, one side of his mouth easing upward. "You've been ignoring me, old friend."

I reached out and shook his hand. "Not ignoring as much as holding you off."

Jaime looked from me to Gia with a slow smirk. "I can see you've been busy."

"Jaime Laredo, Gia Kent."

When she offered her hand to shake, he brought it to his lips, and the feral objection that flew through me at that simple motion caught me by surprise. I barely held back a snarl and had to tuck my hands into my pockets so I wouldn't rip the two of them apart. And when Gia's voice turned light and flirtatious, every inch of my body objected.

Never in my life had I felt jealousy the way I did then.

Not even Ravyn had left my inner animal howling with such rabid possessiveness.

Chapter Nineteen

Gia

RED WINE + WHITE COUCH
Performed by Danielle Bradbery

"*Of all the ranches in all* the towns in all the world, you walk into this one," I said to Jaime Laredo, making sure the flirt and twist of the old *Casablanca* line was obvious.

The man's dark eyes flashed with interest. Desire was in his gaze as it strolled down me inch by inch, as if I was wearing a sexy cocktail dress baring my legs and arms instead of layers of flannel and jeans. It might have felt sleazy coming from another man, but this one, confident and sure, made it look sensual. An offer he didn't have to physically state but hung in the air anyway.

"Have we met, Ms. Kent? Unfortunately, I've never been to Paris or Morocco," he teased back.

Ryder had been relaxed and friendly when Laredo had approached, but the more the two of us talked, the stiffer I felt him grow, until tension all but radiated from him.

"I've been trying to interview you for my article in *Agricultural Sciences Today* on how dude ranching has saved the American frontier."

"Aw, yes. I do remember something about that now. You had a reservation right at the end of the season. But you canceled, didn't you?"

I'd been set to stay at the Grand Laredo in Kentucky

before I'd been called back to D.C. earlier this year to help chase down the Lovato angle with Rory's dad. I smiled at him. "Family duty called, unfortunately, but perhaps we can fix that soon."

I wasn't sure Ryder even knew he'd done it, but he'd somehow inched his way into my space so our shoulders were now brushing. Sparks and awareness drifted between us. Laredo caught it all—the slight movements, the unspoken body language.

The reports on him said he had an IQ over one hundred and sixty, but he hadn't gone to college. Instead, he'd gone to work in the fields in California alongside migrant farmworkers, as if he wasn't the heir to an American ranch dynasty.

"I'll make you a deal, Ms. Kent—"

"It's Gia, please."

He smiled. A suave smirk I was sure had many women handing over their panties to him but was doing nothing to me. "Gia." He rolled the two syllables as if tasting a fine wine. As if he was savoring them. "I'll make you a deal. If you can convince this man to attend the charity gala I'm throwing for the Kentucky Art Institute and listen to my pitch about taking a position on the Eastern Dude Ranchers' board, I'll not only grant you an interview, I'll give you a week free at the Grand Laredo before the season even starts. Full access to every activity you want…and to me."

I could imagine what he'd try to do to me in a week. Wine and dine me before sleeping with me and sending me on my way. Even if Laredo wasn't a potential suspect, I wouldn't sleep with him. My limbs seemed to have turned into a block of ice at even the suggestion. Maybe it was because my body was reacting to Ryder instead, igniting me until it felt as if my skin and bones were going to combust. Or maybe it was because my inner instincts didn't trust the suave player standing before me.

"Only you would try to sleep with the woman you found on *my* ranch, Laredo." There was an edge to Ryder's tone that hadn't been there before, a claim he was staking that should have pissed me off because there was nothing but two kisses, mistrust, and lives that didn't match between Ryder and me. And yet, the possessive growl had my heart spinning in a dizzy dance.

"Don't mind Ryder. He's been pissy all morning," I said with a smile.

Laredo laughed, the low sound echoing through the cold air around us. "Why don't you show me the new cabins, Ryder, and I'll try to convince you to join the board myself? If that doesn't work, I may have to resort to using my powers of persuasion on her."

Ryder's huff was somewhere between another growl and a laugh. "You're incorrigible." The two men started toward the path leading to the cabins, and Ryder looked back at me. "Will you make sure Mila and her friend make it back to Mama for lunch?"

I wanted to tell him Sadie could do it, because I needed time with Laredo, but there was a look in Ryder's eyes—half plea, half command—that made me bite my tongue and just nod.

When the men disappeared around the corner, I headed back into the barn.

Sadie was sitting on a barrel near the bottom of the ladder. From above came the soft laughter and chatter of little girls—the same light talk that had surprised Ryder and me when we'd walked into the barn a few minutes ago. Addy was talking. Complete sentences without a single stutter. I didn't know if it was because she'd finally talked about what had happened to her mother, or if Mila and the kittens had woven a magic spell around her.

"I can't believe it," I said softly to Sadie with a smile.

"The magic of Mila."

We both listened for a moment, and then Mila appeared at the top of the stairs. "I'm hungry. Can we come down now?"

"Ryder asked me to take you to your nana for lunch," I

told her.

"Come on, Addy! We can introduce your jaguar to my unicorns after we eat!"

Mila came bounding down the stairs, spinning away from the bottom, and both her rainbow leggings and bright-pink sweater were covered in straw. Sadie started brushing at her, and I turned to watch Addy as she made her way cautiously down.

When she hit the ground, she gave me a soft smile.

"Did you like playing with the kittens?" I asked.

She nodded without saying anything, and I tried not to be disappointed. I wanted to hear her relaxed and vibrant like she'd sounded with Mila.

The four of us headed out of the barn toward the farmhouse. We were halfway across the parking lot when my skin started to crawl. A weird awareness drifted over me, as if I was being watched. I knew to trust those instincts. They'd been my friend in far worse situations than this. My feet stalled, and I scanned the surroundings, taking in the long, tree-lined drive, the fields, and the fruit trees that would bloom soon. I didn't see anything out of the ordinary.

Sadie and Mila kept going, but Addy stopped and was watching me, seeming to read my tension. I sent her a smile and waved her forward. "Go on. I'm right behind you."

She shifted the backpack on her shoulders, ducked her head, and kept walking toward the steps.

I did a full three-sixty, taking in every single thing that might be out of place and finding nothing. There were two trucks I knew from the last time I'd stayed at the ranch. We'd run the plates on both workers—Shawn and Ramon. Shawn was clean, but Ramon had a drug-related charge in Nashville that had been dismissed in exchange for a stint in rehab. When the task force had chased down Ramon's old dealer, he was hooked into a local gang that had nothing to do with the Lovatos, and Ramon had been clean since getting out.

There was nothing but the sounds of the farm, the movement of the animals, and the banging from the construction. And yet, the feeling I was being watched wouldn't go away.

Ryder had said he'd upped the security here as well as at his house. Maybe that included cameras. I'd ask when he got back.

I headed up the stairs and in the back door Sadie had left open.

The house smelled like vanilla and sugar. Eva was in the kitchen, and if I hadn't had a report on her sitting in a folder on my laptop, I would have wondered if she did anything but cook and bake. Instead, I knew what book clubs she attended and the line dancing she did with her husband.

She smiled at me in welcome, warm eyes sparkling just like her youngest daughter's.

"Gia! Nice to see you again," she said. "Is my son behaving himself?"

I thought about our passionate kiss in the kitchen that I'd instigated but he'd taken control of. I remembered the way his fingers had bitten into my skin and the feel of him pressed into me.

I smiled and said, "Of course. Perfect gentleman."

Sadie scoffed from behind her mother and then said, "You know Mama was hoping you'd say the opposite."

Even years of practicing an expressionless face couldn't stop my cheeks from flushing.

Sadie let out a laugh, kissed her mother on the cheek, and said, "I'm off to the bar. Uncle Phil has me working 'til close tonight." She grabbed a coat and a purse from the coatrack and then sent me another cheeky grin. "Game night at the bar tonight. Ryder usually makes an appearance. You should get him to come. I think he needs a few drinks to loosen up that attitude he's got growing into an ugly beast."

"Sadie!" Eva laughed.

My lips twitched. "I don't disagree with him needing an attitude adjustment, but I highly doubt you're going to get that man away from Addy at the moment." I glanced around for the little girl and was unable to prevent the worry that coasted through me when I didn't see her.

Eva read my concern, saying softly, "I sent the girls to wash their hands."

An older woman came into the kitchen via the archway from the living room. Her face was just starting to show signs of wrinkles, and her black-and-white corkscrew hair was tucked beneath a vivid magenta scarf littered with pictures of unicorns Mila probably adored.

She walked over to me, extending her hand with a smile, saying, "I'm Rianne."

I shook it, flipping through the Hatley file in my mind. She was Maddox's babysitter who was more family than employee. She was also a retired teacher and had taught all the Hatley kids in the third grade.

"Gia."

"Oh, I know who you are. I've heard quite a bit about you." She winked.

I didn't know how to react to the admission, and I was glad I didn't have to respond as Mila came running back in with Addy slowly following her.

"Nana, can we eat at the table in the playroom?"

Addy saw the new person and stopped at the archway. The soft smile on her face turned completely expressionless, and the fingers on her right hand dug into the skin at her wrist on the left. It destroyed my heart to see her react this way. There was a difference between teaching kids to be wary of strangers and the absolute fear Addy seemed to experience.

"Get the tray out," Eva said to her granddaughter, and Mila shouted, "Yes!" before running to the pantry and coming out with a wooden tray. Eva assembled bowls of homemade chicken soup, thick slices of homemade sourdough, silverware, and napkins on it.

"Don't forget the snickerdoodles, Nana!"

Eva shook her head, patting Mila's cheek. "Nope. I

know better. You'll eat the cookies first. Lunch and then snickerdoodles, Bug-a-boo."

Mila looked devastated.

Addy had made her way over to me and was standing so close she was almost pressed into my side. She'd removed her jacket and her backpack by the door, and she kept darting her gaze toward them, as if she was trying to figure out how long it would take her to get away.

"You okay?" I asked softly.

She shrugged, watching as the other people in the room chatted away about Mila's school. I realized with a panicked start that Addy should be in school too. Then, I wondered if she'd ever gone to school. I highly doubted it. Somehow, Ravyn had been able to keep her out of the education system. Maybe she'd said she was homeschooling her. Maybe there was no record of Addy existing anywhere. I wasn't sure. But I did know there was no way the little girl could go to school at the moment. We couldn't afford for people to know she was Ryder and Ravyn's daughter. Not yet.

Eva handed Mila two glasses of lemonade, picked up the tray, and made her way to the archway. She glanced over to where Addy stood with me. "Come on, kiddo. Let's get you settled in the playroom."

Addy hesitated, but then she looked up at me as if to make sure it was okay. "I'll be right here, and Ryder will be in soon."

She didn't say anything, but she went to her backpack, dragged her jaguar out of it, and followed her grandmother and cousin from the room.

Sadie turned toward me and said, "It's so strange. She was chattering away with Mila like she didn't have a care in the world, but now she's retreated into her silent self."

"I was surprised to hear her talking to Mila. I can almost count on two hands the number of words she's spoken to Ryder or me."

Rianne perked up. "She doesn't usually talk?"

I shook my head and explained that she'd gone through a trauma with her mother, a friend of mine, as I shot Sadie a look, trying to remind her no one was supposed to know Addy was Ryder's daughter.

"Did she talk before that happened?" Rianne asked.

"Honestly, I don't know. I wasn't around a lot."

I could tell Rianne wasn't sure how to take my response. Her wheels were turning, trying to put together the puzzle, but instead of asking about the situation, she focused on Addy. "So, she talks to Mila but not really anyone else? What is it like when she does talk?"

"One or two words. Incomplete sentences that feel forced."

"And how does she do around crowds or new people?"

As Eva came back into the kitchen, I started to say I hadn't really seen her around a crowd, but then I thought of her tantrum the day before in the car at the mall. "She melts down a bit around new people and new things. And like with you, just now, she freezes."

Rianne was nodding as if it all made sense. "I had a child in my class once who was a selective mute. It can be triggered by trauma, but it's mostly found in kids with extreme social anxiety. They talk at home or with people they are most comfortable with just fine, but their bodies seize in social situations, especially ones they aren't prepared for or are unknown to them. It can look like defiance to those who don't know better, because they see the child being friendly and talking and then absolutely shutting down and refusing to speak. What people don't realize is that it takes an enormous amount of effort for the child to get even those one or two words out—like talking when you're sick times a hundred."

I frowned, thinking about everything I'd experienced with Addy since finding her. "How do we know if it's the trauma or this selective mutism?"

"Time, I suspect. Either way, I'd suggest finding her a good behavioral therapist. They can put together a plan for her family, friends, and teachers."

Well, that wasn't going to happen. Not yet. Not until we could make sure she was safe.

My mind went to those few seconds outside when I'd felt like I was being watched.

No. There was no way we could get Addy into therapy until we found her mother's killer and either tied them to the Lovatos or not.

But I could research the topic of selective mutism and do my best to help her.

"I'm out," Sadie said, hustling out the door. "If I don't get to the bar soon, Uncle Phil will make me clean up the peanut shells with chopsticks."

"Don't let him bully you!" Eva shouted as the door slammed behind her daughter.

It was quiet in Sadie's wake. I'd never been uncomfortable around the Hatleys. It was part of the reason I'd left, unsure if I could continue to see them as suspects when I liked them so much. But at the moment, with the two older women eyeing me with interest, I felt decidedly uncomfortable. It had nothing to do with my job, though, and everything to do with the feelings I had for the blue-eyed rancher.

Chapter Twenty

Ryder

Jaime asked question after question about the new cabins before admitting he was thinking of adding something similar to the backside of his property. Except, his new cabins would be highly exclusive and available only to those who wanted extreme privacy. His idea was to have limited staff who'd wait on the guests, bringing food and groceries and supplies, but no one else on the ranch would even know they were there. It was a good hook for celebrities who were trying to disappear for a few days. I thought about the cabin up on the ridge that I'd debated converting into a small house. It would be a great retreat, far away from seeing eyes.

As we made our way back toward the parking lot, I debated inviting Jaime in for lunch. Mama would likely skin me alive for not offering, but I also didn't want him to see Addy and ask questions I couldn't answer. So, instead of heading toward the farmhouse, I led him into my office at the backside of the barn.

"Where's Brandon?" Jaime asked, glancing around the office with the two desks shoved together.

"Horse auction in Tulsa," I said before waving toward where a Keurig sat next to a decanter of whiskey above a mini fridge. "Water? Coffee? Whiskey?"

He grinned. "It's a little early for whiskey, but I will have one to celebrate you agreeing to take over the treasurer's position."

I removed my hat, brushed my hand over my hair, and sat down behind my desk. "Truth is, Jaime, I've got some family stuff happening that's going to take up my time for a while."

His smile disappeared. "Nothing serious, I hope."

I bit back an immediate yes. My entire life had been shifted. The last two days with Addy had felt dreamlike in both good and bad ways. How did I move from feeling like she was a guest to making her the focus of my life? If I'd had the chance to learn with her, to grow into being a parent, it wouldn't feel like this—awkward and forced.

"It'll all work itself out," I told him, my voice gruff. "But I'm going to be absorbed with it for some time. I honestly don't think I'd be able to do the job justice."

Jaime watched me with hawklike eyes, and for the first time since I'd met the man, I felt uncomfortable, as if he was peeling back my layers to see everything inside of me. I forced myself to stay relaxed, but tension curled up my spine.

"At least come to the gala. The other board members are coming, and you can get an idea from them of the time commitment. Bring that beautiful woman with you, and let loose for a few hours."

The assumption he'd made about Gia and me landed heavily in my chest even though I'd encouraged just that belief by possessively moving into her space in order to stop his flirting. The unease I was feeling for the first time in his presence grew another round. I hated being pushed and manipulated, but Jaime wasn't someone I could easily say no to. I owed him, and he knew it. He'd never called in the favor. Never even hinted that it was an obligation I needed to pay back, but here he was, leaving all that had come before us hanging in the air.

"You really drive all the way down from Kentucky just

to ask me to attend your shindig?"

He chuckled. "I've been wanting to test out the Porsche on the back roads, and it gave me an excuse." He checked the time on the Patek Philippe gold-and-leather watch that he'd told me his father had won from an Egyptian prince in a card game. "But I should head out. I have a meeting this evening I can't miss."

We walked out, the sharp wind hitting us in the face, stinging my eyes.

"How long you going to keep this one?" I asked, tipping my hat in the direction of the red Cayman.

He chuckled. "Drove well, so I might keep it longer than most."

Jaime had a new vehicle every time I saw him. And not just some off-the-showroom-floor type of car. His required brokers and special handling and cost more than most people had in their pensions. He was the only person I knew who could be that extravagant. He may have turned his family's ranch into a luxurious five-star resort, but they'd never been in jeopardy of losing everything before that. He'd come from a long line of wealth on his mother's side.

But he'd still had to earn his way at the family ranch. He'd once told me his father had been a tightfisted bastard who didn't believe in spending any money. In fact, he'd been so pissed when Jaime, at eighteen, had gotten his pilot's license and then promptly used his trust fund to buy a six-seater Cessna that he'd threatened to cut him out of the will unless he went to work on the farms in California. He felt Jaime needed to work shoulder to shoulder with other migrant workers to appreciate what he'd been born into. He'd wanted his son to experience the hardships his dad's family had gone through coming to the United States.

My opinion was that Jaime's time without money, that time working his fingers to the bone, had only made him more determined to surround himself with luxury. Once his father had died, there was no one to stop him from spending in excess.

Jaime opened the Cayman's door and looked over the top of the vehicle. "I'm expecting you to show up next Saturday. I'll put you down for a plus-one so you can bring that dazzling brunette with you."

I grunted out, "Fine."

Jaime smiled and winked before lowering himself in the driver's seat. The powerful engine roared to life, and he took off down the drive, passing my brother's sheriff's truck on its way in.

Maddox parked next to my truck and slid out, coming to stand next to me. "Who was that?"

"Jaime Laredo. Came to pester me about his charity gala and the ranchers' association."

"Better you than me."

"Thanks, asswipe."

Maddox pulled a paper bag out from under his jacket. "Mama told me you were here, so I brought the DNA swabs."

My jaw clenched again. Everywhere I turned right now, it felt like I was keeping secrets, and it didn't sit well with me. But then I thought of Addy's tiny voice telling us what she'd seen in that hotel room, and determination welled through me. I'd do anything to keep her safe, including a DNA test that the spitfire analyst inside didn't approve of us taking.

Neither of us said another word as we headed for the house. We stomped our boots on the mat and removed our hats as we walked through the door, hanging them on the coatrack.

"Figures you'd both show up just in time for lunch," Mama said, laughter in her voice.

Gia and Rianne were sitting at the kitchen table with her, and they had bowls of soup in front of them, along with homemade sourdough. Addy and Mila were nowhere in sight, and my stomach tightened.

"She's upstairs in the playroom with Mila," Gia said,

reading my worry before anyone else in the room.

"We'll just go up and say hello first," Maddox said.

We headed down the hall littered with pictures of our family, generations worth, including ones of us growing up and new ones with Mila embedded into our lives. Another thing Addy and I had missed out on. Pictures and holidays and vacations together.

Upstairs, we made our way to the bedroom on the end that had once been mine. Mama had converted it into a princess playroom. A little girl's dream space with a castle painted on the wall and flowers hanging from the ceiling. At a child-sized table in the corner, Mila and Addy sat eating lunch. Addy was telling my niece about her jaguar. Complete sentences again, soft and low, but still sure. "Mama told me that Balam can see not only in the dark but into people's souls. He protects good people by sending bad people away."

"We should write a story about him," Mila said. Then, she saw us standing just outside the door. "Daddy!" She came running, hugging Maddox's legs. "We played with the kittens, and are having lunch, and did you know that Addy's mama died? That's why she's staying with Uncle Ryder. She's not only my friend, but she's my cousin! I've never had a cousin."

"Breathe, Bug-a-boo," Maddox said.

"Addy being your cousin has to be a secret for now, remember?" I said with a grunt.

"But it's Daddy! And you told me family knew."

"Maybe we should make a list of people who know," Maddox suggested, looking at me apologetically. "Why don't you go down and get some cookies to bring up to Addy."

"Oh yes! I almost forgot about the snickerdoodles!"

Mila ran out, and I made my way over to Addy. "Did you have fun?"

She nodded, looking between me and Maddox, a

wariness returning to her eyes that I wanted to wipe away. I reached out, took the paper bag from Maddox, and pulled one of the tubes from inside it. "I need your help with something important."

She clutched the jaguar to her chest.

"We need to take a DNA test to make sure the world knows you're my daughter."

Her eyes grew a little wider.

"It won't hurt," Maddox said. "It's just like a Q-tip, except instead of cleaning your ear, we swab your cheek. I'll do your dad first so you can see."

Maddox took the other tube from the bag, cracked the seal, swabbed my cheek, and then stuffed it back in the tube. "See, simple as that."

"You want me to do it, or can Maddox do it?" I asked.

She shrugged, and I missed the new chatter I'd heard all over again. It snagged at my heart that she was more comfortable with my niece than her own father.

I cracked the tube, asked her to open her mouth, brushed the insides softly, and then stuck it back in the tube. "Easy-peasy, right?"

She nodded, a small smile lighting her up.

Mila came skipping back in with a napkin and two enormous cookies.

Maddox's radio squawked loudly, and we all jumped except Mila. He stepped out of the room to listen. When he returned, he looked at me with a seriousness that made my stomach plummet.

"We need to head to the station."

I placed my hand on top of Addy's. "I'm sorry I keep leaving you today, sweetheart, but I promise you're in good hands with Nana. You're safe here."

She nodded and smiled at me softly. "I like Mila's room."

My heart thudded at the complete sentence that

sounded smooth instead of stilted.

"Oh, this is not my room. I don't live here. My room is full of rainbows, but this is my second favorite room in the whole world, and Nana always fills it with the bestest toys. I'll let you pick what we play with after we eat our cookies."

I headed for the door and looked back at the two little girls eating their treat. Addy was at least a year older than Mila, but Addy was smaller, fragile looking, and it burned another hole in my chest.

Maddox's hand landed on my shoulder. "She's fine here. Just like you said, she's safe."

Then, he headed for the stairs, and I reluctantly followed. I wasn't sure I could manage much more bad news, and I could tell by the grim expression on my brother's face that whatever was waiting for us at the station wasn't good.

♫ ♫ ♫

After we'd gone downstairs, Maddox had insisted on Gia coming with us, saying there was someone there who had information about the sketch Gia had posted that morning. We followed Maddox in her car so she didn't have to sit in the middle of the bench seat in the truck. There had to be something seriously wrong with me that I was disappointed by that thought. I wanted her next to me. I wanted that spike of adrenaline she caused, even when I knew I shouldn't.

Gia Kent was everything I couldn't stand. She excelled at lying. She never stayed put. She'd treated my family and our ranch like nothing more than a piece of evidence to be gathered. But she hadn't treated Addy that way. She'd gone over and above to make sure Addy was safe and cared for.

And when we'd kissed… Hell, it had felt like she was everything I'd ever wanted, which was just downright confusing. My mixed emotions were the reason I'd easily succumbed to her driving. Maddox had smirked at me when I'd climbed into the passenger seat, knowing full well how much I hated being there.

As soon as we walked into Maddox's office, Gia smiled at the man waiting there, beelining toward him. He was shorter than me, deeply tanned, with rows of muscles reminding me of a heavyweight boxer. He was dressed in a black T-shirt, jeans, and military-grade boots with tattoos covering almost every piece of visible skin on his upper body.

He and Gia greeted each other with some sort of complicated handshake that ended with her laughing. He slung an arm over her shoulder, but she pushed him away and slammed him lightheartedly in the shoulder with her fist. I wanted to do the same thing. Except, I wanted to shove him clear into the next room so he wouldn't be able to touch her again—teasingly or not.

Maybe the reason I felt this unfamiliar jealousy with Gia when I hadn't for Ravyn was because I couldn't claim any relationship to her. She wasn't mine. I had no rights to her and no right to keep her from touching other men. Or maybe it was because the feeling she evoked in me was stronger than I'd ever felt for another human being.

"What brings you all the way to Willow Creek?" Gia asked.

His eyes turned somber, and his chin nodded in my direction, as if asking if I was okay.

"This is Ryder Hatley. Ryder, this is DEA Agent Enrique Salazar. He's part of the Lovato task force and has spent the majority of his career undercover."

"He the one who gave you the sketch? What did he see?" the agent asked, dark brows furrowing together.

I raised my hat, ran a hand over my hair, and then put it back on before meeting Gia's gaze.

"He's witness adjacent," Gia said, "but knows what we're dealing with."

The man's eyes narrowed, taking me in before shifting back to Gia. "Want to tell me what's really going on? Why a civilian is being dragged into this?"

Gia's face turned as serious as his. "I can't. Not yet. Is that why you're here? You find our guy?"

I could tell the man was uncomfortable with me being there, but if this had anything to do with Addy, I was staying. I crossed my arms over my chest as my brother came in, shutting the door behind us.

"I see y'all met." Maddox easily read the tension drifting through the air. "I vouch for my brother, Enrique. He isn't going to let anything you tell us out of this room."

"I'd like to know why we think he needs to be here at all," Enrique insisted. When Gia and Maddox exchanged a look but didn't speak, he continued, "Fine. I'll tell you. It has to do with the little girl you found in Anna's hotel room."

Concern flew through me, and Gia's face blanched. "Where'd you hear that?"

"You promised me that was under lock and key. Need to know only," I growled.

"It is. But as I also told you both, the only way to truly keep a secret is to tell no one." Her face was furious as she turned to Enrique. "Tell me where you heard it."

"Rory followed the lead on the van she saw outside the hotel where Anna was killed. The guy driving it ended up in Lexington, where I've been undercover, and she needed me to hunt the guy down. I asked why you couldn't do it, and when she clammed up like a bank vault, it made me suspicious. I went digging on my own and found someone who'd talk in Denver," he said.

This clearly made Gia unhappy and raised my concerns to a whole new level. Maddox and I exchanged a look, but before we could say anything, Gia demanded, "Just tell me you found the guy."

"DOA," Enrique said calmly, as if the guy being dead was of no concern. He lifted a manila envelope from the corner of Maddox's desk. He pulled out a picture and handed it over to Gia. I stepped closer, leaning over her shoulder to look.

The guy was lying on a shoreline. He'd obviously been

in the water a while. His skin was bloated. Eyes gray and murky. There was no need to question his cause of death. The gaping wound along his neck made it clear.

"Shit," Gia said, fingers tightening on the corners. "Where was this?"

"Near the Lexington Reservoir."

"Do you know who he is? Or why he was in Kentucky?" Gia asked.

"Best name we've come up with is Vito Jimenez. Word on the street is, if Vito showed up at your door, you could count the minutes you had left to live."

"Why the hell wasn't he brought in?" I demanded. Gia's and Enrique's eyes swiveled to take me in.

"Little something called lack of evidence. Not even enough to get a warrant to tap his phone or computer. Not that the man had either. Burner phones at best. He's been in and out of the country like a shadow, doing dirty work for multiple cartels, not just the Lovatos."

"So, why'd he end up dead if he was so important?" I demanded.

"My guess? He fucked up. He wasn't supposed to kill Anna. Maybe he was supposed to bring her to the Lovatos. Maybe he was supposed to bring both her *and* the little girl to them," Enrique said.

Acid curled its way up my throat.

"You don't know that's the reason. Anna made it clear the Lovatos didn't know about her daughter," Gia shot back. "But you're probably right that he wasn't supposed to kill Anna. There were defensive wounds on her body, and she was key to the organization, so it's unlikely they'd put out a hit on her."

"I heard Rory's idea about her leaking things to the authorities. If she did, they'd end her," Enrique parried.

"Look," Maddox said, tossing his hat onto his desk before dragging his hand through his hair. "He's dead. Unless we can figure out where it actually happened and who slit his throat, there's nothing we can do about it. Way I see it, if he'd known about Addy being in that room when he killed her mother, he would have taken her then. He didn't. And with him gone, there's even less chance they'll come looking for her now. This is good news for us."

"The little girl have anything with her?" the man asked, and for some reason, the nonchalant question made the skin on the back of my neck crawl.

"No," Gia's response was instantaneous. "I pulled her out of that room myself. She didn't have anything but the clothes on her back."

I thought of the backpack Addy wouldn't leave, and I knew Gia was lying. Avoiding eye contact, I stared at my muddy boots. I had to fight every urge in my body to run out of the room, get Addy, and hide her away.

The silence in the room turned thick. "Thanks for delivering the news in person, Enrique, but you made a trip for nothing. You could have just told me on the phone."

"Leland asked me to stick around and be your backup now that we know how easy it was for the information about the girl to get out. I'll be here when they show up."

My blood turned cold for multiple reasons—this man sticking to Gia and my family was the least of them. The fact that these assholes were going to come after Addy made me want to destroy something…someone. Worse, I didn't trust this new dickwad they'd sent to protect her.

I swirled around and headed for the door.

Gia was on my heels. "We have no indication they're coming here, Ryder."

I looked down, anger burning through me. "I see you're as good as your brother at keeping your protectees safe. Maybe you should start a club—Bumbling Agents Unite."

"Ry," Maddox warned, but I didn't listen.

"This time, they'll have to go through me to get to her, and I won't let them. No one is taking her on my watch. No one!" My body was quivering with fury.

"Nobody knows she's here. No one saw the letter but Leland, Rory, and me."

"And now him." I lifted my chin toward the DEA agent just as he said, "What letter?"

I didn't wait to hear her response. I couldn't. I had to get back to the little girl I'd left unprotected with my mother and Rianne. God. What if something happened again? What if another member of our family was shot? I slammed my way out of the office and the station, only to realize I didn't have my fucking truck.

Gia stormed out right behind me with my brother on her heels. She rounded the driver's side of the Escalade, jumping in and starting it up without a word.

Maddox grabbed my arm, holding me back before I could open the door. "Ryder. Look, I know Enrique. He helped me with the case with Chainsaw and the West Gears. He's been working the Lovatos undercover for a long time. If he's here to help, you can be sure he will."

"If he's been undercover for so long, why hasn't he shut them down? What if he's dirty?" I hissed quietly as the man himself appeared in the doorway of the station.

Maddox shook his head. "These kinds of cases take years, decades even. You don't just drop down in the middle of a fucking cartel and say, 'Hey, everyone, we're here to shut you down.'"

"She saw her mother's body being cut apart, Mads. She watched that fucker slice her up. She watched the blood pour from her and then tried to save her mother with her little hands." My throat clogged, and I slammed my eyes shut to prevent the dampness from leaking out.

"Fuck...I know." Maddox sighed, and when I opened my eyes, his brows were furrowed in concern. "All I'm saying is, we can't fight off a cartel on our own. We have to trust this task force, these people who've been working the case for years, are here to help us."

"Maybe that's what *you* have to do because you're wearing that shiny badge. I don't have to trust anyone. And

I'm not going to. She's mine to protect." My voice grew deep and rough. "And I damn well will."

I brushed off his hand, climbed into the SUV, and slammed the door behind me.

Gia backed up, and the wheels squealed as she headed out of town toward the ranch and the little girl I would shield with every bone and breath in my body.

Chapter Twenty-one

Emiliano

JOHN WAYNE COWBOY
Performed by The Trishas

I looked at the pictures Julio had sent me of the little girl walking out of the barn, holding the hand of another child and Hatley's youngest sister. My niece looked so much like Natalia at that age that it made my chest ache, and I felt the fury of my sister's betrayal all over again. She'd betrayed me and slid into this simple-minded rancher's bed—a man who had little to offer her or the child. I could have given them the world, and I would have.

I would still give the girl everything.

She would be mine.

She'd take her place at my side in the way Natalia should have.

She'd be the princess in my kingdom.

A kingdom she'd never escape the way her mother had.

I would decide whether she lived or died. What she did. Where she went. Who she saw.

"I will have my revenge for your treachery, *hermanita*," I said, putting down my phone and picking up the last remaining picture I had of my sister. I'd burned the rest after she'd left the first time, but I'd tucked this one away in my nightstand in a frame made from the hardwood floors that had captured our father's blood as he died. It was a weakness I'd recognized even back then, just as it had been a weakness to let Natalia flit around the globe as if she wasn't bound in chains.

I would never be that weak again.

I swiped my phone to another image Julio had taken, my finger tapping on my niece as she went up the steps into the farmhouse. She was shouldering a beat-up, black backpack that had my intuition flaring. I zoomed in on it and smiled, recognizing the gold NL stitched onto the front pocket. I'd had the backpack made for Natalia during her last year at MIT. Inside it had been the sculpted gold box I'd commissioned for our special code, giving it to her along with my latest instructions.

That idiot, Vito, had been wrong. He'd left more in the hotel room than a suitcase.

He'd left a child and a backpack that both belonged to me.

I would retrieve them.

It would be easy enough to do so.

Then, a plan formed in my mind. A way to exact vengeance against Hatley as much as make Natalia squirm from the heavens.

Ryder Hatley had stolen from me more than once.

He wouldn't live to do it again.

Chapter Twenty-two

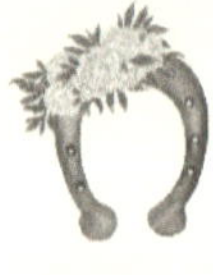

Gia

SAD SONGS FOR SAD PEOPLE
Performed by Megan Moroney

I fought to get my anger under control as Ryder and I drove in silence back to the ranch. I was pissed at Leland for telling Enrique about Addy and sending him here as if I couldn't handle the situation. I was angry at Ryder for tossing my brother's trauma in my face and assuming the same would happen just because my last name was Kent. What happened hadn't been Holden's fault. He hadn't done anything wrong. There was no way he could have known Leya Singh was wearing a bracelet with a tracker on it that had allowed the psychopath chasing her to find them.

But that singular thought had the swirl in my mind coming to a sharp halt.

What didn't I know about Addy?

We needed to go through everything she'd brought with her again. If there was a tracking device, we'd remove it and lead it away from her and the Hatleys. I wouldn't let anything happen to any of them. They'd been through enough already. Too much.

At the ranch, Ryder slammed out of the car, and I barely caught up with him before he stormed into the farmhouse.

I put a hand on his arm, holding him back. "Stop. You go in there like this, and you're going to scare the shit out of her."

He stared down at me, eyes simmering. "What else haven't you told me?"

My jaw dropped. "What do you mean?"

"I can't protect her if I don't know who is coming for her. Who do you have on your list? More of the West Gears?"

"No. They aren't involved."

"Then who?"

"No one locally. Whoever it is will stand out."

"Like you and *Enrique*."

"Enrique is not working for the Lovatos."

"How do you know that for sure?"

"Because his brother was undercover when he was gutted by the cartel, just like Ravyn. No way in hell he'd work for them after that."

Ryder's jaw worked, and I could tell he didn't agree with me, and the distrust in his eyes hurt worse than it should have. I thought we'd started to work past it, but I should've known better than to assume a heated kiss and a shopping spree would change the deep-seated mistrust Ryder felt for anyone who wasn't his family.

He rubbed his beard, tucked his hands into his pockets, and let out a slow breath, as if trying to calm himself down. Then, he turned and opened the back door. Addy and Mila were in the kitchen with Rianne, elbows deep in brown cookie dough they were rolling in powdered sugar.

Addy's eyes lit up on seeing us, and it landed in my heart.

"Hey," Ryder said.

Addy full-on smiled. "We are making chocolate cookies." The complete sentence dug further into my soul.

"Chocolate crinkles," Mila corrected.

"Where's Mama?" Ryder asked, looking around.

Rianne's eyes turned sad, and she scooted around the counter, motioning us farther away. "Sadie called from the bar." She lowered her voice to keep the girls from hearing. "It seems like your Uncle Phil had a heart attack. Your mama went to meet them at the hospital."

My heart skipped a beat. Not even a minute ago, I'd been thinking about how this family had already been through too much. Now, they had one more family member to be concerned about. Ryder's shoulders sagged slightly, and I had to fight the urge to wrap him in my arms and hold him tight.

He yanked out his phone and shot off a text before stuffing it back into his pocket.

"I need to get to the hospital. I'll take Addy with me," he said to Rianne.

When Rianne didn't react to his possessive growl over a little girl who was supposedly attached to me and not him, my chest fell. Someone in the Hatley family had spilled the beans to her. It would be practically impossible to keep the truth hidden in this tiny town.

"I don't think taking her to the hospital is a good idea," I whispered, and he immediately scowled at me. "Ryder, think about how she reacted sitting in the car outside the mall. There's no way she's going to go into a hospital without freaking out."

"I'm not leaving her."

Rianne patted his arm. "Your mama has Sadie with her. McKenna was on call when they arrived in the ER. He's in good hands, and there's nothing you can do there. This is the last set of cookies to go in the oven. Let them finish, and then maybe you can take Mila home with you. Maddox and you can switch off at your house."

"We're all done!" Mila called. Rianne turned back to the girls, helping them add the tray of cookies to the oven and supervising them while they cleaned up.

The silence between Ryder and me continued, taut and full of tension that made me want to strangle him or kiss him or…I wasn't sure what. Anything that would take the beast of an attitude Sadie had claimed he was carrying around and turn it into something different.

Outside, a dark-brown, 1970 Oldsmobile Toronado that was tricked out lowrider-style pulled up beside the Escalade. Enrique's dark hair was visible in the driver's seat. The car wasn't meant to blend in like most undercover vehicles. No, this stood out in a way that would make him recognizable by the low-level street soldiers of the Lovatos he'd worked himself into in Lexington.

Ryder glared at the car and the outline of Enrique inside it.

I stepped closer to him, my hand settling on his arm where Rianne's had been, and the zap of awareness wafting between us settled over me again. He looked down at where I was touching him, and his throat bobbed.

"Look, Rianne's idea is a good one," I said. "We'll go back to your house with both girls. When you need to go to the hospital, Enrique and I will stay at the house. If you want Maddox to show up too, I'm fine with that, but Enrique and I have this covered. I swear on all I hold holy, I'm not letting anything happen to her."

"What exactly is that?" he asked quietly, voice deep and raw as his gaze bored into my soul.

"What?"

"What exactly do you hold holy, Gia?"

My breath caught at the simple challenge. "I love my family just as much as you love yours."

"You run around the globe, lying to them about what you do. That doesn't exactly scream love."

I was determined not to let him rile me up. He was hurting and frustrated, and I was an easy target. "I don't tell them about my job because it protects them and me. That doesn't mean I wouldn't be at their side in a heartbeat if they needed me. It doesn't mean I'd stand by and just watch if they were under fire. Hell, I used a bunch of my CIA contacts to help Holden from behind the scenes when shit went down with The Painted Daisies in Colombia, even if he didn't know I did."

"Somehow, that isn't the reassurance you think it is," Ryder said darkly.

I let out a frustrated sigh. "Bottom line, asshole, is I'm here. I'm not going anywhere. Enrique is here, and he isn't going anywhere. You do what you gotta do. Whether that's staying with Addy or going to check on your mama and your uncle, that's up to you."

I spun on my heel and moved around the counter to where the little girls were putting some of the finished cookies into a Tupperware container. "Looks like Mila is coming back to Ryder's with us."

"Yes!" Mila cheered, doing a little dance. "Sleepover!" She looked at Ryder and asked, "Does that mean I get ice cream for breakfast again?"

"After the way you sold me out to your dad, no way," Ryder said, forcing his voice lighter. "Go grab your things, and I'll get the spare booster seat from the mudroom."

"Come on, Addy!" Mila grabbed Addy's hand, and the two girls went running out of the room, their feet pounding on the stairs.

♫ ♫ ♫

After gorging on pizza and chocolate crinkles and playing more board games than I had in over a decade, Ryder and I tucked the girls into the queen-sized bed in Addy's room. Even with the comforter pulled over her, Mila still chattered away. I thought she'd probably talk until she fell asleep mid-sentence, but Addy seemed comforted by having the other child with her. She'd still put her backpack on the floor by the bed with her shoes next to it, ready to run, but at least she hadn't disappeared under the bed or flattened herself under the covers. Instead, she'd rolled on her side, her stuffed animal touching Mila's unicorns.

It was the sweetest image I'd seen in a really long time, tugging at pieces of me I hadn't known existed. I still didn't think I wanted to have kids. Babies and diapers and breastfeeding didn't appeal to me, but taking care of little kids this age who could walk and talk and use the bathroom on their own…I didn't mind it so much. The hug Mila had given me, unbidden and unasked, had felt like pure love.

Addy had watched the hug, eyes turning shadowy, and then she'd offered both Ryder and me each a one-armed loose hug. It was tentative and brief, but it had still been a hug. Tears had pricked my eyes, and when I'd looked over at Ryder, his jaw had been clenched tight with his eyes blinking fast.

After we left them, he made his way down to the game room, and I followed. We slowly picked up the empty pizza boxes, cups, and game pieces that were scattered around. Enrique had taken the first shift outside, and I was going to switch places with him in a few hours. Knowing Addy's existence wasn't being kept as secret as I'd hoped it was, none of the team would just rely on Ryder's top-of-the-line alarm system to protect her.

While we cleaned up, I told Ryder what Rianne had explained about selective mutism and Addy needing therapy.

"I know it's not possible right now, but I just thought you should be aware."

Before he could reply, his phone buzzed, and he looked down at it with a frown.

"If you need to go, we'll be okay," I said.

He did that thing he and Maddox both did when thinking or upset—he rubbed a hand over his beard. "Uncle Phil isn't doing well. He hasn't regained consciousness, and McKenna says he might not."

I stuffed the last of the boxes into the green garbage bag he was holding. "I'm sorry. Were you close to him?"

"Uncle Phil is actually my mama's uncle. But you probably knew that from investigating us."

I didn't reply. Yes, I knew the basics, but it wasn't the same as knowing the emotions and connections that went with the dotted lines connecting people. I didn't say anything, and Ryder turned away, tying the knot on the green bag, setting it aside, and moving on to putting the board games away. Addy's Switch was on the coffee table, and I piled it in the cupboard with the other gaming devices.

"Mama never knew her dad, so Phil was the only man in her life as a kid. He and Granny ran the bar together right up until she died. Uncle Phil can do and say some pretty inappropriate things, and I think Maddox has had to talk to him a few times about complaints lobbed his way. Mama says Granny was the only one who could keep him in check, and once she was gone, there was no one holding him to a higher standard, you know?"

"But you all still liked him," I said because I'd never sensed any hostility or tension between the Hatleys and their great uncle.

"He was always good to us. When we were little, and things got tight at the ranch, Mama would help out at the bar, and he'd give her more money than she'd earned. He was always sliding cash to us kids too. We spent hours playing in the shed out back of the bar. McFlannigan's wasn't quite a second home to us, but it was comfortable. Still is."

While I hadn't lived in one place longer than five years growing up, I'd spent many holidays and summer vacations with my grandparents on their farm in upstate New York. It wasn't home, but just like Ryder said, it had been comfortable. And even though it hadn't been in our family for generations, it was still a place Holden and I had felt loved and safe.

"Your family has been in Willow Creek a long time. I'm not sure what that's like. The longest my family has been anywhere is my grandparents' apple farm in Grand Orchard, and they bought that early in their marriage. The Kents have always been nomads."

"The Hatleys have been here since the 1800s, and the McFlannigans since 1910. When my parents got married, it was like the town's opposing royalty joining together. Not quite a Hatfield and McCoy situation, but definitely white and dark knights. Half the town thought Mama got pregnant just to trap Dad, but the other half could see they were soulmates. No matter what they believed, everyone showed up when they got married the summer after high school."

I hadn't done the math on his parents' marriage and his birth. It surprised me that he'd been an unplanned baby. Maybe it was why he worked so hard to lift the burdens from their shoulders, feeling responsible for things he obviously couldn't have controlled.

He sank onto the couch, sliding until his head hit the back, eyes closing. He looked as exhausted as I felt. I joined him, careful to keep distance between us, even though the all-too-familiar awareness was flowing like an ocean wave around us.

He turned his head, blue eyes turning dark and moody in the dim lighting. "Don't get me wrong. My parents have loved each other for as long as they can remember. They would have gotten married no matter what. I just rushed it along for them."

It was strange hearing a man like Ryder talk about soulmates and love. He was so gruff, so unforgiving, it was hard to imagine him believing in any of it, even when I knew he'd felt strongly for Ravyn. Strong enough for her to have all but destroyed him.

I had a thousand questions to ask, but instead, I bit the inside of my cheek, waiting to see what else he'd offer up. It was a solid interrogation technique, and yet I wasn't stupid enough to think my interest in what he had to say was work related. No. There was something deep inside me yearning to uncover all the nooks and crannies of Ryder's soul. Things I'd never wanted to know about another person. The stories Eva had told Addy and me while sifting through old albums hadn't been nearly enough. Those had been her version of him. They hadn't been what was going on inside his heart and mind while he'd grown up. Hadn't been his hopes and dreams and the future he'd seen when he'd proposed to Ravyn.

"Mama was determined to break the cycle with us kids, so when Ravyn got pregnant without us being married, I knew it was a blow. But she never once made Ravyn or me feel that way. She was happy as a raccoon before trash day to be a grandma. Just like I was happy to be a father."

I swallowed hard. "You wanted children?"

"I wanted a dozen, but Ravyn laughed me off." His jaw worked as he said her name, throat bobbing, and I felt a spike of jealousy for a dead woman.

"I'm sorry she hurt you," I said softly.

He sat up, hands clenching. "Hurt? Hurt doesn't even come close to what she did to me. She took my soul and ripped it to shreds, ensuring I'd never be able to fix it. Never be able to give it to someone else."

Those words knifed through me—the fact that he thought he no longer had a soul to share. I hated it more than I'd hated anything in a long time, because I knew with a certainty I couldn't shake that Ryder Hatley had more than enough love left inside him. He had so much it would surround the person he chose like a fuzzy blanket, full of comfort and safety and home. A place you'd want to stay tucked forever—which was dangerous to a nomad like me.

I hadn't responded—couldn't—but I wasn't sure he'd even realized. He stood, pacing in front of the coffee table, his eyes distant, as if he were back in the past instead of in the room with me, and heartache dripped from him. "She stole from us. From the people who'd loved on her and made her feel safe when she'd told me she never felt that way growing up. She said her dad was abusive—corporal punishment he liked to mete out to her and her brother for minor offenses. She said it had gotten worse after their mother died. I suspected he might have done more to her, but she never said. I'd thought maybe she'd blocked it out, but now, I think she had more secrets than she'd ever planned on sharing with me."

Those truths caused my wheels to turn, puzzle pieces sliding together. It was clear Ravyn Clark wasn't her real name any more than Anna Smith was, which also made it clear that she'd already been on the run when she'd shown up at the Hatley ranch. She'd said as much in her letter.

She'd said that "they" had found her. Maybe it wasn't just the Lovatos chasing after her for her technical skills. Maybe she *was* a Lovato, and her father had come to drag his runaway daughter home.

When I said as much, Ryder stopped his pacing and stared at me, eyes flashing again.

"You think… That means… Addy might be related to…" His eyes went to the ceiling. "Fuck."

I couldn't stand it any longer. I went to him, wrapping my arms around his waist. He held himself stiff at first, and then after a deep inhale and exhale, he let his arms slide around me too.

"I don't have any proof. It's just supposition."

My cheek was pressed against his chest, and the smell of him flooded my senses—hay and grass and masculinity—sending my endorphins into a tailspin. He rested his chin on the top of my head. It was a tender move that squeezed my already squished heart until I thought it was going to turn to liquid and slide out of my body. I would no longer own it. It would belong somewhere else…to someone else…to him.

That scared the shit out of me.

And yet, I didn't move. I didn't want to. I wanted to stay encased in that warm blanket I'd imagined, the beat of attraction hammering like a conga drum through my veins. The rhythm strong and heady. Intoxicating.

His large hands slid up my back, the heat of them burning through my flannel shirt. His palms were spread wide in a way that allowed his thumbs to caress my sides, coming desperately close to my breasts. He hesitated there for a second then grazed two long, gentle strokes before his hands moved to my back so he was pressing me into him ever so slightly more.

"I'm sorry," he said quietly. "About what I said earlier. About your brother and you. You brought me Addy… You're here trying to help us… I was angry and cruel."

I twisted my head so my gaze met his.

The burning there—the desire—it was like stepping into a full-fledged fire. A furnace that would melt skin and bone and leave me as nothing but ash to be spread over the earth.

He'd removed his flannel overshirt almost as soon as we'd walked through the door this afternoon, leaving him in only his Henley. I slipped my hands underneath it. When my fingers hit bare skin, he sucked in a breath, as if the touch hurt him. But his eyes never wavered. Instead, a question rang through them. A question about how far I'd let this go. Or maybe he was asking himself that question. Maybe we both were.

His head lowered, and my toes automatically responded, raising so our mouths met in the middle. Both our previous kisses had been punishing, merciless. This was so soft and tender and light it felt like the whisper of a breeze on a hot day. A hint of relief. A hint of soothing. But it wasn't nearly enough.

Neither of us had closed our eyes. Our shared gaze was as sensual as the kiss, as if we were learning not only the contours of our mouths but the shape of our souls.

I glided the tip of my tongue along the seam of his lips, and he groaned, but he refused me access. Instead, he pulled back from the kiss, fisting my braid and dragging it backward so I was forced to expose my neck where my pulse beat as frantically as a hummingbird's wings. With hooded eyes, he lowered his mouth until it landed on that erratic rhythm, sucking gently.

My core ignited. My legs wobbled. Hunger consumed me.

I squeezed his sides, fingernails digging into flesh, and my hips slammed into his.

His lips glided down along my neck to the base of my shoulder, nipping softly.

I gasped.

He pushed us closer, muscled thighs widening to pull me in between them.

"Why the fuck do you taste so good?" he muttered, and I heard, in every syllable, his anger and frustration that it was me he was attracted to. The woman he couldn't trust. Who lied. Who would leave. And I suddenly hated that all those things about me were true. I wanted to give him something solid. Something he could count on. To prove to him he still had a soul to share. That he could give it to someone else.

To me.

That scary thought almost had me pushing him away. But then, as if feeling I was about to retreat, he claimed my mouth again, tongue sliding inside, stroking along the soft recesses, and any thoughts of self-preservation, of right and wrong, of my job, evaporated.

There was only him and me and an endless sea of longing and desire I wasn't sure would ever be sated.

Chapter Twenty-three

Ryder

A LITTLE BIT TROUBLE
Performed by Brothers Osborne

It was wrong. Somewhere at the back of my brain, I knew what I was doing, what we were doing, was wrong. But those warm eyes were aglow as she met me stroke for stroke, a blaze inside her burning into me. A blaze I had no desire to pull away from. I wanted it to consume me. I wanted to know what it would feel like when it exploded. When Gia's body came apart and broke mine right along with it.

Because she could break me.

Just like Ravyn had.

Except, I thought maybe Gia could do more damage. And it wasn't because my soul had already been torn apart and would easily shatter again. It was because this…what I felt with my hips pressed up against hers, with my hands and mouth melting into her skin…it was more intense than anything I'd ever felt with Rayvn.

Warning signs were screaming.

And I ignored them.

Instead, I broke our kiss to lift her shirt up and over her head, exposing a plain cotton bra underneath, a pale nude color that blended with her skin. Nothing sexy about it. And yet, it was wildly sensual because it was just like Gia. Sure.

Steady. Simple and yet complex.

I kissed her again, sliding back inside her mouth as my hands caressed her from the waist up, over the bra, pinching taut tips through the material. She whimpered, and the sound went straight to my groin.

She hadn't closed her eyes once during our embrace. She'd watched every move. Every slide of lips and hands, seeing more than I was ready to give.

She fisted my shirt, and we moved apart just enough to pull it off before going right back to where we'd left off. I picked her up, and she wrapped her legs around me. I sat on the couch with her straddling me. Our embrace picked up pace, the slow exploration turning into urgent demands. I unsnapped her bra and lavished one breast while my fingers worked the other.

And that was when her eyes finally fluttered closed. It felt ridiculously like a victory.

I wanted to feast on her for hours. Slow and languorously.

I wanted her every breath, every vibration, every move to be mine.

I wanted to stay this way for years, locked in the warm cocoon of her touch.

Maddox's ringtone broke the quiet, and I still didn't stop.

Instead, I sought her lips again, demanding we both ignore the call, demanding we keep our minds from retreating to reality and the problems facing us.

My phone stopped and then started all over again.

Fuck.

I placed my forehead against her chest. The rhythm of her heart was a soothing beat, the scent of her a tantalizing lure calling me back to the home she'd briefly offered.

I knew as soon as I shifted my hips to grab my phone from my back pocket, she'd be gone. She'd leave. And we'd be back to our verbal sparring, hiding our sexual tension behind walls we were both good at keeping.

My phone stopped and started a third time.

"You should get it. He might get worried and send out a deputy to check on us."

I hated that she was right. And I hated that she did exactly what I'd thought she would, shifting off me as I reached for the offending device. She pulled her bra back on, and then her flannel, and tossed my shirt at me.

"What?" I groused into the phone.

"Uncle Phil passed."

Now, I felt like even more of an ass. I hadn't made it to the hospital to say my goodbyes. Hadn't been there for Mama when she'd lost the last living member of her McFlannigan family. Guilt hit me like a sledgehammer.

"I'm on my way," I said.

"There's no reason for you to come. He never woke, and there's nothing you can do here. McK is working on the paperwork. Mama and Sadie have already gone home."

My throat closed for a moment, and I couldn't even answer him.

Maddox sighed. "Don't go all Ryder on me and feel responsible for this, dipshit. There was nothing you could have done. You were where you needed to be tonight, taking care of our daughters. We all needed that just as much as Mama needed a couple of us here. It allowed her to grieve without worrying about them."

I wasn't used to having a child to think about, but I also realized the truth of what Maddox had said. If I hadn't had Addy dropped into my world, and I'd been at the hospital while Maddox had been home with Mila, I would have understood. We wouldn't have wanted her there, watching Uncle Phil take his last breaths. It was just that it had never had to be me before. I'd always been present where I was able to control the situation if things went haywire.

"How is Mama?"

"Stunned. I don't think any of us expected Phil to ever

die. He was too ornery. Too determined to eke out every last pleasure he could."

"He ate awful. Drank worse. Smoked a pack a day. I'm actually surprised he lived this long."

"He was only sixty-five."

Silence settled down for a second, and Maddox continued, "Mila settle in okay?"

"I'm not sure you're going to be able to tear her away from Addy."

"How does Addy feel about that?" he asked with a laugh in his voice.

"She's talking in full sentences. Her shoulders are relaxed. Mila's magic at work. I'll take it." That damn lump returned to my throat, making it hard to swallow.

"She's gotta go to school tomorrow. What are you doing with Addy?"

"I don't think school is an option yet."

Maddox didn't disagree. "McK and I both have early shifts, so Rianne will be by in the morning to pick her up."

"I can drop her off at the school. I have to get back to the ranch and make sure the build stays on track. I want to see Mama and figure out what she needs help with."

"Mila needs her backpack and school supplies anyhow. Let Rianne do it. Maybe she can help out with Addy's education somehow. A homeschool kind of thing."

It was an option I wouldn't have thought of because I wasn't used to thinking about kids and education.

"I'll talk to her."

"McK just came out, so I'm gonna go. Love you, dipshit."

"Love you too, asswipe."

We hung up, and I turned back to face the woman I'd just had straddling my lap with our tongues tangled. The moment was lost, but just looking at her caused those flames to flicker again. The distance between us felt charged, but it also allowed me enough space to start listening to the warning signs that had been blaring.

She tugged her braid, and I felt the softness of it beneath my hands all over again. Felt the flare of desire that had overcome me when I'd yanked it back to expose the smooth column of her neck and found the rapid beat within her, making it mine for several tantalizing seconds.

"I should get a couple hours of sleep before I relieve Enrique," she said.

I didn't say anything. Didn't know what to say because thoughts of her in bed, spread across silky sheets, did nothing but make me hard, make me want to pick up where we'd left off.

She blew out a frustrated sigh at my nonresponse, turning on her heel and heading for the stairs. She turned back at the last minute. "Don't leave in the morning without us."

"How long do you think we have to live like this?"

Her hand gripped the rail, fingers flexing. "I honestly don't know. But we are closing in on them, peeling back the layers. We'll get to the core soon." When I didn't respond again, she practically rolled her eyes. "Goodnight, Ryder."

"Night, Gia."

Her sock-clad feet were light on the stairs, disappearing in a whisper.

I should have said something more after how close we'd been to tearing off the rest of our clothes and plunging over the edge together. But if I'd opened my mouth, all that would have come out was a desperate plea for her to come to my room, and I still had enough brain cells left in my body to know that would be a catastrophe. So, I let her go and could only hope my callousness would force her to take a step back, because I was pretty damn sure I'd never be able to push her away on my own.

♫ ♫ ♫

I'd barely gotten the two little girls up and fed before Rianne was knocking at the door. Gia hadn't been there like the morning before because she'd taken over from Enrique, patrolling the house like some palace guard. It twisted something savage inside me that objected to her being the first line of defense.

I knew she'd been trained to handle herself, but I still didn't like the idea of her being the one to face the danger alone if it came at us. I hadn't liked the idea of Enrique—who I still wasn't sure I trusted—being my first line of defense either. Worse, he was now asleep in the bedroom I'd already started considering as Gia's, and that pissed me off even more than the idea of her outside standing guard.

When Rianne walked in, Mila stopped mid-sentence and ran to Rianne, hugging her around the legs while giving her a detailed description of our night. When I glanced over at Addy, she was smiling. That singular smile was enough to lighten the dark mood I'd woken in.

"You ready, Chick-a-dee?" Rianne asked Mila.

"Do I have to go to school? Addy isn't going!"

"Yes. School is not an option. Go put your shoes on."

Mila dragged her heels down the hall, and I turned to Addy. "Go get your shoes too. I'll teach you how to wield a hammer today." Addy's eyes widened, but she jumped down from the barstool and followed Mila. I turned to Rianne. "I'm not sure how much anyone's told you, but I can't enroll Addy in school yet. It isn't safe."

"No one said, but I caught the whiff of something funny. Everyone was way too serious about the situation. Plus, I knew she wasn't Gia's friend's daughter. She looks just like Ravyn and has your smile."

My heart clenched. Would it always hurt this badly when people said she looked like Ravyn? I was never going to be able to escape talk and thoughts about my ex now, and I disliked that as much as I loved having Addy here with me. Then again, if I was honest with myself, I hadn't really escaped Ravyn before either. I'd just shoveled her under a pile of mud and dirt, as if she didn't exist, hoping it would all disappear if I left the idea of her there long enough.

"Maddox suggested you might be willing to help us for now. Maybe you could homeschool her until things get settled? I know you're retired, so if it isn't something you want to do, I'll understand."

Rianne's eyes sparkled. "I miss teaching something fierce, even though I was ready to be out of the daily grind. It would be a joy to work with her. Give me a day or two to pull things together. That will give her some more time to settle in. We can work out of the playroom at your mama's place while you're at the ranch, and she can hang with Mila and me on days I get her from school."

Relief hit me.

"Thank you." My voice was gruff.

"Gia and I had a chat about her lack of verbal skills and shyness. Did she tell you my thoughts on selective mutism?"

"She mentioned something last night. We didn't really get to dive into it."

Instead, we'd dived into each other.

"If that's the case, she'll need therapy," Rianne said. "And she'll need a solid individual education plan in place before she's in an actual classroom setting. I can help walk you through all of it."

"She had a bad…scare. Something ugly she witnessed. Do you think it could just be that?"

"Maybe. Maybe not. Either way, therapy and an education plan will mean the adults around her have the tools to help her."

The girls came running back in with their shoes and coats on and their stuffed animals tucked under their arms.

"My Switch? I can't find it," Addy said.

"I think it might be downstairs from last night, but you won't need it today anyway."

She looked uncomfortable.

"You and Balam are going to be my construction forepersons. You get to supervise."

Her eyes turned wide. She shoved her thumb against her chest. "Me?"

"Yep. After I teach you how to use a hammer, you can keep me and my guys on track."

She shifted her feet, uncertainty growing.

"I want to be a foreperson too!" Mila whined.

I ruffled her hair. "Another time, kiddo."

"Thank your uncle Ryder and Addy for letting you stay. We gotta get goin'. Otherwise, you'll be late."

Mila hugged me tight and then hugged Addy, who held herself stiff for a moment before putting her arms around Mila and hugging back. Mila ran for the door, and Rianne said goodbye before following her. Gia passed her coming in, and the two exchanged good mornings.

"I left breakfast burritos in the oven for you and Enrique," I told Gia as she walked in, rubbing her fingerless-gloved hands together. Her hair was tucked under her gray beanie, but her nose was bright red, and I despised all over again that she'd been out in the freezing temperatures because of us. "There's coffee too. Addy and I are heading over to the ranch. Why don't you both eat and catch up to us there?"

"I'll take the coffee with me. Give me two seconds to use the restroom."

"We can go without you."

She shook her head. "No."

She didn't wait for me to argue more, just headed down the hall. While she was gone, Enrique wandered in from the bedroom. He had scruff on his cheeks, his hair was sticking up, and he was wearing the same clothes as the day before. When I'd introduced him to Addy last night, she'd tucked behind my legs. She did the same now on seeing him.

"Gia says we're heading to the ranch." He eyed the coffeepot. "Okay if I grab some of that?"

"To-go cups are in the cupboard above it."

"Thanks."

Gia's hurried footsteps joined us. "Pour me one too, Enrique."

He did as she asked, and I moved to the oven, pulling out the two burritos I'd wrapped in foil.

"Thanks," the DEA agent grunted out.

We headed out the door, locking it and arming the system. Enrique went to his lowrider while Gia, Addy, and I loaded up in the Escalade again. Climbing into the passenger seat was becoming a habit I didn't like.

It wasn't until we were halfway to the ranch that I realized Addy didn't have her backpack with her. The idea that she felt safe enough to finally leave it did something to my heart and soul I wasn't sure I could stand. It made me determined to not let her down. Made me determined to make sure she always felt this safe.

When we parked in the lot in front of the ranch's restaurant, still dark and dim, I looked at Gia and Addy and said, "Why don't you two check on the kittens real quick while I talk with Mama?"

I didn't want Addy to see my mother upset about Uncle Phil dying. She didn't need to see more loss up close and personal. I wasn't sure she could handle it, especially as she hadn't gotten any closure with Ravyn. No funeral. No goodbyes. Why did my heart and lungs feel like a boa constrictor was living permanently inside me these days? Squeezing my chest until it ached.

"That's a good idea," Gia said. "Come on, Addy, I'll race you."

The two of them took off toward the barn, my chest warming as their serious faces grew into wide smiles as they ran. Addy even giggled when she beat Gia to the barn door. I wanted more of that from both of them. I wanted only lightness and laughter to surround them, which was confusing as hell when it came to Gia. I might not have any business thinking of her that way, and it might be the least-smart thing I'd done in a long time, but I couldn't help it. I longed to have all of her. Body. Heart. Soul. Every ounce she had to give. I craved it to be mine.

Enrique pulling in next to Gia's Escalade brought me out of my maudlin reverie to the reality of our situation where we needed armed guards to keep us safe. This wasn't the time to be daydreaming about things I couldn't have. It wasn't the time to be opening my heart again like Sadie had all but begged me to.

I ignored the DEA agent and bounded up the steps to the house.

When I entered, Mama and Sadie were sitting at the dining room table, coffees in hand, scones in front of them, untouched. I hugged them both, squeezing tight before letting go and scouring their faces. They were puffy and tear-stained. "I'm sorry I wasn't at the hospital last night."

Mama sniffed and dabbed at her eyes with a napkin. "He wouldn't have known, and you had those precious babies to take care of. It was how it needed to be."

"What's next? How can I help?" I asked.

"Your daddy is on his way home from Tulsa. He's going to meet Sadie and me at the funeral home, and then we're meeting with Joe O'Halloran at his office."

O'Halloran was our family lawyer and had handled Uncle Phil's legal needs as well.

"Gemma coming home?"

"She was going to buy a plane ticket last night, but I told her to wait until we had firmer dates around the funeral. I don't want her to have to make two trips from LA."

It would be good for Gemma to be home for a few days and be surrounded by those who loved her after her nasty breakup with that dick of an actor. While her homecoming wouldn't be for a good reason, at least she'd be here. We'd make sure she really was holding it together like she said she was.

I shifted my hat from one hand to the other. "What can

I do?" I repeated.

Mama patted my cheek. "Nothing. Concentrate on the cabins and things at the ranch as you always do. That allows your daddy and me to take care of things with Phil. Where's Addy?"

"Out with Gia in the barn." I pointed to the lowrider outside and the dark figure sitting in it. "That's Enrique. He's DEA, and he'll be hovering around for a while. Didn't want y'all to get spooked when you see him. If anyone outside the family takes notice, I'll put him to work and say we hired extra help."

Mama and Sadie exchanged a worried look. "Things getting worse on that end?" my sister asked.

"The man they think killed Ravyn was found dead."

"Good," Sadie said, eyes flashing. "Bastard deserved it."

I didn't want to add to my family's burden at the moment, but I also needed to make sure they kept their eyes open. "They say the cartel behind all this might be looking for Addy now."

Mama inhaled sharply.

Maybe I really did need to take Addy and head out of Willow Creek for a little while to keep everyone safe. But being on the run was all she'd known, and I hated the idea of putting her through it again. Plus, who'd keep things running at the ranch while my parents handled the aftermath of Phil's death? And even if I did run, there was no saying the cartel wouldn't come here first and torture my family for information. At least this way, I was here to face what came at us, and we had extra protection. While neither hightailing it out of town nor staying seemed like the perfect answer, surrounding Addy with family felt more right than wrong.

"I'm going out to work on the cabins, but please let me know if you need anything," I told them.

"Soup is in the crockpot. There's still bread from yesterday. Make sure everyone eats." Leave it to my mother to think about feeding others right in the middle of her own loss. I tugged her close, kissing her temple. She squeezed me back and then let go.

We shared a look filled with love and sorrow and gratitude without a single word. I stepped away, ruffling Sadie's hair as I did, and she ducked with a growl that sounded a bit like mine these days when she used to be all laughter and cheeky smiles. My family had been through so much in the last couple of years. I wasn't sure what we'd done to bring these rounds of bad luck to our door, and I could only hope it would end soon.

I left the house, slammed my hat back on my head, and made my way to the barn.

Giggles greeted me. Addy's soft tiny ones instantly lightened my chest.

"Okay, you two lazybones, time to get to work," I hollered up at them.

Addy's face appeared over the rail first. She was holding the same gray kitten as yesterday. "Puffball keeps following me."

The full sentence made me so happy I wanted to do one of Uncle Phil's Irish jigs.

"Put her in the crate for now. You can come and see her later."

Addy did as she was told, and when she returned to the rail, Gia was with her. They made their way down the ladder, hopping off the last step. Gia landed within arm's reach. I brushed a piece of straw from her ponytail at the same time she went to do it herself, and our fingers tangled. Heat thrummed through me, and our eyes locked for the merest of moments before we both stepped back.

"Come on," I said, taking Addy's hand and leading them out of the barn.

Shawn and Ramon were already in the first of the two partially built cabins, strapping their tool belts around their waists. I introduced them to Gia and Addy, and their eyes widened.

"They're going to help me with the siding today while you two finish up the electrical," I said. We hadn't planned on the external siding going up yet, but it was something I could do with Gia and Addy tagging along.

The men moved toward the bathroom at the back of the cabin, and I sifted through the tools spread around the site, assembling what I needed. I showed Gia how to use the nail gun, and Addy how to follow behind her, supervising and ensuring all the nails got tapped in just right.

I strapped on my tool belt and moved to grab a plank of shiplap siding to demonstrate what we'd be doing, when Addy's little hand stopped me.

"I have?" She pointed to my tool belt.

"Well, sweetheart, I don't have any on-site that would fit you." Disappointment lit her eyes. "Hold on," I said. I went to the next cabin over where we were storing most of the supplies. I found some rope and a couple of extra tools and jogged back to the women.

I squatted in front of Addy and tied some loops in the rope that would allow her to slide a hammer and a pair of pliers I'd grabbed into them. Then I knotted it around her waist. "We'll order you one of your own, but this will have to do for today."

She grinned at me. "That too?" She pointed to the worn brown cowboy hat I had on after leaving my nicer black one at home. This one was nicked and beat up, covered with a fine coat of sawdust from the construction work.

"You want your own hat?"

She nodded.

"I'll get you one, sweetheart."

"Gia too?"

I looked over at Gia, whose brows had raised in surprise. "You want a hat, darlin'?"

She huffed. "Don't call me darlin'."

She turned away without answering me, lifting the plank of siding I'd set down. I reached over to take it from her.

Fine, I answered my own question, *I'd get her a damn hat too.*

I'd get both of these women anything the hell they wanted.

The last time I'd had that feeling, it had backfired on me in the worst sort of way.

I'd lost everything. My pride. My heart. My baby.

Thank God I'd had my family and the ranch to get me through.

They'd be there for me again. They'd likely have to be once Gia took off. But I'd have Addy. I'd have Addy and a life that I'd thought had passed me by. That was going to have to be enough.

Chapter Twenty-four

Gia

SHALLOW

Performed by Danielle Bradbery and Parker McCollum

I considered myself a fit human being. Unlike other NSA analysts who never left headquarters, I spent the majority of my time in the field as part of the Special Collection Service and had to be prepared to defend myself and any team members with me. I'd been trained at FLETC, the government's training center in Virginia, right along with other analysts and agents from multiple federal agencies. After, I'd maintained my strength by spending hours at a CrossFit gym, in a kickboxing ring, and pounding the pavement. All that to say, I wasn't out of shape, but come lunchtime, my body was sore from running the nail gun and helping Ryder hold up plank after plank. Addy had stayed at our side, helping as she could with a quiet determination. Every time Ryder praised her, she glowed like someone had shone a flashlight on her.

By the time snow started to come down in a steady thrum, I was ready for a break. My nose, toes, and fingers were practically numb from the frigid air even as a bead of sweat dripped down my back. Addy looked just as frozen as I felt, but Ryder… He looked as if withstanding the snow gods was something he did all the damn time. He looked like he belonged in a calendar for the good ol' boys of winter.

His cheeks had the barest tinge of red, his cowboy hat

was tilted back slightly, and his dark hair curled out from underneath it. His corduroy work jacket lined with flannel was worn but not shabby, and his jeans clung to his narrow hips and muscled thighs like they were made especially for him. The well-used tool belt accentuated the fact that he wasn't some random model but a man comfortable with hard work. Hands callused and strong. The same hands that had run along my skin and touched my breasts last night, bringing me closer to the edge in mere minutes than any man before him had when I'd been fully naked.

"Lunchtime," Ryder said. He hollered into the cabin at the other two workers, and all five of us headed for the farmhouse.

When we got to the parking lot, Enrique was gone. I pulled my phone from my pocket with fingers that could barely move. I'd missed a text from him, reading that he was following up on a lead, but he'd be back later.

We'd just helped ourselves to huge helpings of the soup Eva had left in the crockpot and the same sourdough bread from the day before when Eva, Brandon, and Sadie walked in. The women's faces looked sad and tear-stained, and even Brandon's eyes looked red.

Ryder's dad gave him a hug that was much more than a masculine back pat. This one clung on and spoke of love. It made me miss my dad and my brother for some reason, made me long to go home and hug my family and make sure they knew how much they meant to me—all thoughts I was unaccustomed to in the middle of a job where normally only the case filled my brain. Except, this case was starting to feel less and less like work and more and more like…nothing I could think of without my heart hurting.

"Sit down," Ryder said to his family. "I'll dish you up."

And my heart twisted again. Ryder was good at taking care of the people he loved. I bet he'd doted on Ravyn, and once he'd found out she was pregnant, I bet he'd waited on her hand and foot. The letter she'd written had said she loved him, loved him even now, but she'd still walked away. While part of me understood—if she was part of the Lovato family and they wanted her back, they'd stop at nothing to get her—the other part of me wondered what would have happened if she'd trusted the Hatleys to help. If she'd trusted Ryder and his sheriff brother to protect her, would the Lovatos have fallen years ago, before they'd embedded themselves right at the top of the criminal world?

It felt like she'd taken the easy way out. It would have been harder to stay. Harder to trust. Harder to risk everything.

What would I have done if I'd been in her shoes? If I had someone like Ryder adoring me, taking care of me, loving me—would I have left? Especially while carrying his child? The idea nauseated me, and I pushed my bowl away to focus on the people in the room rather than my tormented thoughts.

Shawn and Ramon offered their condolences to the family while Ryder worked on ladling soup into bowls for his parents and Sadie.

"How'd it go at the funeral home?" Ryder asked his mama.

"We'll hold the funeral Friday with a celebration of life at the bar afterward," Eva said, rubbing her forehead.

Addy shifted in her seat next to me, and I looked down. Her face had been smiling and open all morning, but now she'd shut down.

"Once Gemma gets here, we need to talk to all four of you about his will and his estate," Eva said.

Sadie shot Eva a concerned look that had curiosity spiking in me—curiosity I shouldn't have as this had nothing to do with me or the case. If Ryder had noticed too, he didn't say anything, letting it drop.

We finished our meal, I helped clean up, and then the five of us who'd been working all morning headed for the door.

As we stepped outside, I halted. The snow was still flitting to the ground in soft, silent waves, and the temperature had dropped another couple degrees. In the forty-five minutes or so we'd been inside, the snow had stuck and begun to build. A few inches was all, but it was enough to turn the world into a black-and-white photograph. A delightful portrait of winter farm life. Buildings and fields and fences all coated with powder. Our breaths left a smoky cloud in the air.

"Well, I think we're done with the siding for the day," Ryder huffed.

"We can still get a few hours in on the electrical," Ramon offered.

"It'll be colder than a frosted frog."

Shawn laughed. "Nothing we aren't used to."

The two men dropped their cowboy hats onto their heads and stomped down off the porch, heading toward the cabins. They left dark, sooty footprints in their wake.

Addy leaned forward off the porch, sticking her hand out, catching the flakes. They melted at first and then stuck to her little palm. She looked up at Ryder with a smile on her face that took my breath away. She was an incredibly beautiful little girl, even when somber and serious, but when she lit up like this, it was almost miraculous.

"Snow," she said softly.

"You ever been in the snow?" he asked.

She shook her head. "Mama didn't like the cold."

Ryder gave a quiet chuckle. "She really didn't. She'd wear so many layers during winter it looked like she was a ball you could roll down the hill. She even wore three pairs of socks to bed."

The little girl looked up with both sadness and interest in her gaze. What I felt was the same jealousy I'd been having over a dead woman. Because Ryder knew what she looked like in bed. Because she'd shared a bed with him. But I also felt a strange affinity with her as we had at least two things in common—I wasn't overly fond of the cold myself, and I found myself strangely attracted to the man Ravyn had been engaged to.

"If you'd like, I can grab some gloves from Sadie for you, and we can build a snowman," he suggested, and Addy nodded, smile growing wider. He turned toward the door and looked back at me. "You need a different pair of gloves?"

My fingerless ones were definitely not up to the challenge of snow play. As a kid, Holden basically had to bribe me to put myself through the torture of wet and ice. But the idea of playing with Ryder and Addy—watching her experience it for the first time—didn't seem like torture at all. I shrugged. "Sure."

He raised a brow at my half-hearted response and then disappeared into the house.

He was back sooner than I liked with a small pair of rainbow mittens and a matching beanie for Addy and a pair of purple gloves for me. "Lucky for us, Mila left these here."

As I pulled on the gloves, Ryder helped Addy tuck her hair into the beanie and tug the mittens on.

We stepped down into the snow, and Ryder led us out past the barn in the opposite direction of the cabins into the wide-open pasture where the animals had grazed when I'd been here in the summer. At the far end of the field, bright-red crabapples shimmered against dark branches layered with pure white, and I wanted to take a hundred pictures of it all from different angles. Ones that included just the landscape and ones that included the pleasure radiating from Addy's face and the gentle smile on Ryder's as he watched his daughter.

Addy and I followed his instructions, patting the loose snow into tight, round balls and then rolling them along the ground. The balls collected sticks and dried grass along the way as the snow wasn't really deep enough yet. But eventually, we had three balls of differing sizes that he helped us pile on top of each other. He jogged to the trees and came back, helping Addy place sticks for arms, not yet fully grown crabapples for a wide mouth, and more crabapples down the front of the snowman as buttons. Then, they searched under the snow for pebbles to make the eyes and a nose.

We all stood back and admired the sad little snowman. He was hardly the perfect shape, and the snow had been too thin for him to be pristine, but it was a snowman. Addy laid a mittened palm on it with a reverence that made my heart skip several beats.

"He's missing something," Ryder said, one eye closed, assessing the crooked mass.

"Hat," Addy said.

He chuckled. "Yep." He pulled his cowboy hat off and placed it on the snowman's head.

Addy laughed, and the sound traveled through the cold air like fairy wings. Soft and light and bringing joy.

"We have to name him if we want him to come alive," Ryder said, voice lowered as if he was telling her a secret. "Only snowmen with names can visit your dreams and grant wishes."

I held back a snort because Addy was eating up his words like they were pure sugar.

"What should we call him?" she asked. Her fully formed sentences kept catching me off guard when they happened, tugging at all those emotions floating around inside me.

"He's your first snowman, so you get to name him."

"Why does it have to be a guy?" I asked. "Couldn't it be a girl?"

Ryder looked up at me, and his smile was as wide as his daughter's. They both were beautiful. Stunning in a way that made them glow as if the sun had come out even though it was still tucked behind dark clouds and shimmering snowflakes.

"It can be whatever gender you want it to be," he said, winking at Addy.

After a moment of deep thought, she whispered, "Rosalinda."

My eyes caught Ryder's. That was such a unique and

specific name that it had to mean something.

"Yeah?" he asked.

"My *abuela* was Rosalinda."

The name tickled at the back of my brain. Something from one of my files. Something about the Lovatos. Damn. I hated not being able to pull it to the surface. I'd go back through them tonight and see what I could find.

"Did you meet your *abuela*?" I asked.

She shook her head. "She went to heaven when Mama was little like me."

"Rosalinda it is," Ryder said, handing Addy a stick. "Can you write her name? Here at the base of the snowwoman?"

Addy took the stick and started to carve the name in the growing layer of snow. She seemed to be thinking about the sounds as she did it, taking her time, and ended up using a U for the As. But at least she could write and spell. She'd had some kind of schooling.

Ryder handed me his phone. "Can you take a picture?"

My throat clogged, thinking about all the pictures he'd missed with his daughter. Thinking of the photo albums at my house filled with pictures of me and my family. Thinking about the ones Eva had shown Addy and me of his childhood. He didn't have those with Addy. He'd had so much stolen from him that he'd never get back. And if those thoughts carved sharply through me, I couldn't even imagine what they did to him.

These two humans belonged together with their matching smiles and love drifting around them. My heart and body ached once more for that "something" I'd never wanted. A man. A little girl. Ties that would tether me to this place instead of letting me float freely around the globe. It was absolutely contrary to everything I'd ever seen for myself. Even growing up, I'd recognized that all the spy heroes I idolized had only received pain from relationships because the life they led wasn't fit for them. Instead, it got people killed. The hero's love interest rarely made it through unscathed or even alive.

Ryder kneeled on the ground, bringing his height in line with our snowman, and tucked Addy up in front of him. They both sent those wide smiles in my direction, and I clicked several shots. I handed him his phone back, and then, without really thinking about it, I dropped down on my knees with them, leaned in, and took a selfie with all of us. It was crooked and blurred with snow, but it had four faces in it, one made of ice and fruit, but they were all smiling.

That moment seemed full of the magic Ryder had accused Mila of having. It made me want to believe in the wishes granted by snowmen. It made me wish for something I knew wasn't mine to have.

I longed to belong to them.

For them to belong to me.

And I really didn't know what to make of it—what to make of this Gia yearning for an unexpected family.

"Come on. Hot chocolate is a must now," Ryder said, standing up and taking Addy's wet-mittened hand in his.

We were halfway across the field when Addy pulled away to turn back and look at the snowman in the middle of the field. "Alone," she said softly, mournfully.

My throat bobbed. Ryder squatted to look her straight in the eye. "Seems like it, doesn't it? But all the snowpeople get together at night. They have a party out by the creek." He pointed out past the pasture. "They use magic to turn snow into candies and rain into punch, and they dance to the beat of the storm. And if they're really lucky, and the moon comes out, it'll cover them in shimmering diamonds. Rosalinda will be all dressed up in jewels, and she'll fill her tummy while having the time of her life with all her snowmen friends."

Addy looked at him like he was a little bit off his rocker, but for me, the story he spun only made those feelings inside me bloom stronger, made me long to always have a person at my side who could turn loneliness and tragedy into joy and enchantment.

When she didn't respond, his throat bobbed, and he tapped her on the nose, saying, "If there's still snow tomorrow, we'll come back and make her a friend. But we're all frozen and need to get warm. I think Rosalinda understands humans are made of weaker stuff. Okay?"

She nodded, and he rose to his full height. Addy tucked one hand back into his and then surprised me by sliding her other one into mine. We finished walking across the field, looking like a single unit. It brought tears to my eyes, and that ache grew wider and more painful inside my chest.

We'd just made it back to the porch steps when Ryder's phone squawked—an ungainly, sharp sound that broke the sweet moment. He yanked it out of his pocket, and his face turned dark. He opened the door for Addy. "Go on inside with Nana for a moment." His voice was calm, but I heard the tension—the spark of fear in it that raised the hair on my neck.

As he shut the door behind her, he showed me his phone with a hand that shook. His voice was a low, animalistic growl as he said, "Someone's breaking into my house."

On the screen, the doorway to his house appeared and a wide-shouldered figure clad in black with his face obscured by a hoodie was fiddling with the handle. As I watched, his gloved hands picked the lock, and in a handful of seconds, he was inside.

I spun around, racing for the Escalade with Ryder on my heels. As I started the vehicle, he jumped in with his phone to his ear, explaining in a torn voice to Maddox what had happened. I wasn't sure I wanted the sheriff's office involved, but I just gritted my teeth and spun out of the driveway with snow flying around the tires as I headed for the gates. After he hung up with Maddox, he called Eva, telling his mother briefly what had happened and asking her to look after Addy.

My heart pounded with anger and frustration at having our beautiful moment torn asunder, but also a teeny bit of hope. If we could catch him, he might lead us to the Lovatos. We might finally find out who their leader was. We might be able to end this for Addy…and Ryder. Waves of mixed emotions flung through me.

"This is why you need cameras inside," I told him.

"I shouldn't need them!" he fired back. I rounded a corner a little too fast, and the car skidded on the icy roads before the four-wheel traction caught. "This is why I should be driving."

I ignored his comment, calling Enrique. "Where are you?"

"I told you, following a lead."

"Someone broke into Ryder's house. He's still there. We're on our way."

Enrique swore. "I'm almost back in town."

The line went dead.

"They either *think* she has something like Ravyn's letter insinuated, or they know she *does*," I said more to myself than Ryder. "It's clear no one is at the house. They risked the alarm and the police showing up for something specific, but we haven't found anything. Just a damn backpack with a few clothes and toiletries."

"And the Switch." Ryder's voice cut through my thoughts, drawing me back.

"Yeah, but it's not like Ravyn hid anything there. It just had a few games and nothing else. I checked. And the coding you'd have to do to hide something else on it would be…" *Fuck*. Ravyn could do it. If she could create a Houdini box like Rory suspected, she could get around the coding on a damn gaming device. I'd meant to go back through it again, but I had let myself get sidetracked…to slip into the cocoon of ranch life and the sweetness of Ryder and his daughter.

"When Addy and I tried to load the games we bought," Ryder said, "It kept saying it was out of room, which didn't seem right because the terabyte drive was huge, and she only had four games on there to begin with. I thought it was broken."

Shit. I'd had the data in my hands for days and missed

it. I'd fucked up, just like Ryder had accused my brother of doing. Except, this was worse than Holden because there was no way he could have known the bracelet Leya had worn wasn't really from her friend. Whereas I knew better than to trust anything in that hotel room—any technology an expert hacker had kept at their disposal, especially after she'd basically told us she'd left something behind.

I gritted my teeth, wanting to pound on the steering wheel and, instead, shoved my foot on the gas pedal.

Ryder's alarm on his phone sounded again.

"He's leaving!"

We were on the bridge when I stomped my foot on the brake. The Escalade slid to a stop with the front end outside the bridge and the back end still under the covered roof.

"What are you doing?" he demanded.

"Blocking his way out," I said, leaping from the car and taking off at a sprint.

Ryder followed me, our heaving breaths the only sound as the snow cushioned our boots. When we reached the house, there was no vehicle in the driveway. Nothing but a gaping front door. I stopped, searching the snow for footprints.

"There," I said, running in the direction of the prints as I pulled my gun from my back. I pointed it toward the trail the burglar had left and headed in that direction with Ryder still on my heels. One set of footprints went toward the house, and the same single set pointed in the opposite direction as he'd left. One perpetrator. After just a few feet, we entered the dark shadows of trees and brush that wound along the hillside on the edge of the Hatley property. I stopped, trying to get my breathing under control so I could listen. A branch cracked behind me as Ryder stepped closer. I put a finger to my lips, tilting my head.

There, down the hill to the right—rustling that had nothing to do with animals tucked away as the snow came down.

I took off again, trying to keep as quiet as possible

while still moving quickly.

"Will he have to cross the creek?" I whispered.

Ryder shook his head. "Not from this angle. He'll hit the emergency fire road first." He pointed the way we were going farther through the trees.

Screw quiet. I had to catch him before he slipped out of our grasp.

I ran as fast as I dared, pushing through the brush, swiping at tree branches, desperately trying not to trip over rocks and downed limbs. The burglar's footsteps were hard to follow here as the snow hadn't made it past the dense blanket of foliage overhead, but we kept going in the direction Ryder had pointed.

When we finally broke out onto the barely visible fire road, there was a dark truck parked several hundred feet away. It roared to life, and I planted my feet, took aim, and let loose. The first shot pinged along the tailgate. Crap. I needed a tire. I aimed again, lowering my sight to the black rubber, and pulled the trigger just as the truck turned a corner. A weak ping let me know I'd hit metal again. Damn it. This is when being a SEAL versus an analyst would have come in handy—where my basic training didn't quite cut it.

I yanked my phone out, calling Enrique. "Where are you?"

"Stuck behind the damn Escalade on the bridge."

"Go back. He escaped in a dark-gray Ford F150. It has a bullet hole in the tailgate and the right rear fender. No license plate." I looked at Ryder. "Where does this come out?"

"State Road Fifty."

I repeated it to Enrique. In the distance, we could hear sirens—Maddox coming in blazing.

Ryder called his brother, repeating what I'd told Enrique.

We headed back the way we'd come, Ryder leading the way this time.

By the time we made it to the house, Enrique and Maddox had both called. There was no sign of the truck, but Maddox put out a *Be On the Look Out,* or *BOLO,* for it.

At the front door, Ryder went to go in, and I yanked him back, tossing him the keys to the Escalade. "I'll clear the house. You move the car."

His jaw worked. The debate clear on his face. I could practically hear his protective instincts clamoring at the idea of letting me go in without him, but I didn't wait to argue about it. I eased into the entryway, peeking around the corner into the kitchen and great room. We'd only seen one person entering the house, but I still had to be sure. I slid with my back to the wall down the hall. Ryder's study was empty. I continued toward the bedrooms. The door to my room was open, but it was empty and looked undisturbed. The bathroom and closet were just as clear.

I moved to Addy's room, and my breath caught. It had been tossed. Clothes and toys were strewn everywhere. The mattress was shoved off, bedding dangling from the sides. Anger filled me followed by a wash of grief. She couldn't find out about this, not after she'd just begun to feel safe enough to sleep in the damn bed. She needed to believe she'd be okay here.

I had to fucking make it the truth. Somehow, someway, that little girl *would* be protected here.

My eyes went to the nightstand where she always left her backpack. She hadn't had it with her today, but it wasn't there either. I did a cursory search of the room and didn't see it. Maybe she'd brought it down to the game room this morning?

I left and headed up the hall to Ryder's room. I hadn't entered his space since I'd been there. And I was surprised to find it full of teak furniture reminiscent of Caribbean hideaways. The vibe echoed in the soft blue-and-tan of the linens. It was soothing and yet somehow masculine at the same time. The windows took up two walls. Gorgeous views of the valley in the west. The room would be full of golden rays and strokes of color in the evenings. I made my way into his enormous bathroom with a sunken tub and a shower with a bench seat and dual shower heads.

Unbidden, images of Ryder's muscled body naked in the shower, an open palm leaning on the beige-and-blue tiles as water sluiced off him, hit me.

I swallowed hard, pushed it aside, and finished clearing the room before forcing myself to leave.

As I was coming down the hall, Ryder showed up with Enrique.

"No one upstairs," I said, heading for the basement.

The men followed me. We searched all the unfinished rooms and found nothing.

I put my gun away, making my way to the entertainment center and cupboards where I'd put the games away the night before. Relief flitted through me when I found Addy's Switch sitting right where I'd left it. I let out a shaky sigh and met Ryder's gaze.

"Her room… It's tossed. They took her backpack. But they didn't get this."

Fury crossed his face as he raced up the stairs. "Don't touch anything yet!" I hollered after him.

"What's on that?" Enrique asked.

"Don't know yet. I checked it out when I first saw it, and it looked like just your normal games. Nothing odd about the menus. Nothing odd about the storage, so I didn't think much about it until Ryder told me on the way over here that it wouldn't load any more games."

"Think Anna was good enough to place information on it?"

"I do."

His eyes turned hooded. We both wanted this. He'd been working on the Lovato case even longer than me. Since before the multi-agency task force had been created, and it had only been the DEA tracking them down. That was when his brother, also an undercover cop in Los Angeles, had been slaughtered and left on the LAPD's doorstep.

I gripped the Switch tightly and jogged back upstairs. We'd just hit the entry when Maddox entered the house with a grim face.

"Nothing?" I asked.

He shook his head. "What happened here?"

Ryder stormed down the hall. "They tossed her room."

"What were they looking for?"

I waved the Switch.

"What's on it?" Maddox repeated the question of the day.

"I'm going to grab my computer from the car and see if I can figure it out," I said. "He had gloves on, but there's a chance we might catch something. A hair. Anything."

"Crime scene techs are on the way," the sheriff said with a curt nod.

The air was full of tension and frustration. The lighthearted sweetness from building the snowman in the field seemed like a dream now. I hated that it had disappeared almost as much as I hated the fact that Ryder's home had been violated, and Addy's beautiful room that had become a haven for her had been wrecked. I clenched my jaw, straightened my back, and slammed my way out of the house toward the Escalade.

A renewed determination filled me. I was going to find something. I'd find something and end this for all of us.

Chapter Twenty-five

Ryder

As I waited for the crime scene techs to finish dusting Addy's room, I called my dad and explained what had happened, letting him know that Maddox was sending several officers their way for protection.

"How is Addy? We left so suddenly… Was she scared?" I asked.

"She asked what happened, and Eva said there'd been a water break. Said it happens sometimes in the snow and ice. They're in the kitchen, making jam."

"I'm sorry she's stuck distracting Addy when she should be—"

"Should be doing exactly this. It helps keep her mind off Phil. Gives her a purpose."

"We'll be as quick as we can, but I want to fix her room after the techs leave. I don't want her to see it this way. If at all possible, try to keep her from knowing Maddox's men are there too."

"You do what you need to there, Ryder. We've got Addy. Everything will be fine here." His words were calm and steady like my father always was. Even when we'd been months away from losing everything, he'd still been cool and composed, positive we'd be okay, even if we had to sell our land. And after Ravyn had stolen from us, and we'd had to pay back the loans without the full income all the cabins would have generated, he'd still been calm while I'd fumed. Sometimes it was reassuring to be surrounded by his serenity, but it could also be frustrating.

"Everything isn't fine, Dad," I snapped.

"No one was hurt. Addy's okay. You're okay. This too shall pass, Son. It'll pass, and you'll have a little piece of you at your side for the rest of your life. That's a blessing. You focus on that, you hear me? You focus on that little girl."

My throat bobbed. "I gotta go."

I hung up and headed toward Addy's room. In mere days, it had become hers in my mind. No longer a guest room. But my daughter's… My daughter.

That singular word turned over and over in my mind.

Maddox was in the hallway, leaning up against the windows opposite the door to her room and watching through the opening as his team worked carefully and methodically inside. I joined him, hands going into my pockets as I pressed my back to the cool glass.

"They're almost done," Maddox said. He was trying to soothe me, but the flames wouldn't die. I was angrier than I'd ever been before. Even angrier than I'd been when Ravyn had left.

"They took her backpack," I seethed. "This is the first time she felt comfortable enough to leave it, and now…"

I wouldn't fucking cry. Not now. Not over a damn backpack.

Maddox bumped my shoulder with his. "You'll get her another one."

"Won't be the same. Just like the jaguar isn't the same. She knows the difference. She knows what she lost. Knows the new one will never really replace the old one."

Maddox's eyes narrowed. "Are you talking about replaceable things, or are you talking about you? Because as far as I can tell, in a handful of days, you've given her a life full of more stability and love than seven years with her mother did. You aren't some lesser replacement."

I hadn't meant that, had I?

The crime scene techs came out of the room with bags and boxes in hand. One of them stopped in front of Maddox. "Not much, Sheriff, but we did get a few hairs and prints. We'll need samples from the folks in residence to rule them out."

"We'll get it to you," Maddox said. "Give me a couple days to gather everyone's prints and DNA."

He was stalling them because we had to keep Addy out of the system as much as possible. But doing so would also limit their ability to find the guy who'd broken into my house and fucked with my daughter's room. My hands felt tied in ways I was coming to despise.

The techs nodded and headed out. I moved into Addy's room and started righting things. Maddox joined me. We worked in silence, cleaning off the dust used to collect latent prints and putting things back where Addy had left them.

Gia appeared in the doorway. "We found something." Her face was excited but cautious, and it made my chest ache. I wasn't sure how much more I could take today—hell, how much more I could take in the next week or month. Hadn't I been handed enough? That old saying about life never giving you more than you could handle was a joke. Life had broken me multiple times.

Gia turned, and I immediately followed her down the hall with my brother on my heels.

She'd set up at the island in the kitchen. Enrique had made himself at home in my house, cupping a mug of coffee while reading something on Gia's laptop screen.

"What is it?" I asked, watching as she slid back onto the stool.

"A bunch of documents and image files. The dates show they started a decade ago. They're encrypted, so I've got Rory working on it, but we think you might be able to help us with the password."

"Me?" I frowned. "I know shit about computers."

"But you knew Ravyn."

I sucked in a breath and felt Maddox go still next to me. I took another deep breath, desperate to calm the pounding in my veins, and stepped closer to Gia and the laptop. Her scent immediately washed over me—fall nights and the comfort of home. There was some strange dichotomy in reading and talking about my ex while standing next to this woman who I ached to make mine. Who'd run after a burglar, gun in hand, ready to defend me and my child.

It was sexy and scary.

It was as enticing as her straddling me while I devoured her body last night.

And just as threatening.

"There's one document that isn't encrypted. I think it confirms the suspicions we talked about last night. About Ravyn being more to the Lovatos than just their tech genius. But more than that, I think she wrote it for you. Can you read it and see if you understand what she means?" Gia asked gently, as if she was afraid of hurting me.

I forced myself to turn my attention from Gia to the computer. Unlike the letter, handwritten in a painfully familiar script, this was typed in a simple font. Impersonal. Merely black-and-white words and a flashing cursor that didn't feel nearly as painful as the letter had. I could remove myself from these generic words that could have been written by anyone. At least, that was what I thought until the story hit me.

> *Once upon a time, a prince saved a demon's daughter from being slaughtered by the demon's son. The prince didn't know he'd saved her, but he still had. He met her, entranced her, and took her to his home, showering her with love and riches she didn't deserve and certainly hadn't earned.*

But the demon, being the evil creation that he was, reached out his inky hands and found her, stealing her from the prince and tying her to his evil deeds by using her love for the prince against her. Ensnared by the demon, she knew she had one chance to save the world before the demon crushed her and turned her to dust.

So, she created a sword that, once wielded, could unravel all the demon's protections and keep the world safe from the demon's dark threats. She waited for the right time to brandish it, working in a fail-safe in case she didn't make it. If she died before she could use it, the person she'd loved with all her soul—the prince—might still be able to use it.

To do so, to free the sword from its bindings and finish the demon forever, all the prince had to do was say her name.

My jaw worked overtime as waves of regret and sadness flew through me. Gia had been right in that this letter made it seem like Rayvn was running from family. From a dark demon and his son. Worse, the story she'd written thrust me right back to lying twined with her on a blanket in the hollow with the trees shading us and the creek bubbling next to us.

The story she'd woven was full of those magical times when we'd been tucked away from the world, and I'd told her the stories my siblings and I had created in our youth. Stories of pirates and fairies and discovering gold. Even back then, she'd been good at spinning our coarse childhood adventures into fairy tales I could almost see, creating new versions. But in all of them, Ravyn had played the villain's daughter, saved by the handsome prince. I'd thought she was trying to speak of the abuse she'd suffered as a kid but wasn't quite ready to talk about, and I'd loved her more for having survived it. For being there, strong and beautiful, facing the world with me. Now, it just added another wound to my already beat-up soul, knowing she didn't feel safe enough to tell me the truth.

Gia raised a brow. "This is the only file that isn't encrypted, Ryder. She wanted you to see this. She left you a clue to unlock it."

"Except, I have no idea what she means," I said right as Enrique said, "I don't think you should get your hopes up. It doesn't prove she's part of the Lovatos or that Hatley has the key. Hell, this could just be some damn fairy tale she wrote for her kid."

"Addy," I groused. "Her name is Addy."

Enrique's eyes met mine across the counter, a standoff that neither of us broke until Gia brought me back to her with a gentle hand on my shoulder.

"No one knew Ravyn as well as you, Ryder. What do you think? Is it a coded message? Or is it a fairy tale?"

Before she'd left, I thought I knew her as well as I knew myself, even with the secrets of her childhood. I'd thought her past didn't matter because I could see the person she truly was. The Ravyn I'd once believed in would have wanted to help others. She would have wanted to save the world if she could. But when she'd left, taking what was ours with her, I thought I'd been duped.

Knowing now that she'd been scared and on the run, it shifted my vision of her again, blending it into some combined version of my rose-colored-glasses version of her and the reality where she was a woman fearing for her life.

"Say her name," Gia said softly.

I swallowed, and it was my brother who spoke instead of me. "Maybe it's just Ravyn, as that wasn't her real name but the one we knew her as," Maddox suggested.

Gia scoffed. "I doubt it's as simple as Ravyn."

But she still brought up one of the files and typed Ravyn's name into the password box. When it was rejected, she tried typing in different iterations, with capitals and without them, spelling it in different ways. Nothing worked.

Gia looked at me with that cautious look back in her eyes. "Did you have a nickname for her?"

After she asked the question, I realized her caution was all for me, because she didn't want to hurt me. Didn't want memories of Ravyn to hurt me. Gia cared enough to look out for me. What did that say? What did I want it to say? Especially when thinking of Ravyn's nickname shoved me back to times tangled with her in bed in the apartment above the barn where I'd lived when we'd first met.

She'd laughed at the nickname I'd tried out before I'd ever tried to make it our child's name, saying, *I could never be Arwen, Ryder. She's an elf full of light, and I'm full of dark. I'm much more likely to be a soldier, wielding a sword than a spell. If I were anyone from that ridiculous trilogy, I'd be Eowyn, bringing the Witch-King down.*

I'd insisted she wasn't dark, that she was my light. But when she'd found out she was pregnant, she'd brought it up again. She'd told me the Witch-King's darkness was in her, had infected her, and that she wasn't sure she could be a good mother because of it. I'd promised her we'd fight the darkness together. As a family. It had been one of the last promises I'd made to her, and it hadn't been until after she'd left that I'd realized she hadn't promised me back.

A hand landed on my shoulder, and I turned my head to meet my brother's concerned gaze. "Ry?"

I scrubbed my face. "Try My Lady Eowyn of Rohan."

Silence settled over the room. My brother covered his mouth, Enrique coughed into the coffee cup, and Gia's eyes went wide.

"Fuck you all. You think I wanted to say that out loud? Just try it," I bit out.

Gia's lips twisted up as her fingers flew over the keys.

The screen came back, red letters denying access. "Let me try a few different versions."

I moved away from her, opened the fridge, and took out

a beer. I needed something stronger. Whiskey. A whole bottle of it. I wanted to head over to McFlannigan's, sit on the corner stool I considered mine, and get so drunk I fell off the damn thing. But those days were now behind me. I couldn't just drown my memories and regrets in alcohol—not if I wanted to be there for Addy. So, instead of giving in to that yearning, I twisted the cap off the damn beer and took a swig.

"Anyone want one?"

Enrique shook his head. "Not while I'm on duty."

Maddox muttered, "I'm good."

Gia didn't respond at all. Did she not like beer? Was tequila or whiskey her drink of choice? She didn't seem like a wine snob, but I knew even less about her than I had about Ravyn. And yet, I was drawn to this spitfire by a lure stronger than even the immediate, undeniable one I'd felt toward my ex the moment she'd walked into the ranch office for an interview.

Hadn't I learned the hard way that when people told you they had darkness following them and they didn't know how to stay, you needed to listen? Gia definitely had secrets—things she did for her job that she'd never be able to tell anyone. And she didn't stay anywhere for long. She flitted around the globe for her work. So, any notion that might be lingering at the back of my mind about making her mine was ludicrous.

I'd downed half the beer by the time Gia gave a sigh of frustration and pushed the computer away. "Nothing. But I'm not giving up. I'll give all of this to Rory and see what she can do with it."

Enrique shoved himself away from the counter. "I'll take the first watch." He glanced at my brother and asked, "Your team has the property perimeter?"

Maddox looked exhausted. "We're spread pretty thin, but I've called over to Sheriff Scully in the next county to see if he can spare us some bodies."

Enrique and Gia shared a look before the DEA agent

said, "If we need outside help, we should bring in more of the task force rather than explain the situation to people we haven't vetted."

Something about that man raised my hackles. "Where were you today?"

Enrique raised a brow. "I don't report to you."

And without another word, he walked out, leaving a vibe in the air I couldn't quite place.

Maddox looked over at me. "I'm heading back to make sure everything from Addy's room gets processed. They want samples of DNA and fingerprints so they can rule out anyone in the family. I'll need yours, Gia. I'll get Barry to keep it off the books, but he can use the sample of Addy's they already have."

"Excuse me?" Gia hissed out. "No one is supposed to have Addy's DNA. I didn't even let the Colorado PD run it in the middle of a murder investigation."

Maddox tossed me a chagrinned look that was decidedly like Mila's when she'd ratted me out for feeding her ice cream for breakfast. "I'll run Mila out to the ranch so she can keep Addy preoccupied until you're ready for her here. Tell me when, and I'll drop her off."

Then, he practically ran out the door, leaving me with one pissed-off NSA analyst.

Her eyes sparked, and it ignited the flame in me that had been simmering all day, waiting for the right time to burst. It washed over me as if it was cleansing me, taking every remaining thought of Ravyn and burning it away. Nothing of my ex existed. Instead, I hungered for another taste of Gia. I wanted to experience again the sounds she'd made while I'd had my tongue inside her mouth. It hadn't been memories of Ravyn that had tormented me all day. It had been Gia.

I closed the distance between us, and she didn't back up. Instead, she raised her chin. All challenge. All defiance. All control I wanted to destroy with my hands and lips, by pummeling inside her until she broke apart in ecstasy.

Chapter Twenty-six

Gia

HELL OF A MAN
Performed by Ella Langley

Annoyance rippled through me as I narrowed my gaze at Ryder, trying to ignore the way his eyes dilated and his warm breath coasted over me. He stood so close that I'd barely need to move to kiss him. Those thoughts only amped up my irritation. "You had her tested? I told you we couldn't afford for her to be in the system."

"Maddox's guy did it for us without entering it anywhere. No names."

"Yeah, well, what if he's working for the Lovatos?"

"He doesn't even know who was being tested. And besides, he isn't."

My temper flared. "You can doubt Enrique, but I can't doubt your guy? I know literally shit about this lab rat. How do you know he isn't flagged in our system as a known cartel associate? You don't get to make these kinds of decisions about my case without me."

"Your case!" His hands went to either side of me on the counter, chest leaning into my space even more. "Your case just happens to center around my daughter. A person. An actual human being, not just some fucking code in a computer, or evidence to log, or a piece of leverage to use."

"Do you actually believe I'd put her at risk to solve

this?" I demanded, hurt cresting deep inside me.

"I think you're very good at your job, and that means lying and conniving and pushing until you get what you want."

His face dropped even closer to mine until our lips were almost touching. My skin broke out in goosebumps, gaze dropping to his mouth. It was set in a firm line I knew to be deceptively smooth when pressed against mine.

I swallowed hard, pressing past the attraction to keep my annoyance at the forefront as I tossed back, "I know you mean that as an insult, but screw you. I *am* good at my job. The fact I know where to push and pull is a good thing. But I also try to be as honest as possible because it's hard to keep your lies straight otherwise. So don't take your trust issues out on me—the one person trying to figure this out for you. For all of us. Do I want to chop off the head of the snake and rid our country of one more ugly cartel? Damn straight. I'll be proud as hell when we do, but I would never jeopardize Addy to get it done."

I hated that my voice cracked at the end of my little tirade.

His hands moved from the counter, gripped my waist, and tugged me into his chest just as his mouth landed on mine. This kiss was like our first one. Brutal and angry and frustrated. Seeking retribution. I wasn't sure if it was directed at me or Ravyn or life in general. But it didn't matter. My body ignited. I wrapped my arms around his neck, angled my mouth to accept the onslaught of his, and got lost in waves of longing.

The intensity of what I felt, locked in this fierce embrace, was nothing I'd ever felt before, and somehow, instinctively, I knew I'd never feel it again. This man, who appeared gruff and callous and severe on the outside, was burning up with love and regrets and sorrow on the inside.

I wanted to take it all away.

I wanted to toss aside the sorrow and heartache until there was none left so this beautiful, gruff man could love and trust again.

Those thoughts scared me, shooting waves of unease through my veins, and yet I didn't break the kiss. It was Ryder who stepped back, fisting his hands on his hips, staring at my deliciously bruised mouth.

"What are you doing to me?" he asked, as if I was the one bewitching him rather than the other way around.

"You act like I'm the one who kissed you. You act like I'm the one weaving a spell around you when you're the one tossing all your breathtaking pieces at me, making it impossible to keep my barriers up. To keep my focus."

He looked startled by my words, and I knew I should stop, knew I should retreat and take back what I'd said or at least prevent myself from digging in further. Instead, the words continued to slip out of me. "I'm entranced by the beauty you craft so carefully for others. The gentleness with which you treat those you love. The fierce way you look after your family."

My voice sounded breathless and tortured instead of calm and sure, and I still didn't stop.

"I find myself wanting to be part of the group you shield and protect and care for, and I don't know what to do with that. I've never wanted to belong to anyone…" I finally was able to jam my mouth shut, looking down and away from those blue eyes that hypnotized me. I could see why Ravyn made up fairy tales about this man. He was worthy of fairy tales.

But did I really want to belong to him? To this life? On a ranch in Tennessee?

I shook my head. No. It would mean giving up everything I'd worked too damn hard for. No way I'd just walk away from it all for a man. No way I'd walk away from the life I'd earned at the cost of my own heartbreaks.

I tried to slide past him, but he caught me with one large hand gripping my elbow. It was a light hold. One I could have easily broken but didn't. Instead, I found my eyes meeting his again. The emotions that swam in them slashed into me, securing the lure he'd thrown out, snagging my heart in a way that would make it nearly impossible to break free.

"She was my soulmate. That was what I thought. But now…" He trailed off, and the intensity of his gaze as it bore into me unraveled me further, leaving me exposed. Raw. Scared. "How could she be the one for me when I didn't even really know her? When what I feel touching you seems a thousand times more."

His words dug deeper into me, making it harder to breathe. This man, the epitome of masculinity, talking about soulmates and true love and weaving his own fairy tales, grabbed my heart and wouldn't let go.

"I've never believed in soulmates and one true love," I whispered.

"Not even when you were a little girl?" he asked as his thumb rubbed along my arm.

"I wanted to play spies with my brother and was bored with the Disney princess movies. And when I did watch them, I loved the battles and mysteries more than the kisses. When I was a teenager, we moved three times while I was in high school. I barely made friends, let alone boyfriends. The closest I got was this guy in college…" I trailed off. I hadn't talked about Kieran with anyone in more years than I could remember.

"What happened?" he asked. My first instinct was to toss it aside as I always did, but looking into those intense eyes, I knew he'd see through it if I did. He was good at seeing between my half-truths. Not even my parents had known how much Kieran had hurt me.

"I thought we were perfect for each other." I rarely let myself think of those days and nights in Kieran's tiny apartment in Philly, surrounded by computers, getting lost in each other's skin after the high of an exhilarating hack. "We were two computer nerds working our way through college together in the tech repair department of the local box store. What I thought was us having fun, hacking and coding and exploring our limits in multiple ways, was really Kieran embezzling money and setting me up for the fall."

Ryder's face turned dark, and he tucked a strand of my hair that had escaped behind my ear. His touch burned, sending chills over my spine in the very best kind of way. "He pointed the finger at you?"

"I caught on to it before he could get that far. Turned him over to the authorities instead."

"What did Kieran say?"

I swallowed, looking away, not wanting to retreat to those memories. "I didn't give him the chance to say anything. It wouldn't have mattered. He'd taken everything I thought we had and tossed it away by using my signature code to steal—the exact opposite of what he knew I wanted for my life. I double majored in law enforcement and computer science. I wanted truth and justice, not virtual robbery."

I never saw him again after the night I'd stumbled onto what he was doing. He'd been naked and asleep behind me when I'd found the hidden folders on his computer. I thought it was a test. A game. We often devised these little traps for each other. What I'd seen had turned my insides to ice.

Ryder bumped my chin up with a knuckle, forcing me to meet his gaze again, and the compassion and understanding I saw there nearly made me weep. Except, it wasn't for the woman I was now, but for the college girl who'd thought she'd found someone who wouldn't disappear just because her family moved.

Ryder's hand had settled on the curve of my collarbone, gently stroking as he said, "For years, I wished I'd been able to say a few words to Ravyn after she left. But I bet getting revenge must have felt just as good."

"Instead of destroying me and my reputation as he'd tried to do, he actually helped build it. What I'd done to trace him and turn him in got flagged somewhere in the NSA's systems, and they came knocking. I've spent nearly six years doing what I'd always wanted to do."

"And protecting your heart against anyone else who has come along," he said softly.

I shrugged. "Even if I believed in true love, not many people get the fairy tale."

"That's where I went wrong with Ravyn," he said, and it was the first time I'd heard her name from his lips without an echo of pain behind it.

"What do you mean?"

"Believing love was a fairy tale. Just because someone is your soulmate doesn't mean it'll magically work if you don't put in the effort. My parents love each other more than any couple I know, but even they have to work at it. They get angry. The baggage of their childhoods rears its head and strikes. The beauty of their relationship isn't in the easy times. It's in the hard ones. In the sacrifices they made to keep each other. It's in the times they choose to stay when it would be easier to walk out the door. Ravyn may have stayed at the first hurdle we faced—when she got pregnant—but she ran when her past came knocking. She didn't even give me a chance to go with her. To face it together."

The fact that he might have gone with her stunned me. That he would have given up his life on the ranch and the love of his family to be at her side was slightly appalling because I couldn't imagine Ryder anywhere else.

My pulse skittered as the reality of his words rolled through me. I'd thought my family didn't know how to stay. That we'd drifted like nomads. And we had, but my parents had done that drifting together. My mom could have thrown in the towel, refused to move any of the number of times we'd had to pull up stakes. Instead, she'd followed the person she loved every time. Because she loved my dad. Because she believed in the life they lived together.

My brother had walked away from the Secret Service to be with Leya, trailing her and her band around the globe. He'd chosen to stay…it just wasn't in a physical location. He'd chosen to stay with her, wherever that was.

As I looked at Ryder, with his dark hair flopping over his brow and his blue gaze whispering of promises I might have in the future if I let us continue down this path, I suddenly understood Ravyn. I understood her with a clarity I would never have gained without the feelings I had for him curling through me. Seeing Ryder with his family and his daughter, seeing the pride with which he managed the ranch, and seeing the home he'd designed and built out of love, there was no way I'd want him to give any of it up. I certainly wouldn't want him to give it up to chase after me as I followed my career, darting around in the darkness with me playing spy. He may not realize it, but taking him from this place would destroy him. The absence of his family, the absence of a purpose, would eat away at his insides until he was no longer the brilliant, generous man I saw before me.

It would be too great of a sacrifice. One not even love could overcome.

Ravyn had known it and ran.

Originally, I'd thought she was selfish, but maybe it had been her ultimate sacrifice.

As much as I was tempted by him, by the beauty of him, I couldn't reach out and take it. Not because it would destroy me—that seemed almost worth risking—but because it would destroy him, and that I couldn't allow.

I swallowed hard, pulled myself away from him, breaking the little thrall he'd surrounded me in. I stepped around the island, determined to put more than physical distance between us. Determined to pretend the intimacy of our conversation had never existed.

I forced my voice to be cold and calm as I said, "I need the guy's name who's running the DNA test."

Then, I walked out of the kitchen before I lost my resolve, dragged him to me, and finished what he'd started.

Chapter Twenty-seven

Emiliano

COLD BLOODED LOVE
Performed by The Trishas

I traced my finger over the NL on the black backpack. Nostalgia I didn't want and despised welled through me before I shoved it away. I flicked open my father's knife and slashed through the letters. Slashed through the bag repeatedly until there was nothing left but long threads of black canvas and plastic zippers. I told myself I wasn't angry. That I wasn't reacting in the heat of the moment but because I wanted to see if she was hiding something.

When all that was left were pieces, and the only thing I'd found was a ring, I shoved the remnants aside. I twirled the jewelry between my fingers. Art Deco style from the 1930s with a box-cut diamond and sidesteps off to each side, creating an elongated geometric shape the period had favored. Nothing I would have expected Natalia to choose. Maybe she'd stolen it, planning to sell it for money. Except, I'd given her plenty of money, and she had access to even more.

I palmed the ring and turned slowly to face Julio.

"Ruiz missed something," I growled.

"He said everything else in the little girl's bedroom was new. No way it came from Natalia."

"Then perhaps the child herself has the key in here," I said tapping my forehead. "Bring her to me."

Julio shifted his feet ever so slightly, the merest of movements, but I still caught it.

"Do you have a problem with that?" I demanded.

"She's covered with family, the sheriff's department, and the task force. Maybe we should wait until things cool off a little. You've gone this long without exposing yourself. This is too big of a risk. None of them are going to just let the child disappear."

Anger roared through me. Impatience. The pieces of my father I couldn't shake that were embedded in my DNA. The pieces I'd sworn I'd overcome. I'd sworn whenever I struck out, it would not be in anger like him. I'd always be in control. I'd strike with a purpose. For retribution and revenge. To take what was mine.

"You're positive the woman is with the task force?"

"Yes. She was in the hotel room in Colorado. She was the one who found the girl."

Gia Kent was beautiful, and Hatley had claimed her. I'd seen it in the way he'd reacted to my flirting. The way he'd entered her space to mark it, like a dog peeing on a tree. Coarse and unrefined.

It would give me great pleasure to take her from him as he'd taken Natalia from me.

I'd take her and the child.

They'd come to the gala because she'd see it as a way into my lair. To snoop and sneak and try to undo me.

She believed she had the upper hand. That she was the hunter.

That excited me, stirred me, and made me hunger for more than just revenge.

I'd let her come. I'd let her stalk.

And then I'd show them all the true meaning of predator and prey.

Chapter Twenty-eight

Ryder

LOVE THE LONELY OUT OF YOU
Performed by Brothers Osborne

After giving me a glimpse of the true woman behind the mask, Gia had nearly run from the kitchen, and I'd let her, even though I'd yearned for her to stay. I wondered how many people even knew she'd tried to give her heart to someone. That she'd had it batted away with even more callousness than Ravyn had treated mine. Because after reading Ravyn's letters, I at least knew that she hadn't set out to con me as I'd thought for years.

What Gia had experienced had been colder—both Kieran's actions and hers in return.

I didn't hold it against her. I would have handed Ravyn over to the authorities without any compunction if I'd gotten my hands on her back then.

But now, the parallels and the differences between Gia's life and mine had me stumbling around for footing.

So, instead of following Gia from the kitchen and showing her just how much a person could be loved, I stepped back. I concentrated on my daughter.

Maddox dropped Addy at home just before dinner, and she seemed quiet and subdued. A step back from the openness of this afternoon when we'd played in the snow. I did my best to tease her out of it as I cooked burgers and made a salad. Gia and Enrique ate with us and then went back to work, him on duty, Gia doing whatever it was she did, tucked away in the guest room, typing away on that computer of hers. Addy and I watched television before I tucked her into bed.

On entering her room, Addy honed in on the bedside table where she'd left her backpack. When she saw it was missing, I was surprised she didn't ask about it, and even though it tugged at my heart, I followed her lead because I didn't want to upset her, because I was just the coward Sadie had teased me of being days ago.

As Addy climbed into bed, I felt the need to distract her from the bag's disappearance, so I asked if I could read one of her books to her. She hesitated and then nodded. I leaned up against the headboard next to her, reading without using the voices Maddox was so good at, but at least it was me, sitting next to my daughter and sharing this time together.

After I closed the book, full of dragons who were brave enough to save the universe, I knew I had to man up and tell her the backpack was gone. I met her gaze and told her it had been wrecked in the water break, which was the excuse my parents had given for why I'd left the ranch so suddenly.

"I'll get you a new one. What color would you like?"

She stared for a moment, as if she knew I was lying. She looked sad in a way I hated, and a tear escaped her eyes that she brushed away. Finally, she just shrugged. What did it feel like to lose everything you knew and loved. Other than the damn Switch that was now evidence and a handful of clothes, Addy had nothing left from before. She'd been forced out of her cocoon into a new life.

"If you ever want to talk…" I spoke past that semi-permanent lump in my throat. "About your mom, or your old life, or just anything…you know you can, right? I may not always have answers or be able to soften the blow of your loss, but I can listen. I can be here for you."

More tears rolled down her cheeks, and suddenly, she was crawling into my lap and clinging to me. I hugged her tight, ran a hand over her back, and tried to let the unexpected and overwhelming love I felt for her encompass both of us.

Eventually, she stopped crying, and when her breathing grew even again, I realized she'd fallen asleep. I sat there for a long time, lost in the feel of having her with me. My daughter was alive. She was here. I may have lost the first seven years of her life, but I had the entirety of our future to look forward to. I'd love on her. I'd make sure she knew she was wanted and adored and cherished.

When my neck started to kink, I was forced to move. I lifted her and tucked her in, drawing the covers up close to her chin. She never even opened her eyes, and knowing she'd felt safe enough to fall asleep on me filled me with more pride than I'd ever had before. More than turning the ranch around.

Addy was the most incredible little person I'd ever met. So damn brave.

I kissed her forehead and left the room with a heart brimming with mixed emotions.

The lights were off in most of the house, allowing me to easily see the glow coming from under Gia's door, announcing she was still awake. I wanted to knock and ask how she was. I wanted to pick her up, carry her down the hall to my room, and give us both a reprieve we desperately needed.

Instead, I turned and went to my room alone, sliding into a bed where the taste of Gia's lips followed me into my dreams.

♫ ♫ ♫

For the next three days, our life slipped into a routine. We drove to the ranch in the mornings, with a team of officers unobtrusively following us. After the stress of the break-in and our suspicions about Addy's family ties to the Lovatos, the only reason I could leave her doing schoolwork with Rianne at the farmhouse was because I knew we had people watching over them. And even then, I checked in on them more than was probably healthy.

When Gia wasn't pulling guard duty, she worked on her computer in the ranch office, scouring the internet for information on Ravyn and the cartel. Enrique and some of my brother's deputies picked up the rest of the protective detail, hovering along the perimeters, keeping watch while I worked with Dad, Shawn, and Ramon on the two cabins.

Unaware of the extra guards, Addy seemed to be coming out of her shell a little more each day with our set routine. She opened up the most when Mila was around, but she'd talk in full sentences to me at times, and she slept in her bed and not on the floor or a shelf. And even though I'd replaced her backpack with a bright-purple one, she hadn't loaded it up with clothes and wasn't bringing it with her as if she was going to need to run at any second.

Every night, she played games with Gia and me. Laughing more, even teaming up with Gia to make sure I lost, getting a kick out of the pretend tantrum I'd throw when I did. I finally got a glimpse of the humor Ravyn had spoken about in her letter. I got to see her devotion to the woman who'd pulled her out from under a bed as well, because if I ever tried to pick on Gia during the games, Addy wouldn't let me.

When we walked next to each other, Addy would often tuck her hand in mine, and she hugged me of her own volition every night at bedtime since the backpack disappeared. In those moments, when Addy chose to reach out to me, I felt like I was the smartest, bravest, most loved man on earth. The fact that she trusted me with her words and affection filled spots in my soul I'd never thought would heal. Spots I thought would always be a gaping wound.

And she wasn't the only one healing me.

Every night, after Addy was tucked into bed, Gia and I found each other, all in the pretense of staying updated on the case. Except, there wasn't much progress to report. Gia said the task force was frustrated with their inability to break Ravyn's encryption on the data from the Switch, and they had no clues about the guy who'd broken into my house. The dead guy who they thought killed Ravyn had been seen by Enrique's gang contacts, talking to a big burly Mexican in Lexington before he'd wound up dead. Enrique was trying to chase that person down, but without driving back and forth five hours round trip to Kentucky, it was hard to work his contacts while staying with us in Willow Creek.

So, while we always started our evening talks with an update about the Lovatos, the truth was we would have sought each other out anyway. We were drawn to one another. Electrical charges seeking an outlet. I hadn't kissed her since our argument over the DNA test, which meant those charges were growing, festering to an unhealthy level that would end up exploding at the worst moment.

Every night, after talk of the Lovatos wound down, we often shared personal things. Talk about our families and our past. We were both careful never to talk about the future. It was too uncertain.

I learned Gia spoke three languages and had been in more countries than I'd been in states. I learned how her love of spy movies and books like James Bond, Jason Bourne, and Jack Ryan had driven her into her career, and how she'd been determined that there'd be more women filling those roles.

For every truth she gave me, for every window she opened up into her soul, I reciprocated by doing the same. I told her about my time at the University of Knoxville, and even showed her some of my early architectural drawings I kept in an overflowing portfolio. But it wasn't the buildings that caught her eye. Early in my life, I'd had a love of the fantastical and had drawn scenes from some of the stories my siblings and I had made up about the hollow by the creek being a haven for pirates and fairies. Spurred by the smooth tales Ravyn had crafted from those stories, I'd drawn more. It was those sketches that Gia spent the most time scrutinizing, knowing they gave her more insight into me than the drawings of buildings ever could.

They showed my belief in true love. My belief in fairy tales no grown man should rightly claim.

Tucked in where I'd forgotten them were a few black-and-white drawings of Ravyn. Gia had stared at them for a long time before asking if she could send one to Rory. She thought it might help refine the reconstructed picture Rory had created. I told her she could do whatever she wanted with the sketches, not because I wanted them gone like I would have wanted weeks…hell, days ago…but because I wanted to do anything I could to end the storm waiting in the distance for us.

One night, when we were sitting side by side, without touching, but still sharing little intimacies of our lives, her phone buzzed. Her brother's name flew across the lock screen before she silenced it.

"Your family really doesn't know you do this for a living?" I asked.

"My father suspects I'm undercover, and he might have used his position as Vice Chief of the National Guard to ferret out where I work, but my mom and brother know nothing."

"You said it was so they wouldn't worry. Is that truly the only reason?"

She shifted, uncomfortable with the question. We both knew I had no right to ask, no right to delve into the depths of her mind, but I needed to know why she lied to those she loved most. Needed almost desperately to understand it so I could believe she wouldn't do the same to me.

"It's the easiest answer I can give. Because I really don't want them to worry. Mom spent so much of her life stressed about Dad being in the line of duty first in the Army, then in the Secret Service, and finally with the National Guard. I saw it eat at her soul a bit. And Holden was single-minded in his determination to join the Secret Service from the time the Twin Towers fell, and he watched our dad protecting President Bush on TV. Holden's job added worry to her shoulders, and I guess I told myself she didn't need me giving her even more."

"What's the real answer, darlin'?"

She rolled her eyes at the endearment and then sat there for a moment, looking inward, as if trying to find the answer deep inside her. And that, if nothing else, made me believe she wasn't lying anymore. "The truth is, I liked that this aspect of my life was completely mine. I didn't have my brilliant, strategist of a father or my perfect, protective brother looking over my shoulder, telling me how to do it better. I don't know…" She trailed off before picking her thoughts back up a second later. "I liked the super-spy vibe of it. The dual life. One in the light, and one in the dark. It was like living in a James Bond movie. It was exciting."

I picked up on the past tense even if she didn't, and I pushed on it, not quite daring to hope that maybe her time here, her time with me was changing how she felt. "Was exciting? It's not anymore?"

Her gaze settled on my lips for a few heartbeats before journeying back to meet my eyes. "The movie always ends, you know? When it's over—when my career is really over—I'm afraid I'll feel empty inside. I'll be nothing but a shell with nothing to show for my years of service but a pile of memories I can't share because they're all deemed top secret."

The idea of Gia feeling empty—of the bright, fiery woman in front of me being an empty shell—made me want to prove to her just how full her life could be.

Except, what exactly did I think that life would look like?

No matter how she was talking to my soul and making me wonder if I could, in fact, give my heart to another woman, this wasn't Gia's world. She was a fish out of water. And if she stayed here, she'd be gasping for breath before too long. There'd be no evil villain for her to catch once the Lovatos were gone.

So, no matter how much I wanted to touch her, embed myself in her, make her mine, I couldn't do it. She couldn't stay, and I couldn't trail after her as I might have if Ravyn had asked me to go with her. Back then, I would have given up everything to keep her and my baby. I would have even given up the ranch and my family. But nothing was that simple anymore. Things like Phil's death proved how unexpectedly life could change, and I didn't want to miss the years my parents had left. Even more, I wanted Addy to grow up here, surrounded by love and stability, not tagging along after some secret agent like she'd been forced to tag after Ravyn. I didn't want her learning to hide and run when she could spread her wings, knowing she had a safe spot to land.

My little girl was now my number one responsibility.

The possibility of having something with Gia couldn't trump that. Even if it meant once again retreating into the life of bachelorhood Sadie had tried to taunt me out of.

So, every night after we talked, I left Gia at her bedroom door without attempting to kiss her again, without relieving the growing tension that zapped through us. And every morning, when she appeared in my kitchen, ready for the day, sometimes beating me there and starting breakfast, I reminded myself of what she'd said. These moments were just a few scenes in the movie of Gia's super-spy life, and when it ended, Addy and I would be left to fill the holes her absence created.

♫ ♫ ♫

On Friday morning, I dressed in the only dark suit I owned, wondering why the hell I was putting it on for Phil. He'd spent his life in jeans at the bar. He wouldn't expect suits from us. He'd probably be laughing his ass off from the other side. But out of respect for Mama and the family, I put it on.

When I walked out into the kitchen and found Gia there with a coffee already poured and pushed across the counter at me, I had to hold myself back, as I had every morning, from kissing her hello. I'd much rather spend the next few hours lost in the scent and feel of her, figuring out what made her gasp and squirm and scream, than attending Phil's funeral.

"Thanks," I said, picking up the coffee while she took me in from head to toe.

"Is that Armani?" she asked.

I shrugged. It was, but admitting I knew that was more than I was willing to give this morning.

"You clean up pretty good, cowboy," her voice dipped, and the sensuality in that nickname made my pulse quicken and my dick respond.

"Just because we live in a tiny town in Tennessee doesn't mean we're clueless."

Her gaze landed on my mouth. "Definitely not clueless."

The air burned between us for several seconds, tempting me, calling to me. I'd clean up for her anytime she wanted if she'd put action behind those words.

"You'll catch me cleaned up even more tomorrow. I rented a tux. Do you have a dress?"

Her brows furrowed. "Damn. The gala? I completely forgot about it."

Images of Gia in a sexy dress that clung to her lean curves filled me, making my body react even more. I wanted to pull her against me, slow dance with her, run my hands along her hips, and press myself into her.

Days and nights of wanting her had pushed me to my limits.

While I was thinking of her in a dress and what slowly removing her from it would be like, Gia was obviously not. Instead, her face held a faraway look I'd come to acquaint with her puzzling out the mystery of the cartel and her job.

"What are you thinking?" I asked.

"Anna's assassin died in Lexington, Laredo's place is in Kentucky, and your place was broken into after he showed up at the ranch."

I shook my head, seeing where she was going. "Jaime is your typical millionaire. Egotistical and arrogant, but he's not running a cartel from his place outside Corbin."

"He have a sister?"

"None that he ever mentioned."

While Ravyn and Jaime shared some resemblance, it could easily be accounted for by their similar heritage. They both had dark hair, dark eyes, and warm skin, but Ravyn had been small and curvy with fairylike features, and Jaime was tall and lean with a long rectangular face.

I glanced at the clock on the microwave, knowing I needed to leave, but I was reluctant to do so. Not just because I didn't really like funerals, but because I wanted to stay here, talking with Gia. I wanted to spend another day with her and my daughter, and now I was walking out the door without either of them.

We'd agreed taking Addy to the funeral wasn't a possibility, not only because we couldn't tell the town about her yet but because we weren't sure how she'd react to seeing the coffin buried. She hadn't talked about her mother or the life they'd led. And other than when she'd helped Gia with a sketch of the assassin, Addy hadn't mentioned the day she'd been killed again.

Just like the charge building between Gia and me, I knew that Addy's emotions were building too. That holding them in for too long wasn't good. That she'd need help. Someone with a degree and the experience to guide her through what she'd witnessed. But until we could ensure she was safe, I couldn't take her to just anyone.

If this thing with the Lovatos went on too long, I'd make sure Gia found an NSA-approved therapist for her. I'd have to do something.

But nothing could be done about it today, so as much as I hated it, I was leaving Addy with Gia and Enrique while I attended the funeral and celebration of Phil's life. I wouldn't be far, just a few miles, and yet it felt like too much. It felt wrong when I hadn't gone anywhere without them in the last week.

As if she read my worry, Gia closed the distance between us, squeezing my shoulder. "She'll be fine, Ryder.

We'll read some of the books Rianne brought her and play some games. You'll be home before dinner. If you had a regular job and she was at school, it would be the same."

Gia was right, and yet something in me still resisted.

I almost leaned in and kissed her cheek. I almost pulled her to me and inhaled the scent that seemed to calm me and wind me up all at the same time. Instead, I grabbed my hat and my keys and headed out the door without saying good morning to my daughter. Because if I stayed even a moment longer, I was pretty sure I wouldn't be able to leave without dragging them with me. And that would be selfish. That would be for me and not them.

Unlike the generations of Hatleys who were buried in a family cemetery on Hatley land, the McFlannigans were buried in the graveyard of a stone church on the edge of town. My family was already there when I drove up.

My sisters and Mama were in simple but stylish black dresses. Gemma had flown in late last night, and I hadn't had a chance to see her yet. Her long blond hair stood out from Mama's and Sadie's dark heads. Gemma and Maddox had inherited their hair coloring from Grandma Hatley, but Gemma was the only one of us who'd gotten Granny's hazel eyes. The rest of us had a shade of blue like our parents. My sister looked thinner than normal, and while her expression was sad for Phil, I suspected it also had to do with her recent heartbreak. As I squeezed her in a tight hug that she returned, Dad and Maddox came out of the church in dark suits that matched my own.

We stood on the steps, greeting what felt like the entire town, before leading the crowd inside where they squeezed into the pews. The church filled until there was standing room only, and even that was packed tight. Uncle Phil may have raised a few hackles, but he'd also been an icon in our community, and Willow Creek had come out to say goodbye to one of their own.

The last McFlannigan.

That hit me so hard in the chest I had to fight back tears.

Carrying Phil's coffin from the church to the graveside with his bartender Ted, my dad, my brother, and the mayor, choked me up again. It was hard to imagine Phil being gone. Hard to imagine the bar without him.

The journey from the cemetery to McFlannigan's was made on foot. A solemn parade where Mama's sniffles and Sadie's quiet sobs seemed to echo through the cobblestones. All the stores and restaurants along Main Street were closed this morning as everyone paid their respects to our uncle.

Sadie had taken care of the arrangements for the party at the bar. She'd been pulling her weight with the funeral all along while my mind had been wrapped up in Addy and Gia. I needed to thank my baby sister for stepping up, for being the one Mama could count on most these days.

Even though it was barely eleven by the time we all crowded into McFlannigan's, the booze was already flowing. Phil would have enjoyed that. Just like he would have gotten a kick out of the fact that there were so many bodies in the room that even the fire marshal, who he'd long since paid off, was looking at the numbers dubiously.

Over the next couple hours, people raised their glasses repeatedly, "To Phil!" as story after story was told that made us all laugh and swear. I could just imagine Uncle Phil's pleased, snarky grin at the talk. He'd be proud as hell that he'd left his mark on the town, one way or another.

As the crowd started to thin, Mama corralled my siblings and me into a table at the back. She squeezed Sadie's hand and said, "Now that we're all here together, we wanted to give you an update on Phil's will."

My sister shifted uncomfortably, a look of guilt spreading over her face, and all my senses went on alert.

"Phil was concerned about the bar's legacy, but he also knew most of you had already built careers and lives that wouldn't allow you to just drop everything to manage it, so he chose to leave McFlannigan's to Sadie." Mama pinned us all with an eye that dared us to be upset.

I looked over at Maddox and Gemma, and neither of

them seemed to be. I wasn't upset because he'd left us out. Hell, I wanted nothing to do with the bar other than having a chance to slide onto a stool and drink a beer from time to time. I also wasn't upset at Phil's attempt to keep the bar in the family. What did upset me was the idea of it tying my baby sister to this town and a business when she should be out creating her own dreams, following her own path.

I held my tongue for the moment, knowing it would upset Mama if I said so, but remained determined to talk to Sadie alone.

"If you thought we'd be upset, Mama, you're wrong," Gemma said.

"Sadie has put a lot of time and effort into the bar. He was right to leave it in her hands," Maddox said.

Everyone's eyes fell on me. "You won't get any fight from me. Damned if I'd know what to do with a bar. I've got my hands full with the ranch and Addy."

Sadie wiped her eyes, and her shoulders sagged in relief. I was surprised she had thought we'd be upset. "He left the house to Mama, told her to do with it what she wanted but asked that we go through the storage shed out back here and the attic in the house and take what we want from all the detritus and crap the family has gathered over the years." Gemma's eyes narrowed at Sadie's wording. "Those were his words, not mine. We'll need to go through it all together. Make sure you get anything you want."

Tillie from the café down the street approached, her long gray hair tied into ponytails and her tunic dress falling to her feet covered in flowers. She apologized for interrupting, saying she needed to skedaddle in order to open the diner for supper. She gave Mama a hug, flicked Maddox and me on the shoulder, and said her goodbyes. That broke up our table, all of us going in separate directions as more people came to pay their respects before heading out.

I held Sadie back with a hand to her elbow before she could disappear.

"You don't have to keep it," I said quietly.

"What?" Sadie turned sad eyes on me.

"Look. Fighting to keep our family's heritage is something I know a bit about. I'm proud of what we've accomplished at the ranch, but this is different. The bar is always going to be a bar, sucking up your evenings and your life. If you keep it, you'll be tied to it and this town, just like Phil and Granny and every McFlannigan before them. I just want you to know you have options. None of us are going to question you if you sell it and go live your real life."

She tilted her head, taking me in. "Is it so strange to think that I might want to do this?"

She had been spending a lot of evenings here with Phil. She'd been the one to reinstate karaoke night. I'd thought she'd been doing it out of boredom while she healed and decided what she was going to do next, but maybe it had been more than that. "If that's the case, I can try and get on board with it. I just think there's more for you out there than this. You had big dreams, Sads. Winning the World Darts Championship, maybe even a triple crown. You talked about a physio degree."

She patted my chest. "Dreams change. You should know that better than any of us."

"It was my choice. I wanted to lead the ranch in a new direction. I'm happy here."

"This is my choice too," Sadie said. She slid her arm around my waist and rested her head on my shoulder. I squeezed her to me.

Maddox's loud laugh drew our eyes to where McKenna was pressed into him. He leaned down and kissed the side of her head. It was a sweet, impulsive gesture I wasn't sure he even realized he'd done. It spoke of intimacy and love. And for not the first time when I watched them, I felt the hole in my life that Ravyn had left. A partner. A person to go through it all with.

I found myself wishing I hadn't left Gia and Addy at the house all over again. If Gia was here, she'd harass me out of my dark mood with her words and a look. I wished I could pull her to me and feel the comfort of her embrace just like my brother did with McK.

"I see the way you look at her, you know," Sadie said softly.

"Who?"

"Don't be dense," Sadie said, pinching me through my suit jacket, and I rubbed at it with a grunt. "It's like how Maddox looks at McK and Mama looks at Daddy. You look at Gia like she's the piece you've been missing."

Her words echoed my thoughts, and it continued to twist those emotions and desire that had been building inside me for over a week.

"She isn't staying, Sads. She'll be here until they can find a way to stop the cartel from coming after Addy, and then she'll go back to her real life." But hadn't Gia told me the life she'd been living felt fake? A movie that was drawing to a close and that would leave her empty afterward? Maybe I could offer her something that would fill us both. I shook my head. It wasn't possible. It was a lust-induced dream. Maybe that was all I really needed—to sleep with her and discharge this built-up energy so it would release us both from its grip. So I could let her go without regrets clinging to me.

Then, why did that idea hurt me more than any thoughts of Ravyn's absence did these days?

"Let me guess, you've made no attempts to ask her to stay?" Sadie asked with a raised brow.

"We're not an item, Sassypants. She's not my girlfriend. We haven't even slept together."

"But you've kissed. You've kissed and felt the world tilt, right?"

"What would you know about making the world tilt?" I started then waved a hand. "Never mind, I don't want to know. This is where Addy needs to be planted so she can grow. She's already come out of her shell in just a handful of days here. She needs the stability this life can give her. One she never got with Ravyn. One that following an undercover analyst around the globe wouldn't give her, and I'm not going to beg Gia to give up her life for us. Asking someone to give up everything is a surefire way for them to resent you in ten years."

"Chicken," she tossed back.

"Being realistic isn't the same as being chicken." But it wasn't the first time in the last week my baby sister had called me a coward, and it rankled some.

"If you don't let her know how you feel, if you don't tell her and show her how important she is, she'll leave because she doesn't think she matters to you. You don't have to beg, but telling her you'd like her to stay, that you'd like to make something work, at least gives her options, allows her to choose which life she'll live instead of just going back to the only life she knows."

How had my baby sister gotten to be the smartest one out of all of us? Maybe being shot, thinking you might not make it, changed your chemical makeup somehow. Maybe it gave you a hint of something that existed beyond this world and a wisdom that came with it.

Deep down inside me, I knew she was right.

I had to talk to Gia. I had to at least put out the offer. Had to extend my hand rather than hide it away. I had to have the courage to risk my heart even if it was risking Addy's too. Maybe we both needed Gia to complete us.

"I gotta go," I said, fishing in my suit pocket for my keys. I glanced over to where Mama and Dad were surrounded by townsfolk. If I tried to say goodbye, I'd be there an hour at least before I could extricate myself. I didn't feel like I had an hour. I had a desperate need to tell Gia what I felt before the courage left me, before I let reality eke away at the fairy tale.

Sadie snickered. "I'll say your goodbyes for you. Just go."

I wrapped my arm around her neck, pulled her into me, and kissed the top of her head.

"Don't tell the others, but you'll always be my

favorite."

"I'm everyone's favorite," she teased back.

I huffed out a laugh, let her go, and took two strides away before turning back. "Sadie?"

"Yeah?"

"Don't forget you have options too."

"Yeah, yeah. Now, shoo."

And I did because every fiber of my being was pulling me home to the two females who were waiting for me.

Chapter Twenty-nine

Gia

AIN'T GONNA DROWN
Performed by Elle King

Addy and I were at the kitchen counter, eating sandwiches, while I started down the rabbit hole of Jaime Laredo's life. I'd been itching to do it all morning but had spent my time with Addy and her schoolwork instead. I'd just brought up his tax return when a call from Rory pulled me from it. The excitement in her voice immediately lifted my hopes.

"Tell me you have good news."

"I haven't broken the encryption."

"Damn."

"But I realized maybe it could help us in a different way."

"What do you mean?"

"Well, the coding has Ravyn's signature all over it, just like the other clues she dropped for us. It made me wonder if we'd missed other breadcrumbs she'd left behind."

I inhaled. "So, you've been searching the internet for her signature."

"Yes!"

"What did you find?"

"It's more what I didn't find."

"Rory!"

She laughed. "I know. I know. But it looks like she's been erasing things for years from multiple databases. She's been scrubbing someone's history."

"Her own?"

"It could be why we haven't gotten any hits on the facial reconstruction."

"I wish she'd been working for us."

Rory got quiet. "I don't think anyone should have what she was working on." She spoke softly, as if she was trying to not be overheard by the other analysts sitting around her. "Certainly not the criminals, but not our government either. I don't trust anyone to have the integrity needed to use it for good and not evil."

"I think you're right."

"Don't get me wrong, I'd love to take a look at the masterpiece of coding required to make it happen, but then I'd want to burn it from my brain so I could never recreate it."

A noise at the back door had me shifting to look down the glass breezeway leading to the garage. I hadn't heard the doors roll up, and the cameras hadn't alerted me to anyone on the driveway. Plus, it was a little too early for Ryder to be home yet.

I glanced at Addy, who was watching a show on Ryder's laptop. My hand went to the butt of my gun, but I didn't want to draw it and freak Addy out, so I eased farther into the breezeway toward the garage before I pulled it out.

I dropped my voice to a mere whisper, "Hey, call Enrique for me, check in with the perimeter?"

"You okay?" Rory's voice sounded worried.

"Just a noise. I'm sure it's nothing."

"If you don't call back in two minutes, I'm sending in the cavalry."

"Deal."

I hung up, stuffed the phone in my back pocket, and tried to creep toward the door, which was ridiculous. With the hallway being made of glass, anyone outside could see me just as clearly as I could see them. A quick glance in both directions showed no one.

And yet, my senses were screaming.

As I neared the door to the garage, the handle started to turn slowly and quietly. My heart skipped a beat, wishing I'd had time to check the cameras. I eased to the far side of the door and took aim at it. When the door cracked open, a Five-seveN pistol appeared in the opening, gripped in a black-gloved hand.

I used my shoulder to slam the door onto the hand, and the gun clattered to the slate floor as a howl of pain erupted from a man on the other side.

"Addy, hide!" I screamed as the door pushed into me with enough force that it jammed my hand to my chest. I stumbled backward, hitting the glass behind me and making the entire wall ripple.

A man with the same build and similar ski mask as the one who'd escaped in the woods the other day surged into the hallway. He attempted a sweeping kick meant to send me sprawling. I jumped over it, raised my gun, and pulled the trigger. The man's body jolted backward, a hole in the chest of his black jacket proving I'd hit home, but it didn't slow him down. He leaped toward me as I pulled the trigger again, and this time, when his body jerked back, I was close enough to see the bullet embed in a bulletproof vest.

I lowered my aim and was just about to take a shot at a kneecap when my body was jerked off the ground from behind with a viselike grip on my waist. I crashed back into a massive chest, feet dangling. Fear lit me up. For me. For Addy. How had I not heard him? Why had the alarms not gone off?

I shifted my hand, trying to aim my gun behind me but mammoth fingers twisted my wrist. I cried out as pain shot through me. Unable to hold on, my weapon hit the ground with a loud clang. The humiliation of losing it was quickly replaced with desperation. I had to protect Addy!

The man holding me wrapped an arm around my neck and applied enough pressure that my breath left my body. I rammed my elbows into his rib cage and heard a satisfying crack, but the hold he had on me didn't loosen, and not even a whimper escaped him. Instead, the grip he had on my neck grew tighter until only gurgling noises escaped my throat.

My panic grew as I fought to remember my training and all the ways I was supposed to dislodge a bigger opponent.

The man I'd shot stormed toward me, waving the pistol he'd retrieved.

"Bitch, that fucking hurt!" he yelled, rubbing one hand over the holes in his vest.

"Do not kill her," the man holding me warned. "The boss wants her alive. Find the child."

His voice was deep. Gritty. It matched the massive body that was holding me as if I weighed nothing. As if I was a mere inconvenience. The fact they wanted me alive should have been a relief, but I knew what cartels did to people. I'd seen the images. Death would almost be better. Except, that meant them getting Addy.

I wouldn't go without a fight. I jammed my foot backward with all my strength, connecting with some part of the man's leg, but he still didn't budge while his chokehold was draining me of every last particle of air. My vision went spotty. My lungs screamed. My attacker's arm was a cement block against my throat. The first man stormed past me into the kitchen as white lights danced in front of my vision. I kicked again, this time landing on the first man's hip as he went by. He barked out an angry curse but didn't stop while the grip on my neck tightened even more.

I fought the instinct to claw at his arm. I needed to hit him somewhere that would make him loosen his hold. His groin. His knee. I dropped my mouth, sinking my teeth into the bare arm with its rows of tattoos. I drew blood. Salty. Appalling. As the man cursed in Spanish, I used my elbows and heels in unison to strike at him.

It was futile. The solid mass continued pushing into my windpipe. Dark blended in with the white spots. My body was shrieking from the impact and the lack of oxygen. Wet lips hit my ear, and my entire being shuddered as his dark voice muttered, "Stop fighting, *chiquita*. It will only be worse for you."

I would not let these men take Addy. I would not.

Blackness filled my eyes as my captor hauled me into the kitchen and down the steps into the living room.

"I can't find her! The little bitch is nowhere." The man with the pistol spat as he stormed back into the room. A hint of relief washed over me. Addy was an award-winning hider.

Outside, I heard the clear ring of a car door crashing closed and Ryder's voice screaming my name. New fear swelled through me. For him. For Addy. For all of us.

Where the hell was the team watching us?

"We need to go," the man choking me said. My vision had disappeared with what felt like my last breath. "We'll take this one with us and come back for the other."

As he dragged my body toward the entryway, I knew I had one last shot at freeing myself, so I let myself go limp, as if I'd passed out. It loosened his grip, and as soon as it did, I used all my strength to jam my heel into the top of his foot before twisting around to thrust my fist into his groin. I was rewarded with a pained grunt.

The front door crashed into the wall.

Sirens blared in the distance.

"Let her go!" Ryder's voice trembled with fury.

Instead of hauling me with him, the giant surprised me by picking me up and tossing me in the air as if I were nothing but a rag doll. I prepared for the harsh pain of hitting the cold tile, but instead, warm arms caught me.

"Where's my daughter?" Ryder's scream was a tormented roar.

I couldn't talk to reassure him she was hiding. I couldn't even see him over the black in my eyes as my lungs gasped.

A gunshot echoed through the house, and I barely had time to fear it was aimed at us before the sound of glass shattering crashed through the room.

I turned my head in the direction of the living room and the sound. My vision was blurry, as if looking through water, hazy and unclear, but I saw the giant who'd been holding me leap through a broken window. He landed with a roll on the rain-soaked leaves and took off running.

"There's another one!" My voice was hoarse and raspy as I shouted at Ryder. "Go! Make sure he doesn't have Addy!"

Ryder's blurred face was a mask of anger and fear as he set me down and whirled down the hall, screaming Addy's name.

Outside, vehicles came screeching into the driveway with their sirens still blaring.

Boots pounding on the tile had me jerking my head around to see two of Maddox's deputies racing into the house with their guns drawn.

"One of them went that way!" I had to use the force of a scream to get the words out as I pointed to the broken window.

The officers followed the beast out the window, sprinting into the woods and relaying their position into their radios.

Ryder came back, face panicked. "There's no one here. But I can't find Addy!"

Desperation and heartache rang through every word.

I wobbled as I stood and forced air into my lungs so I could say, "She was in the kitchen when I told her to hide."

With a mere glance at the empty kitchen, Ryder darted down the spiral staircase to the basement, calling her name, shouting for her to come out, that it was safe.

But it wasn't. It wasn't safe. We'd been so stupid, so ridiculous, thinking we could guard her here. That we could keep her safe in a house made of glass with a handful of officers taking patrol. God, I was such an idiot. The tears that filled my eyes were angry ones. Fury that was all self-directed. What had I been thinking?

I'd spent days getting to know them, as if I was on some reality TV dating show instead of doing my job.

My phone rang, vibrating in my pocket, but I couldn't answer it yet, not until we found Addy.

I used the wall to hold myself up. The world spun, but I forced myself toward the kitchen on legs that trembled with every step. Where would she hide? Where?

I propped myself up on the walls and then the counters, flinging open cupboards.

Ryder's voice calling for his daughter screamed heartache and sorrow. It slid inside my chest like a knife. I'd done this. I'd caused him this grief.

When I got to the pantry, I jerked it open and heard a rustle that brought a spike of relief so hard and so strong it brought the black spots back to my eyes.

"Addy," I said gently, my voice barely audible. "It's me. It's okay."

From a bottom shelf, a bulk-sized box of paper towels was pushed aside, and two terrified eyes found mine. Tears rushed over my lashes.

"Thank God! Thank God!" I whispered.

I held out my hand as Ryder's feet pounded up the staircase, still calling her name. Addy slid tiny fingers into mine, and I'd just pulled her out of the pantry and into my arms as Ryder found us.

"Addy!" Tortured relief pounded through the syllables, stabbing me as much as it soothed.

He didn't yank his child from my embrace. Instead, he wrapped us both in a hug, squeezing tight, holding us with firm bands of muscle and love. Emotions wafted over us that

I didn't know what to do with but felt myself respond to anyway.

"I got you. I got you both. You're okay. You're okay!" It was murmured as if he was still trying to believe it himself. We stayed that way for several seconds before he loosened his hold enough to look down, first into my face and then into Addy's terrified one.

"Are you hurt? Let me see."

When he stepped away to squat down in front of his daughter, running hands along her arms, I felt the loss of his touch in every part of me. Not just the physical loss of his warmth and strength but the loss of his affection that had lodged deep in my soul. How could he ever forgive me? I'd almost allowed them to take her.

The dark spots threatened again.

The adrenaline rush that had held me up while fighting deserted me.

My knees hit the ground. I tried to catch myself. I tried to stop, but as the blackness enveloped me and I crumbled, the only thing I registered was Ryder calling my name.

♫ ♫ ♫

I came to, lying on a bed that smelled like Ryder—hay and spice and soap mixing together in a strangely enticing way. My eyelids felt heavy, but as I forced them open, I was greeted with a pair of vivid blue eyes, the deep color of the sky right before the sun completely disappeared. Except, instead of holding the peace and calm of dusk, the gaze he sent me was tormented.

Ryder's large palm cupped my cheek. "You're awake. Thank God."

I tried to move, tried to sit up, and my entire being objected.

"Don't even think of getting up. McKenna's on her way to check you out."

"Addy!" My voice was raspy and harsh.

A little body curled into me from the other side, and I removed my gaze from Ryder's concerned one to find the little girl on the bed next to me. Her eyes were full of the same worry as her father's.

I hugged her to me, muttering, "I got you," in my broken voice.

Except, it wasn't true. I'd let her down.

I'd let them both down.

Ryder's face shuttered. He tucked his emotions behind a wall that made him look decidedly like Addy when she blanked out. I glanced around, and it took me a minute longer than it should have to realize we were in Ryder's bed.

"Did they catch them?" I asked.

"Darlin', stop talking until you're checked out." It was a growl that tolerated no argument, and I didn't have the strength to fight it. Not yet.

The door behind Ryder opened, and his brother entered in a suit similar to the one Ryder was wearing. They'd been at the funeral. Why had Ryder come home early? Thank God he had.

"They're gone," Maddox said. "Looks like they had two ATVs parked down by the creek."

"Where the fuck was the patrol?" Ryder demanded.

"Bruce was knocked out at the bridge. Don't know where Enrique is."

Ryder's jaw flexed, anger simmering through him that I could no longer say wasn't justified. I still didn't want to doubt Enrique, but this was the second time he hadn't been around and the house had been broken into.

We shouldn't have stayed after the first.

We should have left.

I'd been lulled into placidity. Lulled by lust and the sweetness of a little girl.

Stupid. Stupid. Stupid.

Hadn't Jason Bourne's love for Marie gotten her killed

in the movies? Hadn't it almost gotten him killed too?

I sat up, squirming in my pocket for my phone. When it wasn't there, I glanced around.

"No phone. No talking. Not until you get checked out," Ryder grunted.

"I need to call Leland and the team."

"Stop talking!" he all but yelled.

Addy flinched next to me, and Ryder was instantly remorseful.

"Addy," he said softly. "Can you go with Uncle Maddox? He's going to help you pack a few things to take with you."

Her face fell before the blank look she'd held so often after I'd found her in the hotel room returned to her face. It had slid away over the last few days because she'd felt safe here. She'd unpacked her things and stayed unpacked. She'd laughed and talked. Tears blurred my vision. I hadn't kept my promises to her.

As if reading her reaction just as I did, Ryder's voice was gentle when he said, "It's just for a few days, sweetheart. Just until we put this behind us for good. You'll be back. You are going to be safe here with me. I swear on all I love that I will make that statement true." I felt the force of it in every fiber of my being. He would do anything to keep her safe. If I could feel it in my cynical adult body, I hoped Addy did as well.

Maddox extended his hand, and Addy took it, scooting down to the end of the bed so she didn't have to climb over me. When they'd gotten to the door, Addy turned back to us. It looked like she wanted to say something but didn't. Instead, her head and shoulders dropped, and she let Maddox lead her from the room.

The tears I'd been fighting poured over my cheeks.

Ryder turned to face me, and I easily read the anger and determination written there. But he ran a gentle finger over my tears as they fell, wiping at them.

"Thank you," he said softly, "for making sure they didn't take her."

I shook my head, and my ears rang, and my vision blurred.

"They would have gotten her, Ryder. If you hadn't shown up…" I was humiliated by my inability to defend myself. To defend Addy. Maybe it was time to stop pretending I was some female James Bond and sit down behind the computer with Rory. "My team—"

"Please stop talking, darlin'. Please let McK check you out first. Your phone was ringing, so I answered it. Even if I hadn't shown up, Rory had already called for backup. She said something about my cameras being offline and that she wouldn't apologize for not waiting the full two minutes when she'd seen that."

I was glad she hadn't. Glad she'd listened to the instincts that had me hiring her in the first place.

"I gave her what information I could," Ryder continued. "She knows you and Addy are here and relatively safe. She knows you've been injured and that McKenna is coming to check you out."

"I'm so sorry…" A sob escaped. "I've been so stupid."

Instead of being angry, instead of storming away from me as I felt he should, Ryder did the opposite. He pulled me to him, holding tight, and whispered soothing words into my hair. The sweetness of it undid me further, and I let tears of fury and frustration and mortification fall. I let him hold me up in a way I hadn't let anyone do in so long I'd almost forgotten what it felt like to be soothed.

Chapter Thirty

Ryder

I DON'T REMEMBER ME (BEFORE YOU)
Performed by Brothers Osborne

I'd driven home from the bar, thinking of all the ways to tell Gia how I felt about her when I still wasn't even sure how to express them to myself. I didn't know what or how we could make what was stirring between us stick, but Sadie was right. I needed to let Gia know I was interested in letting these feelings grow, interested in trying to explore them. If I didn't, I'd regret it for the rest of my life.

When I'd seen the gigantic man dragging Gia through the kitchen, it had taken me two seconds too long to realize what was happening. My alarm system hadn't alerted me to anyone outside my door. None of Maddox's men had issued an alert. And yet, a man with a gun was coming down the hallway from the bedrooms, and another held Gia against his chest.

I'd already leaped from my truck as the sirens filled the air behind me. Backup was on the way, but the worst could happen in the minutes it took for them to get here. So I'd raced toward the door with my pulse pounding viciously, dimming the sounds around me.

What I was going to do when I got inside, when I faced a man who looked like he could body slam me with a pinky and another man with a gun, I hadn't known, but I'd do anything I could to prevent them from taking Gia and Addy.

As I'd burst into the entryway, the giant wearing a ski mask and I had shared a steely glare. He'd looked behind me to where the sounds of the sirens were getting closer. Then, he'd tossed Gia at me as if she was nothing more than a toy. I'd barely had time to catch her before she would have hit the floor. The relief that had coursed through me at having her in my arms had been short and bittersweet as terror for Addy burned another hole in me.

It wasn't until I'd come back up from the game room to see Addy and Gia wrapped together that I thought my heart actually started to beat again. And even then, it had been a pained stutter full of anger and frustration directed at the situation and at the cartel. Maybe it should have been directed at Gia and the task force for allowing the men to get this close, but it wasn't.

The person who'd led the cartel to my door was Ravyn.

In my bedroom, as I held Gia in my arms and let her cry, I could almost feel the remorse beating through her. I knew because I'd come to know her pretty damn well through the intensity of the last few days. She'd blame herself for not seeing this coming. She'd feel like a failure for not defending us against a giant and a man with a gun.

Maybe we all held a bit of responsibility for allowing them to come at us so easily. As thrown as I'd been by Addy's mere existence, by the life she'd been leading on the run, and by the feelings that were pummeling me for Gia, I hadn't considered the cartel threat with enough seriousness. Even after they'd broken in and stolen Addy's backpack, it had still felt as if I was watching it all happen from a distance—as if it wasn't real.

And I'd almost lost them because of it.

There was enough regret to go around.

No more. We'd figure out a way to keep everyone safe, and we'd do it together.

A knock was followed by my brother's fiancée striding into the room with an old-school doctor's bag in her hand. McK's gaze bounced back and forth between me and Gia, who was still tucked up against my chest.

"Go see Maddox while I check Gia out," McK said. When I made no effort to move, Gia pushed against me, pulling away and wiping at her face.

"I'm okay," she said, but her voice was still scratchy and hoarse, and when I looked at her neck, there was a distinct purple mark surging to the surface.

I reached out and ran gentle fingers along the discoloration. "You're not okay."

She pulled my hand into hers and squeezed. Her eyes were a soft amber at the moment, spiked with colors of the fields in the spring.

Another knock, and Maddox's head poked around the door. "Ryder, can I see you?"

He and McK shared a look, and I was almost certain she'd told him to come in and get me. My eyes narrowed on the two of them, but they didn't let on that this had been planned.

"Go," Gia said. "I'm fine, but I'll let McKenna check me out."

"If nothing else, maybe you can get her to stop talking and rest her damn voice," I said to McKenna as I rose from the bed. I took Gia's phone from my pocket, hesitating, not wanting to leave it any more than I wanted to leave her.

I set the phone on the bedside table and then walked out without looking back, because if I did and saw the self-incrimination and sadness there that I'd felt in her tears, I'd run back to her.

As I shut my bedroom door behind me, Maddox's face turned grim.

"Where's Addy?" I asked.

"Mom and Dad showed up as soon as I told them what happened. They've got her in her room, packing a few things. Enrique caught one of the men." He turned on his heel, and I followed him into my living room where broken glass allowed a bitter wind to rip through the space.

It wasn't the giant, but another man also dressed all in black. A ski mask covered his face from which two dark eyes glared, and his jacket was unzipped, showing off a bullet-proof vest with two bullets lodged in it. He was zip-tied to one of my dining room chairs with his hands behind his back.

A pistol sat on the table next to a Glock that I was pretty sure was Gia's. Both weapons were out of his reach, but easily within Enrique's. The DEA agent's face was dark with fury.

I had my own fury I directed not at the man tied up but at the man who was supposed to be here watching Gia's back. I crossed the room, slammed a finger into his chest, and demanded, "Where the hell were you?"

Maddox was next to me in a second, hauling me back by my arm and forcing space between us.

"I was in Kentucky!" Enrique said. "I can't fucking chase down leads on Vito from here. Gia knew where I was, and I was almost back when Rory called. I heard the APB on the two ATVs your brother issued and found this dickwad heading up over the fire road at the back of the property. Same escape route he used before. Fucking moron."

I couldn't help it. There was something about the agent that didn't sit well with me. Nothing he could say or do would ever allow me to fully trust him.

Maddox pushed me again, shoving me farther away. Then, he turned to Enrique and said, "What has he told us?"

"Nothing, but I'll have Rory run his face and prints." The DEA agent glowered at me.

Maddox pulled the guy's mask off, and the face that greeted me made my stomach fall.

The man met my stare with a raised chin.

"I know you," I grunted out. The man didn't say anything, but Maddox and Enrique both turned to me, eyes narrowed, waiting for me to expand. "He works at the Grand Laredo. He's one of Jaime's men." I moved forward, leaning down into his face. "Is Jaime mixed up with the Lovatos, or is it just you?"

The man said nothing.

Maddox tugged me away from him as if he was afraid I'd do something stupid. Except, I wasn't sure the idea of beating this man until he talked was stupid at all. I'd never been one to use my fists to solve problems. I'd played football, I'd broken up plenty of fights, and I'd defended my siblings, but I wasn't someone with an innate need to pummel things to the ground to escape my demons. And yet, I was overwhelmed with the desire to beat the living shit out of the man sitting calmly in my dining room chair. I wanted to cause him more pain than he'd caused Gia and more fear than he'd caused my little girl.

I wanted answers. From him. From his goddamn boss.

I thought back to Gia's question this morning about Jaime. I'd been quick to deny his involvement. I didn't want to believe the person who'd taught me everything I needed to know about turning our ranch into a five-star resort could be behind any of this. And yet, here was more proof.

A memory tickled that twisted my insides another notch. After an Eastern Dude Ranchers' Association meeting, just before Ravyn and I were due to get married, Jaime and I had met at the bar of the hotel for drinks. I'd spilled my happy guts, rambling on about babies and marriage, and he'd shaken his head in regret, saying a wife and kids would only slow me down. I'd had a drink too many, and I'd shoved my phone in his face, showing him a rare picture I'd captured of Ravyn and me, daring him to deny how perfect we were together and insisting he'd eventually understand when he found his one true love like I had. He'd taken the phone from me, expanded the screen, and watched it for a long time before returning it. A dark look had taken over his face as he'd said, "She's beautiful. But I've learned beauty is only a shield for deception, my friend. Believe me when I tell you, she does not know how to be loyal."

He'd gotten up and walked away before I could defend Ravyn.

Not once had he indicated he knew her.

Maybe he hadn't. Maybe it was all just one coincidence after another.

But I knew with a sinking feeling that it wasn't.

Jaime had been the reason she'd run. I'd been a fool, spouting love and happily ever afters, and led the demon right to her door.

"He knew her. Jaime knew Ravyn, didn't he?" I demanded of the tied-up asshole. He said nothing, but his eyes flickered to the side and back. An acknowledgment. Rage raced through my veins. They'd taken everything from me once and tried to take it again today. No more. No more! "Who was she to him?"

"She's his sister," Gia's hoarse voice had me twisting around to see her on the entryway steps with McKenna at her side. She had an icepack to her throat, and her phone in her hand.

"What?" It was Enrique who released the shocked question into the room.

Gia swayed as she stepped into the living room, and I took two steps toward her, but it was McK who put an arm around her.

"I'll let Rory explain," she said, sinking onto the couch and putting her phone on the coffee table.

A woman's voice spoke to the room over the line. "I've been scouring the internet for Anna-Ravyn's code. I told Gia this morning that I found a bunch of places she'd scrubbed clean, erasing someone from existence. It took me most of the day to unwind it, but I did. She was born Natalia Emily Laredo to Emiliano Rodrigo Lopez and Maria Rosalinda Laredo. She's six years younger than her brother, Jaime Emiliano Lopez Laredo. She was sent away to boarding school at twelve, spent her life amongst the wealthiest children in the country, and then went to MIT, where she stunned her professors with her computer skills. Both parents are dead. Maria Rosalinda's death was deemed a drug overdose, whispered to be a suicide. Emiliano Senior crashed in a Venezuelan jungle on a small plane, and the body was never found."

"So, their father was involved in the cartel?" Enrique asked.

"I don't think so. The plane crash happened as the Lovatos were just moving up in the underworld," Rory said. "I think this has to do with Jaime's time in California. He's got an IQ off the charts and had a place at the University of Boulder in their engineering program, but instead, he was shuffled off to California to work in the fields alongside some cousins from Mexico." She hesitated. "Why didn't this flag us before?"

"It did," Enrique grunted out. "My time in Lexington was to see if I could tie him to the gang of foot soldiers they had there. But Laredo has friends in high places who insist he's nothing but a wealthy rancher." The DEA agent looked at me as if I'd been the one to insist on it. I would have. I would have bet more than I could afford to lose on Jaime being a decent human. "Any time I even suggested getting closer, I was told to back off."

Silence settled for a moment as the implication of what he was saying ran through all of us. Gia's voice was tortured from more than a bruised windpipe as she said, "You think Leland is covering this up?"

"Someone kept us from following any leads that hinted in his direction. Weren't you supposed to spend time at his ranch?" Enrique asked Gia.

She nodded. "Yes, but when we got the lead in D.C. with Rory's dad, they pulled me back."

"Who pulled you?" Enrique asked.

Gia swallowed, and I could see the doubts that were spinning through her about her boss. "Is the line secure on your end right now, Rory?"

"I'm at my desk." There was shuffling on the other end. "Let me call you back."

She was gone, and silence filled the air. Gia pocketed her phone, a grim look on her face.

The truth settled over me. Jaime was behind this, pulling strings with a suave, confident smile that had fooled everyone, just like he'd fooled me. I'd trusted him, and by doing so, I'd handed Ravyn over to the wolves she'd been trying to escape. My chest felt as if I'd had a knife shoved into it. "I showed him a picture of her a few weeks before the wedding." I rubbed my hand over my face. "Fuck. She was hiding from him, and I led him straight to her."

"You are not responsible for her," Maddox bit out. "Damnit, Ryder, she lied and kept secrets. If she'd been honest with you, we could have protected her. But she wasn't. So don't take this on. There is nothing you could have done differently."

The man in the chair snorted, a dark and unforgiving sound, and all our eyes swung toward him. "No one is safe from the wolf. No one. I'm as dead as all of you are now."

"What does he want with my daughter?" I lunged at the man, but Enrique held me back, only to pick up one of the guns from the table, spin it around, and aim it at the man.

"Talk, and we might be convinced to try to save your sorry-ass life."

The man darted his eyes around, struggled at the zip ties, and then dropped his head. "The key. She has the key to the code he's trying to finish. The box that will allow him complete access to any system in the world."

"She doesn't have it. She has nothing," I snarled just as Gia reached me, pulling at my arm and drawing me away from Jaime's henchman. My eyes met hers. The Switch. The encryption on the Switch. There was definitely something there.

"Even if she doesn't have the key, he believes she does. Worse, he believes she belongs to him by blood. He won't let you have her," the man said with a careless shrug. "He'd rather she die first."

My heart couldn't take it. My heart was going to implode.

As I stared at the man, a red dot appeared on his

forehead—a strange little movement that seemed like I should recognize it. As my mind was trying to place it, Gia's already destroyed voice screamed, "Sniper!"

She dragged me into her with a fierceness that caused us to lose balance and had us tumbling to the floor just as the man's head kicked backward. A hole appeared, blood gushing out, and his eyes rolled back.

In an instant, Maddox had McKenna on the ground, buried under him as he shouted orders into his radio.

Enrique jumped through the broken glass, heading for the woods.

In the silence that followed, I realized I was lying on top of Gia, her thin body having cushioned my fall instead of the other way around. I slid off her, staying low to the ground and assessing her body for injuries that I might have caused.

"Go," she said, shoving at me. "Stay low and get the hell out of this room."

Gunfire echoed through the woods behind my house, and I moved. I stayed as low as I could, clamping Gia's hand in a viselike grip and dragging her with me. She hauled me to stop at the table, reaching up and grabbing both weapons before allowing me to continue tugging her into the entryway. Maddox and McKenna had made it to the hallway and were crawling toward my office doors.

We followed. Once we made it into the room, even though we were on the opposite side of the house from where the sniper had taken aim, we still stayed low.

"I'm going to pull the Bronco as close to the front door as I can. Get Addy and our parents, and meet me there," Maddox told me. He looked over at McKenna and kissed her hard on the mouth. "I love you."

McKenna's face was shell-shocked. Fear and worry scrolled over it. I'd brought this to us. I'd brought this to all of us by hiring Ravyn and then falling in love with her. Gia had been upset with herself for not protecting us, but I was the one who'd really led the devil to my family.

A devil I'd shaken hands with, drank with, and who'd helped me plan my future.

Fuck.

Maddox was gone before I could even think to apologize.

I turned to Gia, overcome with the same desire to kiss her and tell her that I loved her like my brother had just done with his fiancée. Goddamn awful time to figure out what I felt for her was love. Goddamn useless timing to figure anything out.

I stared at her for a moment, gaze dropping to her lips and then back to eyes that were flashing with as many emotions as surged through me. I let myself touch her briefly, a soft stroke of her cheek, before saying, "Get to the front door while I get Addy and my parents."

She swallowed hard, and as I went to leave, she grabbed my hand. I looked back at her, and she didn't say anything. She just gripped my hand tightly. I leaned in and kissed her forehead. "We're all getting out of this. Then we can talk. Get McK to the front door."

She shoved something cold into my hand, and I looked down to find one of the guns she'd grabbed from the table. It wasn't hers. That one was black and smooth. This pistol had a black slide and a bronze-colored grip.

"Safety is off," she said. Then, she turned to McKenna. "Stay low." As I watched, she hovered over my brother's fiancée while they both hunched down and headed toward the front door.

Walking out of the office meant facing the wall of windows in the direction the shooter had been. More gunfire burst through the quiet, but it sounded farther away this time. I had to hope Enrique had forced the man from his perch.

I ran hunched over, flinging myself into Addy's room where Dad had both women huddled in the closet. "Was that gunfire?" he demanded.

I nodded. "Maddox is pulling the Bronco up to the door. We're all going with him."

My father eyed the gun in my hand. He shouldered the purple backpack I'd bought Addy, and my stomach flipped over. She'd been forced back into hiding and running, but I promised myself this would be the last time. She wouldn't have to do this ever again. We would put an end to it even if I had to kill Jaime Laredo myself to make it happen.

Chapter Thirty-one

Gia

IF IT AIN'T YOU
Performed by Smithfield

Maddox's Bronco fishtailed as he turned the corner after the covered bridge. Addy was in Ryder's lap, and he pulled her tighter to his chest. Brandon swore, and Eva and McKenna looked white-faced and terrified, smooshed next to them in the back seat.

I was in the front passenger seat with my gun aimed out the window. My throat throbbed. The force I was required to use to talk was painful as I asked, "Where are we going?"

"Phil's place is empty," Brandon suggested from the back seat. "Go there until you can make a better plan."

Ryder's dad had kept his cool in a way I hadn't quite expected. It was one thing to stay calm on the ranch when you were dealing with animals and nature, but to stay so calm when bullets were firing was something altogether different.

I hated that I'd brought this to them.

If I'd taken Addy somewhere else, to a safe house covered with a dozen agents, none of them would be in danger.

But then again, if Leland was involved, maybe Addy would have been taken days ago.

I bit my cheek as more tears threatened. I trusted Leland

more than I trusted Enrique, didn't I? It was Enrique who'd offered my boss up as being on Laredo's side when we'd been at Ryder's. Still, it was clear Jaime Laredo had been protected by someone with access to the task force. That someone was still unclear. But I wouldn't rest until I uncovered them and saw them punished. Until I brought them all down.

"I'm not calling my guys," Maddox said with a glance over at me. "Whoever has been watching and listening will know if I do. Once I get to a secure line, I'll call over to Dale Scully and have him bring his men over. If we can keep Phil's house dark, make it look like it's still empty, it should buy us a few hours."

I looked down at my phone. Was it being tracked? Did I trust the people on the other end?

I trusted Rory. One-hundred-percent. I'd seen what the Lovatos had done to her mother. I'd seen how she'd reacted to that, chasing them down with her gun blazing. Right now, my only way of staying in touch with her was my phone. I'd get a burner tomorrow.

But tomorrow might be too late.

"Dad," Maddox said. "I'm going to drop you, McK, and Mama off at McFlannigan's with Sadie. Don't go to the ranch tonight. Go to my house. You know the code to my gun safe. You'll find two more handguns in there. I'll be home as soon as Scully's men show up at Phil's."

We pulled up behind the bar, and Ryder's family got out. His mama turned back, eyes meeting mine. "I expect you'll protect my son and granddaughter."

God, I'd failed so many times already. So many damn times.

"Yes, ma'am."

She looked into the back seat, where Addy's face was buried in Ryder's chest, and her eyes softened. "Addy-girl," she said softly.

Addy peeked out.

"I know you're a bit scared right now. I think we all are, and that's okay. But you have some of the bravest, smartest people I know looking out for you. When this is all over, I'll teach you how to make my brown-sugar molasses cookies that I swore I wouldn't teach a soul. You'll be the only one to know. How does that sound?"

Addy's lips ticked upward ever so slightly.

"Love you, Son," Brandon said, his gaze landing on Ryder. "I need to hear from you regularly, otherwise your mama will worry."

They all would. They'd worry until Ryder and Addy were in their arms again.

Whereas my family had no clue I'd even danced with death tonight.

I wasn't sure how I felt about that, but I knew one thing was certain—the Hatleys would get their family back whole and unharmed.

The old Bronco's doors slammed shut, and quiet took over as Maddox put the vehicle in drive. He headed down several blocks to a two-story, rectangular colonial with plain white shiplap siding and a covered front porch. The front yard was small and well-maintained with grass and magnolia trees. Simple and clean but with no flowers or feminine touches.

Maddox pulled around back to the detached garage near the back door. "I'll let you out here. I'm going to run to the station, pick up a few burner phones, and then I'll come back on foot so my vehicle isn't found here."

Ryder climbed out, bringing Addy and her purple backpack with him as I got out of the front seat. "Got the key?" Ryder asked his brother.

"Same place as it's always been," Maddox responded with a head tilt toward the steps.

Maddox drove off, and while Ryder pulled a hide-a-key from under the back steps, I scanned the quiet street. Dusk was falling. A dog barked somewhere a street over. But other than that, there was no movement.

Ryder opened the screen, unlocked the door, and held it open for Addy and me to slide inside.

In the fading twilight, the kitchen we stepped into looked like a 1950s throwback. Black-and-white checkered floor, rounded appliances in shades of mustard, white Formica counters, and straight-faced, white cabinets.

It smelled of stale cigarettes and beer.

"Uncle Phil wasn't much of a homemaker. After Granny McFlannigan passed, he had someone come clean once a month or so, but it definitely became a bachelor pad."

We moved farther into the house, using the light on my phone rather than turning on any lamps. We passed through a dining room cluttered with storage boxes that would have been considered fancy a lifetime ago but now looked tired. Through another arch, we entered a living room that had two antique couches with carved backs covered in crocheted quilts. A leather recliner that appeared to be one of only two things from this century in the room faced an enormous television hanging from the flowered wallpaper over a marble-pillared fireplace.

The house felt…worn-out and lonely.

Maybe that had been Phil as well.

Ryder led us up a staircase with a threadbare runner that must have once been plush, even opulent. The hallway had closed doors on both sides leading down to an arched window at the end. "Bathroom here." He pointed to the door to the left of the landing before opening the one to the right. "Guest room."

"I don't want anyone here," I told him, meeting his eyes. "Too close to the stairs."

He moved to the next room. "This is Phil's. Been his for as long as I could remember." It smelled even stronger of cigarettes. Musty and tired. The brass bed was covered with a handmade popcorn quilt that must have once been a bright blue. The walls were covered in framed pictures of Phil with some of the town's celebrities—football players and musicians.

Ryder's throat bobbed. "Let's just leave it alone for now."

He moved farther down the hall. "This was where Maddox and I stayed sometimes when we were little and Granny Mc was alive." The bunkbeds took up the majority of the room with a small, antique writing desk as the only other piece of furniture. Ryder pointed to a small door that I suspected was a closet. "Leads to the attic."

It would be a good place for Addy to hide. I gave him a small nod, and he bent down to look into her face. "You think you might want to stay in this room? Maddox and I used to argue over the top bunk, but it's all yours."

Addy nodded but didn't let go of his hand. He dropped her purple backpack by the beds and then walked out into the hall where he pointed out two more rooms. "Mom's old room and Granny's."

A door downstairs creaked open, and I whirled around, gun in hand, heart pounding until I heard Maddox's voice softly announcing his presence. We made our way downstairs to the kitchen where Maddox had placed two burner phones on the table and was opening the plastic around a third.

While Ryder tried to distract Addy by scavenging for food in Phil's pantry and then heating canned soup on the stove, Maddox called his sheriff pal and arranged for protection, and Rory and I exchanged new burner phone information. I took out my old SIM card, dug around in the drawers until I came up with a hammer, and smashed the card apart.

"You have your phone?" I asked Ryder, hating the sound of my destroyed voice and the pain that was slowing me down when I needed to be at my best.

He shook his head. "No. I left it in my truck."

He placed bowls on the Formica kitchen table and waved at me. I didn't feel like eating. My throat was throbbing, and my entire body was achy from the hits I'd leveled as well as received, but I also needed the energy to get me through the next few hours. So, I did my best to swallow some of the broth as it was nearly impossible to get down anything more than the liquid.

As if reading my mind, Ryder grabbed a bag of frozen peas from Phil's freezer and set it on my neck. It stung and numbed at the same time. He ducked out of the room before coming back with a bottle of ibuprofen.

"Phil was renowned for his hangovers. I figured he'd have some kind of pain meds."

Addy was almost silent throughout the entirety of dinner. Her face had returned to the blank wall she'd just started to leave behind, and I hated that even more than my messed-up body. The full sentences we'd been getting from her were gone. She was back to single words, nods, and shrugs.

Six of Scully's men showed up. As Maddox and I got up, intending to step outside to make a plan with them, Addy jumped out of her chair and ran at me full force, hugging my legs much like Mila did with her family.

"Don't go!" Addy cried.

My eyes met Ryder's over the top of her head. Pain. Regrets. Love.

I bent down and brushed a kiss along her forehead. "I'm not leaving, Addy. I promise I'm not leaving." But my already torn throat clogged because eventually I would leave, and it would hurt worse than anything my body was feeling. But it wouldn't be until they were safe. "Just going to talk to your uncle Maddox and those officers. I'll be right back."

"Mama said she wouldn't leave."

"Wh-what?" I stuttered out my question.

"She said she wouldn't. But she did. She closed her eyes and left."

Tears rushed over her lashes, and I bent to brush at them, swiping them away, unsure what to say or do. Ryder joined us, picking Addy up and holding her tight to his chest.

"I'm so sorry that happened to you, sweetheart. So sorry. But I'm here. Gia's here. You have all those men standing out there determined that nothing like what happened to your mama happens to you or us."

He nodded his head toward the door, letting me know it was okay to step outside, and I did, but my heart was still in my throat as I listened to Maddox discuss the arrangement with the officers. Four around the house, one on a back street behind the house, and one parked out front. They'd rotate off with another set of officers in the morning if Maddox and Scully hadn't found a safe house to move us to by then.

If Laredo suspected we knew about him, he'd either be running or he'd be hunting, and my money was on hunting. He'd taken a huge risk in trying to grab Addy from a house already being watched. He wouldn't stop now. He'd keep coming.

What I needed to do was lead him away from Addy and Ryder. I just hadn't figured out what that looked like yet. I needed to talk to Rory.

After Scully's team was in place, Maddox headed out for his home and the rest of the Hatley family, and I went back inside to find Addy and Ryder playing cards by the light of his new burner phone. I wanted to join them, just like we'd been doing for the last few nights where I'd teamed up with Addy to make Ryder lose. She'd laughed and smiled and even wiggled her butt in victory a couple times.

Instead, I headed upstairs to check the bedrooms again and talk to Rory.

I made my way into the room Ryder had said was his grandmother's. It had a large, hand-carved oak bed with fairies dancing along the footboard and headboard. The creatures were so lifelike that I almost expected them to burst into song. The bed was piled with light-blue linens that looked brand new—a modern, geometric pattern that seemed to clash with the fairies.

I dialed the new number Rory had given me earlier. It

was an encrypted burner line she was piggybacking around the globe, but I suspected we'd still need to keep the calls as brief as possible. Whoever was giving Laredo information from the task force had the same skills and connections we did. They'd find us eventually.

"I'll only turn the burner on when I need it, so you won't be able to reach me the standard way. You remember the dark website I gave you for dropping coded messages in emergencies?" I asked.

"Yep. Already got it recoded for us."

I inhaled a shaky breath and asked, "Have you heard from Enrique?"

"He contacted me a few minutes after you left Ryder's. He exchanged a few rounds with the shooter but never caught up to him. Enrique said he found blood on the road, so he believes he winged the man."

"If we have blood, we can run him."

"Might not be in the system. And even if he was, Natalia could have wiped him from existence like she did herself."

"Has Leland asked for an update?" I asked.

"He knows about the attack at Hatley's and that you've gone dark. I didn't tell him what we found out about Anna being Natalia, but I also wasn't hiding my work from the task force before now, so he might see it anyway. They all might."

"I'm not sold that Leland is dirty," I told her.

"I'm not either. I'll dig around carefully on this end and see what I uncover. If I find anything, I'll use the dark site to get you a message."

"Can you do me a favor and dig into Enrique also?"

Rory was silent for a moment. "No way, G. His brother was slaughtered by the Lovatos."

"Not all siblings love each other, Rory. Maybe we've got an evil-twin/good-twin thing going on here." When she didn't say anything, I pushed, my voice getting hoarser with each word. "Someone has purposefully kept us off Laredo's trail. Whenever we came even slightly close, we were thrown off to other clues. It had to have been on purpose. And Enrique's been embedded in the gang in Lexington."

"I hate this."

"Me too." I swallowed hard. "We need those encrypted files from the Switch."

"Now that I know her real name, I'll add that into the programming mix and see if we can find a new combination. Have you asked Addy if her mother ever went by a different name?"

"I haven't, but I can. The letter seemed directed at Ryder though."

"I agree, but what we have now isn't working."

The dresser had an antique glass mirror that warped my reflection in the hazy phone light, and I had to do a double-take on the image. My hair was wild, my eyes deeply shadowed, and purple welts were starting to form on my neck. Who was this person staring back at me? I wasn't even sure I knew her anymore. She seemed out of control when I prided myself on having it. She was wanting things I'd never wanted and making mistakes, letting people sneak in under her defenses. I wasn't sure I could trust her.

My gaze fell to the dozens of picture frames scattered along the dresser's surface. Old family photos. Some were taken at the bar and some in downtown Willow Creek when the road was still dirt. My eyes settled on a picture that seemed to be in a position of prominence in the center spot. It was of a couple in thirties-style evening wear with the Hollywood sign in the background, as if they'd just stepped off the red carpet.

My mind whirled. "The gala is tomorrow at Laredo's."

"You can't be thinking of going."

"He's just going to keep hunting until he gets her. I need to stop him somehow. I need proof that he's behind this."

"After what went down today, he's not going to just let you walk in, and if he does it could be a trap."

"As far as Laredo knows, we haven't figured out he's involved. Right? His mole is protecting him. We hardly had time to question the guy today before he was killed. We don't even know his name yet, so if Ryder hadn't recognized him as being one of Laredo's men, we wouldn't have known."

"Those are all huge assumptions, G. If he has figured it out, you'll be in danger the moment you show up."

We were quiet, our minds whirling with thoughts. "Let's use the mole to our advantage. Drop some facts that make it look like we're still clueless."

"I don't like this."

I didn't either, but if we didn't make a move to stop this, Laredo would be the one to come hunting. I needed to do this. I needed to go, get Laredo's attention, and have him whisk me away from the party into the private parts of the ranch. I'd find a way to distract him, have him go get me something, or if worse came to worse, I'd use my gun and tie him up while I investigated. "If he's got the box she created, it ties him to all of this. And we can't risk him finishing the code without her. Just think what he'd do if he completed it."

"At the moment, it's only you, me, and Enrique who know about Laredo and Natalia," Rory said. "If Laredo finds out, we know Enrique is involved. I can craft two or three different scenarios, all with false leads that the Lovatos would want. I'll give them to different people around here, including Leland. If Laredo ends up with any of those facts, we'll be able to trace it back to the person who gave it to him."

"That's a great idea. I don't know what I would have done without you. Thank you for coming on board."

"I want these assholes as much as you do." And she did. While the men who'd been responsible for pulling the trigger on her mom had been killed or taken into custody, our major leads had all ended up dead. Whoever was in charge had ensured the guy closest to the head of the snake had ended up shivved in prison. Rory wanted the Lovatos taken down almost as much as I did.

Before I'd shown up in Willow Creek with Addy, I'd wanted it because I loved my job and was proud of my accomplishments. I was proud of cleaning evil from our world. Now…now I wanted to take the Lovatos down with a desperation that bordered on frenzied because I *needed* to keep Ryder, his little girl, and the entire Hatley family safe.

If anything happened to any of them, it might just rip my soul from my chest, and I'd never get it back.

Chapter Thirty-two

Emiliano

SO BLUE
Performed by The Trishas

I could almost feel the I told you so that was brewing behind Julio's lips, but he was smart enough to keep it to himself. Even though I'd known it was risky to go after the girl while she was at Hatley's, I'd assumed my men could handle the situation. It angered me that they'd been so incompetent. Except, my cousin had never let me down before. He'd always come through, even when I'd pushed us to the edge and back. So, what did that tell me about Hatley and his little sidekick?

Were they just lucky, or did they actually have skills I'd underestimated?

I watched as the doctor stitched up Julio's arm. Blood dripped from his biceps onto the plastic covering the floor and every inch of the room, including the walls and the ceiling. I'd learned a few things along the way. It had been difficult to get my father's blood out of the wood floors in the study when I'd killed him. I'd had to tear up the entire room, which had prompted my remodel of the wing of the house that had become my private lair. That was when I'd used one of the bloody planks to create the frame holding my last remaining picture of Natalia. Reminders of what happened when I used rage instead of intelligence to outsmart my enemies.

After the doctor packed his bag and left, I asked, "What did Ruiz tell them?"

"The DEA agent said Ruiz told them nothing. That they have no clue you're involved."

I didn't believe it, and I didn't think Julio did either. After all, we'd been at this game a long time. We'd been lied to by men with much more skill at it than the undercover agent.

"You let him shoot you."

"So he had something to give them," Julio said, shrugging into a black T-shirt with an ease that belied the fact he'd just had a bullet hole sewn up. It was one of the many things I admired about my cousin. His pain tolerance was almost as high as mine.

"I pretended to play along," Julio continued. "At the moment, it serves our purpose if he can really bring the girl to us." He waved a hand at the plastic room and the lone chair he'd just abandoned. "We'll get the truth out of him once he's here."

It would give me great pleasure to use my tools on Enrique Salazar. Excitement rippled through me. Tomorrow would be full of pleasures both expected and unexpected. The DEA agent. Hatley. His pretty little plaything. And of course, the final retribution against my sister—making her daughter love me.

"You placed a tag on him?"

Julio nodded.

"Good. Make sure he keeps his promise," I said, swiveling on the heel of my dress shoe and heading up the stairs to the ballroom where the event decorators were hard at work.

The decadent splendor I'd planned would take the gala's guests by surprise, just like I would take the world by surprise when I finally had Natalia's code and brought countries to a grinding halt. When I had the most powerful people on earth competing to kiss my feet.

The gala would be the first of many extravagant events I'd hold here, at the White House, the Kremlin. Anywhere I wanted. I'd throw a series of parties all draped like elegant wonderlands, dripping with diamonds and candlelight and champagne. A macabre contrast to the events occurring behind the scenes while the wealthy guests sipped and danced and laughed. Inside, crystal and china. Outside, blood and bared bones.

The idea of it made me hard.

I'd satisfy that need as well.

Gia Kent would satisfy it for me on bended knees.

I'd spend time with Hatley's woman while he was forced to watch. He'd struggle against his bonds. He'd scream and rave and threaten to kill me, but there would be nothing he could do. I'd get the revenge Natalia had first begged me not to take with a promise that she herself had betrayed. I'd get my revenge, and then I'd take both their lives.

I'd have everything Natalia had stolen from me. Nothing would stand in my way ever again. The world was going to be mine to crush or save. I'd have the world's leaders dancing to my tune and calling my name just as desperately as Hatley and his woman.

Chapter Thirty-three

Gia

WHAT I NEVER KNEW I ALWAYS WANTED
Performed by Carrie Underwood

I hung up with Rory, turned off my phone, and pocketed it before picking up the picture of the couple in the Hollywood hills that sat in the middle of the dresser—an elegant and beautiful pair who resembled movie stars from the golden age of the twenties and thirties. I scrutinized their faces, looking for a hint of Ryder and catching sight of him in the woman's eyes. The shape of them was the same as his.

"That's Great Grandma Carolyn and Great Grandpa Harry." His voice startled me, and I almost dropped the frame. Some bodyguard I was if even Ryder could sneak up on me. He walked over to me, took the picture from my hand, and stared down at it. "They met while working at MGM Studios back in the day. She was a costumer, and he worked in props. They got married and had Granny all while living it up in LA, but something happened that had them running back here, to Harry's home. If anyone knew what happened, they never passed it down to us kids. But Carolyn and Harry brought tons of old movie memorabilia with them that we loved playing with when we were little."

I tried to ignore the spike to my pulse that occurred simply by him standing next to me, but it washed through me anyway.

Ryder took in the room, frowning. "Uncle Phil didn't

know shit about decorating. He must have tried to redo the room. None of Granny's stuff is here, but that comforter is awful."

"Where's Addy?"

"She passed out on the kitchen table, so I put her in the bunk in the room across the hall." He set the picture down and put his hands on my shoulders, turning me to face him. His eyes bored into me in a way that made my feet turn to lead. "I almost lost you both today," his voice cracked, and I was right back in the moment at his house after Maddox had kissed McKenna. The moment when Ryder had looked at me like he'd wanted to do the same. As if the *I love you* his brother had given his fiancée was going to slip from Ryder's lips directed at me. But how could that be? We barely knew each other. We'd spent a handful of days together where we'd just started to share a few pieces of our lives. All of it done under intense pressure.

It couldn't be love. It had to be attraction. Respect. Uncontrollable lust. And yet, something deep inside me objected to my brushing the idea of love aside. When I'd seen that red dot on Laredo's henchman's forehead…when I'd thought it might take Ryder too…I'd experienced the most abject terror I'd ever felt in my life. If he'd been shot… God… I swallowed hard, not knowing what to say. Not knowing if I actually could say any of the ridiculous notions I was thinking.

It didn't matter if I said any of it aloud, though, because in the fake lighting my phone had filled the room with, Ryder read my soul anyway.

His hand moved, skating along the marks on my throat—the dark spots that proved I'd failed more than once since I'd shown up in Willow Creek.

"Sadie forced an epiphany on me at Phil's funeral," he said, his already gruff voice taking on an even deeper, rawer quality. "I was coming back to tell you when I saw—" His throat bobbed. "I know this isn't your home. I know you have a life that looks nothing like the one you've been living here with us. But this…" He cupped my cheek, and one long finger slid over my bottom lip, causing every particle in me to ignite. "What I feel when you're next to me… It's worth chasing. It's worth exploring. I don't want you to walk away without me telling you how I feel."

My heart pattered and pounded as if I was a teen girl with her first crush. Except, this was so much more than a crush. It felt like the forever I saw in my brother's eyes when he looked at his fiancée. I didn't know how to assemble the reality of the worlds Ryder and I lived in, but I knew he was right. This feeling… the possibility of having this…it was worth something. I just wouldn't know what *it* was until we'd explored it fully.

Maybe if we gave in to this uncontrollable need for each other. Maybe if we lost ourselves in each other's bodies for a few moments, the feelings would loosen their hold on us. Maybe all of this was just some severe form of lust and desire intensified by the situation. But I was also terrified that it wasn't. That both Ryder and the emotions I felt would end up sticking to my bones in a way that I couldn't shake, that would have me willing to walk away from my future to become part of his. To be his.

As he continued to stroke my lips, staring into those private places of me I'd never shared with another person, I could feel myself stepping over some invisible barrier that I'd never be able to recross. And yet, I did so anyway. I didn't tell him to stop, and when he tugged me closer and our hips collided, I simply slid my hands over his shoulders and down his arms.

He'd removed the suit jacket he'd been wearing, and I was suddenly desperate to touch his bare skin, to feel his warmth radiating through me. I undid the shirt buttons with hands that shook, pushing the white cotton aside to reveal the flat, muscled expanse beneath. His breath hitched as my fingers danced over the dark hair and silky six-pack. When I glanced up, there was a fire raging in his eyes but also the questions I couldn't answer yet aloud. I had to experience this first before I had the conversation he wanted. Before I gave up everything. I needed to know for sure it was what I suspected.

"I can't talk about tomorrow yet, Ryder. It's too much." I covered his hands with my own, moving them to my breasts, curling them over me. "But I want this. I want you. Right now. Make me believe what I feel with your touch."

His eyes closed. Thick lashes rested against bronzed skin before they opened again to reveal a delicious inferno that would devour me. He pulled away from me, and for a moment, I thought he was going to back away even though I could feel the solid proof of his desire pushing into me. Instead, his palms slid under my ass, and he lifted me into his arms, carrying me to the bed full of dancing fairies—a wildness in their movements that I felt growing in us.

I fitted my mouth to his, and heat burst along our lips. Actual flames I hungered to both douse and ignite. When we landed on the bed with him on top of me, pain shifted along my bruised body, and I couldn't help a small gasp that escaped me.

He pushed himself up on his palms, corded biceps working, concern fighting with the hunger in his gaze. "Damn it. I hurt you. You're hurt. I—"

I wrapped my hands around his neck, attempting to pull him back down to me. He fought me. Sinewy muscles pulsed in his arms, but I leaned up enough to snag his bottom lip with my teeth, sucking it into my mouth. He groaned, holding himself tight for a single heartbeat before he gave in and kissed me back with a ferocity that sparked the simmering flames until it felt like they would swallow me whole.

I ran my fingers along the smooth expanse of his back, down over the deep V at his waist, and around to the button of his pants. He stopped me before I could pop it open, pulling back enough to practically tear my flannel shirt off, revealing the same plain bra I'd worn all week.

He growled in approval, one hand finding a pebbled tip through the fabric as his head descended back to mine, lips joining, tongues battling. Theoretically, the embrace was nothing different from what I'd shared with others, and yet this one branded me. I'd never again experience this same intensity. This unbridled desire. This craving that only he could fill.

He unhooked my bra, tossed it aside, and bent to devour one breast with his mouth while gently massaging the other. Every nerve ending in my body sizzled, the energy crackling through the air like lightning strikes. His hands dropped away, undoing my jeans and dragging them down my body, touching, kissing, tormenting as he went with a wet mouth and nipping teeth.

When I was in nothing but my underwear, he rolled back onto me, lips finding mine again, but I sensed he was still being careful. That he was worried about hurting me. I didn't want him holding back. I wanted everything the heavy weight of him could offer.

"Don't you dare hold back on me," I whispered against his lips.

His gaze cut to mine, and I slammed my hips into his, the tension causing a moan to escape us both. He trailed wet, ravenous kisses along my bruised neck before easing down my body, tasting every inch as he went. Savoring me. My thighs shook when the coarse bristle of his beard landed on them. My hips bucked as he sucked at me through my underwear before almost tearing them from me and landing those tantalizing lips on my heat. My body shuddered as my control slipped further away.

His fingers joined his mouth, and I whimpered. It was too much. Too much and not enough. I tugged at his hair, forcing him to look up at me with blue eyes so dark they looked like the depths of the ocean. A soft grin tilted his lips upward.

"Something wrong?" he teased, knowing damn well nothing was wrong. Knowing that every touch and every caress was perfect.

"I'm going to shatter…"

A gasp escaped me as his thumb found home.

"Fair turnaround, darlin'. You've been wrecking me since the day you showed up."

Those words… I loved them and hated them. I wanted to heal not tear more holes.

I pulled on his shoulders, trying to bring us back face-to-face, but he resisted.

"You started this," he said. "And you can stop it any time you want, but if we continue, I need to control it. You don't get to drive here. You have to trust me enough to let go." He waited for my response, eyes dark and glimmering, full of promises and those emotions I was too terrified to say aloud. "What'll it be, darlin'?"

My body needed what he offered. Needed the release waiting for me. And maybe I needed to let go of the control as much as he needed me to hand it over. We stared at each other for several more heartbeats until I swallowed and nodded. His soft grin turned into that enormous smile he gave so infrequently. He dropped his head, tongue and hands turning back to the job of undoing me. The pleasure grew so fast, so furious, that when my release came, I was shaking from head to toe, quivering as the waves flew through me.

My body sank into the mattress, limbs loose but still trembling.

He eased back up me, tongue and hands working still, showering each piece of me with more attention until he reached my mouth and kissed it with a gentleness that was the opposite of the savageness he'd used before. "You taste like my home and destruction all at the same time. How is that possible?" His eyes glittered, staring into me, searching for more answers I couldn't give, but I didn't hold back. I didn't build a wall and look away. I trailed my hand down his jaw, finger caressing those firm lips. He nipped at it, licking my finger before sucking it into his mouth, and my core quivered again.

"We're not done, Ryder. You want to drive, I can let you, but we're not done. I need you inside me. I need to witness you letting go, just like you saw me."

"Tit for tat?" His brow arched.

I swallowed hard. "I'm not keeping score. This isn't a game or a competition. This is two people, giving to each other, but it only works if we both give, if we both receive."

He stared at me, eyes flickering with so much love and desire it drenched me. Drenched me and demanded I believe. That I give in. That I let not only our bodies but our souls touch.

"What'll it be, darlin'?" I tossed back at him, and he laughed softly before his mouth descended on mine once more, the feel of him seeping into every fiber of my being. It would hurt if I decided to walk away from it. Cause permanent damage to us both. But for tonight, I wouldn't let myself think about it.

Chapter Thirty-four

Ryder

DIDN'T KNOW WHAT LOVE WAS
Performed by Kane Brown

With craving beating through every molecule of my being, I pulled myself away from Gia's sweet lips and slid off the bed.

She was always goddamn beautiful, but she was especially stunning like this, with her dark locks curling around her breasts, lips swollen from my kisses, skin flushed from coming apart on my fingers and mouth. Her eyes were flashing with fire and brimstone. Daring me to try to walk away. Daring me to stay. My heart skipped a beat. Several beats. The painful knowledge settled home that I'd tasted something I'd never want to give back.

She'd told me to make her believe in us before she could talk about our tomorrows.

I'd give her that. I had to, because the alternative would bring me to my knees.

If she left, it would break me. Except, I wouldn't be able to collapse like I had when Ravyn left, because now I had a daughter to look after. I wouldn't be able to lock my heart away, because Addy deserved to have a piece of it. So, if Gia disappeared, I'd have to experience every damn slice she left in her wake in order to give my daughter what remained. But that singular thought—of Gia leaving—made something feral beat inside me. Something wild and ancient that needed to mark her and claim her so she'd never want to walk away.

I undid the button on my pants, and she bit her lower lip. As my pants dropped, and my underwear with them, her gaze slid down me, eyes heating. Lust. Desire. The same wild I was feeling.

I pulled a condom from my wallet, tearing open the wrapper with my teeth. Her eyes widened as I kneeled between her legs.

And finally, the simple truth tore out of me. "I'm not ever going to be done with you."

She smiled at my words, sitting up and pulling the condom from my hands. Her sure touch as she slid it on me was liquid fire, searing into me. I loved the confidence with which she did this—did everything. I wanted that to be mine and mine alone.

I pushed her back down on the bed, settling between her hips. As the heat of her soaked into me again, her eyes sparked with a light I wanted to catch like I'd caught fireflies as a kid. She kissed me fiercely, hand guiding me to the one place I yearned to be.

"You wanted to drive," she said, whispering the words in my ear. "So drive."

I responded by sliding in with a barely controlled thrust. As I bottomed out, pleasure rippled through my body, and the world grew hazy until there was nothing but the blaze burning between us and the honeyed taste and smell that was Gia. Our pace was steady and measured at first as we learned each other's shapes and angles—the places that made us both groan in pleasure. The delicious slide of skin against skin. The feel of our connection seeding itself, growing, and blooming until a frantic instinct took over, as if we were no longer ourselves but wild animals linked in a dance as old as time itself.

Those sweet gasps and whimpers of hers, that had almost made me lose it while I'd had my mouth at her core, returned, skimming across my skin as if they were their own touch. And as our thrusts grew harder, fiercer, I desperately held on, determined to watch her face soften and her entire being go lax again before I let go.

My hand drifted down between us, slipping through her curls, and she went off like a rocket, shaking and shivering. A beautiful cry escaped her lips that sounded like angels singing, and in that moment, I went over the edge, my body and heart and soul all landing deep inside her.

We rocked together, bodies slowing until the trembling of our limbs came to a stop. I rolled slightly, bringing her with me so we were on our sides, facing each other.

Her hand pushed at a lock of my hair that had fallen over my eyes. Her lips tilted upward. A softness surrounded her I'd never seen before. This was the real Gia. The one I was certain very few people had ever had the pleasure to see. There may have been other men in her bed, but I doubted they'd seen this. At least, my ego wanted to believe that—wanted to believe I'd shattered her world as much as she'd shattered mine.

"I hate to admit it, but you drive pretty well," she teased.

I huffed out a half laugh. "Only pretty well? Give me a second, we'll get back on the highway, and I'll show you how I can take an exit ramp going eighty."

Her smile grew wider. "That would be something to see."

From somewhere outside, a car alarm sounded before quickly going silent. That simple sound was all it took to tear at the temporary reprieve we'd found in each other, forcing reality back at us. I wrapped my arms tighter around her, kissing her forehead, as cold facts flooded me. Ravyn was Jaime's sister. Addy was his niece. He was hunting her as he'd hunted her mother.

"You need to find proof Jaime is involved," I said softly. "So, let's go get it and end this."

She choked back a little huff. "Rory and I have a plan. I'm going to the gala while you're at the safe house with

Addy."

The image of her being hauled across my house by a giant man filled me again and along with it, the fear, anger, and frustration that I'd felt. For those few seconds as I'd watched from outside my house, I'd been entirely helpless, so the idea of sitting around in a safe house, waiting while she went headfirst into danger, made bile crawl up my throat.

"You go, I go," I grunted out.

"You can't leave Addy, Ryder. After today, she'll need all new assurances that she's safe."

"I can't keep lying to her. We both know she'll never be safe until this is over, and if it takes walking onto Jaime's property to end this and protect her, then that's what I'll do."

Gia's eyes filled with tears she held back by slamming her lids shut. "Let me do this." Her voice was choked, broken and raw from the deep emotions as much as what she'd gone through today. "Let me handle this on my own with my team. Let me do this so that little girl keeps the one person she really needs."

When she'd first shown up with Addy, I'd told myself all Gia cared about was the case. That she didn't care about the humans involved. But the truth was, she'd had to shield herself from others in order to do her job. But it was also a shield she'd learned to create when moving from place to place as a kid so she didn't get her heart pulverized. And yet, over the last few days, I'd watched her fall for Addy and my family. Watched her fall for me. She'd said she wasn't ready to talk about tomorrow, so I'd embedded every last emotion I had into my touch, hoping it would be the proof she needed, but I wasn't sure she believed me yet. Wasn't sure she truly understood how important she'd become to all of us.

"You're wrong if you think I'm the only one she needs," I said softly.

Gia's lids popped open, surprise and hope mixing in those hazel depths. "What?"

"Don't you see, darlin'? We've both fallen in love with you."

She untangled herself from me, clutching at her stomach. She stared at me with fear and yearning and love in her eyes before she turned and reached for her clothes.

"That's ridiculous." She shook her head as if it was more at herself than at me. "All of this is nonsense. You don't fall in love with someone in a matter of days—a handful of hours, really. You don't… You just don't."

I slipped off the bed, pulled on my pants, and then went to her, dragging the flannel shirt from her hands and pulling her to me. She held herself tight, holding back, but I didn't let go. "This is scary for me too. I thought my one shot at true love had come and gone before I was thirty. All I saw before me was a lifetime of empty one-night stands and the love of my family. Then, you tore back into town, bringing me a little girl I thought I'd lost." I had to swallow back a lump of emotions. "Bringing me your fire, drenching me in it, and making me wonder if what I'd felt for Ravyn was all I'd imagined it to be. How could it have been when what I feel simply standing next to you is ten times more than I'd ever felt wrapped up in her?"

I felt her shudder at my words, and then finally, her shoulders relaxed, and her arms went around me. She put her chin on my chest and looked up at me, tears slowly rolling down her cheeks.

"You like everyone to believe you're a brash, grumpy cowboy, but really, you're a poet and an artist full of sweet words and passion you hide behind sarcasm and a wink. I feel lucky that you give me these glimpses of the real Ryder." She took a shuddery breath and then continued, "You're right. What's happening between us is bigger than anything I've ever felt. It makes me want things I've never wanted before, and that does scare me, just like you said.

"But what's even more terrifying is that having these feelings gives me tunnel vision. It put you and Addy and your family at risk today. I was waiting for you to come home to tell me about your day rather than walking the perimeter. So right now…" She breathed in and pushed herself away from me. "Right now, I have to tuck it away. Because if I don't…people might die. *You* might die. Addy. Your family…" A sob escaped her.

Fuck.

I didn't want to agree with her. I wanted to kiss her until she forgot everything again. But she was right. We needed to be thinking about more than just our feelings. We needed to consider Addy and my family—which was exactly why we had to end this.

Then, I could fight with her about what the enormity of our emotions meant.

Then, I'd find some way for us to be together without her giving up everything.

But first, we had to take care of business.

"I agree. We need to end this. But that's not you alone. That's us together. Jaime isn't going to let you waltz onto his property by yourself. He'll expect you to be on my arm. More importantly, he wants me there. That's why he drove all the way down here to personally make sure I came. Like it or not, darlin', I've got to come with you."

"Addy." She said my daughter's name like a desperate plea, and it only made me love Gia more. Ravyn had taken our daughter with her, putting her in danger by keeping her close. Gia would tear herself apart limb by limb rather than drag Addy anywhere near this.

"We'll tell her the truth. We're trying to put a stop to the threats. If anything happens to me, she'll have my family to take care of her. To love her."

Gia didn't respond, moving farther away to finish putting her clothes on. When she finally spoke, she said, "I need a dress. We'll have to stop somewhere on the way."

Her words sent a wave of relief through me. I thought of the piles of trunks in the attic that Granny had kept from her movie days. My siblings and I had created stories and put on performances with them for years. Fancy dress-up clothes, jewelry, plenty of things to sift through.

"I actually think I might have something that will work," I said, grabbing her hand and dragging her toward the room Addy was sleeping in.

We both peeked into the bunk, and I was grateful to see Addy had stayed right there under the covers instead of hiding somewhere in the room. She had her jaguar clutched to her chest, the blanket pulled almost over the top of her, but her face was relaxed in sleep. I swore somehow, some way, I would finish this so she could spend the rest of her life sleeping in peace. Safe in a bed with people she loved around her.

I made my way to the attic door, glad when it didn't squeak as I opened it. The steps were narrow, and cobwebs hit my face as I made my way up them. There were no windows up here, and I felt safe turning on the single bulb that swung from the rafters.

The attic ran the entire length of the house and was stuffed to the gills with the accumulation of McFlannigan lives. Old-fashioned cradles, broken dining room chairs, lamps and knickknacks that had gone out of style, and an abundance of boxes and trunks.

If I remembered right, there was a rolling rack of costumes at the back. I made my way through the maze of our family's leftovers with Gia on my heels.

"No bats up here, right?"

I stopped, turning around, a smile curving my lips. "Bats?"

She shivered. "I'm just saying… I don't do bats well."

A huff of laughter escaped me. "Of all the things for you to be afraid of." I shook my head. "No bats. No way in except the stairs we came up."

I pushed aside several boxes to reveal the clothes rack. All the dresses had been carefully wrapped in garment bags with lavender-scented satchels to keep the pests away. Whenever we'd played up here, we'd been sure to put everything back as we'd found it, otherwise Mama or Granny would have skinned us alive.

I unzipped the first one and grimaced. A dress suitable for a wagon train. Another held a men's suit. Another, a gingham dress that would have made Dorothy proud. Finally, I opened one that held a gown of champagne satin. I pulled it fully out of the bag and shook it. Simple. Elegant. Beautiful. Just like Gia.

When I turned to show it to her, her mouth dropped open a little.

The scooped neck was held up by two slender straps made from crystals. The dress curved in at the waist, and I could just imagine it molding over Gia's hips before flaring out just above the knees and flowing to the ground in a mermaid-like way. It was longer in the back, meaning the dress would trail behind her, and the back dipped decadently low.

She'd be the belle of the ball in this dress. No one would be able to look away.

That made a wad of dread form in my chest.

"Maybe not," I said, turning to put it back, but Gia caught my arm.

"It's gorgeous. Let me at least try it on before you shove it away."

I handed it to her with reluctance. She stripped off her flannel and jeans and pulled the dress on. Even with her no-nonsense bra sticking out the top, it looked beautiful on her.

"You can't wear that," I said, voice gruff.

She looked down at herself, smoothing a hand over it. "It's a little big in the chest, but it's not awful. Why doesn't it work?"

I closed the distance between her. "You wear that, darlin', and I'm going to be the one losing focus. I'll want to punch every man in the room because they'll all be staring at the shimmer of your skin and the soft swell of your curves that dress does nothing to hide."

She flushed a little in the dim light. "Then it's perfect. We want to make a scene, don't we? We want Laredo to pay attention to me."

"And why is that?" I couldn't prevent the growl that erupted through my chest at the thought of Jaime showing any interest in her.

"So he'll take me somewhere private."

"Gia." My growl turned into a possessive roar.

"He's not going to have the box or proof that he's part of the Lovatos hanging around the ballroom. How did you think this was going to work?"

"We're not using you as bait."

But she wasn't listening to me. I could see her mind whirling as she stepped out of the dress and back into her regular clothes. "I've got some comms we can use in my bag back at your house. If I had some jewelry, I might be able to hide a camera in a necklace or earrings." She looked back at the rack I'd pulled the dress from. "Got anything around here that will work?"

I wanted to say no. I wanted to tie her up and make her stay here, safe and sound, while I went and confronted Jaime directly. But I also knew that reaction did no justice to the fierce woman I'd fallen in love with.

I had to trust her.

My chest tightened uncomfortably.

I had to do it. I had to trust her because she needed me to, but also because I needed to prove that I could.

Chapter Thirty-five

Gia

NEVER HAVE I EVER
Performed by Danielle Bradbery

I could almost feel Ryder's internal debate wafting through the air. He didn't want me to do this. I'd said too much about my plan to entice Laredo into taking me somewhere private. I should have known Ryder wouldn't be thrilled about that scenario, regardless of the strategy behind it. Regardless of the fact that I'd used similar ploys to plant devices in places around the world.

I just had to be prepared for whatever Laredo would have waiting if he already knew who I really was, if the leak in the task force had already given him my real job along with my badge number.

Ryder moved past me, shoving his way through the stack of trunks, stopping at a large rounded one with a heavy, old-fashioned lock hanging open off it. I followed him, looking inside to see a slew of movie props. Swords and a fake holy grail. A shield. Sashes and shoes and bags.

Ryder handed me a red velvet bag. "There's a tiara in here that Gemma lent the film crew last year. It has a matching necklace, earrings, and a bracelet. It's all very Art Deco and a bit gaudy, but the large pieces might help you hide a camera."

I drew out a tiara made of yellow gems and diamond-like crystals. Designed with elaborate scrolls of curves and flowers embedded around the large stones on the front, it fell off to more round diamonds on the sides. It was tastefully small but jewel-studded enough to make a statement. A pair of clip-on earrings with large yellow and white gems dangling down several inches matched the tiara along with a three-strand, beaded necklace and a stunning cuff bracelet.

"These are beautiful—gaudy—like you said, but gorgeous. I'll figure out how to add a camera to at least one of them and stream the feed to our burner phones."

I was still uneasy about Ryder coming with me. Every protective instinct in my body had roared to life, determined to make sure he was around for that little girl who desperately needed him. I was terrified I'd miss an opportunity to end this because I was afraid of letting him out of my sight. Alone, I could maneuver through anything. With him… I'd be tempted to watch over him rather than do the job. But also, I needed him to get me in the door.

Worse, I needed another set of eyes at that gala, and right now, I didn't know who I could trust besides Rory. Not with Enrique and Leland both under suspicion.

"I need one of Scully's men to go grab my bag from your house," I told him.

"I'll call Maddox and see if he can do it."

How would Maddox feel about me using his brother? I could almost hear him trying to dissuade Ryder as much as I had.

We made our way down the rickety stairs, and I checked on Addy again. My heart swooshed softly, happy to see her still sound asleep, wrapped in the blankets with her stuffed animal and not hiding under the bed. Today had been terrifying, but maybe the love she felt from Ryder…from me…was allowing her to still believe in some measure of safety.

Ryder grabbed my hand, steering me back to the room we'd lost ourselves in for a few minutes, but I pulled away. "If you could call Maddox, that would be great. I want to check in with the officers outside, and I need to make a few calls."

"You need to rest your voice and get some sleep so you'll heal."

It had been so long since I'd let anyone worry about me, care for me, love on me, that it was overwhelming to have it all streaming at me now from Ryder. What was even stranger was that I actually bloomed under the attention, actively craving his concern and love.

I still didn't know what any of this meant for me going forward. Leland's words about there coming a time when I'd be willing to give up my job for someone came back to me. I'd scoffed at it, doubted it would ever happen, and now…love had hit me like an overwrite virus, destroying what I'd had and making me start anew.

Except, unlike catching a computer virus, I didn't feel frustrated or angry. Love wasn't ugly or vicious. The way it wrote itself on your soul was beautiful. I wanted to keep it rather than scrub it away. Those few moments tangled with Ryder hadn't been nearly enough. I craved more. I yearned to have those feelings every single day, to wake up with his blue eyes taking me in and his fingers tracing patterns on my skin.

I eased back into Ryder's space, rose on my toes, and kissed him. Softly. A quiet pledge. A promise I hadn't been able to say aloud yet. Because what would it really matter if I did say those words? He lived on a ranch in the middle of Nowhere, Tennessee. I lived in Maryland, miles away from NSA headquarters. I traveled the world, and he barely left the ranch. He reveled in being with his family, and I ran from mine in the name of service to a country I wasn't always sure deserved it.

Unlike Leland giving up fieldwork to stay close to headquarters, I doubted the NSA would let me do even an analyst job from the middle of nowhere.

My emotions were ping-ponging all over the place, and I was desperate to get some control back, to talk to someone who would understand.

I ran my hand along his cheek, the beard a dichotomy of soft and prickly. "Let me do two things, and then I'll come and rest."

He brought my hand to his mouth, kissed the knuckles, squeezed, and then turned and walked toward his grandmother's bedroom.

My heart fluttered. He was trusting me—not only to do my job but to come back to him.

After what Ravyn had done to him, I knew how hard it was for him to do just that.

I promised myself I wouldn't let him down, even if I couldn't see the right ending.

After I checked in with the man on guard out back and reassured myself Laredo's men hadn't followed us here—at least not yet—I stepped back into the kitchen. I dialed my brother's number from memory, hoping he'd pick up even though I was calling from a burner phone.

A gruff, sleep-filled voice answered, "Hello?"

I cringed, realizing it was the middle of the night in Toronto, where Holden and The Painted Daisies were, if I'd kept his schedule right.

"Holden. It's Gia."

"What the hell is wrong with your voice?"

I swallowed, suddenly not wanting to lie about any of it to him. "That's not what's important at the moment. I have a question for you."

"Seriously, G, what's wrong?"

"How did you do it?"

He hesitated for a beat, and knowing my brother, he was trying to figure out how far to push me about my voice. He sighed, giving in and asking, "Do what?"

"Your job protecting Leya when you were attracted to her?"

"Hold on." I heard rustling, a murmur of voices, a door shutting, and then he came back on the line, asking, "Where are you?"

"Tennessee."

A small half-laugh echoed over the line. "The Hatley Ranch?"

I wasn't there at the moment, but I knew what he meant. "Yeah. How'd you know?"

"Everyone there was in my face constantly about whatever the hell had gone down between you and Ryder. What did go down? And why are you back there?"

"When I was here last time, he caught me going through his office."

Two long seconds passed before he asked cautiously, "Why the hell were you doing that?"

I inhaled slowly, debating, and then letting the air out with the truth. "You don't really think I work for an agricultural journal, do you?"

"What? Yes, damn it. That is what I thought!" More silence that I didn't fill as I let my smart brother catch up. "What are you telling me? You're CIA?" He was upset. I'd known he would be if it ever came out, but there was more hurt and worry than anger in his tone.

"NSA Special Collection Service."

"Jesus, G," he grunted. "How the hell did you get mixed up with them? And what does this have to do with the Hatleys?"

"I can't talk about the case—you know that. And what? I can't serve my country like my dad and my brother?"

"Is this what really happened in South America? The time you told me you were surrounded by guerillas? They could have chopped you into bits and fed you to the crocodiles, and we'd never have known what happened to you."

I let out a frustrated huff. "Look. I didn't call to talk about what happened in the past. I've done a damn good job protecting myself and my team. I even made sure you had backup in Colombia. So, stop harassing me about my job and what I have or haven't been doing. The only reason I've come clean tonight is because I need some perspective. How did you stay objective?"

Another long silence followed before he asked, "The CIA agent who helped us? That was your doing?" When I didn't respond, he said gruffly, "Thank you."

"Wait, what was that? Did *Golden Holden* just thank me for something? Wow. How bad did that hurt?"

He chuckled. "Come on, I've thanked you plenty of times. You were the reason Leya and I ended up at the Hatleys when we needed a place to stay, and I thanked you then."

"Write it down in the record books. I've gotten thanked two whole times," I teased, my chest lightening just from talking to him.

"Ha ha," he said before clearing his throat and moving on. "So, you're at the Hatley ranch, and you've got what? The hots for Ryder? And you're worried it's making you lose your objectivity?"

"I'd say it's more than the hots, but yes," I said quietly. The way I felt in Ryder's arms… It had felt like…belonging. True belonging I'd never felt, even with my family. Maybe that was my fault because I'd been lying to them for years about who I really was, but no one had ever looked at me and seen me the way Ryder did. Tonight, as we'd lain there, hearts pounding and bodies still shaking, it was as if he read my entire history, every emotion I'd ever had, and still wanted me to stay.

"Want my advice?"

"That's why I called, Holds."

"Leave. Get out. You can't do the job and remove yourself—not if you have feelings for him."

My eyes closed. My heart skidded around in my chest. "That's the one thing I can't do."

My brother heard the words I hadn't said to Ryder in every syllable. "You love him."

"You didn't leave Leya," I said instead of admitting to feelings Ryder deserved to hear first.

"I didn't. And she got kidnapped. I almost lost her." I heard the pain in his admission, what he perceived as his failure, in every syllable.

"What would you have done differently if you couldn't leave?"

"I couldn't leave. I didn't know who we could trust."

"I'm in the same boat," I told him. "Someone's been keeping the truth from us."

"G… Let me see if I can swing some coverage here. Things have calmed down since we found Landry's killer. I'll come to you."

"You have all new responsibilities with the band. I'm not tearing you away from that. I shouldn't have called. I have another task force member here with me. We'll be okay. I'll just put some distance between Ryder and me." I didn't trust Enrique, and I wasn't sure Ryder would let me put any space between us. But I'd called my brother and worried him when there was nothing he could do, so I said what had to be said.

"If you feel even one-tenth of what I feel for Leya, I can guarantee it'll be impossible to put any distance between you."

"Thanks for the vote of confidence."

"I can only hope you don't feel the way I did, G. I don't want you to get hurt, and I don't want your conscience to be filled with my same regrets. If something worse had happened to Leya…" He dropped off, unable to finish. Seeing my brother with his famous wife, I could only imagine the devastation he would have felt. When I saw them together, it was like seeing one person divided into two bodies. Their connection glowed around them like its own aura.

If something happened to Ryder or Addy on my watch, it would tear me apart.

I'd be shattered.

The entirety of these emotions scared me more than chasing a cartel ever had.

"I love you, G."

"Love you too, Golden Holden."

"Keep me posted."

"I will."

"I mean it. If I don't hear from you at least once a day until you tell me it's all clear, I'm going to send some Secret Service buddies to track you down."

I laughed. "Don't you dare. My NSA boss would hate that."

"I know. That's why I'd do it."

When we hung up, I wasn't sure if I felt better or worse. All I knew was that I couldn't fuck up. For those few moments when I'd been lost in Ryder's arms, I'd lost all cognizant thought. There'd been nothing outside his hands and mouth. No job. No cartel. No danger. When the car alarm had gone off, it had slammed reality back into me. I could have been surprised all over again, just as I had been by the giant and his friend at the house.

Instinctively, I knew it wasn't my feelings that were the problem. In fact, the feelings I had for Ryder and Addy—for the entire Hatley family—made me more determined than ever to shield them from anything that came their way. I'd put myself between any of them and a bullet. I'd dismantle, code by code, the world of any asshole who tried to come at them. The problem had been forgetting everything while I was lost in him.

So, the touching had to be put on hold. Not the feelings. Just the skin on skin.

All I had to do was remember who I was—the woman who'd spent years earning her spy badge and proving her merit with the NSA. I knew how to catch Laredo. I had to trust my experience and training to get us through this.

I'd do the research. I'd find all his hidden secrets.

I'd bring Laredo and the Lovatos down.

And then after… After, I'd let myself wander in the shimmering bubble Ryder offered, allow myself to forget who I'd been, and see where the wind blew me.

Chapter Thirty-six

Ryder

PERFECT STORM

Performed by Brad Paisley

As I started to come awake from a deeper sleep than I'd had in days, I registered the warm body curled up next to me in bed with a strange sort of peace. It belonged there. It felt like I'd always slept this way with Gia tucked up next to me and her scent surrounding me. Honeyed goodness I wanted to drown myself in. My eyes flickered open as my brain caught up to the reality.

We weren't in my bed. We were at Phil's house, and we weren't going to get a lazy Saturday morning that we eased ourselves into by making love. Instead, we needed to move Addy to a safe house, I needed to pick up my tux, and then we had to head up to the Grand Laredo, where everything I loved would be at risk.

Gia shifted, rolling in my arms to face me with eyes that were wide awake.

"Did you sleep at all?" I asked her.

"A few hours."

Her voice sounded a little better, but it wasn't back to normal yet. I leaned in, capturing her lips. I'd meant it as nothing more than a sweet good morning, a declaration of the love I felt, but the moment our mouths joined, it was like an inferno erupted. Need slaking through me. Hunger.

Before I'd even registered it, I'd rolled her under me, pushed my tongue into the heaven of her mouth, and slid my hands under her shirt. She met every stroke with her own, palms skimming my back, hips slamming into me.

I broke away from those siren lips, trailing kisses down over the bruises on her throat, tugging the buttons on her flannel open, baring her sweet tips, and devouring them.

"Ryder, I can't do this right—" A breathy little moan took over her words as I pulled her underwear aside, my tongue and fingers finding home.

Her nails dug into my scalp, and I wanted to bury myself in her. I wanted to be lost in the heaven she provided and cursed myself for not having more than one condom in my wallet. Instead, I found satisfaction by taking her up and over the edge, watching with delight as her lids grew heavy, and her body shivered and shook.

The smile that lit my face at watching her come apart felt like a stranger's, larger than I'd given anyone in years.

I found my way back to her lips, kissing her. She cupped my jaw, stroking softly as she whispered a husky, "Good morning."

I smiled against her lips. "Darlin', that was more than just a good morning. That was, 'Welcome to the gates of heaven.'"

She huffed out a little laugh, glanced toward the door, and then pushed me off her with a smile. When she disappeared into the bathroom, I followed, sliding up against her back, hands snaking into the opening of her shirt, pulling her into me, and kissing the side of her head.

"I wish this was all we had to do today. Lie in bed, naked, making love."

She pulled away again, searching the cupboards and coming up with a brand-new toothbrush and toothpaste that might have been a decade old.

"I've never done that," she said almost too casually.

"What?" I asked, trying not to react to the distance she

was pushing between us. A distance that hadn't been there since we'd made love, tapping at doubts I thought I'd put aside.

"I've never spent an entire day in bed, lost in someone."

"Why not?"

She shrugged, looking like Addy when she was unsure. "I always had a million excuses. Even with my college boyfriend, I'd leave, saying I had a thousand things to do the next day. And ever since I joined the agency, I haven't had the time for a serious relationship." She was thoughtful, her hooded eyes taking in my reaction to her. "I don't come to a full stop easily."

She didn't stay. That was what she was telling me, and it hurt my heart. Dug into the wounds I was trying hard to heal. Shook the edges of the trust I was trying to give.

As if reading where my mind had gone, she rose and kissed my cheek softly. "But I find myself wanting those overnights and lazy days for the first time ever. Wanting that and so much more. Wanting you and Addy and a life that means staying put in one spot for longer than a few days."

"Yeah?" My heart slammed harder inside my chest.

She nodded, but then turned incredibly serious as she said, "But for the rest of today, I can't let myself think about it, Ryder. I have to *be* the job today. Otherwise..." She shook her head, throat bobbing.

I wrapped my arms around her, squeezing her to me. I wished I could wave a wand and jump us a day or two into the future, when this was all over, and everyone was safe, and all we had to do was crawl back into bed and make love all over again.

"What do you need from me?"

"Can you go back to being an asshole? Say something that will really piss me off? That might help."

I chuckled and then released her, but as I did, I slapped her on the ass. "Stop trying to seduce me, darlin'. We've got work to do and can't afford to laze around in bed as if we're royalty."

A garbled choke of laughter and irritation broke from her.

"That's a start."

♫ ♫ ♫

Maddox showed up with Gia's bag that she'd requested from my house, along with breakfast burritos from Tilly's café for us and the men outside. After we ate, I sent Addy upstairs to wash up, and we got my brother up to speed on Gia's plan for the gala. As I'd suspected, he wasn't pleased. "I can go in your place. I'm a Hatley. I'm part of the family and the ranch."

"He doesn't want you, Mads," I told him. "And the truth is, I need someone I trust with Addy. She needs someone she knows with her today. You take her to the safe house."

"Scully found a place over in—"

"Don't tell us," Gia cut him off. His eyes widened, and she just shook her head. "You know it's better that way. If we don't know, we can't tell him."

My gut rolled, the burrito I'd eaten trying to crawl back out as I thought of the ways the leader of a cartel might try to get a person to talk.

Addy came down the stairs with her purple backpack over her shoulder and her jaguar clutched in her hands. Her eyes were scared and sad, and I hated it. Hated that she was back to the frightened child I'd first seen in Maddox's office.

I squatted down, hugging her to me, stroking her head. "Uncle Maddox is going to take you somewhere safe today. Gia and I need to go take care of things. I'm hoping that what we do today will make sure you're safe forever. That the bad men won't ever come for you again."

She looked at me with fear growing in her eyes. "Bad men…hurt you? Hurt Gia?" Her gaze turned to Gia, who was standing by me.

Gia kneeled, wrapping her arms around us both. "I'm going to do everything in my power to make sure we're all safe."

I was overwhelmed by the feel of them tucked up against me—the family I'd thought I'd lost and that, somehow, Ravyn had brought back to me. It was shitty the way it had happened, but maybe this was what the universe had intended for me—for us—all along. Maybe Ravyn was supposed to come into my life, give me this beautiful child, and lead me to Gia. Maybe she'd had a purpose I hadn't been able to see. I wasn't the same doe-eyed twenty-something who'd fallen for Ravyn and thought I'd always have her. I'd learned how to appreciate what you were given, and I'd spend the rest of my life showing these two stunningly courageous women exactly just how much I loved them.

"You're the bravest kid I've ever met," I told Addy. "I just need you to be brave a little bit longer. Brave and smart, just like your mom."

Her eyes widened at the mention of her mother, whom we'd mostly avoided.

"You liked Mama?" Addy asked.

"I loved her, but I won't lie, she hurt me good by leaving and not telling me about you." I shook my head to clear it of those last shreds of pain. They couldn't hurt me anymore, not with Addy and Gia at my side. "But when I knew her, I was continually amazed by how smart she was. How beautiful. How courageous she was to start her life over from scratch. I see so much of her in you."

"She didn't like her old life," Addy said, the full sentence twisting inside me. "It scared her. She was scared when people knew her real name."

Gia and I shared a look, thinking of the encryption password and the name I was supposed to know.

"What name was that?" I asked quietly.

"Natalia. We always moved when anyone used it. They wanted her to go back to the ranch where bad things happened, but she promised I'd never have to go there," her little voice cracked.

"You won't have to, sweetheart. Not ever."

"Did she have a name she liked best, Addy?" Gia probed gently.

"She said Papa and me were the only ones who knew her real name. That I should only tell my papa it."

I swallowed, hope pounding inside my chest. I could feel it wafting off Gia as well.

"Ravyn. She loved Ravyn," I said.

Addy nodded, a tiny smile appearing. "She said she'd promised to be Ravyn Eowyn Hatley. She said that was who she really was."

The name hit me hard in the chest for multiple reasons. My past, present, and future all colliding.

I looked over at Gia, and our eyes locked. Was this the name we needed to break the encryption?

"It's a good name," I finally was able to say.

It was a name she should be buried with. I'd make it happen. I'd find out what they'd done with her body in Denver, and I'd have her brought here. I'd have her placed in our family plot in the far corner of the ranch with the rest of the Hatleys, and in that way, Addy would forever have her mom close by.

I cleared my throat and broke away, with reluctance, from the little haven the three of us had made with our tangled arms and joined souls. "She belonged here, sweetheart, and so do you."

Addy looked up at me with so much trust in her eyes I wasn't sure I could hold on to it without disappointing her. Wasn't sure I'd earned it. But I would do my damnedest to do so.

"Okay, Addy, we need to head out," Maddox said, his own throat thick with emotions, and when I looked up at my brother, his jaw was working as he blinked back tears. I couldn't even bother to harass him about it because I felt the same. I felt about to break. As he held out his hand for my daughter, and she moved from me, sliding her hand in his, my entire being clenched.

When she glanced back at me with worry in her eyes, I said the only thing I wanted her to remember if things went sideways. "I love you, Addy. Know that I love you."

She pulled away from my brother, ran back, and flung herself at me. I caught her, hugging her tight, kissing the side of her head, feeling so many emotions that I couldn't quite catch up to them.

"Love you too, Papa."

Tears hit my cheeks. Goddamn tears, but I let them be. I'd earned them, hadn't I?

We stayed that way for a long time, then I set her down, and she went back to my brother.

As I watched them walk down the steps, I promised I'd do whatever it took so we'd be together again. Even if that meant breaking the promise I'd given Mila days ago to never kill another living thing. If it came down to me and Jaime Laredo, I'd be the one who came out on top because I had everything to live for.

♫ ♫ ♫

Scully's men dropped us a town over at the mall, where Gia picked up a pair of low-heeled sandals to go with Great-Granny's dress, I picked up my tuxedo, and we snagged a rental car. Then, we headed an hour north to Corbin, which was the town nearest Laredo's ranch. As I drove, Gia went online and rented a hotel room under an alias, secured a camera to the tiara, and talked with Rory multiple times. Gia gave her the name Addy had told us Ravyn had claimed was her real one, and then the two of them discussed strategies for breaking the encryption on the data from the Switch as well as plans for getting behind the scenes at Laredo's.

No one had seen Enrique since he'd left my house the day before, after having wounded the sniper. The dead man from my living room had been identified as Jose Ruiz, and he'd worked for Jaime Laredo for over a decade. It tied Laredo to the attempted kidnapping, but defense lawyers would poke a million holes in that loose connection, as the dead man couldn't confirm that Jaime had sent him to get Addy.

As we drove into the parking lot of the mediocre hotel Gia had booked, Rory called back yet again with excitement dripping from her voice. "It worked! We broke the encryption!"

The tension that had held Gia's back stiff and straight all morning seemed to ease ever so slightly. I longed to make that tension disappear completely. I could do so easily with my mouth and hands, but Gia had asked for the space to do her job today, and I respected that. Needed that. Needed us both to stay focused on the endgame.

"What did you find?" Gia asked.

"More than enough to get a warrant for every place and device he owns. It lists shipping dates for guns and drugs, people working for him, and even hits he ordered. It also has every financial scheme he ran and the money he took. Ravyn had it all." Rory's voice was almost ecstatic.

"Does Leland know?" Gia asked, and the tension ramped back up in her shoulders.

"No. I figure we need to let our false-information campaign play out first so we know who we can trust."

"I hate that you're right."

"There's something else." Rory was all eagerness again. "She left the final code for the Houdini box. Except, it's not just the final code."

"What do you mean?"

"I think…" Rory took a huge breath. "I think it's a Trojan horse. If we give him this code, it installs correctly at first so he'll believe it's actually working because, well…it does. But then she delivers another little packet, and *boom*, the whole thing gets wiped."

"She can tell that all by looking at some lines of code?"

I asked doubtfully.

Rory heard me and laughed, but I heard the bit of offense in her response. "Do not doubt me, cowboy. I've spent my life swimming in code. I know what these strings mean."

"Won't he know as well?" I asked.

"Maybe." Rory's enthusiasm dimmed. "If he was coding along with her, maybe. But if he was just handing her the ideas, he might not understand the language itself. Plus, he'd really have to take the time to analyze it before he loaded it. If he thinks he's broken you, if he thinks you're giving it to him reluctantly, I'm hoping he just loads it, eager to finally have it complete."

My heart pounded viciously. "What do you mean, 'if he thinks he's broken you'?"

Chapter Thirty-seven

Gia

BACKGROUND MUSIC
Performed by Maren Morris

Ryder's voice was deep and angry. Rory and I had come up with that strategy on text. I'd told Ryder I needed Laredo to pull me into his private rooms at the ranch, but I hadn't told him what I expected to happen once he did. If Laredo didn't suspect me, he'd try to seduce me. If he knew I was with the task force, he'd likely torture me for information. In some ways, that was the better scenario because then I could do exactly what Rory had said—make it seem like he'd broken me and hand over the code.

"Send me what I need. I'll download it to a flash drive and take it with me," I told Rory.

"Gia," Ryder's voice was demanding, staking his objections but also staking a claim. The single word told me he had a right to have a say in what I did. Less than a week ago, that would have infuriated me. It would have had me slamming back at him and doing exactly what he'd tried to stop me from doing. Now…now I wanted to live through this because I wanted to know what it was like to be loved by this man so much that he'd break himself in half to give it to me. I wanted him and Addy, even if that meant walking away from everything I'd accomplished.

It stung. It still hurt, the idea of giving up the spy-like

life I was proud to have created for myself, but I was tantalized by the life this man and his little girl could offer me even more.

The moment with Addy in the kitchen had wiped away the remaining doubts I'd had after making love to Ryder. I wanted them, no matter the cost.

"I'll call you back," I said to Rory and hung up. I turned fully to him in the tiny rental. "I thought you were starting to trust me?"

"This has nothing to do with trust and everything to do with the fact that I'm not sending you into Laredo's knowing you're going to be, what…tortured? No fucking way."

"Do you want this to be over?"

He's eyes were dark and broody. "You know I do."

"Then trust me to do my job."

"Fuck the job if it means you getting hurt." He leaned toward me over the center console, fingers dancing along the bruise on my throat. "I can't… When I saw you being dragged across my house… Jesus… I can't do that again."

"If you can't, you need to stay at the hotel."

"Darlin'…"

"I'm serious, Ryder. We've never been closer to bringing the Lovatos down than we are right now. This is how we end it for Addy and you. For all of us."

"Can't you use the information Ravyn left you to get a warrant and bring him down that way?"

"It would take time. Time we may not have. If Laredo gets even a whiff of this, he has the means to disappear, and who knows what the lawyers will do with it? They could say none of it is admissible. Plus, at this moment, I don't even know who we can trust. What if we hand it all over and it just disappears? Rory planted some false leads, things we want to get back to Laredo so we know who's been working for him. That has to happen before I hand over the data and trust the justice system to do its job."

"Then we should wait. Let whatever you put in motion

pan out and then get a warrant to take him down."

"He'll disappear, Ryder. What happens if all the evidence disappears, like everything on the Lovatos has up until now? This is our chance to make sure he never gets his hands on the final code for the Houdini box. If Rory is right, and Ravyn installed a virus that can cripple his business, don't you think she deserves the chance to make that happen? He took everything from her, from you both. Let Ravyn's work be the final blow."

His jaw worked overtime. Teeth grinding. Fear and desperation in his eyes, but also hope.

I felt that hope deep inside me. Hope and anticipation.

After what felt like an endless minute, he reached for the door handle and got out of the car. He retrieved our shopping bags and the two garment bags from the back. I joined him, slinging my backpack over my shoulder and reaching over to squeeze his arm. When he looked down at me, I said, "Thank you for proving you trust me."

His throat bobbed, but he didn't say anything. He just led me into the hotel, where we checked in using one of my aliases, and headed upstairs to the room.

Once we were inside, I called Rory back.

"Did you send me the code?"

"Put a packet on the dark website we discussed."

I logged into my computer, secured my location by bouncing it around the globe, and then found the website. Sure enough, she'd placed an encrypted file there. I downloaded it.

"You use the same password key as Ravyn?"

"Yep."

I loaded it to a flash drive the size of a nickel.

"G?"

"Yeah?"

"I've been going through some of her files."

"And?"

"It's ugly. Really ugly. There's a journal of sorts that she wrote, and it's clear her dad abused both her and her brother. Savage beatings for the smallest of indiscretions, and after their mom died, I think he might have sexually abused her as well."

My eyes shot over to Ryder, where he was hanging the evening wear in the closet. His hands stalled, turning to me with a look of abject sadness on his face.

"At first, the coding she created with Laredo was supposed to be used as a way to get even with their dad—take the ranch and their trust funds back. Then, Laredo convinced her they could be Robin Hoods, helping the poor, abused, and disenfranchised with it. But when she graduated from MIT and came home, she overheard a conversation between him and Julio and learned what he'd really been doing with her code. The Lovato name, the wolf name, had come from a game they'd played as kids with Julio and their other cousins in California. She dug into the cartel and found out Laredo was selling drugs and guns as well as running financial schemes. In retaliation, she moved some of the funds out of his main offshore account, hiding them. She was throwing it in his face when their father walked in. He demanded a cut, Laredo refused, and their dad drew his knife. Laredo overpowered their father, cutting him to pieces with his own knife while Ravyn screamed. That was why she ran away to begin with. She realized her brother had become an even worse monster than their father."

Ryder sank onto the bed, rubbing a hand through his waves. I wanted to comfort him. To wrap my arms around him and make him forget everything he'd just heard. To retreat to the bubble that was waiting for us.

I forced myself to look away, to think about the information we'd been given and the next tasks that had to happen. "I thought their dad disappeared in a plane crash in South America?"

"Either they put his body on the plane and brought it down, or they just used Ravyn's code to make it look like it happened. I'll have to do some more digging. I'll read more of her files, but my point is that Laredo…he's going to be pissed he protected her, and she betrayed him by running away and then lying for seven years about her daughter."

"He thinks I stole them from him," Ryder said. This grimness in his words startled me. I hadn't thought much about what role Ryder had in this, other than being Addy's dad—the one keeping her from Laredo. With a sinking feeling, I knew he was right.

We'd been chasing the leader of the Lovatos for years, and what we'd found out was that he was savvy and smart and he used deadly force with ease. If he even suspected someone to have betrayed them, if they even screwed up in the slightest, they ended up like Ravyn. Knowing he'd suffered years of abuse may explain how he'd ended up without a soul, but it also shined a spotlight on just what he'd do when threatened.

Both Rory and Ryder were right. Laredo would feel betrayed by his sister, and he'd feel like Ryder had been the reason. I was surprised he hadn't retaliated before now. That he'd kept up a friendship with Ryder even after Ravyn had disappeared. Maybe that was what Ravyn had meant by saying she'd negotiated to keep the Hatleys safe, but if so, that deal would be broken now that she was gone. It wasn't just me who Laredo would want to torture tonight. In fact, if he didn't know who I really was, he'd get great joy out of using me to get to Ryder.

I worked through an enormous lump in my throat to say, "You can't go tonight."

Ryder's eyes darkened. "You go, I go."

He'd said the same thing last night. It was both a soothing balm and a horrendous torment.

"What do we know about the false leads you planted?" I asked Rory.

"Nothing. No one has shown up at either of the locations. Not the hotel Leland thinks Addy's at nor the safe house in Lexington that I dropped to the general task force."

"And Enrique?"

"I haven't heard from him at all, so I haven't been able to give him the Knoxville lead."

Ryder and I stared at each other. My heart slammed inside my chest. I didn't want to put him at risk. I didn't want one beautiful hair on his head to be hurt. Laredo would have a team tonight. An entire team of men at his beck and call. It was stupid to go in there with just the two of us.

For the first time since taking this job, since bringing to life my James Bond dreams of taking down the evil villain alone, I knew the truth. I needed more than just me on the case to protect those I loved. Not because I'd lose focus. Not because the feelings I had were too much. On the contrary, I would do anything to keep every hair on Ryder's head right where they were at. This was simple math. The numbers were against me. Against us.

"If we tell Leland what's been going on, what are the chances of him getting a team here in time to help?"

"In under two hours?" Rory asked with doubt in her voice. "*If* we can trust him to help, there's a chance he might be able to motivate some local cops. But who knows if they're already in Laredo's pocket. There's an FBI residence in Lexington and another in London—as in London, Kentucky. We might be able to mobilize them. But again, that's if we think we can trust them. Just the paperwork to get them all on board might take longer than two hours."

I moved to Ryder, pulling his hands into mine and setting them both on my chest. "What do you want to do?"

He stared at me for a long time, finger trailing over my cheek. "I can't live with a threat hovering over us, and I sure as hell am not letting you go in there alone. We promised Addy we'd try to finish this. I don't want to break that promise to her."

I swallowed hard, hoping—now that he'd given me the trust I'd asked for—that I didn't let him down. That I didn't let any of them down. The weight of it fell heavier than normal on my shoulders. I lifted my phone and said, "Find Enrique, Rory. We need eyes on him. Then, talk to Leland

and see what boots we can get on the ground quickly. If you don't hear from me by midnight, send in whatever cavalry you can pull together."

"Okay, Cinderella. Midnight it is."

She clicked off, and I wrapped my arms around Ryder, setting my head on his chest. The thud of his heart pounded against my ear, echoing my rapid pulse. I wasn't sure we'd walk out of this unscathed tonight. I wasn't sure what would happen to either of us. But if I could plant Ravyn's Trojan horse, and if we could get authorities not in Laredo's pocket to show up, we'd bring down the entire cartel. Addy would be safe, even if the worst happened to Ryder and me.

I wished I'd called my parents and told them I loved them. But if I did it now, Dad would hear my fear, and even Mom would know something was wrong. They'd worry, and their worry wouldn't change the outcome. It was better this way. Better they didn't know until it was over—whatever that ended up looking like.

♫ ♫ ♫

Even though I was covered, I still felt naked after I'd zipped up the dress from Ryder's grandmother's attic. There was no way I could wear a bra with the back dropping down to practically my ass cheeks and nothing more than a scrap of tiny beads holding up the scooped neck. I had nothing on beneath the satin except a thong. And once I'd added the gaudy, thirties-style jewelry, it felt like I was wearing more gems than I was clothing.

The lack of color in the dress had put the bruising on my neck on display. I'd had a hard time covering it with makeup and then decided to let the necklace do the bulk of the work, wrapping it close before leaving a long loop to dangle between my breasts.

I turned, catching sight of myself in the full-length mirror behind the bathroom door, and my feet stalled in the kitten heels I'd bought at the mall. With the gems and the champagne-colored gown, I almost looked bride-like. If I'd ever considered getting married, I would have picked a dress like this. Simple and elegant without all the frills and lace. The thought of wearing this today, walking alongside Ryder in a tuxedo, made my pulse beat erratically. It made visions of a candlelit room and families standing by while whispered promises were made seem suddenly possible.

Tomorrow. If we made it out of this, I'd think about it all then. I'd tell Ryder I loved him, and we'd figure our future out. Something we could both live with.

As I stepped out of the bathroom, Ryder had his back to me, looking out the window. The black tux fit him perfectly, even though it was rented. It hugged his broad shoulders and tapered over his trim waist, making him much more a James Bond image than I'd ever been. As if he felt me watching, he turned from the hotel window, and my breath caught at the beauty of him. His hair was slicked back, putting on display the strong, square lines of his clean-shaven face. I hadn't seen him without his scruffy beard since I'd arrived in Willow Creek days ago. While I missed it, I also found myself desperate to explore all that smooth skin with my lips and tongue.

His gaze slid down me slowly, taking his time. When his eyes finally returned to mine, the longing, the utter fire I'd seen in them since the moment he'd caged me in his office last summer, burned even brighter, like a solar flare ready to leap out and scorch me.

Losing ourselves in each other last night hadn't done one damn thing to tame those flames. It had only added fuel to the already existing pyre.

I couldn't pull my eyes from his. Could barely breathe. Certainly couldn't move. It was Ryder who closed the distance between us, voice dropping as he said, "You're even more stunning than normal. Resplendent."

"Resplendent?" The word jerked me out of my stupor with a laugh, and his lips quirked.

"I hate that he's going to see you this way. That he's going to think about touching you. I don't like the idea of any man touching you, but especially not him." The darkness in his tone wound through me. It wasn't just the possessiveness of it. It was protectiveness too, and it made me want to curl into him when normally it would make me toss my fist and shout my independence.

"You'll have plenty of beautiful women eating you up with their eyes tonight. You think I'll enjoy that? You think I enjoy knowing you've had a sea of women in your bed?"

Jealousy seared me, and he saw it. Instead of making him unhappy, it made his lips curl upward ever so slightly.

"I'm not going to lie to you, darlin'. For a long time after Ravyn left, I tried to scrub the hurt away with sex. But I never brought any woman home. Not a single female besides my family ever crossed my doorstep. The ladies I was with always knew exactly what I was offering, and it was never what I'm offering you."

My pulse skittered around, that love I was feeling bouncing back to the forefront of my mind. But it was the last thing I needed to be thinking about at the moment. I needed to think about Laredo. How to get him alone and how I would make him believe what I had on the flash drive was legit before he did something permanent to Ryder. But still, I let myself savor this one last moment when a man I loved was offering me a future. I leaned in, kissing him slowly, languidly, as if we had all the time in the world, before pulling back and swiping my lipstick from his mouth.

He caught my hand, turned it over, kissing the palm, and I could practically feel the worry vibrating off him.

I swallowed hard. "It's going to be fine," I told him. "You know how to work the camera app. You'll be able to see what's going on with me. You've got a GPS tracker in your pocket, so I'll know where you're at. And if something goes wrong…" I lifted my dress so he caught sight of the gun I'd strapped around my knee where the dress flared out so it wouldn't show. "I have this to help us."

"That's not the comfort you think it is," he said quietly. He reached up to stroke a path from my jawline down to the gem-covered strap at my shoulder. My skin prickled at the fiery trail. He bent and kissed my shoulder softly. More goosebumps broke out, and my nipples hardened, clear as day in the thin material of the dress.

When he lifted his head, there was a pleased look in his eye at my physical reaction to him. I inhaled the heady masculine scent of him, suddenly wishing we were going to a real party. That he was in the handsome tuxedo and I was in an elegant ball gown, attending an event where we'd spend the night brushing fingers, dancing tantalizingly slow, and drinking just enough to enhance the yearning until we could do nothing more than rush back to our room, shed our clothes, and lose ourselves in each other.

My eyes fluttered closed, letting myself enjoy the mirage for one long heartbeat before purposefully brushing it aside once more.

It wasn't just Ryder's or Addy's life at stake. It was our entire civilization. If the Lovato cartel got its hands on a working Houdini box, the destruction would be almost as large as a nuclear bomb. It would change our future.

I couldn't fail. I wouldn't.

I stepped away from the warmth of Ryder's arms, picked up my clutch with the flash drive and my phone, and headed for the door.

He met me there, took my hand in his, and rested it on his arm. Then, he looked down with a smile and a wink, saying, "Out of all the ranches, in all the world, you sneaked into mine. Let's not ruin it by ending tonight with some cliché gun battle, shall we? Let's get in, get out, and go make some movie-worthy memories."

"Wouldn't that be like Frodo tossing the ring into the fire without the torture that came before it?" I teased.

"I was trying to be romantic. I've been told *Lord of the Rings* doesn't cut it."

"I don't know, that moment at Minas Tirith when Arwen marries Aragorn and gives up her Elfin immortality…that seems pretty romantic."

He drew me to a stop, a look of awe on his face. "I don't want you to do that, you know." My heart skipped a beat. "I don't want you to give up your life and everything you love to take a place at my side. But—"

I kissed him. And there was nothing slow and languid about this. It was fierce and strong, and it demanded he shut the hell up, because if he didn't, if he kept going, I'd be back to thinking about tomorrow instead of all the things we had to get through tonight.

"One step at a time, cowboy. Let's live through this evening, and then we can talk about what comes next."

Chapter Thirty-eight

Emiliano

FORGIVENESS DON'T GROW ON TREES
Performed by Bad Flamingo

I stepped out of the closet, clipping the last cuff link into place, and glanced over at Julio in his plain black cotton T-shirt and cargo pants. On nights like tonight, when I got to step out of the shadows and shine while he was stuck in the darkness, I wondered if he ever felt any resentment. But then again, I'd given him everything he had. The nice car, even nicer house, and hordes of women. If it hadn't been for me, he would have ended up in a Mexican jail or dead long ago. I'd been the one who'd turned the handful of drugs he'd been trafficking into something bigger. If I hadn't taken over, turning his tiny drug hobby into a business envied by the Russian, Colombian, and Mexican cartels, he'd have nothing.

Still, as more brother than cousin, he deserved to come out of the shadows. He'd been more loyal than the sister I'd protected with my own blood. Julio deserved a reward. Now that we were on the verge of changing the future of humanity, I'd make sure it happened. He'd rule the world at my side—king to my emperor. After tonight, I was sure I'd have everything I needed to give us the prizes we'd earned.

"Everything in place?" I asked.

"Both rooms are set up as instructed."

"You get anything else out of him?" Unexpected fury

spiked through me. The DEA agent hadn't brought me what I'd wanted, offering an alternative way of getting it instead. It was a minor setback that would end with the same result—Natalia's daughter in my care and Hatley destroyed.

"He's told us everything he's willing to give up. The rest he'll take to his grave."

The man had been stronger than I'd expected. It would have given me great pleasure to seep the last of his strength, to have him begging for death, but I'd give him to Julio as the first of many new gifts for his loyalty.

"Finish him."

Julio's eyes widened. "You don't want to do it yourself?"

My cousin had earned this, and tonight, I had two more gifts arriving that I'd be able to play with. "He's yours."

He nodded, opening the door for me as I strode toward it. The black-and-white halls soothed me, tempering my anger at the minor setback. I'd save my fury for later—for Hatley and his plaything. As we came out of my private corridors, the door latched behind us, the scanner beeped red, and I headed for the ballroom where I could already hear the clink of crystal and the chatter of my guests. They'd been taken to the ballroom by the models I'd hired to do just that. Beautiful women dressed in sequined, see-through gowns that showed off the diamond bikinis and smooth skin glistening beneath.

My mother would have frowned at me for not greeting each guest in person, welcoming them to the Grand Laredo with a handshake and air kisses. But even if I didn't dislike touching people, I'd prefer to arrive with the fanfare I had planned.

Satisfaction welled through me as the animal handler stepped out of the corridor from the kitchens. In his hand was a leather leash studded with black diamonds that was attached to the pacing animal at his feet. He passed the leash over, and I walked the last few steps to the ballroom's doorway. Perfectly timed, the music stopped, the chandeliers dimmed, and a spotlight shone, revealing me and the jaguar prowling next to me. An audible gasp traveled through the room. Yes. This was what I wanted.

The room was draped in decadence just as I'd envisioned, the formal evening wear of the politicians and millionaires adding to the lavishness screaming wealth and privilege. Except, like an eyesore that needed to be carved out, flashes of color splashed through the room, burning my eyes and threatening to ruin the carefully crafted image I'd spent months creating. Not everyone had listened when the invitations had requested only black and white be worn. This made my pleased smile slip ever so slightly.

No matter. I would catalog every single person who hadn't listened, and they'd be the first to be destroyed once I had the final code in hand.

As I stepped into the room with the jaguar prowling at my side, people stepped back instead of closer, slightly frightened.

Awed by the display of power.

This animal was me. I was it.

We were one.

And soon, the entire world would know it.

Chapter Thirty-nine

Gia

BLACKOUT

Performed by Danielle Bradbery

The extravagance of the decorations in Laredo's ballroom was like nothing I'd ever seen before. Sitting on each table was an ice sculpture posed on a silver pedestal, each carved to resemble a famous statue. Scattered around the carving were black and white gems I wasn't entirely sure weren't real. Secured to the center of the ceiling was another large sculpture of marble and flowers from which ropes of pearls, crystals, and fairy lights trailed in glimmering chains to the far corners of the room. Rivulets of what looked like champagne poured down from the statue like magic rain, pooling in a fountain glistening with lily pads fashioned from gemstones. The heavily waxed, black marble floors acted like mirrors, casting the lights from above in all directions in a dizzying display.

The orchestra members sat on a raised platform dressed all in black, playing instruments made of white and silver. There were no colors in the room except for a handful of gowns and the random colored vest peeking from a tuxedo jacket. Vaguely, I recalled Laredo's invitation had requested the guests wear white and black evening wear. It was pure chance the champagne dress from Phil's attic had worked.

As I scanned the crowd, I realized there wasn't even a redhead in the room, as if Laredo had purposefully only invited those whose hair color would fit in with his vision.

Extreme control.

Extreme decadence.

Wealth and power on display.

It was deadly clear that this was much more to Laredo than a simple charity event.

At the head of the room, on a dais, Laredo stood next to a table with only two settings. Beside him was an actual living and breathing jaguar with fur so light its bold black spots stood out, blending with the man's tuxedo.

My nerves went up another notch, and I wondered again if my solo-spy routine was going to get me killed. If I was going to wind up looking like Ravyn with slashes down my torso. Worse, if I'd get Ryder and his precious daughter hurt as well. But just the thought of them being harmed steeled my resolve, forcing back the flutter of doubts.

I could do this.

I just had to pick at that control Laredo craved and felt he had a right to. Pick at it enough for it to unravel. To make him act in haste.

Then, Ravyn would do the rest.

As we entered the ballroom, we were stopped for a picture. A woman with a microphone and a cameraman asked us our names and impressions of the estate and the ballroom as if we were celebrities at some red-carpet event.

As soon as we made it past the camera, a woman in a diaphanous dress similar to the one who'd shown us to the ballroom appeared at our side. "Mr. Laredo has requested your presence."

She led us through the tables to the raised platform, the shimmer of her gauzy dress and the stones that clad the bikini she wore underneath it making her seem like an apparition, as if breathing on her would make her disappear.

She left us at the base of the dais with Laredo looking down upon us. He looped the handle of the jaguar's leash over the knob of the chair and then moved down the two steps with a smooth confidence. He greeted Ryder with a brief handshake before turning to me. I instantly wanted to cover myself from the hunger and the barely restrained fury that lived in his gaze.

He kissed my cheek, and my entire body revolted. A shiver slithered down my spine.

"You're late," Laredo said to Ryder, and the rebuke in his tone was clear. "Your punishment is relinquishing this beautiful woman to sit at my table with me."

My heart skipped a beat, and I looked over to see Ryder's jaw clench. I quickly looked away. This was the plan. This was how we wanted the night to go, but it made me nervous that it was happening so fast. That this man had the same plan with a different ending in mind. I managed a flirtatious smile as I asked, "Won't your date be insulted?"

He raised a brow. "I didn't invite a date."

A flash of confusion crossed over Ryder's face, but I understood immediately. He'd always intended to steal me away—or if it hadn't been Ryder's date, it would have been one of the other guest's companions. It was just another display of power. It said, *I can take whomever I want and make them mine.*

But he'd never have me.

He'd try. He'd try to take me either by smooth charm or by force, but I'd never be his.

"You'll sit at the table to my left," Laredo said, not even looking at Ryder but waving to a table beside the dais. Four other guests were already there. Ryder would be sitting next to a vacant spot because Laredo had claimed his date. Another message—one hand-delivered not only to Ryder but to the rest of the room.

I squeezed Ryder's hand, trying to convey confidence and calm, reminding him with my eyes that this was the plan.

We just had to go with it. Get through it until Laredo took me away from the gala.

When we'd been guided to the ballroom, I'd spotted several potential locations guarded with retinal scanners and keycode locks. Getting into those places would be critical tonight, and the easiest way to make it happen was on Laredo's arm.

Laredo assisted me up the steps to his private table. His touch felt cold, and my body screamed at me to run. I fought back that instinct, easing past the jaguar lying in front of the table. I didn't glance down at it, but I felt the big cat's tail swish against my shoes. What would it take for the animal to pounce? What words or actions would set it off? And did Laredo know them, or was the jaguar controlled by some other person in the ballroom?

He held my chair out for me and then pushed it in. As he did, he leaned down, lips resting next to the shell of my ear, hand sliding over my shoulder in an intimate caress, whispering, "Welcome to the adventure, Ms. Kent."

I shivered again, and he chuckled softly.

"I wonder if my old friend knows what to do with a woman like you."

He removed his lips and his hand, and my body let out a relieved sigh as he moved around the table to sit. A bell tinkled from somewhere in the room, and men dressed in tuxedos as see-through as the hostess's dress came out from hidden doors, carrying trays of glittering silver.

Our table was served first, the cut crystal plate layered with black caviar and creamy white brie on white and black crackers. The monotone-colored array was mimicked in every course that came after it. Shades of black and white and gray, with an occasional hint of red. A surprising flash of color that hit with an almost brutal force.

Throughout the meal, Laredo talked to me about nothing and everything—what it had taken to make tonight happen in just this way, the ranch and his plans to expand it. He was charming and confident. If it weren't for the coldness of his gaze and what I knew about him, I would never have suspected he was anything but an extremely wealthy man showing off for his guests.

My eyes kept catching Ryder's over Laredo's shoulder. Neither of us was eating much, and we were drinking less.

"You should eat," Laredo said when I'd left the majority of my blackened swordfish on my plate. "You're going to need your strength."

When I met his gaze, barely controlled annoyance flashed through it, either because I wasn't eating the food he'd arranged or because I kept looking at Ryder. The flare disappeared as quickly as it had appeared, but the stony look that remained wasn't much better.

"Why would I need my strength?"

His jaw clenched. Another challenge he didn't like. "You wanted an interview and a tour of the estate for your little journal, didn't you? You'll need some stamina to get what you want tonight." Each word held innuendo, not just the sexual promise he'd intended, but also a hint of the real threat.

Any remaining shred of doubt I'd had of whether he knew who I was or not disappeared. But it gave me an idea I hadn't thought of before—a play that would make me sick to my stomach to make but was perhaps the only one a man like Laredo would respect.

"Do you really know what I want?" I said, lowering my tone and adding my own innuendo.

Interest sparked. "Perhaps I want to hear you say it."

"I have something to offer you. A trade."

He laughed, and to all the guests around us, it simply looked like he was enjoying himself while wooing his friend's date. "What makes you think you're in a position to bargain?"

I hesitated for a mere second. Going with my instincts while in the middle of an operation had always been my strength, but if I did this, there'd be no going back. I would be giving away any chance of retreat. But maybe this would keep Laredo busy enough to forget about Ryder.

Behind Laredo's back, Ryder's brows were furrowed, concentrating on me and paying no attention to the others at his table. It made him look like exactly what Laredo wanted—a jealous boyfriend. Ryder couldn't hear what we were saying. Even if he pulled his phone out and opened the camera app to reveal my vantage from the tiara I'd tucked into my updo, he wouldn't be able to hear it. I only had cameras without mics in my kit.

As Ryder's eyes burned into me, I could almost hear his silent plea for me to play it safe.

But safe wasn't going to cut it.

I pretended to sip at the champagne, running a finger along the rim and hearing the glass sing before setting it down. I leaned in slightly, feeling the neckline of the dress dip even more. Laredo's eyes skimmed along the exposed skin.

"I have the last piece of Natalia's code."

Fury drifted through his eyes at her name, but his face remained frozen in a suave smile, so the rest of the ballroom saw nothing but a charming host.

"You should have kept that to bargain with later— when you needed to beg for your life."

I forced my hand not to shake as I played with the beaded necklace Ryder had loaned me, finger trailing downward, drawing Laredo's gaze once again.

Ignoring the threat he'd issued, I continued as if he hadn't said anything. "I want a place at your side." I waved to the table and the room. I picked up one of the diamonds glittering on the tablecloth. "I want all of this to be mine."

He didn't react to my offer. Didn't do anything but quirk his finger to the waiter, and our plates were removed only to be replaced with dessert. Perfectly formed dark-chocolate cakes twined with white rose petals. They were beautiful, but I had no interest in it.

I sipped at the champagne, yearning for water instead. As beautiful as everything was tonight, it would never be anything I'd want. What I loved were jeans and T-shirts, unraveling clues, and—more recently—the smell of grass and hay. The scent of a man who spent his days outdoors and his nights loving his family. I wouldn't want anything Laredo had to offer, even if he wasn't the head of an evil cartel.

"You're beautiful, Ms. Kent, and the pure Americanness of your lineage is tempting. It would be like making Captain America's daughter mine. But I'm not convinced of your honesty, nor am I sure you could be loyal. After all, you came with Hatley and are here offering yourself to me. Perhaps I would do better to bequeath the permanent spot at my side to one of the socialites who have actual blue blood running through their veins and knowledge of what it takes to follow their husband's commands."

"None of those boring little socialites have Natalia's code, and they'd be a cardboard cutout standing next to you. While I"—I flicked a look toward the jaguar at our feet and back to him—"would always require a bit of taming."

His eyes narrowed ever so slightly, and his mouth parted. I was confident I'd set that icy heartbeat pulsing just a bit. If I could keep him off-kilter, it might just save us.

"You will dance with me," he commanded. "Then, we will go somewhere quiet, and you can convince me of just how deeply you want this bargain to work."

He rose from his seat, and the jaguar sat up. Laredo grabbed the leash and held out his other hand for me. I took it, forcing myself to not jerk out of his hold the minute our skin touched, barely holding back the shudder of revulsion that threatened to spin through me. I'd never felt such extreme dislike for someone in my life.

We made our way down the back of the dais and out onto the marble dance floor gleaming with a nearly blinding ferocity. Once we'd made our way to the middle and the room turned hushed, he drew me close. Our hips collided, and he wrapped the leash of the jaguar around me at my lower back. The big cat's fur brushed along the thin satin of the dress, but I was less afraid of the animal than the man whose eyes were glittering at me.

I was scared Laredo knew everything. Not just the truth of my job and what I intended to do with Natalia's code, but the love I felt for Ryder that escaped with every breath and heartbeat. What would it take to convince this coldhearted villain that I was willing to give up everything for him? How could I prove I wanted a place in his evil empire?

The music started, and we were moving. The music was violent and yet sensual. What should have been an elegant glide, an opening dance befitting the image Laredo had created in the ballroom, instead showed an ugly underbelly. The song was almost lewd, adding to the statement he'd already made. He'd taken Ryder's woman, and he'd do whatever the hell he wanted with her. With all of them.

We weren't alone for more than a minute before a tall body showed up beside us—a cowboy with a glower on his face, anger radiating from every pore. Instead of having a guest accompany him, Ryder had dragged one of the women in the diaphanous dresses.

"Jaime, I think it's time we switched partners."

Laredo laughed. He didn't even respond. He just whirled so he had his back to Ryder. My eyes met tortured, brilliant blue ones over Laredo's shoulder. I silently begged Ryder to continue to trust me, to stop what he was doing before he got himself hauled away.

More people slowly joined us, and the dance floor quickly became crowded. I risked looking at some of the people's faces. Shock was the predominate one followed by an attempt not to watch as Laredo pressed himself to me, hands lingering in places that weren't appropriate for an audience.

When the song ended, relief flew through me because it allowed me to take a minuscule step back, only to collide with the jaguar. I froze. Laredo laughed. It was cruel—a predator having caught his prey.

Without a word, he led me away from the dance floor toward a door at the back of the room. There, he handed off the jaguar to a man standing in a suit that didn't quite fit while I felt Ryder's eyes burning into my shoulders.

He'd known this would happen. It was what we needed.

And yet, I could almost feel Ryder's panic join mine, crawling through my veins as Laredo used his eyes and a ten-digit code to open the locked door. When he pulled me through and the door shut with a formidable click, I almost lost the little bit of food I'd put in my stomach.

I thought of all the things I hadn't said to Ryder. The *I love you* I hadn't given him. The tomorrow I'd offered but not figured out.

I thought of Addy and my parents and Holden. All the people I loved and might not see again. Was it worth the risk? Was the trauma and grief I'd add to their life if I died tonight doing a job I thought I'd loved really worth it?

It was too late. I'd already offered up not only myself but all of them.

I squeezed my clutch with the flash drive tucked inside it and rubbed my knees together, allowing the cold metal of my gun to reassure me. I inhaled slowly, holding my breath for several seconds before letting it out.

I had to keep the panic at bay.

I had to believe it was worth it, because it wasn't just my fate or my loved ones' fate on the line, but the entire world we lived in.

Chapter Forty

Ryder

MAN OF STEEL

Performed by Brantley Gilbert

Just before the door shut behind Gia and Jaime, he sent a cold look in my direction. A smile that radiated evil. How had I never seen it before? How had I only seen friendliness and confidence and not the demon underneath?

It wasn't just his look that had me wanting to break through the door and chase after them. It had been the hungry, brutal gaze he'd given Gia and the way he'd all but fucked her on the dance floor. My body burned with hatred and jealousy.

This man had ruined my life once by destroying his sister's.

I wouldn't let him ruin it again.

I wouldn't let him hurt a hair on Gia's head. He couldn't have her. Oh, he'd try to take her and use her, but she'd never be his. I wouldn't let him, but even more importantly, Gia wouldn't let him either.

Right now, I had to find a way to get back there with them. Should I create a scene to do so? Or try something stealthier?

As I got closer to the door, I saw the scanner and the keypad. Gia would know a way past the electronics. Or Rory. Why hadn't I put Rory's number into my phone? Why had I just assumed we'd be able to reach her through Gia?

Jesus, I was an idiot. Definitely not cut out for spy work.

I headed in the opposite direction, out the ballroom doors, requesting directions to the restrooms, but before I could get there, a large beast of a man showed up at my side. Dressed in the black gear one might expect of the special forces, I recognized him as the animal who'd nearly strangled Gia in my house. It took everything in me not to lunge for his throat and repay the favor. My body instantly stiffened, fists clenching as I fought to hold myself back.

"Mr. Laredo has requested your presence."

It wasn't really a request. It was a command, but it was one I would easily follow if it meant getting behind the party walls and closer to Gia.

"Lead the way," I grunted in response.

He took me down several hallways to another door guarded with scanners and keycode locks. The walls beyond it were black and the floors a checkerboard pattern. I'd been in the Grand Laredo before and had been impressed by its luxury and elegance, but I'd never been hit over the head with the pure black and whiteness of it. Was it a recent change?

The outside of Laredo's home—as well as the barns and the other outbuildings—were warm greens and browns that blended in with the trees and mountains at the edge of the Daniel Boone National Forest. But inside, the house lacked any hint of color. I tried to remember a time when I'd seen Jaime himself wearing anything but black or white and couldn't. His red Porsche was probably the only color I'd ever seen around him. It felt like it was a statement I'd need another encryption key to unravel.

At the bottom of another set of marble stairs, we moved past another key-coded lock and along another monochrome hallway to double doors, which the man opened with his thumbprint. Inside was a sitting room filled with black leather and white brocade. The walls were stark white, and the tables were black marble. There was a large television hanging over an ivory-colored buffet.

I was surprised when Gia and Jaime weren't in the room. I'd been sure he'd want us all together so he could rub in my face his ability to seduce her, to show he could take what he wanted while causing the utmost pain to me. My pulse spiked, and my stomach rolled as unease crept through me.

"Enjoy the show," the man said, head nodding toward the television.

He took a step back but didn't leave the room. Instead, his arms crossed over his chest, revealing the gun tucked in at his waistband.

I turned my head to the screen as it came on, revealing another black-and-white room. This one had a large bed with black satin sheets. At the foot of it were two tufted armchairs. In one of them sat Gia with her back straight. Granny's gems in her hair and on her body glittered in the light cast by the enormous chandelier glowing above her.

Standing beside her was Jaime. He'd removed his tuxedo jacket. It was draped over the back of the chair next to her.

"Tell me, Gia. Has Hatley made you come with his fingers and tongue as well as his dick? Or have you kept him dangling while using him for your job?" He ran a finger along the shell of her ear, and I was filled with the need to rip his hand off and shove it down his throat until he choked to death.

"A girl's got to do what she's got to do, right?" she said, voice colder than I'd ever heard it. Even when she was angry with me, there was emotion in Gia's voice. Fire I loved. That same fire I'd felt as I'd embedded myself in her last night. I hated that he was trying to turn what had happened between us into something dirty. Something ugly. It had been a little piece of heaven—heaven I needed back, needed in my life with a desperation that would make me do just about anything to keep it.

"He fucked my sister. For that alone, I should have killed him," Laredo said, but there was no heat to his voice. He was in complete control. "Instead, I will make his daughter love me more than she ever loved him or my traitorous sibling."

Gia stood, entering his space with a saucy dare as she pulled the flash drive from her clutch. "Do you want this or not?"

He stared at her for a moment and then grabbed her chin. Even over the screen, I could see he was holding it with a fierceness that made his fingers go white, that might leave more marks on her than the ones already on her neck. My nails dug into my palms, and my teeth ground together, shooting pain through my jaw.

"The first lesson you need to learn is that you do not set the terms. You don't demand. There is only one of us who will ever set the rules."

She dropped her lids, and I knew it was so he wouldn't see the hatred and fury those words caused her. Gia wasn't built to capitulate. She was meant to burn and scorch and lead. But even as I had the thought, I realized just how much she'd relinquished control to me—not only last night but multiple times since she'd returned to Willow Creek. She'd trusted me enough to give me power over her and her body. It was a gift. One I'd never take for granted.

He jerked her chin higher and smashed his lips on hers. My entire body jerked, twisting to scan the room, looking for a way out. A way to get to her.

The giant stepped closer, reading my thoughts.

"Let's see what you've brought," Jaime said, drawing my gaze back to the screen. As he walked away holding the flash drive, Gia scrubbed at her lips with the back of her hand, and I caught a hint of red. He'd made her bleed. Fuck this. Fuck all of this.

"Take me to them!" I demanded of the man beside me.

"Soon."

I whirled toward the door, and the man calmly pulled

out his gun with a silencer screwed on the end and aimed it directly at my heart. "You are to watch first. Then, I will take you to them."

My blood was pounding so harshly it filled my ears.

My eyes returned to the television, hating every moment that I was forced to stand there, knowing this was exactly what Jaime wanted. He wanted me to feel helpless, jealous, and angry.

But what he didn't realize was Gia didn't really need my help. Not yet. Maybe never. She knew what she was doing in that room. I'd said I trusted her, and I would. I'd trust her to get herself the hell out of there. I had to believe she could, because if I didn't… I couldn't even let myself think it.

Jaime moved to a table at the side of the room where a laptop awaited. He plugged the flash drive in, hit some keys, swiped the screen, typed some more, and turned to glance at her with narrowed eyes. "Where's the malware? The back door the NSA loves to plant."

"I don't expect you to trust me right away, but I've already told you why I'm here. The NSA doesn't even know I broke the code. I'm here for myself and the life I can have if I choose correctly."

What was she talking about? What life was she choosing? What had she told him? My heart rate spiked. Not with doubt, but with fear that whatever she was playing at might backfire.

He fiddled with the computer some more, checking for who knew what. He messed around for so long I was afraid he'd find the Trojan horse Rory had said Ravyn had planted. Laredo turned back and said, "It's encrypted. Just like the one I already have. How does this help me?"

"Because I have the key."

He laughed, a dry, cynical laugh. "If I couldn't figure out my sister's password, there is no way you could. You know nothing of Natalia. I am the one who spent my childhood playing games with her and spent my teen years shielding her from our father. I am the one who gave her the freedom she tossed back in my face. I know everything there is to know about my sister, and I still couldn't unlock it."

Gia moved toward him with a grace and confidence that took my breath away even over a damn screen. When she reached him, she gave him a careless shrug.

"I've spent years lying to my family about who I am. My brother knows nothing about the real me."

"I knew my sister." His voice was a barely controlled warning, screaming at Gia to stop, even though he hadn't raised his voice.

Her chin went up, defiance in those eyes. "You didn't know she was screwing Ryder Hatley. You didn't even know she had a daughter. Ryder knew more about the real her than you did."

His hand collided with her cheek, sending her face jerking to the side and requiring her to step back and steady herself on the table. My arm swung automatically in response, connecting with the beast next to me, and the hand holding his gun flung upward. I followed the first hit with a thrust to his nose and a knee to his groin. He grunted, countering my movements before shoving the gun into my temple.

I stilled.

"He wants you alive. Do not make me kill you and anger him," the beast said just as, on the television, Jaime said, "Is this how you would try to win my trust?"

"You said you would require honesty. I'm giving it to you."

Jaime's hand wrapped around Gia's neck, drawing her close. "You've overplayed your hand. I don't need you."

"If you didn't, you'd already be using the Houdini box she created. You'd already have taken over the world one system at a time."

His eyes narrowed, but his lip curled up, making him look a thousand times more demonic than ever before. "But a wolf whelp brought me a present today. A way to get the code without ever having to accept your offer. Would you like to see it?"

He turned on a television hung on the wall across from the bed, flipping through several screens until he found the one he wanted. As I registered what was on it, my heart shattered and broke, and I let out a roar of agonized fury.

A cot was the only thing in the cinderblock room, and lying on it, covered entirely by a black blanket, was a slight body. Next to the blanket was a stuffed jaguar, and on the floor beside the bed was a purple backpack I knew well. I knew every item stuffed inside it. They were things my daughter loved most and ensured she had when she needed to run.

Gia was talking. I could see her mouth moving, could see Jaime respond, but I couldn't hear any of it over the thundering need to get to Addy, to save her from the demon her mother had run from.

My gaze landed on a large marble bust on the table next to me. I hunched, clutching my stomach as if in despair and ensuring the barrel of the gun dropped from my forehead as I picked the bust up and swung at the beast's head. In his attempt to block it, he moved the gun, and a shot went off with a quiet puff. I swung again, catching him on the cheek this time with a satisfying crunch. His fist connected with my jaw, sending my head reeling and blood bursting from my lip. I ducked the second punch, spinning around and catching him in the temple with the bust, using a ferocity I'd never applied in my life. He'd barely crumbled to the floor before I'd stolen the gun from his slack fingers and headed for the door.

It was locked. A panel required a thumbprint on this side as well as on the outside. I aimed the gun at the pad, shot it, and was satisfied to hear the lock click open. I pushed out of the room just as I heard a moan behind me. The black hallway greeted me. Where the hell was Addy?

I raced to the next door, shot the keypad there, pushed it open, and was greeted with an office. I spun around, heading for the next door. I couldn't shoot them all open. I'd run out of bullets. But what other option did I have?

"Addy!" I screamed, listening for a quiet response. Could she even find her voice enough to respond if she was scared out of her mind?

Behind me, the door to the room I'd been in slammed against a wall, the noise shattering the silence.

A bloodied beast emerged, fury registering in those cold eyes.

I spun, banging on the next door with the butt of the gun, calling my daughter's name again.

The man stalked toward me. A deadliness in his look left me with no doubts he'd easily anger his boss now to get revenge for the blows I'd landed.

I aimed the gun in his direction. "Take me to my daughter!"

From behind me, another voice spoke. "He doesn't have her."

I spun around to find Enrique—or what once had been Enrique—easing toward me. One arm hung useless at his side, blood trailing down it. His chest was bare, and large bloody circles covered his torso. His nose was crooked and swollen, the skin on his cheeks drooping as if the bones beneath them were no longer there to hold them up, and cuts over his entire being oozed blood. His eyes were hollowed and his brows bloodied from a gash on his forehead. He used the wall to prop himself up. In his hand was a stick that looked like it had been broken off from a broom or a mop, long and jagged.

"Keep the gun aimed at Julio," Enrique groused, his voice barely recognizable.

I turned back to see the beast had closed the distance between us to mere steps. The giant's eyes shined with a deadliness that promised no mercy. He would kill us. He would kill us in a way that was even more painful than whatever Enrique had already been through.

"How did you escape?" Julio's voice was as dark as his look.

"Never leave someone else to do your cleanup work," Enrique said.

Fuck this cozy little chat. "Take me to Addy, or I will pull this trigger."

"He doesn't have her," Enrique insisted. "He only has things that look like hers."

I didn't know if I believed him. All my doubts about the man flooded through me.

"He lies," the beast—Julio—said. "He brought us your daughter. Handed her over for nothing. For a few thousand dollars and a position in our organization. The only reason he tells you this now is because he realized we would never let a coward and traitor inside our doors."

I put my back to the wall, gun swinging between the two men.

Julio eased a hand into his jacket pocket.

"Freeze, asshole," I demanded.

"It is just my phone," he answered. Calm. Cool. No fear. He pulled the device from his pocket, swiped a few screens, and then Enrique's voice came from it.

"I'll bring you the girl. I just want in. I want Vito's old position and fifty grand to set me up."

My insides coiled and seethed. Anger burned through me, making me want to use the bullets to end both these men. I barely stopped myself from pulling the trigger, and I only did it because I might need the ammunition for our escape.

"Someone take me to my daughter before I start aiming for heads," I growled.

"He can't take you to her. He doesn't have her," Enrique insisted. "I wouldn't give her to them."

"Come, I'll show you." Julio spun on large feet, heading back toward the staircase.

I waved my gun in Enrique's direction. "You go first. Follow him."

He did as I requested, using the wall and the broken stick to keep himself up. Every movement looked pained, but I had no sympathy for the man who'd brokered a deal with the devil for my daughter's life.

"It was a play, Hatley," he said quietly. "It backfired, but it was a play I had to make."

"Giving them Addy!"

"No. I swear on my brother's grave, they don't have her. Call your brother. You'll see."

And if they didn't have her—God, my heart burst with hope at even the thought—what would happen if I called? Would they triangulate my signal? Find my brother? Find Addy? Could I risk it?

Waiting for Enrique's slow movements, I lost sight of Julio, as he'd reached the staircase well before us. I'd never been in this part of Jaime's house. I didn't know what was down below waiting for us. When Enrique and I hit the landing, the giant was at the bottom with another pistol in his hands, pointed up at us.

I barely had time to react, pushing Enrique to the ground. As I dove, Julio pulled the trigger, and a bullet scorched by my ear. I twisted, aiming my gun. I wasn't a crack shot. I wasn't trained to pull a trigger in these situations, but I'd done a fair share of shooting in my lifetime, so when I shot at Julio, it found home in his chest. As my body slid to a stop, I took better aim and followed the first shot with a second. Julio's body jerked again, his hand went to the wound on his chest as if he could stop it from bleeding, and then he fell to his knees, crashing face-first to the cement floor.

I rushed to my feet, and the damn dress shoes I was wearing skidded out from beneath me on the cement. I found myself sliding down the stairs. Pain ricocheted through my elbow and hip. As my back hit the edge of the bottom step, my breath was knocked from my body. I lost my grip on the gun, and it went flying as I collided with the beast's body.

My lungs screamed, attempting to breathe. I was frozen, struggling to regain the air I'd lost as Enrique's bloody hand picked up the pistol Julio had dropped. Everything slowed as he whirled in my direction.

My heart joined my frozen lungs, forgetting to pump, forgetting to function.

I'd teased Gia about the cliché of a shoot-out.

It had been a taunt because, somehow, I'd expected the good guys to win, just like in a real movie. I'd expected her plan to work because she'd made it with a surety, a confidence I couldn't doubt, hadn't wanted to doubt.

Looking down the barrel of the gun held by a man I'd doubted from the moment he'd shown up at the ranch, I knew any chance of us surviving had disappeared long before the credits had rolled.

Gia

THE CHAMPION

Performed by Carrie Underwood

$\mathcal{P}$ain tore through me at the sight of Addy's stuffed animal lying next to a blanket-covered heap on a cot. Her backpack was next to her on the floor of the cell. Somehow, some way, Laredo had gotten to her. I'd promised Ryder she wouldn't be hurt. I'd sworn she'd be safe.

What the hell had happened to Maddox? To the deputies guarding her?

Nausea twisted through me.

Ryder! God. Ryder would never survive this. And even if he did, he'd never forgive me.

I'd never forgive myself.

Laredo's face was dark and gratified as he took in my stunned expression. I had to pull myself together. Had to continue the play. Had to find a way to get her to safety. She wasn't harmed. I didn't think he would hurt her. What had he said? He wanted her to love him more than she loved Ryder and Ravyn. He wanted to have her at his side where he could get his revenge every day for the rest of Addy's life.

I buried my emotions, finding that calm I'd been taught to show in the worst of situations.

Summoning the strength of every fictional spy

character I'd ever loved, I gave Laredo a careless shrug. "I liked the kid. It'll be nice to have her here. But she doesn't know the code."

Something flickered through his eyes. The first sign of uncertainty.

"You don't believe me?" I asked. "Bring her here, ask *her*. Even if you can get her to talk—because she doesn't really talk to anyone—she still won't know the answer."

Irritation rushed over his face, and he yanked me to him with a brutality that had me slamming one hip into the desk. He put his hands around my neck and squeezed. The bruises that were already there, the wounded windpipe, screamed at the touch.

"Tell me. Tell me the code, and I promise not to destroy the Hatleys, your family, and anyone you care about when I'm done with you."

"That's hardly a promise I can believe in," I choked out.

He let me go, and air rushed into my lungs. I forced myself not to clutch at my neck, to act as if he hadn't just tried to strangle me.

He stepped away, reasserting a terrifying calm. "Reacting in anger is never the right answer." He looked down at his hands. "I *will* burn my father's responses from my body." He glanced up at me, tilting his head as if finding something curious. "Maybe you are the answer. Maybe your defiance will be the way I learn to control it."

My pulse was pounding, my breath hissing out in sharp puffs. Every nerve was on alert. Fight-or-flight instincts screamed at me to do both. I rammed those reflexes down, knowing I couldn't do either. I had to stay the course. I still had a chance to get Addy out of this. To get Ryder and Addy to safety. If I were truly turning traitor to join Laredo, what would I demand from him? What kind of assurance for my safety would I request in trade for the code?

"Give me the key code," he commanded.

"I need some assurance you won't kill me once I've given it to you. Some assurance you'll keep me at your side like I want."

He chuckled. A dark sound that made me believe in the demons Natalia had run from. "There are no assurances you would believe. I will always be able to kill you if I choose. You can die now, without having given me the code, and I'll set my people on it and figure it out eventually anyway, or you can risk giving it to me, knowing that, at the moment, I'm fascinated with you, and my reaction to you is enough to keep you. Perhaps, if you always entertain me, if you continue to surprise me, I will always want you at my side. It will fall on you to make it so. That is the best I can offer you."

Our gazes locked. I battled those flight instincts more as my veins pounded with fear and heartache. Would a woman who wanted to rule the world accept these terms? Would a cornered animal relent so easily?

"I can see you are running through all your options," he said, a hint of pride there that made my stomach curl. "Unfortunately for you, there is only one door open. You closed the rest when you showed your hand."

"I want Addy to travel with me. Wherever I go, she goes with me."

His mouth tightened, and his fingers curled into his arms, but he smirked. "You will both go where I go. I learned my lesson with Natalia. From now on, I keep the people who belong to me close. There will be no escape. Be warned, you are giving up your freedom in order to get what you want."

Was he delusional enough to believe anyone would accept these terms?

Maybe he was. Maybe he believed the temptation of having the world at your feet was enough.

It didn't matter. I only needed him to think I was agreeing long enough for Ravyn's virus to take effect.

I released a long exhale and said, "Fine, but don't hate me for the code she chose." I waited a beat and then shrugged, saying, "It's Ravyn Eowyn Hatley.

His eyes narrowed, and he swore in Spanish under his breath but typed it into the screen. When the passcode was accepted, and the encryption started to clear, he smiled and did the worst thing he could possibly do—he forgot about me.

I backed away as he concentrated on the screen, fingers moving, doing exactly what Ravyn had thought he would by logging into a critical system to ensure the code worked. The one he chose was the FAA, where it would now be easy for him to bring down a plane. I sank onto one of the armchairs, and he must have caught the movement in the screen's reflection, because he glanced back at me.

I purposefully dropped my shoulder so the strap of the dress slipped down and the neckline of the gown with it, revealing the tops of my breasts. I acted like I didn't feel it, like I didn't notice even as his eyes skimmed over me.

"Take it off," he demanded.

"What?"

"You heard me. Take the gown off. Get on the bed. When I'm done running this little check to ensure my sister didn't betray me once more, I'll expect you to be ready for me."

"How on earth can I keep you entertained if I acquiesce so easily to every command?"

Heat flared. "I punish those who don't listen."

"Promises. Promises."

He took a step away from the laptop. A step toward me. I slid out of my sandals. Easier to run barefoot than in those low heels. My hand slid the hem of the dress up, baring my ankle and calf, but not quite far enough that he would see my gun strapped to my knee.

He eased toward me, undoing his belt buckle and sliding it off.

My stomach rolled. It was a deadly dance I'd engaged in, and for the second time tonight, I realized how much I didn't like it. I didn't want to engage in hand-to-hand combat I wasn't adequately trained to win like Jason Bourne. I didn't want to face a gun or a knife or a computer code that could ruin the world. I wanted the excitement of a puzzle and finding the answers, but I no longer wanted to have my life or the lives of people I loved on the line to do so.

I did my best to keep my emotions from showing, forcing my eyes to remain on his face and not the screen glowing behind him. How long would it take for the Trojan horse to be unleashed? How long did I have before I wound up dead?

When he reached me, his hand landed in my hair, jerking my head back with a brutalness that brought tears to my eyes, and I slid my hand farther up the dress until it collided with my holster.

"Just remember, you asked for this," he purred, an ugly sound of a predator who'd captured his prey.

I closed my fingers around the grip of my gun and slid it slowly and quietly out. I reached for his arm as if to caress it, and then I shoved the barrel of my Glock into his stomach.

"Remember that you asked for it too," I hissed back.

He glanced down, and a surprised huff of laughter escaped him. Not the reaction I was expecting. A playfulness took over his face. A cat batting at a mouse.

"This is exactly the reason you've lived as long as you have tonight."

He yanked me to my feet by my hair, pivoting to the side just as my finger pulled the trigger. The gunshot echoed through the room, but the bullet went wide, hitting the door behind us.

It was then that I heard it. Ryder's desperate voice calling Addy's name. Calling mine.

Any playfulness Laredo had exhibited disappeared into a cold, dark wall of hatred.

He twisted my wrist holding the gun in one quick movement. Bones cracked, sharp pain sliced through me, and I cried out. The gun hit the floor, but he didn't even bother to pick it up. Instead, he dragged me with him to the door by my hair. When I tried to resist, he put pressure on my broken bone, and I gasped, air rushing out of my lungs as the pain spiraled through me.

"With such a low tolerance for pain, you never would have been able to please me."

He twisted my broken wrist again. The agony would have knocked me to my knees if Laredo hadn't hauled me to his chest as he yanked me into the hallway.

"Let her go!" Ryder's furious snarl drew my eyes down the dark corridor, settling on the gun he held in his hand.

Love and hope twined with fear inside me. I barely bit back a scream, telling him to run, to find Addy and get the hell out of the devil's house.

Laredo still held my wrist in one hand, and he barely had to put any pressure on it for me to cry out. Concern skated over Ryder's face as he aimed his gun, trying to get a clear shot at the man using me as a shield. With his free hand, Laredo pulled a switchblade from his pocket, flicking it open and placing it on my already bruised neck.

"It's over, Jaime," Ryder said, continuing toward us slowly but surely. "Everything you thought you were getting tonight is gone. Ravyn got in the last word. She's destroying you even as we speak with that flash drive you installed. You have no one coming to save you, because your giant is dead. The world will know exactly what you are and any respect you might have garnered will disappear."

The tip of the knife pierced me. I bit my cheek, refusing to cry out again, as I felt blood drip down my neck, staining the beautiful gown Ryder's family had lovingly preserved.

"What did you do to Julio?" Laredo demanded.

"Shot him. Just like I'm going to shoot you for marking her."

"You lie."

"Unfortunately for me, lying is not a skill I learned,"

Ryder said, stalking closer. "While you and Ravyn excelled at it. Fooled the hell out of me and everyone around you. But it seems like she was even better at it than you are. I guess she'll have the last laugh."

"He has Addy," I gasped out and was punished by the tip digging farther into my neck.

Ryder shook his head. "No. He has a stuffed animal and a backpack that looks like hers. There's no one in that room."

Laredo pushed harder on both my wrist and the point of the knife. My eyes watered, and the inside of my cheek bled as I tried desperately not to scream.

A voice from behind us said calmly, "What's that line? About bringing a knife to a gunfight?"

Laredo jerked, pulling us so his back was against the wall, but it also caused the knife tip to slide farther in. I choked, a garbled noise escaping me as I registered Enrique limping down the hall, bloodied and battered.

I did the only thing I could, flinging the elbow on my good arm back into Laredo's stomach, tearing hair from my head as I attempted to pull away. The moves barely budged him, but the miniscule space I'd created was all I needed. Two suppressed shots rang out, the air by my ear burning before both bullets struck Laredo. One to his head, the other to his left shoulder.

He sagged, his body taking me and the knife in my neck with him.

I tried to catch myself, tried to find the hilt, but I was already tumbling.

And then, warm arms caught me. Ryder's strength surrounded me.

And every nerve in my body surrendered.

I'd finally found something worth staying for.

♫ ♫ ♫

Six hours later, I had a bandage on my neck, a temporary wrap holding my wrist, and a cowboy who wouldn't leave my side as we finished up at the Grand Laredo. Once it was clear Laredo was dead, and with the FBI, DEA, and local cops invading the place, Laredo's staff at the ranch either took off or surrendered. Those who escaped wouldn't get far, because Ravyn had given us a complete list of every person who worked for the organization. They'd be hunted down one at a time. There was no way any of them could pick up where Laredo had left off because Ravyn had destroyed it all. She'd given all the money away, uncovered every single trafficking lane they'd used, and handed over every contact who'd ever helped them.

Her work would do more than just end the Lovato cartel, as it also gave up resources used by other cartels as well. It was a true shake-up in the criminal world.

The minute Ryder was sure I wasn't going to bleed out, he'd called Maddox. Addy was secure, tucked in a bed at the safe house, surrounded by officers. If he hadn't already been tortured, I would have wanted to bust Enrique in the face several times for giving Laredo the idea to make Ryder and me think he'd taken her in.

After the EMTs loaded Enrique onto a gurney, I walked with them toward the waiting ambulance. "I'm mad as hell that you offered Addy to Laredo, but I also have to thank you for saving my ass."

His dark-brown eyes were a mix of sadness and relief. "I would never have let him have her. But for the first time, I knew what he wanted and could use it to get to him. He had to be stopped, Kent. For ten years, I've been searching for the bastard who slaughtered my brother. I wasn't going to let him get away once we'd found him."

Would Enrique have killed Laredo even if he hadn't had a knife to my throat? In the end, it didn't matter. The man was gone. He couldn't hurt Addy or Ryder or any of my family again—a family that included every single one of the Hatleys.

As we reached the ambulance, the reporter who'd been covering the gala shoved a microphone toward Enrique and me, demanding answers about what had gone down and why. After, "No comment," ripped from both our throats in a similar growl, the woman backed away. But it wouldn't be long before more news crews showed up, camping out along the edge of the drive and attempting to get statements from guests as they were released.

"You're going to be feeling the aftereffects of tonight for a long time," I told Enrique. We both knew I didn't just mean the physical healing. I wasn't sure he'd be able to go back to the DEA after he'd gone dark, even if he'd done so to bring Laredo down. I wasn't sure anyone would trust him again.

He glanced over my shoulder, and I didn't have to look to know who'd caught his eye. I could feel Ryder's heat as he made his way toward me, the tether of the bond that joined us reaching out like its own embrace.

"I think we'll both be feeling the ramifications for the rest of our lives," he said, but there was a smirk on his lips that had mine twitching up in return.

The EMTs lifted the gurney inside and shut the door just as strong arms surrounded me. I eased back into him, and Ryder growled, "He used my daughter as bait. He's lucky I didn't shoot him when I had a chance."

I turned to face him. "He never would have given her up."

Ryder's jaw worked. "I'm not sure I agree."

"Did you see the state of him? If he was going to give her up, it would have been while they were torturing him."

"Nothing you say will make me like or trust the man."

I didn't want to argue with him about it. Enrique would have to remain one of the things we disagreed on, and I wasn't sure it mattered. With the task force disbanded, I wasn't sure I'd ever see the DEA agent again.

As the ambulance pulled away, Ryder ran a hand along my jaw in a tender caress, leaned in and placed a tender kiss on my forehead, and asked, "Can we go home now?"

Home. Willow Creek. The glass house that he'd built because of his love for another woman that had somehow become a haven in the last few days for me.

Before I could respond, I caught sight of a disappointed face weaving through the sea of vehicles on the drive. My heart fell as Leland reached me.

"G."

"Leland."

We stared at each other for a long moment before my boss's gaze flicked to Ryder, whose arms had tightened protectively.

"How'd you get here so quickly?" I asked.

"Once Rory came clean about what you'd been hiding, I commandeered a company jet and landed outside Corbin in under two hours." His eyes were sad as he shook his head. "After all we've been through, I have to say, it stings that you doubted me."

My throat bobbed, emotional pain joining the physical ones, both sure to scar me. I hadn't just respected Leland, I liked him as a human being and thought of him as a friend as well as a boss. It had taken a lot to doubt him, but I didn't say any of that because, in the end, it didn't matter. I *had* doubted him. Instead, I asked, "Did we find the mole?"

"Tech analyst with the DEA."

"Enrique's going to destroy him."

My boss didn't respond immediately. When he did, he looked Ryder straight in the eye and said, "I need a moment with G."

Ryder wasn't happy. I could feel it vibrating from him, but I squeezed his hand and said, "Give me another ten minutes. Then, I'll let you take me home. I want to hug Addy, and I want to fall in bed and sleep for a day at least."

His eyes lit up at me saying home and Addy in practically the same sentence. Or maybe it was the idea of staying in bed for a day in that way we'd both wanted to do this morning. He kissed me on the forehead and stepped away, pulling out his burner phone and texting someone while he waited.

"The virus destroyed everything he had online?" Leland asked.

After Ryder had ripped his tuxedo shirt up and tied it around my neck to stop the bleeding, I'd insisted on searching for the Houdini box. I'd brought Laredo's laptop with me as we hunted, shooting our way through locked doors and watching as Natalia's virus ate its way through the Lovato businesses before destroying itself as well.

Once we'd found the safe in Laredo's office, we'd hauled Laredo's body into the room to unlock it with his eyes and his fingers. Inside was an Art Deco ring and two gold-encrusted external drives. Ryder had gasped at the ring, fisting it and closing his eyes as if he'd found the Holy Grail.

I hadn't had time to ask him about it, but I suspected it was the ring he'd given Ravyn. I turned my attention to the drives, called Rory, and used the key code to unlock them. The Houdini boxes were missing the final string of code Rory had found on the Switch, but it too was gone now into the etherland of ones and zeroes that Ravyn had burned up. Even knowing the last piece was missing, Rory and I had still made the executive decision to smash the drives to pieces. No one should have the power that code would have given.

I nodded at Leland. "Yes. The virus did its job, but Ravyn left us enough evidence to dismantle what's left of the Lovatos' physical business."

"The bigwigs won't be happy to not have the Houdini box in custody. They'll want to know how those drives got destroyed."

"I made the decision. If they want a badge for it, they can have mine. Leave Rory out of it."

"Or maybe Laredo destroyed those drives in a hissy fit before he was shot. You know, if he couldn't have them, no one would?"

My chest squeezed tight. Even after I'd doubted him and hid things from him, my boss still had my back. I didn't respond, because if I did, I might start crying, and I'd be damned if I'd do that in front of the range of law enforcement crawling over the ranch.

"I'm thinking you need to use up some of that vacation time you've accrued," my boss said. "Maybe in two months, things will have died down enough for you to come back in." His eyes darted over to Ryder and back, and his lips twitched. "Unless you've got other plans."

"I honestly don't have an answer for you today, Leland."

"We'll figure something out, G. We need you."

I didn't tell him the truth. How, in those minutes when I'd thought I might die at Laredo's hands, all I cared about was telling Ryder I loved him and making sure I saw Addy and my family again. This job wasn't worth me risking any of them.

"Get the hell out of here," he said with no heat. "If the task force needs an update from you, I'll reach out. Otherwise, we'll talk in a few months."

He walked away, and the moment he did, Ryder was at my side.

I put my arms around him, my wrist screaming and my body shivering as the icy January air finally registered through the thin fabric of the satin evening gown. I reached up with my good hand, brushing at a lock of hair that had drifted over his forehead. Blue eyes seared into me. Concern. Love. A hint of doubt that I hated to see.

"We need to get that wrist set," he said gently.

I nodded. "There's something I need to say."

His throat bobbed. "Okay."

"I love you."

A smile emerged for the first time since we'd teased each other in the hotel room. It was a stunning smile that made me feel like I'd stepped into a spotlight. I was on a stage with an audience of one, but it felt better than having the entire world watching.

"That's it?" he teased. "No reasons. No grand gesture. Just three words said like you were ordering a steak?"

I huffed out a laugh. "Those three words have changed my life, even if they haven't changed yours."

"It wasn't the words that changed me, darlin'. It was you."

He leaned in and kissed me softly, and even tired, stabbed, and broken, I felt the spark of it in every piece of me. All the way down to my soul.

He drew back, put his forehead to mine, and said, "Just in case it wasn't clear when I was talking about soulmates, you're it for me. The true love I thought I'd never have. I love you. I love you, and I'll do anything to make your world whole."

The fact that he thought my world wasn't whole slid through me almost as painfully as Laredo's knife, even as joy flooded my veins at his sweet promise. I had to make sure he understood, that he truly heard the truth and felt it deep inside, just like I'd felt it with the honesty of words.

So, I put every ounce of love I had into every syllable as I said, "All I need is you and Addy."

Chapter Forty-two

Ryder

GROWING OLD WITH YOU
Performed by Restless Road

Gia insisted on picking up our things from the hotel and driving straight through to Willow Creek. I wanted her to go to the hospital, but she demanded we see Addy first, that we get *home* first. And the fact that she was so desperate to reach my home and my daughter, along with the *I love you* she'd given me, did something funny to my heart. Sealed it. Healed it. Branded it. I wasn't sure which. Maybe it was all three. All I knew was that I loved her.

I loved her and was in awe of what she'd accomplished tonight.

The cool she'd maintained while I'd thought I was falling apart at the seams.

She'd taken some over-the-counter pain meds offered by the EMTs but nothing more. I knew she was still hurting when she winced as I took the turns too fast in my hurry to get us to our family.

I took my foot off the gas, easing the speedometer down a notch. There was no fire anymore, no piano waiting to fall on our heads. There was just a long future strolling ahead of us that we still had to figure out, but it was there, waiting.

"You should sleep," I told her.

"Too wound up," she said. "I need to call my family

before they see something on the news. Do you mind?"

"You don't ever have to ask something like that. Family always comes first."

Her eyes glimmered at me the same way they had when she'd said she loved me. My heart swelled. I listened while she called her brother and then her dad, giving them a very condensed version of what had happened, letting them know it would probably break with the morning news. Then, I'd listened as her mother came on and chewed her out for keeping her job a secret. But the lecture was followed by love and a deep relief that Gia was okay.

When she hung up, she closed her eyes, resting her head against the back of the seat. The sun was creeping over the horizon as we reached the mountains twenty minutes from Willow Creek. For a moment, I thought she'd actually fallen asleep, but then she turned those amber eyes flashing with hints of green in my direction and said, "I don't want to do this anymore."

My heart sank. Part of me knew she didn't mean me…us…and yet a moment of panic still snuck over me. Old habits. Lack of trust that wasn't caused by her but by those old wounds that, while healed, could still flicker back to life occasionally. It would be a work in progress for a long time.

"Do what?" I finally asked.

"This job. I don't want my mom and dad to get a call that says they lost me in some jungle in South America. I don't want you and Addy to lose someone else you love."

I swallowed hard, throat bobbing. "I told you before, and I'll say it again. I'd never ask you to give up what you do. That isn't who I am."

She smiled, and it lit up the entirety of the darkened car even more than the weak sunrise. "I know. It's part of why I love you. That you don't expect me to just walk away." She extended a hand as if to caress my shoulder, and pain drifted across her face again.

"I'm calling Maddox. I'll have McKenna meet us at the

hospital." After I did that, she returned to the conversation as if we hadn't stopped.

"I don't have a back-up plan." There was a whisper of sadness in that tone. She'd told me she didn't sit still well, and I'd witnessed that myself ever since she'd rolled into town. She'd need action. Something meaty and gritty to keep her occupied. Puzzles to solve.

"It's not the same—not the same at all—but Maddox is shorthanded at the station."

She winced again, and this time, I wasn't sure if it was because of the pain or because of the job I'd suggested.

"Your boss is right. You don't need to figure it out right now. Take the vacation he suggested. Rest and recover. That should be your primary focus right now."

"Shall I call your mama for a reservation?"

Even though I knew she was teasing, eyes flashing with humor, I still growled out my response, "You stay at the ranch, and we will have a problem. There's only one place you're sleeping while you're in Willow Creek."

"So bossy."

"You love it."

"From you…I do."

Those two little words sank into me. *I do.* I wanted her to say *I do* in a very formal way. I wanted her to let me slip a ring on her finger in front of our families and declare to the world that we were forever. The ring I'd taken from Jaime's safe was burning a hole in my pocket. I wouldn't give that one to Gia. It had too many tainted memories now, but I'd give her another one—one that was just about us.

The moment I'd closed my fist around my great-grandmother's ring, I'd been overwhelmed with relief at having back the family heirloom Ravyn had stolen. Mama had tried to hide how sad she was that it was gone, because she knew I was already carrying around enough remorse, but losing the ring had felt like losing part of us. While Granny had never married, she'd worn the ring on her right hand until she died and then passed it down to Mama. By that time, Mama already had a ring Dad had bought for her, and she didn't want to trade one for the other, so she'd saved it for whichever of us kids got engaged first and wanted to use it. I'd had the dumb luck of being that sibling.

Having it back felt a bit like saving our land from being auctioned off piece by piece, as if I was setting right our family history. Restoring it. Keeping it whole.

Gia had allowed me to do that.

She'd brought me gifts I'd never expected to have again.

Addy. Her. They were the most important ones.

Everything else was like adding whipped cream to one of Mama's pies—sweet but unnecessary.

♫ ♫ ♫

When we got to the hospital and McKenna reviewed the X-rays with us, it was clear that not only had the asshole broken Gia's wrist, but he'd twisted it so the bones had been shifted out of alignment. This meant Gia needed a cast. So, it was almost lunchtime by the time we actually headed out to the ranch where Addy was waiting for us with the rest of my family.

I'd barely helped Gia out of the car and turned toward the porch before a tiny body was flinging itself at us. My heart rushed, pounding fiercely as I picked Addy up, wrapping her in one arm and tugging Gia close with the other.

Addy buried her face in the crook of my neck, and her little body quivered. It took a rush of water hitting my skin for me to realize she was crying.

I kissed her temple, squeezed her even tighter, and did my best to try to comfort her. "It's all over, sweetheart. We're here. We're all safe. And no one is coming after you again."

Addy lifted her face, tears flowing down her cheeks as

she looked from me down to the bandage on Gia's neck and then the cast. "You're hurt!"

"Nothing big. In six to eight weeks, I'll be good as new."

Addy stared at the bandage amidst the purple bruising on Gia's neck. The blood stains trailed down onto the bodice of the evening gown. Addy's eyes were big as she reached out tiny fingers to touch the bandage.

Gia grabbed her fingers and kissed them. "I swear, Addy, I'm going to be okay."

"Was it a knife?" The question was whispered so quietly the wind almost took it away.

"Yes," Gia said, throat bobbing and eyes filling with tears. "But they're all gone, Addy. All the bad men. They aren't going to be able to hurt any of us ever again." Gia's words were sure and confident, and even if I hadn't seen the end of the Lovatos with my own eyes, I would have believed her.

"They died?"

Gia nodded, and I loved her for being honest even when it was hard to hear. The truth was always better.

"Mama died too." Addy's little voice was so sad it almost broke my heart all over again.

"She did," I acknowledged. "But we're going to bring her here. To the ranch. We'll bury her with the rest of my family in the Hatley plot, and you'll be able to walk over and talk to her whenever you want."

"She can't talk back."

"No, but I believe she'll hear you," I told her. We stood that way for several minutes, hugging each other and reveling in the fact that we could, until Mama hollered out at us from the back porch.

"I need some of my own damn hugs, you three. So shuffle those feet on over here."

And we did what we all did when Mama gave an order. We followed it.

That first night, we stayed at the ranch to be close to family. The three of us slept together in Maddox's old room that Mama had made into a guest room with a king-sized bed for nights just like this when some or all of her kids stayed there. I wasn't sure what had forced my eyes open. Maybe nothing more than the dawn starting to creep through the blinds, as I'd always been an early riser and working on the ranch meant even earlier starts. But the first thing I saw was Addy's tiny body snuggled up between Gia and me.

My heart felt like it grew and expanded until it threatened to leap from my chest. This was all I needed. Family. This little unit I'd never believed I'd have again and that I was going to cherish until death knocked at my door in another hundred years. And even then, it would be too soon.

Addy's sweet face was completely relaxed, and her lips were curved upward, as if she were dreaming of only good things. I promised myself I'd give her a lifetime full of just that. She'd earned it in her first seven years, suffering more than most grown adults had. I ran a hand over her hair, amazed that she was there. That she existed. That I got to touch her.

When I moved my hand back to Gia's waist, warm eyes greeted me. A slow smile took over my face, and I leaned over the top of Addy to give her a gentle kiss, a welcome-to-the-day kind of kiss. What I really wanted was to give her a kiss that would leave her gasping and calling my name.

There'd be time for that. Time for all the things I wanted to do to Gia's body.

And that thought made my heart grow and expand a bit more. I wasn't sure I'd be able to contain it for much longer.

"Morning, darlin'. How you feeling?" I asked, glancing down at the bandage on her neck and then the cast on her arm.

"All I feel right now is lucky and loved."

I ran a finger along her cheek. "That's a mighty good way to start the day."

♫ ♫ ♫

The next night, we went back home. Gia and I watched Addy carefully, worried the events that had taken all of us from there would make her feel unsafe and scared. It helped that Dad and Shawn had replaced the broken window, and Mama and Sadie had helped them clean up. No sign of anything bad having happened remained, even though I could still see it in my mind like a horror movie on repeat.

As soon as we'd set our bags down, Addy asked to play *Pac-Man*.

So, we spent the day in the game room, where nothing bad had ever happened. We played video games and board games and taught Addy how to play pool. Gia promised she could beat me with her eyes closed once she had use of both hands, and I was pretty sure she could, even though I was the undefeated billiard player in my family. It wouldn't bother me at all to lose to her. It only added to her sexiness and my desire to take control in other ways once our bedroom door closed.

The three of us collapsed at the end of the day on the sofas in front of the entertainment center with pizza and movies that Addy picked out. When Addy's eyes started to droop, we headed upstairs where Gia helped Addy get ready for bed. I read her a couple stories until her eyes closed, and then, we quietly left, shutting the lights off behind us.

It had been a good day. Good memories. Moments I would always cherish because I'd already missed too many of them with Addy, and yet, I hesitated outside her door, suddenly panicked at the thought of leaving her on her own after all that had happened. I'd lost her once before she'd been born and thought I'd lost her again when I'd seen her things next to that cot on the video at Jaime's.

Gia pulled my hand into hers. "If we don't believe she's safe, she won't ever feel it." I tucked a lock of her hair behind her ear but didn't say anything, and she let out a breath, as if she'd been holding it for a century, before saying, "She's safe, Ryder. We're all safe."

My throat bobbed. I hated that her voice was still raw and rough. Hated what had happened to her as much as I hated what had happened to my daughter. But Gia was right. Nothing was coming after us anymore.

All we needed to do now was let our bodies heal while we loved on each other.

And loving on people…I was good at that. I'd once been *great* at it.

For Gia and Addy, I would become a world-champion lover and dad.

I whisked Gia into my arms, and she gave out a startled little cry as I marched her down the hall to my room. I kicked the door shut behind me, punched the button by the light switch to shut the blinds, and tossed her onto my bed, being as careful with her arm as I could while still getting my point across.

She laughed but didn't move. Instead, she just directed a long, slow gaze over me from head to toe, slowing along the expanse of my chest and settling on my jeans, where my hard-on pressed against my zipper.

I returned the favor, taking in her dark hair spread across my sheets, skimming over the hard tips pushing against her thin sweater and the black leggings that were clinging to her hips. The cast and bandages sliced into me, but when my eyes found hers again, the unconditional love there eased that pain. There were no more secrets. No hidden agendas. Just love. My heart exploded, sending a burst of confetti of passion and devotion into the air. It spread over us, coating everything with a hazy glow.

I didn't remember moving, but I found myself devouring her like I'd consumed her at Phil's. She met me stroke for stroke, not yet surrendering control to me, determined to do just like she'd said that first night and give as much as she received. Hands and mouths nipped and glided over each other. Clothes were shed, and I'd settled in between her thighs just as the moonlight shifted out from behind a cloud and shone on her through the skylight. It made her look ethereal. Fairylike. If Ravyn had been Eowyn, Gia was absolutely Arwen, giving up her way of life to be part of mine.

I'd never let her regret it now that she'd chosen to stay.

Our gazes locked, and she brushed a soft palm along the stubble on my jaw, which was already turning back into a beard.

"Make love to me, Ryder," she said. "Make love to me in a way that screams this is where I belong. That proves to my heart and body they belong to you. Make me feel it with every touch and caress. And I promise, I'll do the same. I'll write myself onto your soul and never let go."

I let out a low, guttural moan, half pleasure and half pain, before I captured her mouth with mine, searing into us the promises we were making to one another. Fingers trailed over hot skin, lips following the same path. Her movements echoed mine, every touch and caress returned with equal fervor. A battle to see who could show who how much they cared most. A battle to prove this was the only place we belonged. We slid together, the sweet glide of silk against silk. Two souls merging as the moonlight surrounded us and the rest of the world disappeared.

Chapter Forty-three

Gia

TAKE MY NAME
Performed by Parmalee

Two months passed in what felt like the flash of code along my computer screen. I spent my days alongside Ryder, helping him with the construction of the cabins. At first, he wouldn't let me do much with my cast and bruised neck, but as I grew stronger and my body healed, I was able to wield a nail gun, one-armed, in a way that made his eyes grow heavy with lust whenever he stopped to watch me. It often ended with us taking breaks that Brandon, Shawn, and Ramon chuckled over and made my cheeks flush.

But I never said no. I liked the breaks. I liked being needed so much he couldn't wait.

What I tried not to do was think about the Lovatos, the NSA, or anything to do with my job.

I worked my body to exhaustion and spent my nights being worshipped by a man who loved me more than I'd ever imagined a person could be loved.

While we finished the cabins, Addy studied with Rianne, learning and growing stronger in a different way. She now talked to all the family in complete sentences without ever wavering. But if Shawn or Ramon or any of the farm workers talked to her, she clammed right up. We weren't sure if she'd ever adjust to a regular school, but there was no hurry or pressure to make her do so, even though

Mila begged her almost every day to come with her so they could play together at recess.

I had a feeling Mila would get her way eventually. She usually did.

But as the cabins wound down to paint and decorations, which I wasn't much help with, I had less and less to do. Eva seemed to read my restlessness and ordered me into the kitchen with her one day. Gearing up for six months of guests took more time and prep work than I'd expected. With Sadie's hands full at the bar, Eva needed help baking and canning and freezing food, so I became her sous chef. After my cast came off and I had full use of my arms again, she taught me to roll dough and bake bread. She taught me to cook and bake in ways that would stun my mom when I finally made it home for a visit. I needed to make that happen soon, as everyone in my family called daily to make sure I was okay.

While I worked my body to exhaustion, I could forget about what I was going to do next. I loved the bubble I was in, even though I knew it couldn't last. It would pop, and life would expect me to move in one direction or the other. For now, I concentrated on the satisfied feeling I had at the end of the day when I went home with Addy chatting in the back seat and Ryder sending me looks that promised another night with him in control and me being worshipped.

I always got in some adoration of my own.

Whatever else happened during the day, I always felt complete when Ryder and I were lying skin on skin in the moonlight.

Everything about my life felt right in those heartbeats.

In early March, Maddox came to the house one evening to pick up Mila after she and Addy had spent the afternoon playing together. He asked if he could have a word with me.

"Don't give her a hard time," Ryder grunted out.

And my stomach clenched. Was it something about the Lovatos? After the dust had settled and the initial questions had been answered about what had gone down with Laredo,

I hadn't responded to any of Leland's messages. I'd done more than just take a vacation. I'd basically gone dark.

I'd answered Rory's texts, but only when they were about personal things and not about the job. She and I often checked in on each other to make sure the relationships we'd chosen over the futures we'd seen for ourselves weren't falling apart. When I'd left her in Cherry Bay with a boyfriend and his two siblings to raise in December, I hadn't envied her the ready-made family. Now that I had Ryder and Addy, I couldn't imagine giving them up, and I understood everything she'd done to keep her new family.

Maddox waved his cowboy hat in Ryder's direction. "If she says no, she says no. I won't push."

Ryder headed downstairs to the game room where the girls were playing. I went to the refrigerator and pulled out two beers, waving one at Maddox in offering, who said, "No, but thanks. I'm not staying long."

I put one back, cracked the top of the other, and took a swig.

"Four of us sheriffs with small offices around these parts have been discussing ways to combat the online crimes that are growing faster than we can say possum. None of us has the resources to hire a full-time cyber-crime investigator, but it's clear we need one. We thought we might be able to pool some dollars together and create a multi-county unit. We'd be able to hire one person for sure, maybe two. My first thought was to offer the position to you."

My throat clogged with a whole slew of emotions, and before I could respond, Maddox continued, "Now, it might look like nepotism, or like I'm offering you this in some attempt to get you to stay because I've never seen Ryder this happy in his entire life. Not with Rayvn. Not with anyone."

"Maddox—"

"No, let me finish, please. I love my brother, and I want him to stay happy, but I also know that no matter if I offer you this job or not, you aren't leaving him. You'll figure something out. I also know you're a damn good analyst. You brought down an entire fucking cartel with a few swipes of code."

"Really, Rory did more of the coding."

He huffed out a laugh that sounded very much like his brother. "What I'm saying is, we'd be lucky if you took the job. It likely won't pay anywhere near what you're getting with the NSA. The benefits are shit, and the hours would probably be even worse because we'd be dividing you over four counties."

"You're making this real tempting," I teased, and he grinned.

"The advantage would be that you'd pretty much be your own boss. You'd be creating the unit, so you could do it the way you want without a ton of oversight."

I took another sip of my beer. I'd put years of blood, sweat, and tears into my job at the NSA, crafting myself into a respected analyst. Living the spy dream. I'd loved the brain power it took to figure out the puzzle from the pieces left behind by the criminals. I'd enjoyed feeling like I'd done something worthy. I wanted that feeling again, but I also didn't want to leave the bubble I'd created with Ryder and Addy.

"Would I be in the field?" I asked.

"Do you want to be in the field?" he responded.

The night at Laredo's had changed everything for me. I didn't want to leave my loved ones anymore. I didn't want to risk Ryder and Addy losing someone else.

"I don't think so," I told him honestly with a shrug.

"Well, like I said, we aren't sure exactly what the unit looks like, so you could shape it how you want. Toss the fieldwork to our deputies."

It was hard to imagine something coming up that would be more handcrafted for me, for my skills, and for what I needed to keep me close to this family I'd embedded myself into. So, what was holding me back from jumping at it?

"Give it a thought. No rush," he said just as the girls came up the stairs with Ryder on their heels.

Mila pouted and begged to stay, and Maddox held firm that it was a school night. They said their goodbyes and left us to our nighttime routine—Addy getting ready for bed and the three of us cuddling together as Ryder read stories from the growing pile of books in her room.

Once we were alone in our room, I slipped on a T-shirt and shorts, although, most nights they ended up on the floor.

Ryder drew me to him. "You've been quiet since Maddox left."

"You knew what he was going to ask?" I didn't know if I should be irritated by that or not.

He nodded, easily reading me, and said, "He told me. Not because he thought he needed my approval, but more as a heads-up so I wasn't caught off guard."

Brothers taking care of each other. I understood that, even though Holden and I were hardly able to do that for each other anymore with the way our lives were pulled across the globe in different directions. I didn't say anything as I moved away, dragged the covers back, and climbed into bed. Ryder joined me, tugging me into his arms and holding me close. I could feel the pulse of his heart against my cheek. I'd never realized just how much of a comfort that could be, feeling the rhythm of his body seeping into mine as we ended our day.

I'd felt lonely that first night I'd arrived in town with Addy. Seeing Ryder with his family jumping to help at a traumatic moment had been overwhelming. But since the moment I'd kissed him, that loneliness had all but disappeared, and I never wanted it back.

"You don't want the job?" he finally asked.

"It feels too good to be true, honestly."

"But?"

"The NSA is all I've known. Leland has been more than a mentor. He's been a friend. I brought Rory in, and now, if

I walk away, I feel like I'd be letting them both down."

Ryder didn't say anything for a long time, but when he did, I knew he was right. "If they're real friends, they'll want you to be happy."

"I need to talk to them."

He nodded. "Not tonight. Tonight, I have plans for you."

"You always have plans for me."

"And I will every night for the rest of our lives. Take off those clothes, darlin'."

And I did because I loved what he would do—what we would do to each other—once I did.

♫ ♫ ♫

After another night spent in the arms of the man I loved, I talked with Rory and Leland. Leland was both happy and disappointed, saying, "I thought I'd get at least another ten years out of you, G. That cowboy is quite a bit older than you, isn't he?"

I'd never considered the difference in Ryder's and my ages before. Six years wasn't all that much, was it? It didn't matter, even if it was.

"I've already given him my heart. Promises I won't break. I can't. It would break me too," I told him honestly.

"That county job won't pay much. Let me put you in our consultant database. Rory can run things by you. It can supplement what you're getting there."

"As long as I don't have to travel, I'll consider it."

When I talked with Rory, she was nothing but happy for me.

I hung up and went in search of my growly rancher, who was hardly ever grumpy these days, with my heart full and at peace. I'd have to close up my apartment in Maryland and go get my things, but there wasn't anything there I couldn't live without. The only things I really needed I already had.

♫ ♫ ♫

Two weeks later, spring had finally sprung fully, sending the scent of magnolias into the air as flowers and trees bloomed across the ranch. With the cabins completed, the first guests due to arrive in a week, and my new job with the four counties' cyber-crime unit starting the following week, Ryder and I had been reveling in a few unencumbered days. We'd woken late each morning, slowly getting ready, and arrived later and later at the ranch. Instead of working, Ryder took Addy and me riding, teaching us both how to handle the horses, and leading us to all his favorite corners of the property.

We often stopped by the cemetery where Natalia was now buried with a headstone that read RAVYN EOWYN HATLEY, the name she'd chosen for herself. Addy always brought wildflowers she'd collected, and we typically left her alone so she had a few quiet moments with her mama.

Every moment with Ryder and Addy felt real and poignant and sweet.

Daily movie scenes I wanted to keep forever. That I felt lucky to have made mine.

The Thursday before I was set to start my new job, Ryder stole my jeans from my hand as I was getting ready and tossed them on the bed.

He hooked me around the waist, placed a kiss on my neck, and said, "Mama and Sadie are taking you to the spa at The Beehive Lodge today. Full works. Massage. Facial. Whatever the hell else a spa day means."

"What?" I'd barely registered his words because, like always, his kisses were sending all thoughts from my head.

"You're going to be spoiled on your birthday," he grunted out.

I spun in his arms so I could face him. "How did you find out?"

"You're not the only one with sleuthing skills."

I chuckled. "Holden told you?"

My brother and Ryder had been sending sporadic texts ever since the night at Laredo's. It was as if my family needed someone to verify I was actually healing—as if I wouldn't tell them the truth. At first, it had stung a bit, but after years of lying to them about what I did, it wasn't necessarily surprising. And truth be told, I was secretly pleased my brother and the man I loved had found some common ground. I wanted my family to love the Hatleys as much as I did.

Ryder shrugged. "Maybe. Or maybe I just read the date on your driver's license."

I huffed out another laugh. "Thank you for trying to do something nice for me, but I'm not really good at letting people touch me."

Ryder's eyes grew dark, and his fingers skimmed along my bra. My nipples instantly went hard, and my core ignited. That was all it ever took. A simple touch and I was gone. I kissed him, tongue tangling with his, and our bodies notched together automatically. Coming home.

He pulled away, waving a finger at me. "Don't distract me, darlin'. As I'm not sure I'm in love with the idea of someone touching you either, I don't care if you skip the massage. But you will go with Mama and Sadie. They want to do this for you, and I have other stuff to take care of."

My lips quirked upward. "Bossy much? And what other stuff? What exactly are you planning, cowboy?"

He pushed a lock of hair behind my ear, saying with a sudden gentleness that captured my heart all over again, "Let me keep it a surprise for a few more hours."

He never lied to me. Never. And now this was his way of asking me not to force him to while he did something nice for me. How could I ever say no to that?

"Fine. I'll go with Eva and Sadie."

The smile he gave me was enough to make me want to

give him anything he ever asked just to see him light up like this. When he was happy, he looked more like Addy than ever. Or she looked like him? All I knew was that when they both let their guards down and let the joy overtake them, they were absolutely radiant. Stars that I felt lucky to call mine.

♫ ♫ ♫

After Eva and Sadie picked me up, I'd bypassed the massage but agreed to the facial, manicure, pedicure, and hair trim that made me feel a bit like a movie star. Pampered. Rested.

We feasted on chicken and dumplings for lunch at Tilly's Café, with Tilly hovering around us, yapping about all the latest gossip in town, including how Willy the mechanic had found himself a new girlfriend. Everyone was hoping this one would last so he didn't spend another two years crying into his beer at McFlannigan's.

After our meal, I was whisked away to the mall where they pushed me into a chair in the makeup aisle and hmm'd and ha'd while a makeup artist lined my eyes and my lips. Then, they insisted I pick out a dress and new shoes, as if I'd put up a fight. Little did they know…I didn't mind shopping. I just rarely had the time anymore, and my simple wardrobe had been what I needed while working for the NSA. But there'd been a point in my teen years when I'd thought shopping was the only good solace for a broken heart. Now, my heart was full, and I still didn't mind shopping.

I chose an off-the-shoulder floral dress that it was a little too chilly for yet but would be nice and cool once the Tennessee humidity kicked in. I skipped the shoes, insisting I liked the way my blue cowboy boots, scuffed and scraped as they were, looked with the bright magenta and blue flowers. So, they took me to a shoeshine station and had my boots buffed and polished.

By the time we were done, it was nearing dinnertime, and they said we were due back in Willow Creek at

McFlannigan's. That was when I felt the first flutter of nerves hit my stomach. Ryder had said he'd had a surprise, but I thought it was nothing more than dinner and cake at our house with his family showing up.

"Anything I need to be prepared for?" I asked.

Eva and Sadie exchanged soft smiles, and my heart tripped again.

We parked in front instead of out back in the parking lot like the family usually did. What exactly was I walking into? I drew my shoulders back, lifted my chin, and swallowed hard, wishing for the first time in two months that I'd had time to do my sleuthing and uncover enough of Ryder's secret not to be nervous.

Sadie and Eva walked inside in front of me, but as they stepped to the side, a bar full of people screamed, "Surprise!" and then burst into the happy birthday song. In the dim light, my gaze settled on Ryder with Addy next to him. Shock flew through me as I saw her in a dress for the first time since I'd met her. It was purple, and she wore it with a pair of tan cowboy boots. Her long black hair was twisted into two braids, and she smiled shyly, tucking into her dad when she saw me.

When I turned my eyes to Ryder, my heart slowed to a complete stop as it often did when I saw him after a few hours apart. He had on dark-washed jeans that hung low on his hips and a striped blue button-down that made his eyes pop even at a distance. His cowboy hat was missing and his dark hair gleamed, making me want to run my hands through it and mess it up. But it was the smile on his face as it widened and grew that made my feet come to a complete halt. I wanted to shout, "I love you!" across the bar. I wanted to run to him like one of those romance movies I'd never wanted to watch, where the heroine and hero find their way across a field of flowers.

As my feet seemed frozen, Ryder came to me. He picked me up, shoved his face in the crook of my neck, and spun me around. When we came to a halt, I was facing the door again. He put me down, kissed me softly, and whispered, "Happy birthday, darlin'." And my entire body burst into flames.

He grinned, eyes slowly strolling down over my body in the lightweight dress in a way that made me afraid I'd be showing nipples to the entire bar. "Damn, you look beautiful. How the hell am I going to get through the next few hours with you looking like this?" he asked quietly, leaning in to kiss my forehead.

"You should have thought about that before you threw me a surprise party in a very public space."

"There's always Phil—Sadie's office." He winked but then took my hand and twirled me around so I was facing the entirety of the room. "But first, there are some people who've come a long way to see you."

When I saw them, tears filled my eyes, and then I was pulling away from Ryder to run through the tables and chairs until my dad caught me in his arms and held on tight.

Standing at an impressive six foot three that my brother matched, Dad appeared exactly the military man he was, even in jeans and a dress shirt he rarely wore. The white at his temples was hardly noticeable with his dark-blond hair shaved down to stubble.

"You're here!" I practically shouted, turning from him to my mom.

Her face was one large smile that was echoed in her eyes, the faint lines around them barely visible. Her dark hair was still thick and full without a hint of gray, which I was vain enough to hope I inherited.

Mom hugged me tight, saying, "Happy birthday."

Ryder joined me, my smile widened, and I grabbed his hand, squeezing tight, trying to communicate how much what he'd done by bringing my family to me meant. "You've all met, I see."

"Ryder picked us up at the airport," Dad said, voice booming through the bar. "Set us up in some very nice cabins at the ranch."

"How long will you be here?" I asked.

"A couple of days. Holden and Leya wished they'd been able to come, but they said to give you a squeeze from them," Mom replied, giving me another hug.

Eva and Brandon joined us, and pretty soon, everyone was chatting and talking. My heart skittered around at seeing them all together. It was almost like that flash I'd gotten when Ryder and I had been all dressed up for the gala—with our families together, getting along. It sent a chill up my back in the very best kind of way, and my eyes filled with tears I refused to shed.

Instead, I concentrated on the people and enjoyed the food, cake, and alcohol that had been served, drinking enough to be just a bit tipsy.

I was watching Sadie teaching Mila and Addy a line dance when Mom found me again, tucking her arm through mine and pulling me close. "You're happy."

"More than I ever thought possible," I told her the truth.

"I'm pretty excited myself," she said, and I turned to look at her, brows furrowing. She smiled. "I finally have a grandbaby." She looked back at Addy, and I thought my chest might just explode with joy and love. Then, she looked at me with a sly smile. "Think I might get another one?"

I laughed. "Ask Holden. He's the one getting married in, what, three months?"

"I'll take all the grandbabies I can get."

"Then you should have had more kids."

She laughed and patted my cheek as a muscled arm wrapped around my middle, tugging me into a solid chest. The song changed, a slow and broody rhythm bursting through the bar.

"Can I have this dance?" Ryder asked, gritty voice low and sexy in my ear.

Next to me, Mom said, "I think I'll get what I want sooner than you think," before she walked away with a grin on her face.

Ryder pulled me onto the dance floor, tugging me close, an arm around my lower back and a hand twining in my hair at the base of my neck. "What did she say she wanted?" he asked.

"Grandkids," I said with a raised brow.

If I'd expected it to freak him out, it didn't. He just smiled that slow, knowing smile that had once made me want to knock it off his face. "Yeah. How many?"

"She'd like a whole schoolroom full of them, but she's not getting her way."

His smile grew, and the beauty of it made me wish we were alone in our room with the moonlight pouring in. "No? How many is she getting?" he asked.

I leaned up, kissing him softly. "We'll have to negotiate. I remember someone saying he wanted a dozen. I think I can compromise somewhere around two."

"That's not a compromise, darlin'. That's cutting it to the bare bones."

"For someone who never saw kids in her future, two sounds like a hundred."

His smile slipped slightly. "You're right. You've already given up enough. I'll settle with whatever number you decide works."

My chest tightened. "You once told me you didn't want me to have to give up everything I wanted to be with you. Same goes for you. We'll figure out the right number."

He kissed me, tongue sneaking in and taking the kiss in a flash from a sweet one, acceptable on a dance floor with our families watching, to one that would need a dark room and no witnesses.

"Perhaps, before you need to get a room, you should remember Gia's present!" Sadie laughed walking by.

We broke apart, grinning.

"There's more?" I asked.

Ryder spun me out of his embrace, holding my hand and then spinning me back. As I got closer to his body, he bent down on one knee, and all the breath left my body.

He held out something small and glittery, but I couldn't look at it because I was mesmerized by the look of love and joy in those bright-blue eyes.

"Gia Kent, you whipped into my life with a gun, a badge, and snark that I thought I'd hate but was really the missing part of my soul. You brought me a daughter I'd thought I'd lost, filling cracks in me I'd been trying to heal for years. And then, you did me the honor of giving me your love on top of it, giving me the gift of a partner along with a child. While I don't need this ring or the words *I do* or a piece of paper to tell me how permanent the bond we've forged is, I'm hoping you'll agree to marry me anyway so the rest of the world can see what our hearts already feel. I love you, darlin', with all my damn broody heart has to give. So, what do you think? Will you marry me?"

I rubbed my hand over the bristles of his beard he'd long since grown back and that I absolutely adored, then covered his hand holding the ring with my other one and tugged him to his feet. "I thought giving control of my life to someone else would be impossibly difficult. But instead, giving you my heart, my life, and my future has been the easiest thing I've ever done. The easiest decision I've ever made. I'm yours, and if that means walking down an aisle and saying *I do*, it'll be my joy to do so."

"Make it easy for the man, G. Just say yes," my dad shouted.

I laughed, leaned in, and kissed Ryder quickly before saying, "Yes. It would be my honor to marry you."

The bar erupted into shouts of joy. Addy collided with our legs, hugging us tight. Ryder lifted her so she was between us. Our faces were full of light and love and happiness.

And all I could think was, this was the life I'd been intended to have all along.

No spy movie. No sleuthing.

Just forever, giving and receiving.

Epilogue

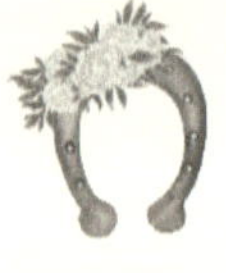

Ryder

UNFORGETTABLE
Performed by Darlinghurst

One Year Later

How was it I was back in this same damn situation? Shooting at crows and hoping like hell I didn't clip one. Mila would never forgive me after the promise I'd made to never hurt another creature. Those black beasts were cackling laughter through those caws. I just knew it.

I aimed to the left and high above the trees, hoping the sound would be enough to scare them and cursing Willy for taking off on a damn honeymoon while my sound machine needed repairs.

Even after I'd let two shots ring through the icy air, the birds just sat there, feasting on Mama's crabapples and making faces at me.

"Let's try something else," Gia's voice rang out behind me.

I turned to find her and Addy stomping over the snow-crusted field, both of them covered in so many layers of clothes that nothing but their rosy cheeks peeked out.

"What are you doing out here? You'll freeze to death," I groused. It was too cold for my girls. The temperature had plummeted to an unusual two degrees this morning. It never got quite this cold in Willow Creek.

Gia waved a black box she was carrying. As she got closer, I realized it was an old-school boom box—an antique she'd found in the attic of Phil's house when my family had gotten together to go through it all.

When they reached me, I tugged gently on one of Addy's braids hanging out from beneath her beanie. "Aren't you supposed to be in school, sweetheart?"

"Snow day!" she all but screamed. Her volume sounded more like Mila's than her normal quiet self, and it did crazy things to my heart. I loved that she was coming out of her shell and finding a way to feel safe and secure.

I leaned in and kissed Gia. I couldn't help myself. Every time we were apart and came back together, my instincts took over, my body demanding to be reunited, even if we'd only been apart minutes. In this case, we'd been apart for several hours. I'd left her when our room was still dark to drive over to the box store a town over and then headed back to the ranch to handle Mama's pesky crows.

"Business first," Gia said, pulling back with a smile that tugged her cheeks up and her color-changing eyes flashing.

She marched away from me, closer to the crows that took a moment to go silent, as if they too were in awe of the beautiful figure she made, crunching over the frozen earth in a bright-red jacket and matching snow boots. Addy twirled along behind her, and I brought up the rear.

Gia set the boom box down, clicked a few buttons, turned a few knobs, and a classic-rock song burst into the air at a volume that made me want to cover my ears.

The birds squawked in objection before taking flight.

I watched in awe as black wings filled the air, heading out over the trees and up into the mountains.

Addy grabbed my hand with her mittened one and started dancing. My girl was an amazing dancer. It had taken months of line dancing with Sadie for us to figure that out. Now, Addy was enrolled in a class that she only freaked out at attending once in a while. No performances for her. She couldn't handle the audience and probably never would, but she could participate. She could do something that brought her as much joy as the video games and coding she did with Gia.

Gia rejoined us, and the three of us twisted and twirled, leaving a path of wild footprints in the snow. A year ago, I'd been in this field, pinky-promising my niece, my chest filled with an ache for something I'd lost and never thought I'd have again—a wife and a child. And now, through life's twists and turns and wild adventures, I'd ended up with both.

Thank God, Gia had wanted a simple ceremony here at the ranch that we'd been able to pull off within months of me proposing. I hadn't wanted to wait to make sure the world knew we belonged to each other.

It was a gift I'd never take for granted. I'd never treat these moments with them with anything but the precious respect they deserved.

When the song ended and a slower one started, Addy pulled away, picking up a pail she'd set down by the boom box. "I'm going to collect some crabapples for Nana."

My heart always leaped with pleasure when she called Mama that.

Gia and I watched as Addy started picking up fruit from the ground, reaching up to the low-hanging branches for more. Then, Gia pulled me to her, hands going around my neck, tucking our hips close together—or as close as they could be with her in layers of clothes and me in my thick work jacket and jeans.

She swayed us to the beat of the music. Slow and sultry.

"You danced with me to this song before proposing," she said with a soft smile.

"Damn good song."

Her smile grew. "Do you remember what we talked about?"

I furrowed my brow, trying to remember.

"Mom had been harassing me about grandkids. We

were negotiating how many we were going to have."

The conversation fell into place. The one when she'd said she wanted two kids and I'd said I wanted a whole bushel of them. Enough to fill up those empty rooms downstairs. "I remember," I said quietly.

"I think we should get to work on that."

My feet ground to a halt, hope and joy flooding my veins. "What?"

She laughed, and it tinkled through the air lighter and more beautiful than any snowflake.

"Let's make a baby, cowboy."

My hands slid down to the hem of her jacket, trying to sneak under it, trying to find the smooth expanse of her flat stomach. Just the thought of it going round and full because our child was growing inside her made me hard, made me uncomfortably aware of Addy singing and dancing as she collected fruit behind us.

"You're wearing too many clothes, darlin'. We're in the middle of a damn frozen field. Addy's with us, and you tell me that now? That's cruel and unusual punishment."

Gia brushed her lips against mine. They were cold and yet hot at the same time, and my body flooded with desire. If Addy wasn't with us, I would have taken her down to the cold hard earth and seen just how we could melt the ice around us.

"You can take your revenge when we get home," she whispered.

"Addy, Gia and I have to go. Grab the pail, and you can help Nana bake some pies," I hollered.

Gia laughed, but I swung her up in my arms and started marching across the field.

"Put me down. You can't carry me all the way back to the house."

"Watch me."

"Addy, get the boom box!" Gia called out over my shoulder.

"Leave the damn box! When it runs out of batteries, I'll send Ramon out to replace them," I shouted back.

I was halfway across the field before Addy caught up to us. She looked up at Gia with a concerned look in her eye. "Is Gia okay?"

Damn. I hated that I'd worried her. I let Gia slide down my body and steadied her while she found her footing. "She's fine. I was just in a hurry. We have some business I forgot to take care of."

When she still didn't look sure, I tweaked her braid. "Promise, sweetheart. Everything here is really good. Better than any dream I could ever imagine. You. Gia. This family we've made. My heart is so full every damn day I can't believe my luck."

Addy's face broke into a huge smile I was proud to say looked a hell of a lot like the one I saw each morning in the mirror. "You owe a dollar for the curse jar, Papa!"

Then, she took off, running toward the farmhouse where Mama would tuck her up next to her in an apron and have her stir and pat and bake. As soon as our daughter's feet hit the steps, I twirled Gia back into my arms and slanted my mouth over hers. I devoured those pretty pink lips like I had every day for more than a year. Like I would every day for another hundred years.

She'd always be mine. I'd always be hers. There was nothing that would come between us.

…Except too damn many clothes.

♫ ♫ ♫

Thank you for reading Ryder and Gia's happily ever after. If you're not quite ready to let them or the Hatley family go yet, you can catch more of them *in three ways*.

1. You can get a sweet little **bonus epilogue where Gia shows her true fear…of bats…and Ryder makes her beg with olallieberry pie**, in which you

also get a sneak peek into a mystery involving Sadie. It's FREE with a newsletter subscription.

DOWNLOAD BONUS EPILOGUE NOW
https://BookHip.com/DNQJRPN

2. You can read **Gemma Hatley's short story with the A-list actor who sweeps her off her feet**, breaks her heart, and then earns it back. Available in eBook and paperback on Amazon, or you can get the eBook for FREE with a newsletter subscription.

   DOWNLOAD PERFECTLY FINE at
   https://www.ljevansbooks.com/freeljbooks

3. Finally, **while you wait for SADIE'S HEA,** coming in EARLY 2025, you can read Maddox and McKenna's second-chance romance if you haven't already done so. Read a sample here:

The Last One You Loved – Sample

Ten Years Ago

Maddox

AIN'T ALWAYS THE COWBOY
Performed by Jon Pardi

The lake shimmered in the moonlight. The warm

breeze stirred up tiny waves, sending white sprinkles shifting across the surface as it drifted toward the shore where we were parked.

We were on the tailgate of my beat-up Bronco with our hands and limbs joined. McKenna's jean-clad legs were flung over my lap, and her head rested on my shoulder. Her cowboy boots were off, lost somewhere behind me in the chaos of blankets and food wrappers. I ran the fingers of my free hand over the gentle arch of her foot, and she jerked it away, laughing.

"Don't you dare tickle me unless you want to end up with a busted nose," she teased, her soft voice washing over me.

It wasn't like I hadn't known she'd pull away. Ten years of knowing her meant I knew just how ticklish her feet were, but I'd done it anyway in an attempt to lighten the mood. But the sound and scent and feel of her made it almost impossible to feel anything but sorrow. It might be the last time I would hold her like this, and my heart screamed as if it could change what was happening by merely twisting inside my chest.

"Wanna go for a swim?" I asked.

It was still humid outside, even though the sun had set hours ago. Long enough that the twilight sounds of the bugs and wild animals had almost disappeared. Instead, a quiet had taken over the space, a preview of what would happen once she drove down the road tomorrow and my life was forever changed.

In answer to my question, she slid off of me and started discarding clothes. She was wearing a string bikini under her jeans and floaty blouse, as if she'd known I'd ask for this—us in the water. I swallowed hard at the gentle curves I'd spent years getting to know as well as my own. I glanced down at my sinewy body toughened from years of working on the ranch. She'd always said my muscles were the very best kind—built from hard work. Would anyone else ever care about them the way she had?

I hadn't been as prepared as she'd been for a swim, so my boxer briefs were going to have to do. Once I'd stripped down, I recaptured her hand, determined to touch her for as long as possible, and led us toward the water, picking our way through the twigs and rocks as we went.

As soon as we hit the cool water, I shivered. It was a soothing relief to the heat and heaviness of the day. If only it could lift the weight inside me as easily as it chilled my skin.

We swam toward the makeshift dock someone had fastened

to the middle of the lake decades ago. We didn't pull ourselves up on top. Instead, we hid in the shadows. She wrapped her long limbs around my waist, and I looped an arm through one of the ropes hanging off the wooden slats to hold us steady while my hands continued to touch her.

She kissed me. Wet and wild. Slow and torturous. Love and goodbyes blended into the movements as we rejoined our bodies in the way we'd been doing over the last couple of months. Like a flame on the wick of a firecracker, burning, burning, burning until it finally ignited into a shower of light and sound.

Until it became nothing but us.

She moaned into my mouth when my fingers slid under her bikini, touching pieces of her that were aching for me. I wanted to cry out as well, but with a different ache. I wanted to let my tears wash into the lake.

But it would be selfish because I wouldn't be crying for her. I'd only be crying for me, and that didn't seem fair. McKenna deserved the future she was heading toward—her dream of becoming a doctor finally starting. But her desire to escape this town and her mother hurt because it meant she was escaping me and my family as well—the people who'd loved and sheltered her.

Knowing it was coming hadn't eased the pain of its arrival. As much as I wanted to follow her, I couldn't. My life was here with my family, and the ranch, and my own dreams of serving my community. Even if everything at home had been perfectly fine, I wasn't sure I'd want to leave our small town for a place where you couldn't see the stars. Here, they were so bright it seemed like you could grab them, put them in your pocket, and take them with you. If I was forced to live in a city, I'd burn out just like those faraway suns. If you forced her to stay, she'd wither like the roses I'd given her last week. Dust into dust.

We loved each other more than I'd ever thought was possible, especially considering we were just two kids, barely legal. I knew her smiles and looks and moods better than she knew them herself, and vice versa. But this was where the road we were on finally divided after a decade of running side by side. A bitter taste rose inside me because I wasn't sure our roads would ever cross again.

"I'll come visit," I told her, breaking my mouth from hers. "Thanksgiving or spring break. Whichever works."

Could I get through to spring without seeing her? Touching

her? Loving her? How would I even come up with the money for the trip?

She rested her forehead on my shoulder, placed a gentle kiss there, and then looked up at me with sad, tormented eyes.

"Maddox…between college, medical school, and a residency, it'll be at least eleven years before I'm done. I'll always be your friend. I'll always love you…but…I just…" A choked sob broke free from her, and my throat bobbed, eyes watering.

"You want to break up. You don't even want to try?" I asked, that bitterness coating my tongue and my mouth growing. She had choices. She could have applied to Tennessee State. She could have kept us closer, but even as I said it, I knew she couldn't. McKenna needed to put her childhood behind her…even if that meant giving me up along with it.

She put her hands on my cheeks, cupping them and kissing my lips sweetly.

"You're my favorite thing. My favorite memory. My favorite gift. My favorite person," she said quietly.

I could no longer hold the tears back. I didn't know how to let her go. But I'd have to because it wasn't always the cowboy who ran away.

Sometimes, it was the golden-haloed woman with a future so bright the gods had to be jealous.

That was my McKenna.

And tomorrow, she'd be gone.

No longer mine, but the world's instead.

Now

Maddox

SLOW BURN
Performed by Zac Brown Band

I pulled back just in time, letting the fist barely graze

my chin. The movement was enough to send my Stetson flying, landing amongst the straw where it was going to get trampled. It was the sight of my hat on the ground that pissed me off more than the fist or Willy Tate's drunken, angry snarl as he lunged for me again.

I ducked the second shot and shoved my shoulder into his gut, taking him down to the ground with me. The music had stopped, the customers in the bar quiet as they watched two burly men wrestle. Several chairs were tipped over, tables were bumped, and drinks were spilled as we rolled around. It took me one too many moves before I finally had him pinned facedown with his hands behind his back and my knee holding him in place.

"Damn it, Willy, you owe me a new hat!" I growled.

Clapping filled the air along with hoots and hollers that made my eyes roll.

"Thanks for the show!" someone in the back yelled as someone else shouted out, "Brings me back to my sheep-tying days!"

"Thanks for the help, y'all," I said sarcastically, eyeing my brother sitting calmly on a stool at the bar with a crooked grin.

"Why, Sheriff Maddox, no one would ever presume to think you needed help." Ryder's grin grew, and then he had the audacity to wink at me as he raised a beer in my direction. I barely resisted flipping him the bird as laughter erupted from him, causing his blue eyes that matched mine to crinkle at the corners. He brushed a hand over his perfectly tousled dark-brown hair that should have been smashed flat after wearing a hat all day but instead looked like he'd stepped off the page of a damn magazine.

I was not anywhere near picture-perfect. My dark-blond hair was standing up in places, and the stubble on my chin—a day past trendy—was dripping and sticky from the whiskey Willy had thrown at me. The alcohol had stained my tan shirt, and our scuffle had snagged the ends of my olive-green tie, almost ripping it from my neck.

"She left me, Maddox. For a goddamn suit from Knoxville." Willy was crying now, and it almost looked ridiculous on the six-foot-three mechanic with the hair and beard of someone who'd been lost in the wild for one too many years.

"Taking it out on everyone here isn't going to make the pain go away, shithead," I grumbled. "You gonna start swinging again if I get up?"

Willy shook his head. I stood and then helped the man to his feet. His sad, puppy-dog eyes were full of tears that tumbled down his cheeks.

"You going to arrest him for hitting a lawman?" Gemma asked, trying not to giggle. My sister was sitting next to Ryder at the bar. Her long hair was the same color as mine, but her hazel eyes were full of our brother's laughter. Ryder tapped her elbow with his in appreciation of the taunt she'd thrown my way.

Willy hunched his enormous shoulders. "Fuck. I forgot you're the sheriff now."

"I've been an officer of the law for damn near six years, Willy. Hitting me before or after I'd been elected wouldn't change a damn thing." I leaned down and picked up my hat, brushing it against my thigh and shoving him toward the door of McFlannigan's. It was the only bar in town and normally looked as Irish as my uncle who owned the place, but on Thursdays, they had two-dollar beers, line dancing, and a live band. Uncle Phil brought hay in from the ranch to make it more *Tennessee barnyard* than *Dublin dive*.

I'd told him more than once the hay was a hazard, but as he was friends with the county health inspector, who just happened to be in one of the booths tonight with his wife, my uncle clearly didn't have to worry about being fined. That was the way everything in this town worked, and while I'd been able to turn a blind eye to some of it as a deputy, since I'd been elected, it had been harder to do.

The people of Winter County had put their trust in me. Maybe it was because Sheriff Haskett had thrown his hat in my direction when he'd stepped down, or maybe it was because the Hatley family had been in Willow Creek since its inception. Regardless, they'd taken a chance on a green twenty-seven-year-old last year, and I'd spent twelve months proving to them it had been the right choice.

Willy and I were at the door when Ryder called out, "Going to come back and have a beer with us after you get him home?"

I shook my head.

"Come on, Maddox, one drink!" Gemma called.

I had no desire to sit at the bar, shooting the shit with my siblings, after the long day I'd had. If the bar hadn't been mere blocks from my house when the call had come in as I walked out the station door, I would've let one of my deputies handle the call.

Now that I'd done my civic duty for the night, I had only one goal, and that was getting home to my girl.

I directed Willy into the passenger seat of my ancient green and rust-covered Bronco, wishing I'd driven my sheriff truck instead. But the Bronco had called to me this morning—the date dragging at me as it did every year.

The date I tried to ignore and failed miserably to do.

I got Willy tucked into the small apartment above the garage his family had owned almost as long as mine had owned the ranch and then headed to my 1950s-style bungalow two streets over. After three years of hard work, the house was pretty much how I wanted it. The wood siding had a fresh coat of pale-yellow paint, new black shutters edged the multi-paned windows, and a burnt-orange custom door invited you in, just like the swing tucked in the corner of the front porch.

An antique lamp on the hall table cast a gentle light onto the dark plank floors as I let myself in, and the murmur of the television in the open-space living area greeted me. Rianne looked up from the cushy, leather couch I'd spent a small fortune on as I hung my destroyed hat on the rack by the door.

Her bright-red lips curved upward in greeting, and her dark-brown face was just starting to show signs of wrinkles even though she was as old as my grandparents. Her black-and-white corkscrew hair was tucked beneath a vivid-blue scarf littered with pictures of baby ducks. She had so many head wraps I thought she could wear a different one every day of the year and still have more.

"How is she?" I asked.

"Like always. Pretending to sleep but really waiting for you," she said, turning off the TV and rising. She was wearing soft jeans and a long tunic top, looking far more casual than she ever had as my third-grade teacher. When I'd been a rowdy eight-year-old, I'd adored her, and now that she'd turned in her teacher badge and taken on helping me, I loved her almost as much as I loved my mama.

"You smell like a liquor cabinet." Rianne's nose squished up, but there was a smile on her lips.

I sighed, ran my hand over my half-assed, alcohol-soaked beard, and grimaced.

"Had to pull Willy out of McFlannigan's before he tore it

apart."

Rianne's face fell. "Aw, he's taking the loss of his woman pretty hard."

I nodded. It was why I'd tucked him at home instead of locking him up in a cell at the station. I knew what it felt like to watch your woman drive away. The agony I'd felt didn't make me want to bleed out on the floor anymore, but the reminder on this day, more than any other, made the hurt tumble through me as if it had happened yesterday instead of a decade ago.

Rianne gathered her things, and I walked her out.

"Try to get some rest tomorrow, and I'll see you on Sunday," she said before leaving.

I was technically off the clock for a whole day, but that never meant much when you were one of only twelve people holding down the only law enforcement agency in the county. We didn't have a lot of crime in Willow Creek, but we did have a lot of work. On any given day, I might be helping round up stray chickens one moment and taking beer from underage kids at the lake the next. The biggest pain in my ass was the motorcycle club, The West Gears, who used their headquarters up in the mountains right at the county line to deal drugs and store stolen merchandise. The Gears were the reason I was dead on my feet tonight after a day of hunting them down.

I headed down the hall, feet stalling as I passed Mila's door. She'd expect me to crawl into bed with her, and I didn't want to do that smelling like whiskey, so I continued on to the one room I hadn't let Mama or my sisters help decorate. Instead, the main bedroom reflected me like almost no other part of the house. It was full of dark woods, navy linens, and black-and-white photographs of the lake and the ranch.

I locked my weapon away in the gun safe, showered in the bathroom filled with teak woods and blue linens, and then changed into sweats and a long-sleeve T-shirt before padding on bare feet back to Mila's room. I turned the knob as quietly as possible in a vain hope that she might actually be asleep but chuckled to myself when I saw her dart her head under the covers.

Her room looked like a rainbow had thrown up in it. She was obsessed with them. She'd even convinced me to paint her white headboard in rainbow stripes. Between that, her four pastel-colored nightlights, and the pile of stuffed unicorns that filled an armchair in the corner, it felt like walking into a cartoon world. I crossed the faux-fur white rug and stood looking down at the rainbow comforter that shed glitter like it was a cat changing seasons.

"Oh good, Mila is asleep. I don't have to read *The Day the Unicorns Saved the World* for the one-thousandth time," I said softly.

The covers were thrown back, and beautiful wheat-colored eyes stared at me under thick brows that were almost black and contrasted with the honey-blonde hair spiraling in waves around her round face. "I'm not sleeping, Daddy! You *have* to read it, or I'll be up all night."

There was a little whine to her sweet voice and a pout to her lips that made my mouth twitch. I sighed dramatically, looked up at the ceiling, and pretended to contemplate the fate of my life before pulling the book from her nightstand.

"Scootch over," I said.

She pulled back her covers and moved to the side as I slid in with her. Her tiny, five-year-old body curled up against me, and I put one arm around her, holding her tight. She smelled like the berry shampoo Mama had bought for her birthday, and she had on a pair of fuzzy, pink-striped pajamas that had been from my sister. Her body was warm and her tiny hand soft as she placed it on my arm. My heart filled to near bursting just by having her there.

"How was your day?" I asked.

"I learned that the letter L says *lllll* like in lion, and that five and two more is seven. Seven is my birthday number, so Mrs. Randall let me use the butterfly pointer and lead the class in the alphabet song."

Kindergarten. My baby had started kindergarten at the end of August. I hadn't expected it to be as hard as it had been to drop her off at school and walk away. I mean, I'd been leaving her every day for the four years of her life that she'd been mine. But there was something different about leaving her with Rianne versus taking her into a classroom full of kids who I couldn't guarantee would be nice and adults who were strangers. I'd run the name of the principal and every teacher at the school to make sure there weren't any scumbags hiding in the system, even when I knew the state wouldn't have given certificates to criminals. I'd sort of gone off my rocker for a day or two. The only thing that made it easier was knowing Mila liked being there.

"That sounds like a really good day," I told her.

"Yeah. But Missy wouldn't give me a turn with the hula hoop." She pouted, and every vein in my body tightened. The need to protect her, even from other five-year-olds, was a strange sensation. There was a time in my life when I hadn't wanted to be a dad, when I'd promised another blonde-haired girl that we wouldn't have kids because she was adamantly opposed to having them.

"I'll buy you your own damn hula hoop tomorrow," I told her, voice gruff with emotions. She giggled.

"You cussed again, Daddy. You owe me another dollar for the cuss jar."

I smiled with my lips against her hair. She'd have enough money in that jar to go to college if I wasn't careful. The thought of her being grown up and going away to college threatened to rip some more at the scars that had already cracked open today.

I pushed the pain away, opened the book, and started reading as my girl snuggled deeper into me. My heart expanded until it was quadruple the size it should have been. This was perfect. I didn't need anything else in my life but this.

Keep reading *THE LAST ONE YOU LOVED TODAY.*

https://geni.us/TLOYL

Free in Kindle Unlimited

https://geni.us/Hatleys

Acknowledgements

I'm so very grateful for every single person who has helped me on this book journey. If you're reading these words, you *are* one of those people. I wouldn't be an author if people like you didn't decide to read the stories I crafted, so THANK YOU!

In addition to my lovely readers, I need to acknowledge these people:

My husband, who never ever lets me give up on myself, even when the battles seem endless. Your sacrifice, your strength, your laughter is what gets me through.

Our child, Evyn, owner of Evans Editing, who remains my harshest and kindest critic. Thank you for helping me create my stories and driving me to be a better human. Love you, kiddo.

My sister, Kelly, who made sure I hit the publish button the very first time and reads my crappy first drafts, still loves my stories anyway, and is never afraid to say, "You can do better."

My mom, who tells me the truth, even when it hurts her to do so, as she beta reads my stories and then loves them enough to buy them repeatedly and reread them over and over.

My dad and my father-in-law, who are my biggest fans and take my books to the strangest places, telling everyone they know (and don't know) about my stories.

Michelle Fewer, who patiently reads, uplifts, and plots without judgment and so much grace. Thank you for giving me your time, energy, and love.

Jenn at Jenn Lockwood Editing Services and Karen Hrdlicka, who have been on this journey and continue to have faith in me no matter how far apart we get pulled. Your edits and proofs are always the perfect polish that my words need.

The entire group of beautiful humans in LJ's Music & Stories who love and support me. I can't say enough how deeply grateful I am for each and every one of you.

The host of bloggers who have shared my stories, become dear friends, and continue to make me feel like a rock star every day. Thank you, thank you, thank you!

A host of authors, including Stephanie Rose, Erika Kelly, Kathryn Nolan, Lucy Score, Hannah Blake, Maria Luis, Annie Dyer, Aly Stiles, and AM Johnson, who have shown me that dear friends are more important than any paralyzing moment in this wild publishing world. MWAH!

All my ARC readers, who have become sweet friends and true supporters. Thank you for knowing just what to say to scare away my writer insecurities.

Leisa C., Rachel R., and Stephanie F. Thank you beyond words for being the biggest cheerleaders, partners, and friends I could ever hope to have on this wild ride called life.

I love you all!

About the Author

Award winning author, LJ Evans, lives in Northern California with her husband, child, and the three terrors called cats. She's been writing, almost as a compulsion, since she was a little girl and will often pull the car over to write when a song lyric strikes her. A former first-grade teacher, she now spends her free time reading and writing, as well as binge-watching original shows like *Wednesday, The Mentalist, Veronica Mars,* and *Stranger Things*.

If you ask her the one thing she won't do, it's pretty much anything that involves dirt—sports, gardening, or otherwise. But she loves to write about all of those things, and her first published heroine was pretty much involved with dirt on a daily basis, which is exactly why LJ loves fiction novels—the characters can be everything you're not and still make their way into your heart.

Her novel, **CHARMING AND THE CHERRY BLOSSOM**, was *Writer's Digest* Self-Published E-book Romance of the Year in 2021. For more information about LJ, check out any of these sites:

www.ljevansbooks.com

FaceBook Group: LJ's Music & Stories

LJ Evans on Amazon, Bookbub, and Goodreads

@ljevansbooks on Facebook, Instagram, TikTok, and Pinterest

Books by LJ

Standalone

After All the Wreckage— Rory & Gage

A single-dad, small-town, romantic suspense

He's a broody bar owner raising his siblings. She's a scrappy PI who's loved him since she was a teenager. When his brother disappears, she forces aside years of pining and family secrets to help him.

Charming and the Cherry Blossom — Elle & Hudson

A contemporary romance with hints of magical realism

Today was a fairy tale…I inherited a fortune from a dad I never knew, and a thoroughly charming guy asked me out. But like all fairy tales, mine has a dark side...and my happily ever after may disappear with the truth.

The Hatley Family Standalones

The Last One You Loved — Maddox & McKenna

A single-dad, small-town romance

He's a small-town sheriff with a secret that can unravel their worlds. She's an ER resident running from a costly mistake. Coming home will only mean heartache…unless they let forgiveness heal them both.

The Last Promise You Made — Ryder & Gia

A single-dad, small-town, romantic suspense

He's a grumpy rancher who swore off all relationships. She's a spitfire undercover agent who brings danger to his life. Not even a common enemy can force them to trust each other. Desire is an inconvenience. Falling in love is absolutely out of the question…

Perfectly Fine — Gemma & Rex

A fish-out-of-water, celebrity romance

He's a charming, A-list actor at the top of his game. She's a determined, small-town screenwriter hoping for a deal. They form an unexpected connection until heartbreak ruins their future. Available on Amazon and also FREE with newsletter subscription.

My Life as an Album Series

My Life as a Country Album — Cam's Story

A boy-next-door, small-town romance

This is tomboy Cam's diary-style, coming-of-age story about growing up loving the football hero next door. She vowed to love him forever. But when fate comes calling, will she ever find a heart to call home? Warning: Tears may fall.

My Life as a Pop Album — Mia & Derek

A rock star, road-trip romance

Bookworm Mia is trying to put years of guilt behind her when soulful musician Derek Waters strolls into her life and turns it upside down. Once he's seen her, Derek can't walk away unless Mia comes with him. But what will happen when their short time together comes to an end?

My Life as a Rock Album — Seth & PJ

A second-chance, antihero romance

Recovering addict Seth Carmen is a trash artist who knows he's better off alone. But when he finds and loses the love of his life, he can't help sending her a host of love letters to try to win her back. Can Seth prove to PJ they can make broken beautiful?

My Life as a Mixtape — Lonnie & Wynn

A single-dad, rock star romance

Lonnie's always seen relationships as a burden instead of a gift, and picking up the pieces his sister leaves behind is just one of the reasons. When Wynn enters his life just as her world is disintegrating, their mixed-up pasts give way to new beginnings neither of them saw coming.

My Life as a Holiday Album – 2nd Generation

A small-town romance

Come home for the holidays with this heartwarming, full-length standalone full of hidden secrets, true love, and the real meaning of family. Perfect for lovers of *Love Actually* and Hallmark movies, this sexy story intertwines the lives of six couples as they find their way to their happily ever afters with the help of family and friends.

My Life as an Album Series Box Set

The 1st four Album series stories plus an exclusive novella

In the exclusive novella, *This Life with Cam*, Blake Abbott writes to Cam about just what it was like to grow up in the shadow of her relationship with Jake and just when he first fell for the little girl with the popsicle-stained lips. Can he show Cam that she isn't broken?

The Anchor Novels

Guarded Dreams — Eli & Ava

A grumpy-sunshine, military romance

He's a grumpy Coast Guard focused on his job. She's a feisty musician searching for stardom. Nothing about them fits, and yet their attraction burns wild when fate lands them in the same house for the summer.

Forged by Sacrifice — Mac & Georgie

A roommates-to-lovers, military romance

He's a driven military man zeroed in on a new goal. She's a struggling law student running from her family's mistakes. They're entirely wrong for each other…except their bodies disagree. When they end up as roommates, how long before attraction shatters their resistance?

Avenged by Love — Truck & Jersey

A fake-marriage, military romance

When a broody military man and a quiet bookstore clerk end up in the same house, it isn't only attraction that erupts. Now, the only way to ensure she gets the care she needs is to marry her.

Damaged Desires — Dani & Nash

A frenemy, military romance

A grumpy Navy SEAL reeling from the loss of his team fights an overwhelming attraction for his best friend's fiery sister, until a stalker puts her in his sights, and then he'll do anything to protect her, even if it means exposing all his secrets.

Branded by a Song — Brady & Tristan

A single-mom, rock star romance

He's a country-rock legend searching for inspiration. She's a Navy SEAL's widow determined to honor his memory while raising their daughter. Neither believes the intense attraction tugging at them can lead to more until their futures are twined by her grandmother's will.

Tripped by Love — Cassidy & Marco

A broody-bodyguard, single-mom romance

He's her brother's broody bodyguard with secrets he can't share. She's a busy single mom with a restaurant to run. They're just friends until a little white lie changes everything.

The Anchor Novels: The Military Bros Box Set

The books + an exclusive novella

Guarded Dreams, Forged by Sacrifice, and *Avenged by Love* plus the novella, *The Hurricane*! Heartfelt reads full of love, sacrifice, and family. The perfect book boyfriends for a binge read.

The Anchor Suspense Novels

Unmasked Dreams — Violet & Dawson

A second-chance, age-gap romance

Violet and Dawson had a heart-stopping attraction they were compelled to deny. When they're tossed together again, it proves nothing has changed—except the lab she's built in the garage and the secrets he's keeping. When she stumbles into his dark world, Dawson is forced to break old promises to keep her safe. But when the swells subside, will their hearts still be intact?

Crossed by the Stars — Jada & Dax

A second-chance, forced-proximity romance

Family secrets meant Dax and Jada's teenaged romance was an impossibility. A decade later, the scars still remain, so neither is willing to give in to their tantalizing chemistry. But when a shadow creeps out of Jada's past, seeking retribution, it's Dax who shows up to protect her. And suddenly, it's hard to see a way out without permanent damage to their bodies and souls.

Disguised as Love — Cruz & Raisa

A chemistry-filled, enemies-to-lovers romance

Surly FBI agent, Cruz Malone, is determined to bring down the Leskov clan for good. If that means he has to arrest or bed the sexy blonde scientist of the family, so be it. Too bad Raisa has other ideas. There's no way she's just going to sit back and let the infuriating agent dismantle her world…or her heart.

The Painted Daisies

Interconnected series with an all-female rock band, the alpha heroes who steal their hearts, and suspense that will leave you breathless. Each story has its own HEA.

Sweet Memory — Paisley & Jonas

An opposite-side-of-the-tracks, second-chance romance

The world's sweetest rock star falls for a troubled music producer whose past comes back to haunt them.

Green Jewel — Fiadh & Asher

An enemies-to-lovers, single-dad romance

He did it. She'll prove it. Her body's reaction to him be damned.

Cherry Brandy — Leya & Holden

A forced-proximity, forbidden, bodyguard romance

Being on the run with only one bed is no excuse to touch her…until touching is the only choice.

Blue Marguerite — Adria & Ronan

A celebrity, second-chance, frenemy romance

She vowed to never forgive him...not even when he offers answers her family desperately seeks.

Royal Haze — Nikki & D'Angelo

A bodyguard, on-the-run romance with a morally gray hero

He was ready to torture, steal, and kill to defend the world he believed in. What he wasn't prepared for…was her.

Free Stories

All available with a newsletter sign-up at
https://www.ljevansbooks.com/freeljbooks

Perfectly Fine

A fish-out-of-water, celebrity romance

He's a charming, A-list actor at the top of his game. She's a determined, small-town screenwriter hoping for a deal. They form an unexpected connection until heartbreak ruins their future. Also on Amazon.

Rumor

A small-town, rock-star romance

There's only one thing rock star Chase Legend needs to ring in the new year, and that's to know what Reyna Rossi tastes like. After ten years, there's no way he's letting her escape the night without their souls touching. Reyna has other plans. After all, she doesn't need the entire town wagging their tongues about her any more than they already do.

Love Ain't

A friends-to-lovers, cowboy romance

Reese knows her best friend and rodeo king, Dalton Abbott, is never going to fall in love, get married, and have kids. He's left so many broken hearts behind that there's gotta be a museum full of them somewhere. So when he gives her a look from under the brim of his hat, promising both jagged relief and pain, she knows better than to give in.

The Long Con

A sexy, antihero romance

Adler is after one thing: the next big payday. Then, Brielle sways into his world with her own game in play, and those aquamarine-colored eyes almost make him forget his number-one rule. But she'll learn…
love isn't a con he's interested in.

The Light Princess

An old-fashioned fairy tale

A princess who glows with a magical light, a kingdom at war, and a kiss that changes the world. This is an extended version of the fairy tale twined through the pages of *Charming and the Cherry Blossom*.

www.ingramcontent.com/pod-product-compliance
Lightning Source LLC
Chambersburg PA
CBHW022254310726
48973CB00001B/62